OLD BILL'S LAST WILL and TESTAMENT

LEE STUESSER

◆ FriesenPress

One Printers Way
Altona, MB R0G 0B0
Canada

www.friesenpress.com

Copyright © 2022 by Lee Stuesser
First Edition — 2022

All rights reserved.

No part of this publication may be reproduced in any form, or by any means, electronic or mechanical, including photocopying, recording, or any information browsing, storage, or retrieval system, without permission in writing from FriesenPress.

This book is protected by copyright. No part of this book may be reproduced or transmitted by any person or entity, in any form or by any means, without the permission of the author.

This book is a work of fiction. The characters in this book are fictitious and any resemblance to real persons, living or dead, is purely coincidental.

ISBN
978-1-03-912685-5 (Hardcover)
978-1-03-912684-8 (Paperback)
978-1-03-912686-2 (eBook)

1. FICTION, THRILLERS, CRIME

Distributed to the trade by The Ingram Book Company

IN MEMORY OF

An Old Friend

ACKNOWLEDGMENTS

A book is never the work of an author alone. I was fortunate to receive advice, input and suggestions from a number of people who proofed and read the manuscript in progress. In particular, my wife, Linda, was a fount of common sense, and my children, Kelly, Jenny and Brett, provided youthful insight and learned much about the summer of 1972. John Michaels provided a lawyer's perspective. Finally, Kathy Hodgson, did a preliminary edit, which did much to improve my writing. I thank you all.

As always, any and all errors, omissions and oversights are my responsibility alone.

CHAPTER 1

"Get the hell off my property," the old man yelled, in a thin strained voice. But his words carried little authority and were smothered by the surrounding bush. The two men paid him no mind. They walked in single file. The one in the front was the leader and kept advancing, saying not a word. The second man had a younger man's gait, walking with his hands in his pockets, wearing a baseball cap, pulled down over his face, and sunglasses. They were far bigger and stronger than the feeble old man, who retreated. The old man picked up a worn grey axe handle from a nearby woodshed and turned to face the advancing men. He stood his ground.

"Get the hell off my property. Get out." He threatened the men with the axe handle. They did not stop. The leader, who was now face to face with the old man, grabbed the end of the axe handle, gave it a twist, pulling it out of the old man's hands and casually flipped the axe handle so he had hold of the grip. Then with a quick two-handed swing he hit the old man on the side of his head with a powerful blow. There was a crack of bone and the old man crumpled to the ground. Dead.

The leader knelt and felt for a pulse. There was none. He dropped the axe handle and motioned for his follower to take the old man's arms and he took his legs. No words were exchanged. Together they carried the old man's body down the forested path to the river. The path ended at a dilapidated timber dock. Two logs were tied to the dock on one side and on the other was moored a small wooden row boat. "Throw him head first into the logs," was all the leader said, and they did, waiting as the old man's body slowly slid off the logs into the river. No movement. The two turned and walked away. At the murder scene they stopped; the killer picked up the axe handle, and ran his gloved hand down its length, seeing there was no blood on the handle, he put it back in the woodshed. The follower used his feet to spread dead leaves over the area where the old man had fallen. Not to worry there was little blood. Satisfied, they left. No rush. No one was around. No one would care. They showed no emotion. No humanity. Life was cheap. Their job was done.

CHAPTER 2

Tuesday May 16, 1972

The murky, swirling waters of the North Saskatchewan River marks the great divide between the prairie grasslands to the south and boreal forest and lakes to the north. Driving over the Diefenbaker Bridge, Josef Manne took a moment to enjoy the view of the river below. The cloudless morning sky foretold of warmth for the rest of the day. In May the weather in Saskatchewan is a crapshoot: snowing one day, blazing hot the next and everything in between.

A good day for a funeral Josef thought. He had about an hour and a half drive from Prince Albert to Blue River, where the funeral for Old Bill was to be held. On Wednesday, May 10th, Josef received the news from Mrs. Maggie Cameron, who lived next door to Old Bill. She was stoic, matter of fact and told what she knew. Josef listened in silence, holding back his grief. Earlier that morning she had gone down to the river, as was her routine, and there she saw Old Bill's body floating in the river next to his dock. The doctor and police figured Old Bill fell, hit his head on the dock or logs tied up to the dock and drowned. Josef and Mrs. Cameron consoled each other with the fact he had lived a long life and must have died quickly, presumably without pain, at his favorite place by the river. After hanging up Josef sat at the kitchen table, not moving, staring at nothing, numb. Old Bill was a dear friend.

The following day he received a surprise phone call at his office, this time from Mr. Benjamin Wallace the manager of the Royal Bank in Blue River, which was the last bank left open in the town. In a very officious way, Wallace told Josef that Old Bill had entrusted a letter with him, which upon his death, was to be given to Josef. Strange, Old Bill wasn't family; maybe he had no family. Josef agreed to drop by the bank when he came for the funeral. What was Old Bill up to?

Josef turned on to the highway and stepped on the gas. The '68 Mercury Parklane surged forward powered by its 390 cubic inch engine and purred down the highway. The Parklane was his father's last car. He always drove a Ford Mercury. Josef thought of him, thought of Old Bill and missed them both. His parent's generation were now gone from Josef's life and he was alone.

Memories dominated his mind as he drove. Funny, he had never thought of Old Bill dying. For him, Old Bill never aged. He was as much a presence as he was a friend. Just there smoking his pipe, always happy to see Josef. It was human nature he reasoned; people are naturally in denial and blind themselves to the inevitability of death. Old Bill was now gone and Josef regretted not doing more, not visiting him more, not writing to him more.

Growing up in Blue River, Josef knew Old Bill all his life. He lived on a small acreage about a mile outside of town along the shores of the Blue River and every Saturday he'd walk into town for supplies. He had no car. Without fail he'd drop in for a visit. There was a bond between him and the parents. They had pioneered the area; opened up the land. He'd sit down at the kitchen table have a coffee and they'd talk. Josef fondly remembered Old Bill reading the Saturday comics to him. He was only three or four, couldn't read, and Old Bill would ask him very formally whether the Saturday paper had arrived and whether he would like to read the comics with him. Josef would drop everything and run to get the paper and they'd sit together on the dark brown sofa. Old Bill would read the comics caption by caption using different voices for the characters as he went. Josef's favorite comic strip was Popeye, and he loved Old Bill's voice for Wimpy. It was a moment in the life of a child not to be forgotten.

Old Bill lived alone, never married. Josef's mother thought he was engaged to be married shortly after World War I, but his fiancée died in the Spanish flu epidemic of 1919. Old Bill was a loner, but not lonely. Josef concluded he liked the serenity and independence of living on his own totally self-reliant. He had served in the Boer War, World War I and in World War II. Imagine three wars! Yet, he never said much about the wars.

Josef's family moved away from Blue River when he was ten. No jobs. More opportunity was to be had in Prince Albert. However, they still farmed north of town and travelled back regularly – spring seeding, fall harvesting. Each time they'd stop in to see Old Bill, who was sure to be home. He lived in a one room 'shack', his term, which was painted white with forest green trim and a green door. It was small, maybe 20 feet long by 8 feet wide. Inside he had a table placed below the only window. A pot belly stove provided heat. His bed filled the back wall. He had a comfortable horsehair chair, which was his reading chair. He had electricity. No television, but a radio and books, lots of books. It wasn't much, but was all he needed or wanted. No fridge, but he did have a cold cellar. He built a box in the floor of the cellar to hold ice blocks cut from the river and insulated by sawdust. The ice kept things nice and cool even in summer.

His yard was lined by the biggest wood piles Josef had ever seen. Or maybe they just seemed gigantic to a little boy. Saskatchewan winters are long and cold and a great deal of firewood is needed. A path led down to the lake and to his dock. That dock was solid. Wooden piers were pounded into the soft bottom of the river. The piers supported thick beams, which, in turn, supported the three-inch-thick rough-hewn deck planks. The dock needed to be strong enough to withstand the winter ice. With the ice out, his handmade wooden row boat would be tied to the dock. It was a 'rescue boat' he used to salvage wayward logs sent downstream by logging camps up river. He'd retrieve the logs and soon they would be cut and split.

As Josef grew older, he travelled back to Blue River, however, after the farm was sold visits became fewer and fewer. After both his parents died, he was too busy with work to return to Blue River very often. He'd send a Christmas card each year as a way to keep in touch. Old Bill had no phone. Josef thought of the last time he saw him; it was last spring. He'd gone to fish at Blue River and spent the day at Old Bill's. They sat together on the dock. Josef fished. Bill smoked. They didn't talk much, simply enjoying each other's company. The fish were fried for supper — a memorable day. Josef would miss him. He was alone, 28 years of age, single, no prospects and no family.

He shook his head. Stop feeling sorry for yourself he admonished himself. As he continued to drive, the radio talk shows bombarded the airwaves with arguments about the forthcoming Canada Soviet hockey series. Every hockey pundit had an opinion and wasn't afraid to tell the world. Josef turned the radio off. In the silence his mind wandered and work seeped into his thoughts. Work was always there. Was it his escape? Perhaps. He was a lawyer, practicing criminal law in Prince Albert. Tomorrow he had a sentencing on a theft charge and on Friday he had an impaired driving trial, which is the cash cow for defence lawyers. He freely admitted that he was a product of television. He had grown up with Perry Mason, who was so smooth, so cool and never lost a case. On the other hand, the prosecutor, Hamilton Burger, was a sour unappealing sort, who never won a case. Defence for Josef. He was an associate with a small five-person firm, McNeil and Associates. Two of the lawyers did criminal law, one did real estate and solicitor work, one did family law and Mr. McNeil was the civil litigator, company law man and all-round mentor.

After three years, Josef was becoming more comfortable with his practice. For the first few years every file was new in terms of the law. There was so much to learn. Now things weren't so new. Thus far he had eight jury trials, winning seven. He was no Perry Mason. His style was more soft-sell, low key. He'd converse with witnesses and reason with the jurors and judges.

Josef was told his persona changed when he was in court. Outside of court he was quiet, somewhat shy, soft spoken; in court he became stronger, more confident, with a voice that could be kind one moment and biting sharp the next. So, he was told. His secretary, Shirley, called him a workaholic. She was probably right. He had to confess he lived to work. Such was his life.

Josef ruefully accepted he was somewhat insecure. He remembered his first day of law school. He was terrified. All the other students seemed so brilliant, so confident in themselves and then there was him. Maybe he was admitted into law school by mistake? In fear of being exposed he threw himself into his studies. Perhaps it was another escape from life. His sister had died a few years before; she was a drug addict and died of an overdose. Then his mom died when he was in law school. Josef lived and studied.

His father died a couple years ago. He was now alone. These losses, all too soon, perhaps molded him into a loner. Oh, he had friends and would go out with them and play all sorts of sports, but depth of friendship was missing. There were girlfriends, but they never lasted. It was him. Josef knew he probably pushed them away. Fear of rejection. In high school he was too shy to ask the girls out – insecurity. Instead they were snatched up by the confident, egotistical types; usually older students and usually complete jerks. He was not bitter, just honest.

He was alone with his work. Sad really.

Soon the forest grew denser and coming to the crest of a hill he saw the Blue River valley in the distance, a rolling sea of green spruce. It was almost 9:30 am and he had arranged to meet Mr. Wallace at the bank before Old Bill's funeral, which was at 11:00 am. The highway was the main thoroughfare through town. It followed the gradient down towards Blue River, where the town dock was located, then it made a ninety degree turn west following the river. The Royal Bank was located at the turn.

The bank was the only brick building in the town. The intent, no doubt, was to give the bank gravitas and an aura of security. The blue and gold Royal Bank of Canada signage looked stately atop the red brick. Two tellers acted as the bank's reception and Josef could see an older, somewhat rotund, bald man in an inner glass walled office. That would be Mr. Wallace. Josef went up to one of the tellers and told her he had an appointment with Mr. Wallace. She went to get him. The bald man came out of his sanctum hand outstretched.

"Mr. Manne, nice to see you, Benjamin Wallace. Nice to put a face to a name." He shook Josef's hand vigorously and escorted him to his office, where he gestured for Josef to take a seat and he took his chair behind the desk. "You know, your parents banked with us when they lived in town. I was sorry to hear of their passing."

Josef accepted his condolences. Mr. Wallace had done some background checking or, perhaps, it was just small-town knowledge.

"Now Mr. Manne."

"Please, Josef."

"Okay, Josef. I have a few other things for you beside the letter." Mr. Wallace was getting right to business, which was refreshing. "First, I have a bank record book for a chequing account and some blank cheques. But before I give these to you, and please don't take offence, I do need some identification. A driver's licence would be fine."

Josef was taken aback. "I don't really understand. I have no bank account here."

Mr. Wallace smiled. "Mr. Jones came into the bank towards the end of March, just before Easter. He told me he wanted to put his affairs in order. That day he opened this chequing account and he insisted it be a joint account in his and your names. You see Mr. Jones wanted to leave you some money outside of his estate. A joint account means when one of the account holders dies the other account holder receives all the funds in the account."

Josef handed him his driver's licence and Mr. Wallace recorded the details on a form. Next, he took out two signature cards passed them to Josef and indicated where he was to sign. Once done, he passed the account book and cheques to him.

Josef looked at the amount in the account and was shocked. There was $30,000 in the account! Mr. Wallace continued talking, "Mr. Jones was adamant about putting this money aside for you." He chuckled. "Came into the bank with a bag of cash including rolled coins. I explained the chequing account would pay no interest and suggested he might want to open a savings account. However, the interest on the savings account would have to be declared and I would then need your social insurance number. He didn't want that and so the chequing account was opened. I hope you don't mind."

"Of course, I don't. I'm just surprised Bill did this for me." Josef was still reeling; $30,000 was a lot of money. You could buy a nice house in Prince Albert for about $20,000.

"The money is now yours." Mr. Wallace opened his top drawer and pulled out the letter addressed to Josef. "Here is the letter Mr. Jones left with me. I will leave you alone to read it."

Mr. Wallace left and closed the door. Josef fingered the letter. His name, address and telephone number were printed on the envelope in a shaking hand. He felt a small hard object inside and gently opened it. There was a one-page letter and a safety deposit key. The letter read:

Old Bill's Last Will and Testament

March 29, 1972

Dear Josef,

Since you are reading this I am dead. Don't grieve. I have lived a long and full life. One of my joys has been watching you grow into a fine young man and a lawyer to boot. Your parents would be proud.

I have one request of you from the grave. I have made you the executor of my estate and I trust you to see that my wishes are carried out. I never had the courage to do what was right when I was alive. In death I hope to make things right. The will is in a safety deposit box in the bank and you now have the key.

Your old friend,

William Maurice Jones

Josef smiled. The letter was so Old Bill. He was a man of few words and liked to speak at times in riddles. What was it he wanted to set right? The will would probably provide the answer.

Mr. Wallace knocked and Josef motioned for him to come in. Josef showed him the safety deposit key. "I assume this is a key for a safety deposit box here?"

"It is. Mr. Jones opened a box in your joint names the same day he opened the chequing account. One of the signature cards you signed was for the safety deposit box. Do you wish to look at its contents now?" Josef nodded yes. "Very well, we'll have to go into the vault. This way."

They went into another room, where the vault was open. Mr. Wallace found the safety deposit number. Each box was secured by two locks. Mr. Wallace had the bank key for one and Josef had the key for the other. Mr. Wallace took out the box and escorted him to a separate room, where he could have privacy.

Josef opened the box. On the top was a heavy brown paper envelope with a printed title, '*Last Will and Testament of William Maurice Jones*'. It contained a one page will. Josef cringed, a holograph will. In other words, it was hand written by Old Bill and not prepared by a lawyer. Trust him to write his own will. The will read:

MY LAST WILL and TESTAMENT

This is the last will and testament of me, William Maurice Jones, of Blue River, Saskatchewan.

I have no other wills.

Anyone who does not survive me by 45 days will be treated as having died before me.

I am a bachelor, always have been, and my only living relative is my younger brother, Bruce Nathan Jones, who is to receive absolutely nothing under my will. He and his family have only brought dishonour upon our family name. You reap what you sow.

I appoint, Josef Manne, of Prince Albert, Saskatchewan to be my executor and to look after my estate paying all debts and dealing with all my assets as he sees fit. As executor he is entitled to be paid a reasonable lawyer rate for his work.

I give my entire estate to Connie Thornton and her daughter, Rebecca Thornton, of Goondiwindi, Queensland, Australia the wife and daughter of Flight Officer Charles Thornton, of the RAAF, who died on January 31, 1945 in a Prisoner of War Camp at Niigata, Japan.

Signed,

William Maurice Jones
March 26, 1972

Josef folded the will, put it back into the envelope. Who were Connie and Rebecca Thornton? And why? He had no idea.

The safety deposit box contained a number of other documents. There were about twenty Canada Savings Bonds with coupons attached, a stock certificate for 10,000 shares in Morrison International Agriculture Inc., three titles to property in Blue River Township, a wad of $100 bills and a savings account in Old Bill's name showing a balance of $56,342.10. Time was short, he'd return again later in the day and left for the funeral.

CHAPTER 3

The funeral service was held in the small Anglican church in Blue River, built in 1922. Josef knew the church well; he remembered the uncomfortable pews, where he, as a young child, would fidget, squirm and generally be a nuisance for his mother, who had insisted they go to church and that was non-negotiable.

Josef looked around for a place to sit. Mrs. Cameron was seated in the third row. She saw him, waved and indicated she had saved him a spot. Normally Josef was a back-row person, however, he could not deny Mrs. Cameron.

He took his seat and surveyed the people, trying to recall names. He asked Mrs. Cameron about the people seated in the front row. She whispered, "The heavy-set man in the brown suit is Bill's brother, Bruce, next to him is his wife, Mary. She's a nice lady. Too bad she married him. Next to her is their son, Ron. Don't know where his wife is. I think she took off. Better off without him. Next to him are his sons, Alex and Tyler; Alex is the older one. They are bad news. They take after their father and grandfather. The men in the family have crossed a lot of people in town. Bill didn't have much to do with them and here they are sitting prim and proper at his funeral looking as if they care. I saw the boys rummaging around Bill's house a day or two ago. God, I hope they don't move in. There'd go the neighbourhood."

If only she knew what Old Bill had in store for them.

She continued in a quiet church voice. "You know the minister had a right row with Bill's brother over the funeral. Bruce Jones did not want a service at all. Just plug Bill in the ground. Nice and cheap. But Minister Knox would not have it. Bill had given him money and instructions for the

Old Bill's Last Will and Testament

funeral and unless Bruce had a will saying otherwise he was going to fulfill Bill's wishes. Bill gave the minister $5,000 to cover all funeral costs, with what is left over to go to the church. There will be plenty. Doesn't cost more than a thousand or two to have a proper funeral. I never thought Bill had that kind of money."

If only she knew.

The church was now full and his eye caught a group seated in the back. There was an older man and woman, Josef assumed they were together, and a man in his fifties. They stood out: well dressed, confident, strong people. Definitely not from the town. The people from Blue River were hard working, quality folk, but they struggled against the odds to make a living in this harsh country and it showed. These people weren't struggling. He asked Mrs. Cameron, she'd know.

She turned and took a peek. "No idea. Not from here. Notice of Bill's funeral was in the Saskatoon Star Phoenix."

Minister Knox entered and walked to the front of the church to stand beside Old Bill's simple pine casket. The service began. Josef struggled to pay attention. His mind was elsewhere, thinking about Old Bill's will and knowing his brother would not be too pleased. The minister's eulogy was witty, touching and caught his attention. Minister Knox told the assembled the story of Bill's life and there was much Josef did not know.

He told the story about the under-age 16-year-old signing up to fight in the Boer War. The British needed mobile mounted cavalry. Although Bill was under-age, he had worked and lived on ranches all his life and was a skilled horseman. Evidently the recruiter was skeptical of signing up young Bill, until that is, Bill took to his horse and showed him how he could ride. Horse prowess trumped age and off Bill went to South Africa.

Although Josef knew Old Bill had fought in World War II, he never knew that he was one of the Canadians captured after the fall of Hong Kong in December, 1941 and spent over three and a half years in Japanese prisoner of war camps. It explained the reference to the prisoner of war camp in his will. Old Bill had never mentioned being a POW to Josef in all the years he knew him and Josef had pestered him, as children do, to talk about the wars. He would say to Josef, "Wait. You're too young fella. Remember war brings out the worst and best in people."

Minister Knox turned to Bill's life in Blue River. He highlighted its simplicity. Josef found it interesting that when he mentioned Bill had no refrigerator, but a cold cellar instead, there was a quick exchange of glances between the two Jones' boys. One reached over and nudged his father and whispered in his ear. The father nodded. To that point they had been sitting impassively, barely awake. The cold cellar had gotten their attention. Strange.

The most poignant part of the service was the end. The local Legion provided an honour guard and a trumpeter. All rose as the trumpeter played the Last Post and the honour guard carried Old Bill's casket out of the church. Tears came then.

The assembled followed the casket out. It was loaded on to the hearse for the short journey to the local cemetery for burial. A reception was to take place at the local Legion hall. Mrs. Cameron had to go to the hall as she was one of the church ladies looking after the food. Josef was to drop by her place for supper. He decided to go to the cemetery.

When Josef got to the cemetery the honour guard placed the casket on braces over the freshly dug grave. Ropes were looped through the casket handles and lay by the grave. There was only the minister, the funeral staff, the honour guard, the three 'strangers' and Josef present. No family. So much for grieving relatives. Minister Knox said a number of burial prayers and the honour guard lowered the casket into the grave. The burial ended with the Lord's Prayer. The honour guard left and Josef thanked the minister for the service and complimented him on the eulogy. "How did you know so much about Bill's life?" Josef asked.

Minister Knox gave him a wry smile and replied, "Truth be told, Bill outlined the service and wrote most of the eulogy. I was but the messenger. He came to me a month or so ago and wanted to have his funeral all arranged. He gave me a sum of money with clear instructions on what to do upon his death and I carried out his wishes."

The 'strangers' and Josef were left alone at the graveside. The cemetery caretaker appeared and asked, "Sorry to bother you? I do need to fill the grave in."

The older lady quickly responded, "Oh could you give us more time? It will be our last opportunity to say good-bye. You don't mind, do you?" It

Old Bill's Last Will and Testament

was more of a statement than a question. The caretaker mumbled that he'd take his lunch and leave them in peace.

They stood awkwardly by the grave. The older lady broke the silence and introduced herself, "My name is Margaret Morrison, this is my husband, John, and our son William. We are friends of Bill's going back a long time. And you are?"

"I'm sorry, rude of me, I'm Josef Manne, also a friend of Old Bill's. Nice to meet you. You're not from around here."

"No, we live in Saskatoon. But couldn't miss coming to farewell Bill. I noticed you called him Old Bill."

Josef smiled. "I've known Bill all my life and he has always been old to me. I will miss him."

Mrs. Morrison looked at him knowingly and said, "I don't think you're from around here either."

"No, I came up from Prince Albert this morning, but I was born and raised in Blue River."

John joined the conversation, "What do you do Josef?"

"I'm a lawyer, and work with a small firm in PA."

"A lawyer. What type of practice do you have?"

"My practice is mostly criminal defence work."

"Sounds very interesting. Must be in court a great deal."

"Yes, almost every day and the one thing for sure is that there is never a dull moment." The conversation was easy and it then dawned on Josef, "You aren't the 'Morrison' as in 'Morrison Elevators'?"

John gave a quiet laugh. "Yes, we are that Morrison. I am the President of the company. William here is in charge of our brokerage branch and Margaret is the boss."

Margaret interjected, "I wish, but I do try to keep these two in line." She then changed topic. "Please tell us how is it that you know Bill?"

Josef gave an abbreviated summary ending with, "And I found out this morning Bill named me the executor of his estate. Little did he know that as a criminal lawyer I know nothing about estate work."

Margaret jumped in and looking at John said in a jubilant voice, "There is a God! We told him to put his estate in order." She turned to Josef. "Bill knew he was dying. He was in Saskatoon towards the end of March and

19

dropped by. He told us he was in town to see a specialist at the University Hospital. We prodded. The specialist was an oncologist. Bill had lung cancer. It was inoperable. He was given about six months. We urged him to prepare a will. He said he'd think about it. But you know Bill; he is an independent cuss. I am so glad he did it. The cancer took him quickly."

Josef corrected her, "Oh he didn't die of cancer. He had a fall on his dock, probably getting ready to winch some logs out of the water. Hit his head and drowned." Josef could see the surprise on the Morrison's faces. He tried to soften the news, "It would have been quick and doing something he loved."

Margaret smiled verging on a laugh. "Trust Bill to be doing that at his age."

John then asked, "Would you like to join us in giving William Jones a proper farewell?"

Josef was puzzled. John continued, "We've brought a bottle of champagne with us to toast our Bill and would be honoured, very honoured to have you join us." Margaret nodded her approval.

Josef could not say no. William went to the car and returned with the champagne and a box of champagne glasses. Josef re-arranged the wooden folding chairs left at the grave site to a level grass area. He noticed John had a bad leg and used a cane. William uncorked the bottle of G.H. Mumm champagne and filled each of the glasses.

They stood by the grave. John raised his glass. "A toast to William Jones, my friend, my brother in arms, my guardian angel." All stood with glasses raised.

Mrs. Morrison elaborated, "My husband served with Bill in both World War I and World War II. Bill saved my husband's life in both. We owe him a great deal."

Josef was intrigued, "In both wars. Do you mind telling me about that? Old Bill never told me much about the wars."

John took a sip of champagne and nodded. "It deserves telling young man. And now's the time. Let's have a seat. It is a long story." He started:

"In World War I we served in the 5th Battalion (Western Cavalry). Bill signed up early and was an original. They left for France in February, 1915. I was only 17 when the war broke out and my parents insisted I finish high school and turn 18 before enlisting. I think they hoped the war would be over by then. It wasn't. I signed-up as soon as I turned 18 and my father pulled a few strings to get me into officer school. I came out a green lieutenant and shipped off to France. This was early 1917. I was brash, inexperienced and knew so little about the fighting. Bill was my sergeant and took me under his wing. By then he was a veteran of many battles. He knew the front and taught me survival. Funny, in war survival is so much luck. Why does a man right beside you get shot and you don't? Dumb luck."

"When I arrived, I was thrown into the thick of it, Vimy Ridge. The Canadian Corps was in the final stages of planning that attack. It was my first combat. My first time going over the top. Bill was at my side. After our success at Vimy Ridge in April 1917 we were thrown into Passchendaele in the fall of 1917. What horror." His voice saddened as he relived that time. "The rains came and came. The front was a muddy cesspool. Man and beast disappeared swallowed up by the mud. How could anyone think about attacking in those conditions? It was slaughter. I remember our unit followed a creeping barrage, where our artillery pounded a path forward. We slogged through the mud, each step an exhausting effort. Then the artillery barrage stopped and the Germans returned to their trenches and counter-attacked. They started shelling our position. I remember hearing the explosion of the shell. After that, nothing. I was told I was buried by the explosion. It was to be my grave. I was concussed and shrapnel had cut through my thigh, breaking my femur. Bill survived the blast, dug me out, put a tourniquet on my leg and carried me back to our lines where stretcher bearers took me to a field hospital. I would have bled out, died right there in that horrible battlefield if it hadn't been for Bill."

"After months of recovery I returned to my unit and was so happy to see Bill still alive. Together we survived the last months of the war. Afterwards we kept in touch through battalion re-unions. There was always the bond of battle between us. In 1922 Margaret and I had a son and we named him William."

John went quiet, sipped the champagne, gave a painful smile and said, "Then war came again."

"In 1935 Margaret, William and I moved to Winnipeg, which was and is the center of the grain trade in Canada. Times were tough. The Depression hit. With the rise of Hitler, I felt obliged to enlist in the reserves with the Winnipeg Grenadiers and was made a captain. War came and I received a letter from Bill. He had never written to me before. He wanted to enlist but was told he was too old. He told me he was 49, which was a lie, and asked to be my batman. I was a little taken back, because a batman is essentially an officer's personal servant, and I never had one or wanted one, too British aristocracy for me. Yet, I owed Bill, and went to my commanding officer and made my case. It wasn't hard, given Bill's war record, provided Bill could pass the physical he was in. Of course, he passed the physical and became my batman."

"The Winnipeg Grenadiers were a green unit with no combat experience. We were sent to Hong Kong in October 1941. It was British military stupidity. Hong Kong was not defensible. The Japanese attacked on December 8, 1941. We had no hope, but we put up a fight for seventeen days. Bill was by my side throughout. We surrendered on Christmas Day. Frankly, if we had known what surrender would bring I think many of us would have chosen to fight to the death."

"We were taken prisoner. At first, we were kept in a POW camp in Hong Kong. The conditions were bad and became worse. As an officer I was treated half decently; the enlisted men suffered. They worked often in terrible conditions, like slaves. Officers, under the Geneva Convention, did not do manual labour and we fared much better. Bill, as my batman, could go back and forth between the officers and enlisted soldiers. I also think because he was older, the Japanese tended to show him a measure of respect. And Bill earned respect. His bearing was proud. He wouldn't say much, but would stand his ground. They'd beat him at times, but he never cowered. That was Bill."

"In August 1943 Bill and I were part of a group of Canadians transported to Japan to work in their slave camps. I was one of only a few officers sent along. The Japanese wanted officers to keep military discipline. We were taken to a camp at Niigata on the coast north of Tokyo. It was hell. We lost a third of our men. The enlisted soldiers provided slave labour unloading coal from ships or working in the ship yard. The men were starved, beaten and worked to death. And it was so cold. In late 1944, early '45, I took ill with dysentery and pneumonia. I was dying. Somehow from somewhere

Bill got sulfa tablets to fight the infections. We all knew medicines were in our red cross packages, but the packages never reached us. Bill found a supply. My fever broke and there was Bill by my side. The doctor told me Bill had saved not just me but many. He never told me his source. Some things are better kept secret. I owed my life again to Bill. The Yanks then saved us." He stopped.

All sat in silent tribute to Old Bill.

There were certain things, which Josef had to ask. "Mr. Morrison, in Old Bill's will he mentions an Australian officer at Niigata. Do you remember him?"

John sat thinking, searching his memory. "At Niigata most of the prisoners were Canadian and American. Sorry, I don't recall an Australian, he may have been with the Americans."

"One other thing, in Bill's documents is a certificate for stocks in Morrison International Agriculture Inc. Is that your company?"

John smiled. "Yes, that is our company. It went public in 1947 and I gave Bill a substantial number of shares. It was the least I could do. I think the shares were worth about $1.00 per at the time."

"Well he still has them, 10,000 of them."

William gave a whistle. "Dividends have been paid out every year since 1947 in the form of shares and the current share value is $33.00. Ballpark, the market value today in those shares may well be about $350,000 to $400,000."

More surprises. Did Old Bill know the value of the shares? He knew. Josef had to laugh, the money meant nothing to him. He had everything he needed living in his shack by the river. The four remained, warmed by the sun, sipping champagne, talking and remembering. It was comforting.

The time came, however, for the farewell to end. All rose and went over to the grave, each with their own thoughts, and said goodbye to William Maurice Jones one last time. Josef thanked the Morrisons for sharing their farewell. It was truly special. Mrs. Morrison gave Josef a hug and Mr. Morrison in shaking his hand looked him in the eye and said, "A friend of Bill's is a friend of ours. You remember that young man."

CHAPTER 4

Josef returned to the Royal Bank and asked Mr. Wallace if he would help take an inventory of the items contained in the safety deposit box. Wallace readily agreed and came up with an inventory form. They itemized everything and Wallace witnessed the document as accurate. They then made photocopies of the will and letter.

It was a little after 3:30 pm and Josef decided to go and see Mrs. Cameron and at the same time check on Old Bill's property. When he arrived at her place, he noticed an older black Ford pick-up and Harley Davidson motorcycle parked at Old Bill's. Mrs. Cameron met him at her door. She was not a happy lady.

"Glad you're here. The two Jones' boys just arrived at Bill's a moment ago. I can't stand it having them mess around with Bill's stuff. Two loud-mouth louts is what they are. At the reception today, they sat at the bar all the while drinking themselves silly, getting loud and obnoxious. That's what free booze will do to white trash. White trash is what they are. I guess nothing I can do. It's their property now."

Josef debated, should he or shouldn't he tell her about the will. He decided. "Well it is not their property yet. I found out today from Mr. Wallace at the bank that Bill named me executor of his estate. I think I'll go over and talk to the boys." Mrs. Cameron's mouth could not have opened wider and then it was replaced by a satisfied grin.

"Be careful. They're boozed up," she said, "I'll go and get Betsy just in case."

"Betsy?"

"My shotgun. Handy at times."

As Josef walked over to Old Bill's shack, he mulled over how he'd approach the two. They'd not take kindly to him kicking them out, but he'd be damned if he was going to let them ransack Old Bill's home. Josef preferred wits over fists. Besides being outnumbered two to one he'd likely come out the short end of any fight. No, calm, lawyerly pomposity was the order of the day. Josef would let them come to the decision to leave. The door was open and he saw one of the brothers, the bigger one, Alex, seated in Bill's chair looking through a wooden box. They'd found the cold cellar, which was what had excited them at the church, and the other brother, Tyler, was in it. Both had changed into blue jeans and T-shirts. Josef stood in the doorway. "Excuse me, can I help you gentlemen?"

"Huh, what. Who the fuck are you?" Alex asked in a slurred nasty sort of way, which Josef assumed was his general disposition. Tyler popped his head up out of the cold cellar, much like a gopher poking its head out of a hole.

"My name is Josef Manne, a lawyer, and Mr. Jones named me the executor of his estate. And you are Alex Jones, Bill's grand-nephew." He looked at Tyler. "And you are Bill's grand-nephew, Tyler. I'm glad it's the two of you, I thought someone might have broken into Bill's place. Can't be too careful, can we?"

Alex was leery. "How do you know our names? We don't know you. And what's this about an executor?" Josef knew this would throw off the two brothers.

"I was at the funeral this morning and Mrs. Cameron, next door, pointed you out. I wanted to know the family members."

Alex was now standing. He was heavyset, part muscle, part fat. He had a couple tattoos on his bare arm and 'hate' and 'love' knuckles, crude jailhouse work. Definitely not artistic. Most noticeable were his eyes. They were dark, unfeeling, black coals. The eyes of a psychopath.

He spoke, "I asked you, what's this about an executor." His voice belligerent.

Josef calmly replied, "Mr. Jones made a will naming me the executor and I'm here to secure his property. I know you are family and all, but it's best that you leave."

"Best that we leave," Alex smirked, "well, we got some things to look for before we leave. You just hold off until we're finished with our business." Josef could feel his aggression and saw Alex flex his knuckles. Tension was rising.

Josef in a controlled tone explained, "I appreciate, as family members, you'd like to go through your uncle's personal things. But I'd advise against it. You see, it's my job to protect Bill's property for everyone who is a beneficiary under the will, which might well include you both. Think about it, say some money is missing and the finger points to the two of you. Tampering with an estate is frowned upon by the courts. It is in your best interests to leave, and I'll be doing an inventory of everything. Here is my card." He took a business card out of his wallet and gave it to Alex. Giving him something to think about. Without question Alex's first impulse would be to hit Josef, but by now confusion was eating into his aggression.

Tyler crawled out of the cold cellar, and said to his brother, "Nothing in there anyway."

Alex was the leader of the two and he was hesitating. Before he said anything else, Josef heard a gruff voice behind him. "What's going on here? Who are you?"

Josef turned, it was Bruce Jones. He and Bill were brothers in name only. Whereas Bill exuded warmth, sensitivity, with a twinkle in his eye, Bruce displayed none of that. He was a hard, cold, bull of a man, not tall, solid, big boned, big head, no neck. He had a short crew cut, which accentuated a harsh demeanour. His eyes were a cold grey.

Tyler jumped in, eager to please. "He's a lawyer, grandpa."

"Mr. Jones, Josef Manne, I am the executor named in your brother's will."

Josef could see the flash of surprise in Bruce's eyes. "I didn't know Bill had a will. No one told me."

"I just found out this morning. Your brother left his will with Mr. Wallace at the Royal Bank."

"What! I went to see Wallace last week about Bill's affairs and he never mentioned any will. Lying bankers."

Josef came to Mr. Wallace's defence. "In fairness, Mr. Wallace would not have known about any will last week. The will was kept in a safety deposit box at the bank and I only had access to it this morning."

Old Bill's Last Will and Testament

"I'd like to see that will." Not a request, but a demand.

"Of course, the will has to be made public when we proceed to probate."

"As the only surviving relative, I want to see the will. I have a right to see the will."

"I don't disagree with you at all, and that certainly will occur when we move to probate."

"When will that be? I don't like hanging in the wind while you lawyers squeeze the fees."

"Look, Mr. Jones I just found out this morning. I will be going back to my office in Prince Albert tonight, and our firm will move as quickly as possible in dealing with the estate. Here is my business card." Josef handed it to him and Bruce grabbed it without bothering to look at it, which was good because it touted his speciality in criminal law and not estate law. Josef continued with his lawyerly façade. "I'm here to secure the property to protect the estate. I explained that to your grandsons."

Bruce gave Josef a penetrating look of distain and said, "You'll be hearing from my lawyer." He then turned and said to Alex and Tyler, "Come on let's get out of here." He was finished talking and walked away. Rude, but Josef concluded such was his nature. The boys followed in tow like trained dogs. Alex deliberately brushed by Josef. They left in protest, engines revving, stones spewing and tires screeching.

Josef went into the shack. Books were sprawled about, boxes pulled out and the cold cellar was open. The boys had been looking for something, probably money. Bill had beaten them to the punch by putting his money in the bank. Old Bill probably expected his brother and family to descend on his home the minute he was dead. Josef started cleaning up. Mrs. Cameron poked her head in the door.

"Thank God they're gone. Look at what they've done. Bill was always so orderly. I was ready to call the police. So, Bill had a will."

Josef knew she wanted him to tell her more. "Yes, he had a will, but that's all I can say right now." He wanted to be alone. "I have to secure the place. I'll come over when I'm done. Shouldn't be too long."

"Okay, I'll put Betsy away and start working on supper."

"Oh, just a sec, do you know where Old Bill keeps a key?"

"It's under the ugly dog boot scraper by the door."

The boot scraper was made of iron. Two dogs stood on their hind legs holding a thin iron cleaning blade between them. It was ugly indeed and heavy. He tipped the boot scraper on its side and there was the key.

Josef tidied. The books were put back. Old Bill loved historical fiction and he loved Tolkien's Lord of the Rings. There on the shelf was a leather-bound early edition of the trilogy. It was Old Bill who insisted Josef read that classic tale. What a glorious read. Old Bill's array of pipes was on the window sill. He had lent Josef a pipe for a Christmas play when he was in grade one. Santa Claus needed a pipe. His clothes were neatly folded or hung with military precision in a cedar armoire smelling of pipe tobacco and lemon laundry detergent mixed with a hint of moth balls. There was a wooden crate filled with papers, mostly newspapers. Josef flipped through them and found a thin, paperback entitled, "Making your Will", written by Simon J. Witherspoon. The store sticker showed it was purchased from 'Saskatoon Books'. No doubt this was Old Bill's guide in writing his will. Josef decided to take it with him.

He went down into the cold cellar. All looked in order. He closed the floor hatch, sat in Old Bill's chair and picked up the wooden box Alex was going through when he arrived. It was precious. First, it contained his war medals. There was a Queen Victoria medal from the Boer War and all his other medals. Josef was thrilled and so happy Alex hadn't pinched them. Next, it contained a bundle of letters. When he untied the bundle, he found a number of Christmas cards Josef had send to Old Bill over the years. Josef felt pleased he had kept them. Finally, there was an old photo album and pile of loose photographs, some with cryptic comments, others were camera dated. He shuffled through the photographs and found a few of Old Bill with him and his parents. Memories came exploding back. Josef decided to take the wooden box, its treasures and photo album with him. He locked the door and returned the key to underneath the boot scraper.

Leaving the treasures at the door, Josef walked down to the dock. It was so peaceful. Two logs were tied to the dock and there was Old Bill's wooden boat. He stood on the dock embracing the serenity. The river glistened and sparkled in the afternoon sun. It was a peaceful place to die; if there is such a thing. Sure beats lying in a hospital bed surrounded by sickness and false sterility. Josef sadly thought of his parents. Both had suffered. His father had cancer and his mother had ALS, Lou Gehrig's disease. Her body strangled her to death.

Sadness, grief, loneliness enveloped Josef. They were all gone. As he looked out over the river he thought that this may well be the last time he would stand on Old Bill's dock, the last time in Blue River. There was nothing for him to return to. He stood in silence. Finally, he turned and walked back up the path, past the woodshed, and past the wood piles, which didn't seem quite so large as he remembered as a boy.

CHAPTER 5

Josef arrived at the office early, knowing Straun McNeil would be there. This was his firm, his home; he was the first one in and last one out. From the staff room he heard Straun's cheerful voice. "Coffee's on." Josef went to get a coffee.

Straun was standing by the coffee pot, leaning on the counter. He was early 60's, still had a full head of white, thick hair, was a little on the heavy side, had a pale complexion, rosy cheeks and an ever-present smile. He was a positive person and knew everyone in town. Josef loved working for him.

"How was your trip to Blue River?"

"Interesting," Josef replied pouring himself a cup of coffee. "I went up a mourner and came back an executor. My friend who died made me the executor of his estate."

Straun chuckled. "You had no idea? How'd you find out?"

"He left a letter addressed to me with the local bank manager and the will was kept in a safety deposit box at the bank."

"You're kidding. How big is the estate?"

"Actually, quite large, which is even more of a surprise, because my friend lived in a small one room house. The estate could well be about half a million dollars. I'd like you to have a look at the will and get your input. If you have a few minutes? Everything's in my office."

"I've got to see this."

They adjourned to Josef's office. Straun leaned back in his chair reading Old Bill's letter and will. Without looking up he said, "Got to love folks who can't spend $100 bucks to get a lawyer to write a will for them and then go and cut their family out of it. Invites a very costly fight and the lawyers win."

"That's what I thought too. But I'm not an estate lawyer."

Straun looked at Josef over his reading glasses. "You mentioned the estate could be worth a half a million, how do you figure that?"

Josef outlined the contents of the safety deposit box, and had checked the price of Morrison International Agriculture stock in the paper. Yesterday the stock was selling at $33.18 per share. Straun gave a knowing nod. "That's a big estate, do you want Gabe to help you out? He's our will expert."

"I was thinking the same."

"First things first, you need to open a file, and put the money you have in trust, with the remainder put in our safe." Straun was already working through the file. "Want to see if Gabe is in? He usually is by this time."

Gabriel Forest was a quiet, bookish person with a dry sense of humour. He was a solicitor, more comfortable with paper than with people. Josef gave a quick rap on the door. "Morning, got a moment? Straun and I have a will for you to look at in my office."

Gabe countered, "A will? You? How many times have we told you to get the money up front from your clients?" Gabe loved to give Josef a rough time about his criminal clients.

"Very funny. Want to come?"

Josef filled him in as they walked to his office. Straun handed him the letter and the will. Gabe spoke out loud as he read. "William Maurice Jones certainly had high regard for you, Josef. Interesting his phrasing about doing right. A holograph will. Good in Saskatchewan. Has to be entirely written in the hand of the testator. I assume we can easily prove he is the writer. No other writing on the will, which would make it invalid. Revokes all other wills. Puts in a survivorship clause of 45 days. I bet he was copying from a will kit. Doesn't like his brother or family. They will not be happy. Probably contest the will, if the estate is worth a half million, I would. Names his executor. Too bad he's a criminal lawyer. Full authority is good. He was a prisoner of war. Interesting. Leaves entire estate to the wife and daughter of Charles Thornton. They better be alive otherwise the will lapses. Why did he leave his estate to them? Was he of sound mind? Was his mind wandering back in time? I've seen it, old folks start travelling back to their youth." He finished and turned to Josef smiling. "And you said estate work was boring."

"Is it a valid will?"

"Yes, a few years back a Saskatchewan farmer was pinned under a tractor and he scratched with a pen knife on the fender of his tractor a will giving everything to his wife. He died. The writing on the fender was recognized. Here we have much more thoughtful writing and it's clearly intended to be a will."

Josef showed Gabe the book he found at Old Bill's shack. Gabe laughed. "Ah, Mr. Witherspoon strikes again. What's the saying, a little knowledge is a dangerous thing."

"You mentioned a few problems as you were reading through the will. You mentioned the will lapsing. Why?" Josef was showing his ignorance.

Gabe was all too happy to elaborate, "As he has it, the will has two beneficiaries, Connie Thornton and her daughter, Rebecca. Everything goes to them. That is if they survive him by the 45 days. If you find out both are dead, there are no beneficiaries. The will lapses, which in this case would mean the entire estate lapses. It would be as though there was no will. The intestacy laws would apply and his brother, who is next of kin, would get the entire estate. Mr. Jones should have put in a residuary clause, something like: If they do not survive my death then my estate goes to their surviving family members. Something! Anything! There is nothing like that in the will."

"But he clearly indicates his brother is to receive nothing. Surely the will would still stand to cut him out of receiving anything?" Josef argued.

Gabe's answer was short and clear, "No. The will lapses. Tell me, when did Mr. Jones die?"

"May 10th, at least that is when his body was found."

"Okay, so 21 more days in May. June 24th would be the 45 days. The beneficiaries have to be alive until then."

Straun, ever the optimist, piped up, "I'm confident they're alive."

Josef then queried about the survivorship clause, "Why is that clause about surviving his death by 45 days in there in the first place?"

"You did take wills in law school, didn't you? How soon we forget." Gabe was enjoying this. He went on, "I know it seems like a strange clause, but there is a reason. It is designed to avoid double probate fees and taxes. It makes sense to have a survivorship clause for people who live together and are more likely to die in a common accident. For example, assume a husband and wife are killed in a car crash. The wife survives the crash for a day. The husband is killed instantly. Without a survivorship clause, the estate of the husband first would go to the wife, and she'd have to pay all the fees and taxes. Of course, the wife is dead, so you have to go through the probate of her will as well and pay more taxes before it gets to the children, who are the beneficiaries. Double taxes and fees. I don't think it should have been in this will at all. I bet Mr. Witherspoon tells people always to put it in a will. What does he say?"

Josef had Witherspoon's book and looked up survivorship clauses in the index. "Yup, page 23, Mr. Witherspoon says, 'Every will should have a survivorship clause.' And he suggests 45 days."

Straun took charge. "Gentlemen, we have a substantial estate. I suggest the two of you work together. The will provides for reasonable legal fees, use your standard billable hourly rates. Josef you open a file and any money goes into trust. Gabe what do we need to do?"

"I can go about putting the estate together, putting a value on the lands he owned, stocks, and bonds. I'll also start preparing the application for probate. We really don't know if there is another will; I'd like us to be the first to file. It's critical to find the beneficiaries, and I think Josef, that's for you. Other issues can wait, such as his state of mind when writing the will. I will prepare a short memo on those issues and the evidence we may need."

"Sounds like a plan gentlemen. Josef are you good with this?" asked Straun.

"I'm not only good with it; I'm relieved. I really didn't know where to begin."

Meeting over, Josef turned to his sentence hearing, which was scheduled for the late morning. When he got back from court there was a letter waiting from Mr. Sebastian Wright, who had a small law practice in town. Josef didn't like him much, he was shady and a bully. Wright was proud of his moniker 'bull dog'. He was the local 'gang lawyer' and, like his clients, he often relied on intimidation. Josef had seen him in action and he didn't like to see nice people beaten up by a lawyer in court. The letter he sent to Josef was typical — a 'demand letter'. He acted for Mr. Bruce Jones and demanded a copy of the will be sent to his office by the close of business today. Josef was not surprised Bruce Jones hired Sebastian Wright as his lawyer. They were a perfect match.

He went to see Gabe and showed him the letter. "Well, do we send him a copy of the will?"

Gabe thought for a moment. "A will is a private document, until it is filed for probate. Normally beneficiaries under a will are shown a copy or at least told of their inheritance. No one else is entitled. However, it's your call."

"If we don't send him a copy what can he do?"

"He'll probably go to court for an order compelling us to provide him with a copy."

"Okay, how long will it take for us to file for probate?"

"We aren't even close. We need property valuations. We need addresses of the beneficiaries. Christ, we don't even know if they are alive. It will be at least two, three weeks, a month or more just to start the process."

Josef thought things through aloud, "If we don't provide a copy we invite a court action. If we provide a copy he'll be pissed off and probably litigate."

Gabe added, "Of course, keep in mind, at the hearing it will definitely come out that he and his family get nothing under the will. He'll find out anyway."

Josef sighed. He didn't like playing litigation games. Bruce Jones was going to find out sooner or later Old Bill cut him out of the will. "Augh, let's give him a copy, not today. We'll send it to him tomorrow." In hindsight this decision was a mistake.

CHAPTER 6

Josef pondered, how to find Connie and Rebecca Thornton? Who to contact in Australia? Surely a lawyer in Queensland would be a good starting point. He needed telephone numbers and called the Australian Consulate in Ottawa. A helpful consular officer provided him with the phone number for the Queensland Law Society. The officer also kindly advised him to remember Australia was 15 to 16 hours ahead by the clock. Josef hadn't thought about that.

He waited until late afternoon to make the calls, which by his calculation would be Friday morning in Australia. The Queensland Law Society had a referral list of solicitors. In Goondiwindi, there were eight solicitors listed. His game plan was simple, he'd go through the list alphabetically and if a lawyer answered directly he'd hang up. The reason was simple, he didn't want a lawyer who couldn't afford a receptionist or secretary. It wasn't scientific, but was logical.

He made his first call to Fred Armstrong, Solicitor. "Hello Armstrong speaking". Click. His second call was to Kenneth Barnes, Solicitor. "Mr. Barnes' Office, Judith speaking." Contact made. Josef gave Judith his name, told her he was a lawyer from Canada and asked to speak to Mr. Barnes. "I'll see if Mr. Barnes can take your call." He loved her lilting Australian drawl.

Mr. Barnes came on the line, "Ken Barnes speaking, a Canuck eh?" He laughed.

Josef hadn't expected that greeting. "Yes, Josef Manne, from Prince Albert, Saskatchewan, Canada calling."

"PA, I know PA, I did some training in Saskatchewan during the war. The Commonwealth Air Training Program. Do you know Dafoe? I did bomber training there."

What a small world! "Sure do. It's just outside Saskatoon, pretty desolate."

"And even more desolate after we bombed the hell out of it. Great clear skies for flying. But it was God awful cold. Pretty girls, loved us Aussie flyers. Good memories."

He had a clipped way of speaking and you could tell he was a jovial sort, a glad hander for sure. Josef bet he would know everyone in Goondiwindi. He told him his reason for calling. Barnes did not know Connie or Rebecca. "Here is what I'll do. I'll have Judith call the Queensland Registry for Births Deaths and Marriages. She's a cracker at getting through the bureaucrats. If they died in Queensland we'll know. I'll also go for a beer today at the RSL and ask around. They'll know about the flyer. Give me his details again?"

"Charles Thornton, RAAF, died January 31, 1945. He was in a prison of war camp in Japan. What's the RSL?"

"Oh, it's the Returned and Services League of Australia, for veterans. They'll know. Died in a POW camp. Damn, we lost too many that way. Japan you say, I lost a buddy of mine working on the Burma railroad."

"The testator of the will was captured at Hong Kong and spent three and a half years as a POW. Then he was taken to Japan to work as slave labour. That's where he met Thornton." Josef asked about paying Barnes for his work.

Barnes wouldn't have it. "What we find at the registry won't take but a few minutes of our time and a beer at the RSL is long overdue. I'll tell you what, you come through Goondiwindi some time, you owe me a beer. It's the least I can do for a fallen RAAF mate. No worries."

They chatted for a few more minutes. He gave Josef his personal phone number and told him to call the next day, which was Saturday in Australia. In his words it shouldn't take much time to find something. Josef hit pay dirt with Kenneth Barnes.

* * *

After receiving a copy of the will Sebastian Wright called Bruce Jones, who insisted on seeing it. Wright knew Bruce would blow his top at being cut out of the will and wanted to milk that anger. Will contests meant good money for the lawyers involved. No legal aid retainer, but real money and Bruce Jones had deep pockets.

The meeting played out as Wright expected. He sat back listening to Bruce. Let him stew, let him rant, feign compassion and plant the seed to attack the will. But first he needed to know whether there was anything to fight over.

"What the fuck," Bruce roared, "this wasn't even prepared by a lawyer. Load a crap. I'm his brother for fuck sake. Can he do this?"

Wright took his time answering, "Yes, a hand written will is still a will. The real question is whether it is a valid will. You see, a properly prepared will has two witnesses present who, if need be, can attest to the testator's state of mind. Here there are no witnesses. Was he of sound mind? Don't know. Sure raises a lot of questions."

"Can we get it thrown out?"

An opening to test the waters thought Wright. "Whoa, slow down, contesting a will can be expensive. There might not be anything worth fighting over."

Bruce looked hard at Wright and simply said, "There is, believe me. Bill owns two parcels of land along the Blue River and I want them. I don't know how he got them, but he has them."

"What's so special about those parcels?" asked Wright, probing. How much is this land worth to Bruce?

Bruce was too clever and too mistrusting to bite. If Wright knew the true value of the parcels, the fucking lawyer would increase his fees for sure. He replied, "Call it sentimental. All you need to know is I want them."

"That's fine, so long as you know these things can cost." Wright was celebrating on the inside. He had a nice will contest. "There are a couple other things. I had one of my associates look at the will. We may not need to fight the will at all. If the two named beneficiaries are dead then the will fails and there is an intestacy and you, as the heir-at-law, would receive the entire estate."

"Then we need to find out if they are dead or alive," Bruce snapped.

"Let the executor do that. We'll find out in due course."

"No," said Bruce. Impatient by nature, he needed to know now. "I want to know ASAP. You find out."

"Alright, alright I'll get on it."

"As in right now." Bruce then asked about the 45 days. Wright explained, "That's standard in a will. The beneficiaries have to live at least 45 days after the testator's death in order to receive under the will."

"I hope they're fucking dead," said Bruce.

Wright thought, 'I hope they're not'.

* * *

Josef's drunk driving trial went through most of Friday morning. It was a two-witness case, the two arresting officers. No breathalyzer was taken, so the case rested on the officers' observations of intoxication. Unfortunately for them, their notes were not complete, and their memories seemed to improve and get more detailed with time. Funny about that. The Provincial Court Judge, formerly a seasoned Crown, was not pleased with the police work, had a reasonable doubt. Josef's client was acquitted. Justice was done.

Josef phoned Ken Barnes in the mid-afternoon, which turned out to be pretty early Saturday morning in Queensland. Barnes laughed, "We get up with the sun in Queensland. I was up. I have something for you. Got pen and paper?"

He continued, "First, sad to tell you, but Connie Thornton died on February 19, 1968. Her full name was Constance Marie Thornton, born September 14, 1921. Her maiden name was Booth. She married Charles Winston Thornton, January 15, 1943. He was born March 5, 1920. They had a daughter Rebecca Rose Thornton on October 8, 1943. No record of her marrying. Judith didn't have time to contact the other state registries. She'll do that on Monday. Easier now that we've got a birth date for Rebecca. At least we can find out if she is dead or alive. I'll get copies of the death and birth certificates for you."

"That's a big help. Any word on Charles Thornton?"

"There is. He is listed as one of the fallen on the cenotaph and on the wall of honour at the RSL. None of the vets I talked to served with him. Although, none were in the RAAF. The military might have more information."

"Do you know of any relatives?"

"Sorry, don't know about that. Thornton and Booth are not common names in these parts. People around here tended to settle in family packs, brothers, sisters, aunts and uncles all taking up parcels of land in the same area."

"Anything on the possible whereabouts of Rebecca?"

"Nothing there either, sorry mate."

"Okay Mr. Barnes, Ken, do you know of any private detectives I can contact?"

He laughed. "Those wankers. Most are either drunkards, no-goods or both. In my twenty odd years of practice never used one. They cost too much and provide too little. Goondiwindi is too small to have any. You'd have to bring a bloke in from Brisbane. Mind they'll charge you plenty."

Josef thanked him profusely for his information and agreed to call him early next week to find out the results of Judith's search for Rebecca in the other state registries. Barnes promised to continue to 'snoop around'.

Shortly after getting off the phone with Barnes, Josef received a call from the local Crown, Roger Peters. They had a three-week murder trial scheduled for the last court sitting in June. It was Josef's first murder trial. His client had stabbed a man to death. He said self-defence. The Crown said murder. Roger called to tell Josef that after reviewing the file the Crown was prepared to take a plea to manslaughter. Josef had proposed manslaughter a few weeks back, which was rejected by the Crown. Something wasn't right. He asked Roger if all his witnesses were available. Roger paused and then told him a key Crown witness had died. Josef said he'd get back to him. He was torn. He was really looking forward to handling a murder trial, but knew a manslaughter conviction was a good result for his client. He would recommend his client take the Crown offer. His client had stabbed the guy four times and a jury may well not accept self-defence. Maybe for the first stab, but not the additional three. Good result for his client, but no jury trial for him and all that preparation gone to waste.

* * *

When Bruce got on the line, no greeting, Wright simply said, "One's dead. Connie Thornton, the mother, died in 1968. Just got the word from an Australian law firm."

You could hear the excitement in Bruce's voice, "One down; one to go. Any word on the daughter?"

"No record of her death. We know she was born in 1943, so she is pretty young. No record of marrying. Assuming she is still in Australia."

"What are your thoughts?" asked Bruce.

"I'd bet she's still alive," Wright replied.

"So, she would get the entire estate, if the will is valid."

"Yah, if it's valid." Wright quickly added, "And if we aren't successful in overturning the will. Want me to have the Australian law firm try to find her?"

"No, no, waste of time and money. If she's alive, she's alive." Bruce didn't want the Australia law firm nosing around. It created a paper trail.

"Okay. I'll have the Australian law firm send me the certificate of death."

After Bruce hung up the phone he turned to his son Ron, who had been sitting quietly listening. "Mother's dead. No word on the daughter. Wright thinks the daughter is still alive." Bruce pounded his desk. "That fucking Bill. That fucking Bill. He was a problem when he was alive and is still a problem dead. Bugger wouldn't sell me the parcels. Kicked me off his property. Who'd have thought he'd have a will?"

Ron was a man of few words. Sullen. When he spoke, he got right to the point, "I don't like relying on lawyers. Can't trust them. We got to let Mel know. He'll be pissed."

Mel Laxon was head of the Rebel Motorcycle Club in Saskatchewan. He and Ron had a few dealings together. Last year there was some talk amongst the men of unionizing at Jones Trucking. Ron felt the company needed some muscle and approached Laxon. Contact was made by his son, Alex, who was already a patched member of the Rebels. Problem solved. Their relationship grew. Laxon became a silent partner in the business, which was good for the Rebels, who needed a place to launder money. Jones Trucking obliged with a nice return on the laundering.

"I'll have Alex set up a meeting with Mel. Alex tells me there's a Rebel chapter in Australia."

Old Bill's Last Will and Testament

Bruce agreed. "Just be fucking careful."

* * *

Josef called Barnes on May 22nd. There was no record of Rebecca Thornton dying or marrying in any other state or territory in Australia. Barnes also had made some inquiries and found little. She had worked as a barmaid at the Victoria Hotel in Goondiwindi, but had left a few years ago for parts unknown. Not much to go on. Josef asked again about hiring of a private detective. Barnes just laughed. "You must have money to burn. Hell, it would be cheaper for you to come down here yourself!"

Actually, Josef had been thinking the same thing. His June calendar was open now that the murder case had folded. Further, he had Old Bill's money left to him in the joint account. Josef had dropped into a travel agency and found out Qantas had started flying the new Boeing 747 between Los Angeles and Sydney. It was a possibility.

Josef mentioned it to Straun and he was enthusiastic for him to go. "Go, go. You can charge the estate for travel expenses. Your jury trial folded, and we can cover anything that comes up. We need to find her and you need a holiday too." Talk about not feeling indispensable.

Josef met with Gabe, who had been busy determining the value of Old Bill's estate. He put the value at $540,000. The Morrison International Agriculture stocks alone were worth $387,000. He had a real estate agent do an appraisal of Bill's properties. The home property was worth only $8,000. The two sections of land north on Blue River were appraised at $30,000 each, which was less than the going rate for agriculture land. The problem, according to the real estate agent, was the two sections were mostly sand and poor pasture land. Bill had bought them from the Crown in 1950, using a veteran's land loan. The real estate agent did note the existing gravel road that ran parallel to the Blue River was going to be paved in the near future and pushed through to Northern Alberta, which could increase the value of the land. Gabe had a survey map of the parcels. Josef knew the area well. It was called the 'Sand Cliffs' because of the sandstone cliffs coming to the shore. The beach there was pristine and it was a favorite swimming spot. In total, Old Bill had two miles of river front.

Interestingly, when Gabe did a title search in the Prince Albert land titles office he noticed on the property ledger that a 'Bruce Jones from Blue River' had searched both parcels of land in February of this year.

Josef told Gabe he was thinking about travelling to Australia in search of the missing beneficiary. Gabe quipped, "If you don't go, I will." The decision was made and Shirley booked the flights. Josef would indeed be flying Qantas in the Boeing 747. She too seemed pleased he was going. Less work for her. Josef sure wasn't going to be missed.

He phoned Barnes in Goondiwindi. "Ken, you know that beer you wanted me to buy. I'm going to buy it for you."

"You are now," replied Barnes, "sounds like I might be seeing you soon. Do I have that right?"

"You do. I'm flying to Australia on June 1, arriving I guess on the third and I return on June 22. I have three weeks to find Rebecca Thornton."

"Where are you flying into, Sydney or Brisbane?"

"I land in Sydney and then take another flight to Brisbane. In Brisbane I'll rent a car and drive to Goondiwindi. How long will that take?"

"About eight hours. Don't rent a car. Rent a Ute, mate."

"Ken, what the heck is a Ute?"

"It's a truck, what do you call them? It's a pick-up, but not a pick-up. Has a bigger load tray. And you need roo bars on it. Don't rent one without roo bars."

"Alright, what are roo bars?"

Barnes was laughing again. Laughter came easy to him. "In Canada you probably would have deer bars or bear bars. Whatever – critter bars. You know bars fitted on the front of the truck in case you hit a deer. Around Goondiwindi we've got big mobs of kangaroos and they are dead stupid. Road kill everywhere. Mate, you need a roo bar."

They discussed what he needed to wear. Queensland was going into winter. Barnes offered to put him up, but Josef didn't want to impose. He'd get a hotel.

"How old are you? Married? Attached?" Barnes asked mischievously.

"I'm 28. Not married. Not attached. Any other questions?"

"No. Just asking. Our Aussie Shelia's might want to know."

Josef was really looking forward to meeting Ken Barnes in person.

Old Bill's Last Will and Testament

* * *

Jimbo Hooper, head of the Taipan Motor Cycle Club in Toowoomba, Queensland looked at the money and shook his head in amazement. There was $10,000 in Australian dollars. Hard to believe. He got a call from Vic Beltorino, head of the Rebels in Brisbane, a week ago. Vic had a favour. He had a request from a Rebel's Chapter in Canada. They wanted a job done in Australia. Vic was too busy, couldn't be bothered and wondered if Jimbo would be interested. Jimbo's aim was to have the Taipans become full patch members of the Rebels. He couldn't say no.

What followed were a series of phone calls with a Canadian contact. No name given. He wanted a woman found and 'taken care of' and it had to be done by June 24. Jimbo set the terms: $10,000 up front to cover search expenses and $15,000 to be paid once she was 'taken care of'. Jimbo really never expected to see the money. Yet, here it was. Unbelievable.

He could just sit on the $10,000, which was tempting. No, better to show Vic Beltorino the Taipans could be trusted to get the job done. Jimbo decided to give the hit to his younger brother, 'Stump'. The name originated from the fact Jimbo was big and tall, 250 pounds and 6'5". He was like a tree. His younger brother was stocky and short – hence the name 'Stump'. He was smart. He'd find the woman. It would do him good. He needed to prove himself. A hit would toughen him up. Stump was the man.

CHAPTER 7

Saturday, June 3

Josef slept little throughout the flight. He was simply too excited. It was his first overseas flight. Movies were shown, and he watched, but don't ask him what was playing. The flight landed in the early morning hours in Sydney. Josef could see the Harbour Bridge in the distance. From Sydney he had a two hour wait before his flight to Brisbane. He napped on one of the terminal benches. Jet lag was sneaking up on him and he fell asleep on the short flight to Brisbane. Upon arrival he was semi-revived.

The young attendant at the car rental agency was not convinced Josef wanted a Ute. "Mate, are you sure?" He took Josef out to the lot to show him the vehicle, which had been returned to the airport the day before from the Northern Territory. In North America it would be called a ranchero, half a car with an open back. The Ute he had was a white Ford XY, raised suspension, roo bar in the front, oversize tires, a canvas cover for the back. Josef nicknamed it 'The Beast'.

"It's a manual, mate. Can you drive a manual?"

Josef looked at the young man and all he said was, "Raised on a farm."

He took possession of The Beast. The attendant's parting words were, "Remember drive on the left!" Josef sputtered and jerked off the lot, having to get used to shifting gears with his left hand. The drive through Brisbane was an adventure. He invariably turned his windshield wipers on each time he wanted to signal a turn; the indicators were on the right-hand side. He found the roads much narrower than he was used to and The Beast seemed much bigger. Frustratingly, lanes seemed to end without reason. He cursed Ken Barnes a few times for talking him into renting a Ute; a mini would have been much better. After a little more than an hour he emerged from the city on the right highway to Goondiwindi through Toowoomba.

It was early afternoon and he was driving on adrenalin. By his estimate he had been in transit for over 38 hours. He fought to stay alert, which was not good. Toowoomba was only a few miles ahead and he needed to stop. There was a long incline leading to the city up the Great Dividing Range. The Beast protested, engine roaring stubbornly up the hill to the top. Josef stopped at the first motel he saw. It was a little before 4:00 pm. He managed to change out of his travelling clothes, flopped on the bed and fell fast asleep within seconds. Jet lag had caught up with him.

* * *

Stump cruised along on his pride and joy, a 1968 Harley Davidson FLH. He was in a fine frame of mind. He had money in his pocket, $2000 of it, had three weeks to find his target and it didn't matter if he did or didn't. Fun was to be had.

Stump always had an inferiority complex, largely because he followed in his big brother's footsteps. Jimbo was a leader; he was a follower. Stump had fought his way through life. He made up for his small size with sheer bullheaded tenacity and meanness. He had shaved his head and tattooed his body. The one constant for him was his brother. Jimbo protected Stump from their abusive father. It was Jimbo who stood up to the father and in a mighty fight ended the father's reign of pain, abuse, and terror. Stump was devoted to Jimbo and the Taipans. He'd find that woman and see the job done.

It was early evening when Stump arrived in Goondiwindi. He checked into a small hotel on the outskirts of town. He'd stayed there before, knew the owner and knew a few of the girls. With money in his pocket he was going to have himself a time. And he did.

Sunday, June 4

Josef awoke at 2:00 am. Not a good time to be awake. With no reason to get up he lay in bed his mind racing. Not much of a start to his search for Rebecca Thornton or for a holiday, wasting his time in bed in a no name motel. He decided at first light he'd take a look around Toowoomba and then travel to Goondiwindi.

He was up and ready to go at 6:30 and headed to a nearby park to watch the sun rise. Looking east, through the morning mist the view was absolutely spectacular. Josef now felt more touristy. His soul was refreshed. The air was crisp and clear. He figured it was a few degrees above freezing. The sky was solid blue and the birds were busy greeting the day. Beautiful.

He was ready to start the journey to Goondiwindi, which would be about a three-hour drive. Barnes had invited him for an afternoon lunch at his home once Josef arrived. Driving west through the Darling Downs he was reminded of the prairies. Big sky, flat land, wheat and cattle. He marvelled at the size of some of the fields; they were gigantic. Josef wasn't in any hurry and a few road trains, semi-trucks pulling two trailers, ran up his back. He bailed and let them pass. He had never seen such road monsters before. He stopped at a wayside rest spot, which was located beside a dry river. Dry! He had never seen that before either.

Josef arrived in Goondiwindi shortly before noon. He appreciated the wide streets; easy for equipment to maneuver. Marshall Street was the main drag. There he found the Victoria Hotel, where he had a reservation. The Vic was an eclectic mix of Victoriana with a strong Australian flavour. He called it irreverent Australiana. From its rectangular two storey base there was a tiered tower, which, if he was not mistaken, seemed to have a slight tilt. The hotel's brick and timber were painted white with black trim. The entire building was adorned with lattice work and decorative pillars. There were wraparound verandas on both the ground level, where the public rooms were located, and on the second storey where the hotel rooms were found. This was a character hotel dictated by the whims of its owners over time. Josef loved it! He checked in and called Barnes. They'd meet in the bar in about thirty minutes. Barnes said, "I want that drink you owe me before you skip town."

Josef went down to the bar and sat at a table. No server came. It finally dawned on him to go to the counter and order. Disaster. Did he want a pot? A schooner? A pint? What beer? XXXX? VB? Toohey? He had to tell the bartender he had no idea. As soon as he spoke his ignorance was revealed. American? No, Canadian. The bartender showed him the sizes and suggested he order a schooner of XXXX, which was Queensland's beer. He got his beer and retreated to a table. Barnes arrived a few minutes later. He looked around the room and found Josef.

Coming towards him hand outstretched, he said, "You've started without me, Canuck. Welcome to Goondiwindi." Josef got up and Barnes gave him a strong, warm handshake with his right and a pat on the back with his left. "I'll have that beer. Thank you. A XXXX." Josef went over to the bartender and ordered a second XXXX.

Barnes was exactly how Josef had pictured him. He was fiftyish, tall, over six feet, not fat but healthy. His light brown hair was thinning, but still worth combing. His face had a suntanned, reddish hue and his green eyes danced. He had noticeable crow's feet, which in Josef's view were true laugh lines. Barnes took a deep swallow of the beer and asked, "How was your trip? Did you get a Ute?"

After talking to him on the phone Josef was used to his staccato way of speaking. "The trip was long, but enjoyable and yes, I did get a Ute, which I call 'The Beast'."

"The Beast, hey. Good name. You'll need it around here. Did you fly Qantas?"

"Yes, and it was the 747."

"Wow, good on you, I'd love to fly in that plane. Did you know Qantas has never lost a passenger? It's a fact. Safest airline in the world. How's your room?"

"Great, I front on to the main street. I'm going to enjoy standing on the balcony watching life in Goondiwindi go by."

"Not much life, except Saturday nights can be entertaining. The Vic is the place to be. We'll have to get going, Ruth has been busy preparing a special lunch. I'll drive. It's not far."

They finished their beer and Barnes directed Josef to his black Holden Ute, roo bar and all. Barnes gave a quick tour of the town as he drove. Goondiwindi had about 3,000 people and was a distribution centre for the surrounding farms and stations. The Macintyre River marked the southern boundary of the town. He told of past floods. "In the flood of '56 a guy rowed his boat into The Vic." Josef could see protective levees. He mentioned to Barnes the dry river bed he had seen. "Lots of those. It is the dry season, although we do get some serious winter storms. When it rains in this country, it rains."

Barnes' home was close to the river. It was a Queenslander, built on stilts, wraparound porch, ornate wrought iron canopy work and pillars, heavily painted green, which complimented the yellow and white siding. A double split stairway led to the upper living area finished with decorative lattice work. As they drove into the yard, Barnes' wife, Ruth, and their 15-year-old daughter, Lucy, came down to greet them.

Ruth was small, slim, active-looking. Her skin had been aged by the sun, but she, like her husband, had similar laugh lines. Lucy, in contrast, was tall, a full head taller than her mother; she was blonde and her skin still healthy and freckled. Ken and Ruth had two other daughters, who were studying nursing in Brisbane. Not surprising, Ruth was a nurse.

She prepared a bountiful lunch topped by a delicious pavlova. Conversation was lively and fun. Time passed quickly, late in the afternoon, Barnes invited Josef to come for a ride. The sun was low in the sky. They travelled a short way out of town, got out of the Ute and stood on a small knoll with a vista of surrounding fields and the highway. Barnes simply said, "Wait a minute." The air was filled with the cry of birds announcing the end of the day. The wind whispered quietly. Then Josef saw them, 10, 15, 20 or more kangaroos hopping through the grazing land. The mobs were out. Barnes pointed to the highway. There they were standing, like sentinels, by the highway. Occasionally one or two would hop across the road. Barnes told Josef the smaller ones were wallabies. "Now you know why you need a roo bar, especially at dusk."

Josef saw some tall cacti in the surrounding brush and asked Barnes about them. He swore, "That's fuckin' prickly pear. Pardon my French. Damn near ruined all the farming land here and in New South Wales." Barnes was just getting warmed up. "You couldn't get rid of the damn things. Try what you might they'd come back. You should see the pictures, fields of prickly pear."

"Where did they come from?" Josef asked.

"They were brought in by the early settlers. You see an insect that feeds on the cacti provided a form of scarlet dye, which was used for the soldier's red uniforms. The pears really didn't take off until the late 1800s, but by

1900 the damn prickly pear were invading farmland throughout Australia. It was terrible, folks were forced off the land. Goes to show how fragile Australia is."

He continued, "The government posted a reward on how to eradicate prickly pear and a group of scientists, just prior to World War I, travelled the world in search of a solution. They went to areas of the world where the prickly pear was natural and searched for something to attack it. And they bloody well found it. A bug, the cactoblastis, eats the pears and kills them. And it cleaned them out right quick. Bloody amazing. The settlers came back and reclaimed the land."

"What an amazing story. You sure are an expert on prickly pear."

He gave a hearty laugh. "Believe me, as a boy living on a farm, I had plenty to do with prickly pear: burned them, axed them, dug them up. We farmed south of Inglewood, which is prickly pear territory. I had my fill of prickly pear believe me."

They got back into the Ute. Barnes turned more serious. "My office is just down the street from The Vic, same side of the street to the west. I have a spare office and it's yours. Judith is a gem in talking to people." He gave Josef a few of his business cards. Josef thanked him and said he'd drop in the next day to say hello to Judith. The Vic tower was now in sight and they said their goodbyes. Josef headed back to his room and fell asleep in front of the television. Jet lag winning again.

* * *

Stump did not get up until late morning. It was quite a night. His head told the tale. Booze, marihuana and sex. Life was good. Stump didn't mind paying for women. Sex was sex and Betty was worth every cent. Sunday, no day to start searching for the Thornton woman. He'd do it tomorrow. Plant a few seeds, drop a few dollars. His plan was simple, pay for information. Money was the greatest incentive and the locals needed a few bucks. He'd drop the word he was looking for a Rebecca Thornton, money was to be had and let the locals do the searching. Today he needed to recover.

CHAPTER 8

Monday, June 5

Today was going to be a work day for Josef. It began with breakfast and he asked the server, Gloria, if she knew Rebecca Thornton, who had worked at The Vic. Gloria was non-committal. She wasn't sure. The name sounded familiar, but there was a lot of people on staff. She asked why he was looking for her. Josef told her the truth, "Rebecca is named in a will in Canada and I need to find her." Nothing more. Gloria didn't remember her. Strange, since when she first took his order they had chatted and she had worked at The Vic for over ten years. They'd be employees at the same time, if his information about Rebecca was true. The front desk receptionist also did not remember Rebecca. Josef got the distinct impression they did not want to talk to him. They were chatty about everything else under the sun, but clammed shut when he mentioned Rebecca's name. No follow-up questions. No further inquiries. Strange.

After breakfast he dropped in at Ken Barnes' Law Office and met Judith, who was delightful. She had a permanent smile, a little on the heavy side, pleasantly plump, more to love. On her desk were photographs of her two young boys, James and Scott, her 'darlings', and she was more than happy to tell Josef all about them, as a proud mother should. She showed him the empty office, and gave him a quick lesson on the phones. Josef had a home base.

His next stop was the local police station. At the front counter was a young officer. Josef showed the officer one of his cards and told him he was looking for a young woman, Rebecca Thornton. Josef noticed the officer's eyes widen a bit. He asked Josef to stay for a moment and he went and spoke with another officer, no doubt his superior, who got up from his desk and came to the front. "Hello, I'm Senior Constable Stan Malton of the Queensland Police."

Josef introduced himself. In a few seconds he sized up Senior Constable Malton as a thug in uniform. His deportment was impeccable, boots polished, shirt ironed, pants properly creased all in order. This was a man who liked wearing the uniform. His eyes were cold. No glimmer of humour. "My officer tells me you are looking for Rebecca Thornton."

'My officer'. Most supervisors would have said, 'Officer so and so tells me'. Yes, Malton was full of himself. Give a person a uniform is dangerous, give them a gun with the uniform is even more dangerous, and give them a measure of power is sure to result in abuse. Josef was wary of Malton. "Oh, you know her?"

He ignored Josef's question. "She is a person of interest to us. Why are you looking for her?"

"I'm a lawyer in Canada and Rebecca Thornton of Goondiwindi, Queensland is named as a beneficiary in a will and our firm is the executor of the will."

"It must be a substantial estate for you to come all this way in search of her?"

"Not really. I'm here on holiday and am just trying to wrap this up at the same time."

"How much is the estate worth?" he persisted.

"Sorry I'm not at liberty to divulge that. You mentioned she was a person of interest to you. How so?"

Malton gave a thin smile. "Sorry I'm not free to divulge that. What did you want from us?"

It was Josef's turn to be evasive. Malton wasn't going to give him the time of day. "I just thought the local police would have their sources and I might get lucky and find her."

"Sorry we don't know where she is. Can't help you. But we'd appreciate it if you'd let us know if you do. I trust we can count on you to do that?" Malton emphasized the last sentence.

"Rest assured, I will let you know," Josef lied. Why was she a person of interest? And if she was running from the police it would be even more difficult to find her.

They shook hands, but it was a mere formality. No warmth. Malton didn't believe Josef and Josef didn't trust Malton. So much for the police.

Next stop was the local paper. Josef had Connie's date of death and wanted to read her obituary. The lady at the front of the Goondiwindi Gazette was on the phone when he entered. The Saturday paper was on the coffee table in the waiting room. The front-page news was about a grey horse, Gunsynd, The Goondiwindi Grey. Josef quickly read the article. Gunsynd was one heck of a horse. And he noticed the horse could win over a variety of distances. The article was all about Gunsynd taking a break before the forthcoming spring carnival of races. Josef studied the photograph. Gunsynd was majestic and a grey horse too boot. His dad always backed greys and almost invariably lost. He'd have loved Gunsynd.

The lady was off the phone. Josef went to the counter. "That is quite the horse you have."

She brightened. "Yes, we are very proud of him. He's a good one. You're from America?" she asked.

He told his story. The horse had broken the ice. The lady, Agnes by name, took the details Josef had about Connie Thornton and went to the archives. Given the death was only a few years old, it was stored with the actual paper copies and not on microfiche. She came back a few minutes later with a few copies of the gazette around that time. The paper only published on Tuesdays, Thursdays and Saturdays. Josef found the obituary. Connie Thornton died after a 'courageous' battle with cancer. Her parents had predeceased her, as did her husband, Charles Thornton, and she had only a surviving daughter, Rebecca, and a sister, Muriel Thomas, from Talwood, Queensland. Josef had his first lead! Agnes photocopied the obituary for him and Josef rushed back to Ken Barnes' Law Office.

He showed Judith the obituary. She got out the local telephone book and three Thomas numbers were listed. Josef asked if she would mind making the calls. Her voice would not be as startling as his. Judith freely admitted to him when he had first called the office she was taken aback by his accent. Josef, of course, denied having any such accent. On the second call she got through to Muriel Thomas. Yes, she was Connie Thornton's sister. Yes, she'd be happy to talk to a lawyer from Canada. Judith asked, if she'd mind if he came out to speak with her in person. That was fine and Judith got the details, 2:00 pm today was perfect.

After hanging up, Judith explained, "I do hope you don't mind, but Muriel sounded a little muddled on the phone and I really think you would get so much more out of her in person. Talwood is only an hour drive west of here. I know, I should have asked you before I made the appointment. I'm sorry."

"Nonsense, you did the right thing. Best in person. I'll get my map." Judith looked relieved.

The road to Talwood was deserted, except for the odd road train. The countryside became drier, wilder, and the vibrant red soil of the outback became more prominent. Talwood was not big. It was a small rail stop and grain depot. Josef had little difficulty in finding Muriel's house. The Queensland ranch was built on timber piles, crudely placed tree trunks in various shapes, never perfectly round. The house was in desperate need of fresh paint. The corrugated iron roof was rusting. She was waiting for him seated on the front porch. He had expected a fiftyish lady. The woman he was introduced to looked far older. Life had been hard on Muriel Thomas. She was as tired as her home, frail, weak-looking, and seemed tied to her rocking chair. She insisted on getting them tea, but it was an effort. Judith was so right; better to speak with her in person.

Muriel was Connie's older sister by ten years. Josef did the math, she'd be about 60, and she looked 80. There had been three other siblings. All died young. Connie and Muriel kept in contact over the years, mostly through letters and the odd phone call.

"Connie went up north of Moonie to work at the Foster Station. She was their cook. Connie was a good cook. Always was, loved to cook. We never saw much of each other. She came down when I married George. That was about it. I never went up to the Foster's for Connie's wedding. It was wartime and she got married quick. Charles Thornton was a crop duster. Connie told me he was so handsome. That is how they met. Charles was spraying the Foster property. They dated for a while. She wasn't interested in marrying until the war broke out. Charles signed up. They needed experienced pilots. I guess it was when he was getting ready to go overseas that they got married. It was good for Connie, at least she got a bit of a military pension when Charles died. You know I don't think he ever saw his daughter, Rebecca, in person. Sad, really, isn't it? Connie so loved that man. Never married again."

"How did she die?"

"It wasn't pretty. I went to see her when she was brought down to the hospital at Goondiwindi. She had cancer, breast cancer. Fought it hard for a number of years. But I could see the death mask on her face. Rebecca was so good to her. She came back to Goondiwindi to care for her mother. They rented a small house in town. Connie's death was a blessing. She suffered terribly and Rebecca had no life, she was a full-time nurse for her mother."

"Have you been in contact with Rebecca?"

"No, last time I saw her was at the funeral. With Connie gone, our connection with each other disappeared."

"Do you have any idea where Rebecca might have gone? Any idea at all?"

"No. No I don't." She paused, thinking. "But Rebecca really loved living on the Foster Station. I'd talk to them. Sorry I don't have more information for you."

Josef thanked her for the information, her time and the tea. George had died five years ago and Muriel lived alone. She managed. Her son, who lived in Talwood, checked in on her regularly. Josef's sense was that Muriel had given up living. She rocked her days away waiting for the end.

Josef now had a new lead, Foster Station, and he drove back to Goondiwindi. With the light fading, he noticed the kangaroo sentinels on watch. Fortunately, he made it into town before dark. After cleaning up he went downstairs to the bar. Josef sat at the bar, nursing a schooner of XXXX. Two regulars were on either side of him, James and Walter. They were tradies. James was a chippie, which is carpenter, and Walter was a sparkie, which is an electrician. Both were quite impressed when the conversation turned to Gunsynd, and Josef knew about the horse. They were now fast friends. Josef enjoyed listening to the two of them, although he needed a translator at times. Australian slang is a language on its own. He told them he was looking for Rebecca Thornton. They knew her.

"Beckie, gosh she went rack off a year or two ago. She was a right nice Sheila, and I mean that with respect," said James.

"Too right," affirmed Walter. "Everyone loved her. She had life, and wouldn't take no guff from us blokes."

Walter then turned to the bartender. "Ben, you know where Beckie headed off to?"

Ben busied himself cleaning the bar counter and gave a mumbled reply, "No idea."

James and Walter lingered at the bar, which was their end of day sanctuary. They introduced Josef to other regulars, which provided an excuse for further rounds of drinks. Their families could wait. Eventually they went home to their family duties. Josef moved to the Vic's lounge restaurant for dinner.

His server, Roberta, was fortyish. He asked her how long she had worked at The Vic. She smiled and said she was a "lifer". She'd been there for over twenty years. It was then that he asked her about Rebecca Thornton. Her response was too quick. "I don't know where she is. Just left one day. It happens." Then she asked, "Why are you asking after her?" Strange she asked that. Why would that be of any interest to her? He gave her the usual generic response, which ended the conversation. Why did Josef get the feeling he was being stonewalled?

* * *

Stump had spread some money around, not much, but the Goondiwindi locals weren't a greedy lot. Stump visited three of the road houses and spread the word he was looking for Rebecca Thornton. For twenty bucks he found out she had worked at The Vic. As far as Stump was concerned that was a good day's work. He'd visit The Vic tomorrow. For tonight, well he had money in his pocket and needs to be satisfied.

CHAPTER 9

Tuesday, June 6

Ethel Foster told Josef he couldn't miss the gate to Foster Station. She was right. Two stone pillars rising 12-15 feet high stood on either side of the entrance road and each had a large iron figurative F in a circle. Josef had spoken to Ethel earlier that morning and after initially sounding somewhat dubious she warmed to the conversation. She certainly knew both Connie and Rebecca. He asked if he could drive up to talk to her and without hesitating she suggested he get there for lunch at noon. She provided meticulous directions to the station from Goondiwindi. Obviously, she'd given the directions many times before. The two-hour drive through the Darling Downs went quickly. As he turned on to the entrance road, Ethel warned him the Foster homestead was still five miles distant. In total Foster Station was over 10,000 acres.

The station had more rolling hills than the surrounding Downs. He could see cattle grazing in the various paddocks. Over a slight rise, the homestead came into view. The main house was low and long with a veranda on three sides. There were other smaller houses nearby with large gum and fig trees providing shade. Off on one side was an equipment building, two large barns and a number of grain storage bins. Josef drove to the front of the house and parked. A tall woman walked down the steps to greet him. She was wearing an Akubra hat, boots, blue jeans and a flannel shirt sleeves rolled up. It had to be Ethel. She was about 60 but wore her years well. She was slim, stood strong and erect, Josef could see her skin was weathered by the sun, which accentuated her wrinkles.

She put out her hand. "Ethel Foster, welcome to Foster Station." Her handshake had strength. Her green eyes were penetrating, yet not threatening. She was the boss of this domain and he could see why.

"Josef Manne, it is my real pleasure to meet you and thanks for the lunch invitation."

"You made good time. Lunch will be ready in about 15 minutes. Would you like something to drink after your trip? Water? Tea? Lemonade? A beer perhaps?"

"Too early for a beer for me, thanks. I'm good."

"I can tell you aren't an Aussie. Never too early for a beer." She laughed. "Come on, I'll show you around the homestead." She then toured him through the large house. It was filled with Foster family history. Her husband, who had died a few years before, was the fourth generation to farm the land. The station grew with each generation. The house was immaculate. The wooden floors glistened and each piece of furniture had its place. Although it was ordered, the house did not put on airs, rather it was comfortable and had a manly feel.

At noon a bell called the workers in for lunch. Ethel finished the tour a few minutes later and they went to a dining hall, where at least fifteen men sat around a large table devouring a bountiful lunch of assorted cold cuts, chicken, soup, veggies and fresh bread. Ethel motioned Josef over to a smaller table set off to the side. Plates of food were already on the table and there was water, tea and coffee for the taking.

They chatted as they ate. Josef learned many of the workers were itinerant hands and there were protocols to follow. Ethel explained casual workers were always in short supply and dependable casuals were especially treasured. Therefore, she liked to treat the workers well. Shearers, for example, travelled from station to station and there were strict requirements for a morning and afternoon smoko, food and lunch to be provided. Ethel explained, given Josef's visible bewilderment, that a smoko was a break, a short break; enough time to have a smoke and something to eat.

He learned that Ethel was a Melbourne girl. She met Graham Foster at the 1930 Melbourne Cup. "Phar Lap won the race. The place went mad. And a bloke behind me spilled his beer over me. The bloke was Graham Foster. I turned and was furious. He was so apologetic in a sweet kind way.

I couldn't get rid of him. We married six months later. Graham used to joke that was the most expensive beer he ever bought and he never even had a sip of it."

"What did your parents think of your marrying?"

"They weren't too happy about it, but in a way, they were relieved. You see I was 20 at the time and they desperately wanted to see me wed. But to a Queenslander from the outback!" She laughed.

"It must have been difficult for you, a city girl, to move to the station."

"Oh, bless me, it was. I cried every day for a year. But I'm stubborn and Graham was so supportive. It took time, but I grew to love the life out here. The people are genuine and the battle with nature is a never-ending challenge." She stopped. "But you don't want to hear about my life. You're a lawyer, you'll want to ask me questions. Let's go to the main house where we can talk in private."

They walked over to the main house and Ethel showed him to her study. They sat down in the deep leather armchairs. "Fire away," she said.

Josef began, "Tell me about Connie Thornton."

"Connie was like a younger sister to me. She came to the station in 1940-41. We needed a cook and Connie loved to cook. She was young, only 20, but she learned fast. She was a delight to have around. Rest assured a lot of the lads had their eyes on her. I tended to protect her, but she didn't need much protection. She was a strong-willed young woman. Her man had to be special."

"Was Charles Thornton special?"

A smile whisked past her lips. "Yes, Charley was special. He loved to fly and had a beat-up old bi-plane. He'd come to the station to do some spraying. We had a few fields in crops and he'd turn up at mustering time to help spot cattle. Charley was tall, blonde, a good-looking young man. He was also serious, well read, and worldly. Yes, Charley was special. They fell in love. Charley would find all kinds of excuses to turn up at the station. The marriage took place here. That was a grand day. Charley had leave for two weeks and I think they went to the Sunshine Coast north of Brisbane for a honeymoon. Then he was off to war."

"Did he ever come back and see Connie?"

"No, never did. He was posted overseas. In the Pacific. I think at one time he was flying with the Americans."

"So, he never saw his daughter?"

"No," said Ethel, "no, he never did."

"Tell me about Rebecca?"

"Ah, Rebecca. She was a little monkey. She followed my boys around like a little dog. A real tomboy, and mischievous. We treated her as one of the family and supported Connie. You know, Connie was alone. She never talked much about her family, I think she had a sister, but that was about it. Connie's life revolved around Rebecca."

"When did Connie find out that Charley died?"

"Oh, that was painful, so painful. Connie got a telegram from the war office. Charley had been shot down and was missing. This was in, I think, late 1944, yes, before Christmas, for sure. Connie hung on to hope he was alive. Then she got another telegram in March or April that Charley had been taken prisoner. Connie was so happy. Charley was alive. The war ended. We waited for Charley to return. We waited. I remember the day Connie received the news. It was horrible, just horrible."

She paused, her eyes welled with tears, she looked away, remembering. "It was towards the end of September 1945. The war had ended over a month before. Still no news. I saw a car driving up. I knew it was a military car and I saw the two officers, dressed in air force blue. I knew. They said they'd like to speak to Constance Thornton. I knew, I knew. I went and got Connie." She took a sip of water, and continued, her voice soft and pained. "I held Connie's hand as we walked to the porch. One of the officers told her that her husband, Charles Thornton, died in a prisoner of war camp in Japan. Connie shook. She didn't cry. She shook. I held her. Hugged her. Then, and I shall remember this to my dying day, little Rebecca ran up. She saw the officers in uniform. She ran up crying out, 'dadda, dadda'. You see Connie had a photograph of Charley in uniform and they prayed for him each and every night for his safe return. Little Rebecca, almost two, thought her daddy had returned. Connie swept Rebecca into her arms and hugged her tight. No tears. I had to hold it together. Connie thanked the officers and took Rebecca to her bedroom to tell her. I asked the officers for any details. Unfortunately, they had little. Evidently the Japanese destroyed many of the POW records before the Americans arrived. Do you know anything about how Charley died?"

Josef could see that Ethel needed a moment. She was dabbing her eyes. He replied slowly, "No, all I know is he died on January 31, 1945. I have no other details. I'm so sorry to raise this with you."

In a voice far away, Ethel went on, "That was a horrible day. Little Rebecca healed quickly, because she had never met her father. Connie was stoic. She kept on working. I wanted her to take some time off, but she refused. She said she needed to work to keep it together. Connie stayed with us until 1967."

"She never married again?"

"No, I think her heart was broken. She poured herself into raising Rebecca. She was a good mother; tough when warranted and loving when needed."

"How long did Rebecca live here at the station?"

"Oh, she lived here until grade nine, she would have been 15. Connie homeschooled her. For kids in the bush, we have School of the Air. Rebecca was bright. She was also very artistic. She used to draw Christmas and birthday cards for us all. I think Rebecca loved it here. She'd ride horses, help muster the cattle, did chores. She did everything with my boys."

"In grade nine where did she go to school?"

"She went to a Catholic school in Goondiwindi, St. Mary's. A number of the farm kids boarded with families in Goondiwindi and went to school. Every school break she'd be back at the station."

"Mrs. Foster, Ethel, do you have any photographs of Connie and Rebecca? I don't know what they look like."

She smiled, got up and went to the bookshelf and took out a photo album. She took an armchair by Josef and walked him through Rebecca and Connie's life at Foster Station. Josef saw a beautiful, proud-looking Connie, who rarely smiled in the photographs, and a shorthaired tomboy, Rebecca. She grew slowly into a strong athletic young woman, never wore a dress. Jeans were more to her liking. When younger, she had dimples and freckles. They faded over time; her smile never did. In many of the pictures, she had her arm around her mother.

"What happened to Connie? I know she died in 1968."

"1968 was a bad year. Graham died on February 8, a heart attack. Quick. No lingering. At least he made it to 60. Connie died too young. Stricken with breast cancer, which was diagnosed in 1966. Rebecca was off travelling the world. Connie never told her. She didn't want to worry Rebecca. Connie got weaker and weaker. Finally, Rebecca called one day. She was in London and I took the call. I spoke out of turn and told her Connie was sick. She should come home, but not to tell Connie I said anything. Rebecca arrived at the station a week or so later. This was in the winter of 1967. Connie needed treatment in Goondiwindi and they moved there. Rebecca got a job and cared for her mother. Connie wasted away. I visited whenever I could. Connie passed about two weeks after Graham died. At the funeral I told Rebecca there was always a home for her at Foster Station. Rebecca thanked me, but told me she was fine. She'd work a year or two, save and travel again. You see, there was no one else in the world for her."

"When was the last time you saw Rebecca?"

"I had coffee with her, oh, a year or two ago in Goondiwindi. She then left. To travel I suppose."

"What did Rebecca do after high school?"

"She went to UQ, University of Queensland. Connie was so proud. Rebecca got a scholarship. I told you she was bright."

"Do you know what she studied?"

"Yes, it was fine arts, as I told you, Rebecca was very artistic. She also got a scholarship to study in London for a year. Connie plastered the postcards all over her fridge. She was such a proud mother. Brave of Rebecca to go overseas to study and travel, but that's Rebecca. She is a tough, independent woman. She learned how to handle herself by fighting off the outback boys."

"Do you know anyone who might be able to help me find her now? The boarding family in Goondiwindi for instance?"

Ethel thought. "No sorry. I imagine that St. Mary's might have a list of boarding families."

"No boyfriends?"

Ethel laughed. "A mob of wannabees, but none who could corral her."

"Well, you have been very helpful. I rest my case. I have no more questions."

Ethel looked at Josef and smiled, "You'll find her I know."

"Why do you think that?"

"Because you listen. You let people talk. You learn a great deal that way. Do you mind if I ask you a few questions?"

"Not at all."

"The fact you travelled around the world to find Rebecca tells me the estate you are administering is quite large. Is that the case?"

"Yes, there is a lot of money involved. She would be well off. Not a millionaire, but well off."

"Good, and tell me about the Canadian who named her and Connie in his will."

Josef gave a condensed version on Old Bill. Ethel was intrigued. She loved his simple life. "But you don't know why he so wanted to give everything to Connie and Rebecca?"

"No, it's a mystery. They were prisoners together in Japan. At this point that is all I know."

"You've no wife, I see no ring, you've no attachments, which allows you to travel here alone?"

Josef felt himself blushing. "No attachments. Both my parents and my sister have passed away."

"Are you lonely?"

Ethel was perceptive and Josef felt compelled to be truthful. "At times I am lonely, but I am a loner. I guess by nature. Always have been. I like people and get along well with people, but I don't need people."

She was watching him closely and said in a soft voice, "I like you Josef Manne and when you find Rebecca, will you tell her to give me a call."

"I will."

Josef returned to Goondiwindi. When he got back to The Vic he showered, changed and headed down to the bar, which in his view was the best gossip source for him. James and Walter were seated on their usual stools and Josef joined them.

"Have you found Beckie?" Walter immediately asked.

Josef shook his head no. "But I did have a pleasant drive to Foster Station."

"That be north of Moonie?" asked James.

"Yes. I do have a few questions for you, if you don't mind." Both of the tradies perked up. "First, do you know a horse by the name of Phar Lap?"

"Phar Lap, Christ every Australian knows Phar Lap." Walter replied in a loud voice. The two of them commenced to tell Josef the legend of Phar Lap. Walter gave his opinion, "The race officials bloody well almost killed that horse, weighed him down like a pack animal in the '31 Melbourne Cup. Bloody unfair."

"But Phar Lap won the 1930 Melbourne Cup, didn't he?" Josef knew that would surprise them. They laughed. He had to ask, "What's the Melbourne Cup?"

That brought a mighty roar of disbelief from the two of them. "Holy Jesus," said James. "It's the race that stops the nation. First Tuesday of November at Flemington Race Track in Melbourne. It's a brutal two-mile race. Most famous race in the country. Everybody, everywhere puts a bet on and stops to listen or watch the race."

Walter gave Josef a pat on the back, "You've got much to learn m'boy." He then ordered a round for them all; apparently it was his shout. They filled Josef in on St. Mary's school, which was going to be his first stop next day. They were enjoying each other's company when three workers came into the bar. Josef noticed Ben the bartender tense. He made a mental note to keep an eye on the three. They ordered at the far end of the bar, and one of them, after taking a deep swallow of his beer, came over. Heading straight to Josef.

"I hear you're looking for Rebecca Thornton?" The man was in Josef's space. James and Walter stopped chatting and watched in silence. Josef turned to face him. He was dirty from the day's work in the fields. Grime and sweat covered his brow and neck. What was most noticeable was a nasty scar on the left side of his face, around his eye. The scar was jagged, semi-circular and the eye was partially closed. He was solidly built. Perhaps a tad overweight. He had meanness written all over him. His one good eye was cold. Josef had seen many men like him before, losers who intimidate through violence. But he was at a loss as to why this man was wanting to talk to him.

Josef calmly replied, "Yes, I am. I'm a lawyer from Canada and Rebecca Thornton is a beneficiary under a will our firm is administering. And your name is?"

The man ignored the question. Instead of giving his name he said, "I suggest you mind your own fucking business and stop poking around here for her. Understand?"

Conversation throughout the bar had stopped and all eyes were on the two. "Well, we do need to find her, so I'm afraid I'll have to do some poking." Josef looked right into his eyes. The man flinched a bit and then without warning hit Josef in the stomach with a powerful uppercut. Josef doubled over winded, gasping for breath, his body heaving. The pain shot through him. All his senses focussed on getting his breath back. His attacker stepped back to watch, proud of his sucker punch. Josef's old football coach used to say he was like Ferdinand the Bull, all peaceful and mild on the field, until he got hit and then Josef became a raging bull. Fighting also wasn't foreign to Josef. It was part of life growing up in Prince Albert, especially when boys from the hill ran into boys from the flat. Funny how those thoughts raced through his mind. His body calmed, he got his breath back. His attacker leaned into him, grabbing his hair, moving his head closer to him and he whispered in Josef's ear, taunting him, "I said do you understand me?"

Rage consumed Josef. He stopped thinking and reacted. He clinched his right fist and delivered a powerful upper cut to the man's stomach, who let out a loud gasp and folded over holding his mid-section. Josef then grabbed the man's head with both hands and slammed it down into his knee. His attacker was out cold and fell to the floor in a heap. Josef learned from a friend, in a street fight always finish the job – no half measures. The attacker's two buddies moved forward, until James and Walter stood up and blocked their path. James snarled, "You two calm down. Take Rupert and get out of here." They paused and seeing their leader was down and out and they were outnumbered three to two they chose retreat over attack. Each took an arm and hoisted Rupert up, carrying him out of the bar. James turned to Josef, slapped him on the back and said, "You must be a goddamn Canadian hockey player." Ben poured Josef a beer and nodded his approval.

Rubbing his still tender stomach, Josef asked, "What was that all about? And, who was that guy?"

"Don't know what it was about," said James, "but that was Rupert Malton. He is a mean son-of-a-bitch. His brother, Stan, is the senior constable in Goondiwindi. You couldn't have hit a more disliked fella in the town. Good on you, mate!"

Ben interjected, "Rupert had a fancy for Beckie. He thought she was his property."

After the beer, Josef went for dinner in the restaurant. Roberta was his waitress, once again; however, her attitude towards him changed markedly. Her reserved presence from last night was replaced by friendliness. Towards the end of his meal, she came over. "Can I get you anything else? The sticky date pudding is always good."

"Thank you, no. I'm too full. It was delicious."

In tidying up the table she bent over and whispered, "I'm off at ten. Meet me in the park back of the hotel. I'll tell you more about Rebecca." She quickly left. Josef wondered about her change in attitude. A trap? He didn't think so, but why so cloak and dagger. Was it fear of Rupert Malton? Or of Stan Malton? He'd find out.

It was dark and quiet outside and Josef found the small secluded park back of The Vic. He was a few minutes early and stood across the street watching the park for any uninvited guests. He saw Roberta, she looked around and stood hiding in the shadows. He went over.

"I'm here," she whispered as he came closer. "Come out of the light." He did as he was told and stood beside Roberta. "Sorry to meet you like this, but Rupert Malton is crazy."

"I figured that from tonight."

"Yes, I heard about the fight. We didn't want to talk to you before because we didn't know if Rupert or Stan had brought you in as a plant to find Rebecca."

"What do you mean a plant?"

"They're desperate to find Rebecca, and I don't want to think about what they'd do if they found her. You saw the scar on his face. Beckie gave that to him. It was about a year and a half ago. Rupert was besotted with her. Wouldn't leave her alone. Finally, Beckie had enough and told him in no uncertain terms to get lost. You don't do that to a Malton and not in public. Later that night he followed her home. She rented a small apartment on the edge of town. He tried to rape her. Beckie fought back. She glassed him and ran. She came to my house, covered in blood and with a fat lip, swollen face, black eye. She couldn't go to the police, because Stan would cover for Rupert. He always does. Rebecca needed to get out of town. Rupert would kill her for sure. I had my husband drive to her home. Rupert was gone. My husband packed a few personal things, her clothes and such. I cared for Beckie. After she took a long shower, my husband returned and drove her to Toowoomba. And she disappeared. All of us at work, her friends, vowed to protect her. That's why Ben and the others didn't tell you anything."

"So, my hitting back at Rupert proved my honesty."

"It did, and a good hit it was, I'm told."

"Alright, do you have any idea where Rebecca is? I do need to find her."

"Sorry, all I can say is she went east. That's all I know. I just wanted to warn you about Rupert and Stan. You don't know them and in Queensland the police are God. Be careful. I also wanted to tell you a bikie was in The Vic today asking about Rebecca. He was willing to pay. Didn't get any takers."

"You don't think he was sent by the Malton's?"

"Don't think so. Could be. But it would be pretty strange to bring a bikie in paying for information when they could do that themselves."

"Roberta, thanks for this. And pass the word, I'm a friend of Rebecca's. If you think of anything else you know where to find me or call Ken Barnes." Josef gave her one of Barnes' business cards.

Roberta scurried off into the night and Josef kept a vigilant eye walking back to his room. This certainly explained why Rebecca would not want to be found. Great. It would also mean she'd want to stay under the radar. No taxes paid, no driver's licence, no registrations of any kind in fear of Stan Malton finding her. No doubt Stan had told Rupert about him.

* * *

Stump had a good day at The Vic. He arrived at lunch time and asked around about Rebecca. No information. The staff gave him the cold shoulder, until he talked to the young front desk receptionist. She didn't know

Rebecca, but asked Stump whether he was working with the Canadian lawyer who was looking for Rebecca. Stump's street smarts took over; he replied, "As a matter of fact I am. I hadn't expected the Canadian to arrive so soon. Is it Dan; Dan usually is sent from Canada?"

The young woman, looked at the registration, "No, his name is Josef Manne."

"Joe, oh yah, Joe sometimes comes instead." Stump was on a roll. "What room is he in? I'd better touch base with him."

"He's in room 309, but he was heading out and told me he'd be gone most of the day, back for supper. I'm sure you'll find him in the bar or restaurant tonight."

"Thanks, I'll see him when he gets back."

Stump headed towards the front door. When the young woman turned her back, he detoured to the stairs leading to the first-floor hotel rooms. The hallway was empty. Stump gently knocked on the door to 309. No answer. The door had no deadbolt. He took a credit card out of his wallet, slid it down the gap between the door and the frame, forced it behind the lock and pushed the door inwards. The door opened. The room had been made up and was tidy. What interested him were the papers on the desk. The lawyer made notes. He was documenting his search for Rebecca Thornton. A quick read showed he had visited an aunt in Talwood yesterday and today Stump saw a note to meet with 'Ethel Foster – Foster Station – north of Moonie'. Stump smiled to himself, let the lawyer do the work. Stump would watch and follow his trail. He checked everything was back in place and left the room. He'd return to The Vic later in the day to see this lawyer.

Stump arrived back at the bar shortly after 5:00 and took a table in the corner, next to the front window with a full view of the bar. He nursed a beer, waiting. The lawyer arrived a few minutes later. He stood out: no tan, no windburned face, new clothes. The lawyer met two locals and they started chatting. Shortly before 6:00 three drovers came in. Stump watched the fight between Rupert Malton and the lawyer with amusement. After Rupert's sucker punch, Stump assumed it was all over. Then, what the hell, the lawyer fought back. The guy had balls. He did a real job on the drover. Stump admired that. He decided to take a room at the hotel; better to keep the lawyer under surveillance. He got a room on the first floor near 309.

67

CHAPTER 10

Wednesday, June 7

The ladies at St. Mary's were most obliging. Josef anticipated a bureaucratic battle. Instead of resistance, he was met with assistance. He was shown to the small library, where the librarian, Mrs. Cathy Cox, helped him hunt down old school yearbooks from 1958, 59 and 60. Mrs. Cox had only recently started at St. Mary's, and didn't know Rebecca. Josef took a seat and leafed through the years. He found Rebecca Thornton in 1958. Her yearbook picture showed a freckled, independent girl, who seemed to look at the camera with a degree of defiance. She had attitude. This was no meek timid country girl. She was on the school netball and track and field teams. You could see her natural athleticism. As the years proceeded, she blossomed. A young woman replaced the school girl. Below her graduation picture the caption read, "The world awaits Rebecca: travel, UQ, more travel." He noticed she and a classmate, Susan Ford, were often photographed together. Her best friend?

Mrs. Cox made some copies for him from the yearbooks and he asked her whether the netball coach, Mrs. Smythe, was still at the school. She was. The bell rang for morning tea and Mrs. Cox walked Josef to the staff room to find Mrs. Smythe, who had aged since 1958-60, but was still the netball coach. She remembered Rebecca very fondly.

"Rebecca was a determined, driven girl. She played hard that one and was the heart of the team. We won the regionals two years in a row." Josef imagined if he asked for details, Mrs. Smythe would have the game stats.

"What about Susan Ford? Is she still around? It looked like Rebecca and Susan were best friends."

"Oh, they were – inseparable. They did everything together. Rebecca was maid of honour at Susan's marriage a few years back."

"Do you know where Susan lives?"

"I think she still lives in a small house on Andersen Street near the river."

"What's her married name?"

"Let me think. I was at the wedding. Blake, yes, Blake. John is her husband. They had a baby four or five months back."

"Mrs. Smythe, you don't happen to know where Rebecca is? I have to find her."

"Sorry, can't help you there. Last time I saw her was at the wedding and that was a few years ago."

The bell rang and Mrs. Smythe returned to work. Josef went back to the library and checking the Goondiwindi telephone directory found a "Blake J. 130 Andersen Street". He decided to drive over right away. Forget a phone call. Time was slipping away.

130 Andersen Street was a cute wooden cottage surrounded by a white picket fence, freshly painted. The house had ornate ironwork on the porch façade. All was well maintained. He knocked on the screen door. A voice answered his knock. "Just a moment I'll be right there." Susan Blake appeared, babe in one arm. Josef recognized her from the yearbook. She was now a little fuller, but her athletic body was still visible. She had a perfect, white, Nordic look. Josef could only assume that she worked very hard at staying out of the sun. She opened the door, stood at the threshold and said, "If you're selling something; I don't need it."

"No, no I'm not selling anything. Susan, Susan Blake? I'm sorry to bother you and arrive here unannounced. My name is Josef Manne and I'm a lawyer from Canada and I'm looking for a friend of yours, Rebecca Thornton. I've just come from St. Mary's School and Mrs. Smythe tells me you and Rebecca were best friends." Josef wanted to give Susan as much of an introduction as he could.

She smiled. "Well I could tell as soon as you opened your mouth you weren't from round here. I'm sorry. What's your name again?"

"Josef Manne. Please let me explain why I'm looking for Rebecca."

"Gonna have to be in the kitchen. I have some cookies in the oven. Come on in." She turned, walked inside and casually added, "I'll just put Benjamin down for his nap. Kitchen's straight through."

Josef followed the smell of the baking to the country kitchen and took a seat at the table. Susan arrived a few moments later. He heard no protests from Benjamin. "Your son never cried when you put him down. I'm impressed."

"Benno likes two things in this world: food and sleep. If I give him plenty of both all is good." She checked the oven and turned to Josef. "You know, I haven't seen Rebecca for years. Why are you trying to find her?"

He went through the story of Old Bill and the will. Susan busied herself baking, whilst at the same time plying him with cookies and coffee. She listened carefully – saying little. When he was finished he asked her directly, "We need to find Rebecca, and any clue might be helpful. She stands to inherit a fair bit of money."

Susan took her time replying. "I just can't help you. I have no idea where she is. No idea at all."

Josef decided to try a different tactic. "I know all about Rebecca and Rupert Malton. I know that she had to flee town. In fact, I've already had a run-in with both Stan and Rupert Malton." He was looking for a reaction and saw surprise in her eyes. "You are welcome to check me out. Phone Ken Barnes, who is a local lawyer in town, and the staff at The Vic will vouch for me." He gave her one of Barnes' cards.

Susan took a sip of coffee and began talking, "Rebecca hasn't told me exactly where she is, but we have kept in touch. She sent me a card and gift when Benno was born. There was no return address on the parcel. I can tell you this, and it's all I know, she's in the Gold Coast hinterland. She's an artist and sells her paintings and whatever at the local markets. Cash only. No receipts. If you visit the local markets around the Gold Coast you'll find her. I'll show you something." She got up and went into another room returning with an embroidered bib that she handed to Josef. In the corner of the bib was sewn, 'Artisan made, Coolangatta, Qld Market'.

"Susan, thank you so much. This is the first real lead I have."

"But you can't tell anyone in case it gets back to the Malton's. Rupert's crazy and wants revenge. He lost his eye you know when Rebecca glassed him. He'll kill her; he'll kill her for sure. I'm telling you this because maybe, just maybe, the money from the inheritance will give Rebecca a way out, a life away from hiding. Promise me you'll not tell anyone."

"You have my word. I'll do whatever I have to do to protect Rebecca."

With business over, they enjoyed each other's company for the next hour. For Susan, it was nice to have an adult conversation. She wanted to know all about Canada. Josef plied her with stories of winter snow and cold. She replied with outback tales involving wild boars, venomous snakes, deadly spiders, floods and droughts. Their tales were cut short by Benno's cries for food. Josef begged off and she in a good-natured way said, "A typical male. As soon as a baby cries, you panic and flee the scene. I know, go, go." And she laughingly flicked her hand dismissing him. She went and got Benno. Her last words to Josef, "Tell Rebecca, when you find her, that I love her and Benno would like to meet her."

Josef left with a lighter gait. A burden was lifted. He now had a specific search destination. He decided to take the rest of the afternoon off and went to the Macintyre River to enjoy the day. A hike was in order. Susan told him in Australia, "watch where you walk". Given his terror of snakes, he was super vigilant and when he found a nice spot on a sunny hillside by the old bridge he checked round and round to ensure he could lie down free from any and all critters. He lay basking in the sun. For a change his mind rested. He was free to take in the now; no thoughts of tomorrow; no thoughts of work; no thoughts of life; just enjoy the sun, enjoy the day.

* * *

Stump rented a car. He reasoned a car was less visible than a loud motorcycle. His nondescript grey Datsun fit the bill. He followed Josef to St. Mary's and to Susan Blake's house. Stump didn't like hanging out for much of the morning on surveillance, but upon seeing Josef leave the house he sensed he had found something. Josef returned to the hotel and then went out for a walk. To Stump this was a signal Josef had indeed found something. Stump watched Josef cross the river bridge and he returned to The Vic. Stump entered room 309. There he found the yearbook photographs. There were three copies of each photograph. Stump decided to take one, which was of the two girls standing together. He flipped through Josef's notes. Nothing new. Stump too decided to take the day off and went to see if Betty was up for a good time.

* * *

Josef invited Barnes and Ruth to have supper at The Vic and told Barnes he was leaving tomorrow morning. Where to? All he said was east. Ruth couldn't make it; she had a prior ladies' supper at the bowl's club. Barnes arrived promptly at 6:00 pm. He'd heard about the altercation with Rupert Malton and wanted all the details, blow by blow. Josef obliged and went on to fill him in on the trouble between Rupert and Rebecca. Barnes nodded his head. "Makes sense for her to go to ground. The Malton boys are bad. They take after their old man, who was a mean bugger."

The less Barnes knew the better, at least that was Josef's reasoning. His fear was if he confided in him about Rebecca's whereabouts the secret would eventually leak out. Keeping a secret in a small town is a real challenge. Barnes respected his silence. They did agree to keep in contact through his travels. The steaks were served – tender and perfectly cooked. Their meal, however, was interrupted.

Stan Malton entered the restaurant with the underling officer Josef met the other day. They marched up to their table. Without so much as a greeting, Senior Constable Malton, addressed Josef, "I've heard there was an assault here at the hotel last night and you were involved. I'd like you to come to the police station to make a statement." It was not a request, but an order. Josef continued chewing and gave him a long look. Barnes put his knife and fork down and wiped his mouth with a napkin. He had a twinkle in his eye.

Josef finally spoke. "Good evening officer. I assume you are talking about the assault committed by your brother?"

"That's not the information I have. The information I have is you knocked him unconscious."

"That so? Do you usually investigate crimes involving your brother? In Canada we call that a real conflict of interest." Josef had his fill of the Malton boys, was baiting him and was succeeding; Malton's face took on a crimson hue.

"I still need to get all the facts. A complaint has been made. Better to discuss this at the station."

"No." Josef said firmly, "I'm not going anywhere with you. I know why you want to find Rebecca Thornton and I assume further it was you who told your brother about me. So, seems to me, you may well be some kind of accomplice to his attack on me." He saw the anger in Malton's eyes. He had marched into the restaurant full of authority and now Josef was calling his bluff.

Malton snapped, "Look, there is an easy way or hard way for you to come with me to the station. I'll arrest you if I have to."

Barnes stepped in, and in a quiet, but firm voice said, "Officer Malton, my client will not be going anywhere with you. You know as well as I, you cannot take someone to the station for questioning. If a person refuses, that is their right, and you know that. You are also in a terrible conflict of interest and should be recusing yourself. You also know that. Therefore, I suggest you calmly ask my client whether he wishes to make any statement and, if he does, it can be taken here. If he doesn't, then you will say good day and let us finish our meal in peace. Those are your options Senior Constable Malton and those are your only options." Barnes emphasized the last sentence.

Malton hesitated. It was one thing to roll a few deadbeats or drunken farm hands; it was another thing to pick a fight with two lawyers in a crowded public restaurant. Especially when what he was doing was clearly illegal.

Malton turned to Josef and with gritted teeth asked, "Do you want to make a statement?"

"I do not," Josef replied, giving him a steely look.

"Very well." Malton turned to his underling. "Nothing further here. Let's go." He turned and marched out, underling in tow.

Once out the door, Barnes gave a deep laugh. "That was so much fun. Malton is such a prick. Let us drink." He lifted his glass in a toast. "To the rule of law. May it ever prevail against tyranny." They celebrated into the evening. Ruth eventually arrived to say good-bye and to give her husband a ride home. Josef had much to celebrate: new friends and for the first time he felt confident he would find Rebecca Thornton.

CHAPTER 11

Thursday, June 8

Josef rose early feeling invigorated and wanting a fresh start. He decided to take a different route back to the coast. Instead of going to Brisbane he would travel via the Cunningham Highway to the Gold Coast. He paid his bill, said good bye to the hotel clerk and set off. It was a clear crisp Queensland winter morning.

The town of Inglewood was about one hour down the highway and was the ideal place to have breakfast. His waitress proved a wealth of information. She had lived on the Gold Coast for a number of years. In her view, which was not to be questioned, the place to stay on the Gold Coast was Burleigh Heads. "Best beach in the world, in the world," she bragged. Markets? She knew of markets taking place throughout the Gold Coast each and every weekend. Josef left well-fortified and much better informed.

He travelled through the Cunningham Gap and took the road to Boonah. The Beast mildly protested the lengthy ascent to the gap. The highway was replaced by a narrow single lane bitumen road, which wound its way through the rough mountain terrain towards the Gold Coast. Although the mountains were not high, like the Canadian Rockies, they were rugged with steep cliffs, very inhospitable and most likely snake infested. Josef had a workout shifting gears, and became accustomed to The Beast's foibles. The Beast preferred gentle clutching as opposed to quick forced gear changes. The driving slowed. Couldn't be helped. The twists, turns and one-way bridges would not tolerate speed. The road was an adventure through Beaudesert, Canungra to Nerang and finally the Gold Coast. It was late afternoon when Josef arrived and, as directed, he went to Burleigh Heads. He checked in at the Gold Coast Hotel, which was an older Queenslander build at the base of Burleigh headland across the road from the beach.

He dumped his luggage into his room and went to explore, crossing the road to the beach. It was beautiful, just beautiful. Burleigh Beach was anchored by two headlands, and the beach itself was a wide expanse of pristine white sand, gradually sliding into the Pacific Ocean. The warming sun glistened off the clean turquoise water. There was no protective reef, and the ocean waves relentlessly crashed into shore.

Stately columns of Norfolk Pines rimmed the beach and a footpath and esplanade followed the shoreline to the north. The sun was setting and Josef's ears were assaulted by the shrieking of hundreds of colourful birds. A lady was close by and he asked her what the birds were. "Those are rainbow lorikeets. At dusk they come out to feed and make a heck of a racket. Watch yourself. They drop a lot." She smiled and walked off. Josef adjourned to the hotel. He had booked one of the few rooms with an en suite bath. He looked forward to a bath, meal and sleep. Tomorrow he'd enjoy the beach.

* * *

Stump was panicking. Where was the lawyer? As he walked down the hall he saw the cleaners in room 309. He rushed down to reception. The young woman he'd first spoken to a few days earlier was on duty. "Hello, I was to meet Mr. Manne this morning, but I see his room, 309, is being made up. Is he in another room?"

"Oh, no he checked out early this morning," she replied.

"Damn," said Stump. "Did he say where he was heading?"

"No, no afraid not."

Stump retreated to his room. Think. Think. He had to think. The lawyer was his key to finding the girl. He had to find the lawyer. Think. The only reason the lawyer would leave was because he got some information and was following up on it. Think. Who was the last person the lawyer talked to? The woman on Andersen Street; she was in the school photograph. Stump pulled the photo out. The caption said, "Susan Ford and Rebecca

Thornton co-captains netball". Susan Ford, that was her name, she had told the lawyer something. He had to talk to her. He put on a clean shirt and packed his bag, checked out of the hotel, returned his rental car and hopped on his motorcycle.

Stump left his motorcycle at a park down the street from the house and watched it for a few minutes. All was quiet. No one seemed home. No car was parked in the driveway. Good, the husband would be at work. He put a pen in his shirt pocket and got out a small writing pad he used to jot down notes and things. He checked her name from the school photograph. He was ready. He walked up to the door and knocked.

Susan had just finished breast feeding Benjamin. "I'll be there in just a moment," she called out. She cleaned and burped Benno and with him in hand went to the door.

"Mrs. Ford, sorry to call on you, but Joe Manne, he talked with you yesterday, wanted me to come back just to get some further details." Stump put on his most charming front.

"It's not Ford. That's my maiden name. My name is now Blake."

Stump replied quickly, "So sorry." He flipped through his note pad. "Oh yes. Joe told me that. I see it here now. So sorry."

Susan opened the screen door. Doors were never locked in Goondiwindi. "Come on in. I don't know what more I can add to what I told him yesterday. Have a seat in the living room." Stump came in and took a seat. Susan was a little uneasy. This man was nothing like Josef Manne. He also had called him 'Joe'; however, yesterday Manne distinctly introduced himself as 'Josef'. Probably nothing she thought. But this man lacked polish. He was more like a farmhand than an office worker. He didn't have dress shoes; instead he wore scuffed work boots. Where was his car? It wasn't parked out front. She decided to do more probing. "You never introduced yourself, what is your name?"

"My name is Steven Conway."

"You didn't walk, did you? I don't see your car."

"I had trouble finding the right house, and I parked down the street by the park." Clever, he thought.

"You're not Canadian, how is it you work for Mr. Manne?"

76

"Oh, when he comes to Australia he often hires our firm to provide local support. On the ground help so to speak." Stump was proud of his quick-witted response, using the same ruse he had used with the hotel clerk at The Vic. Yet, he was wondering about this interrogation. Did she know? If so, he'd have to go to plan B.

"So, you have worked with Mr. Manne before?" Susan was now getting nervous. She bounced Benno on her knee to relieve some of her anxiety. Josef had told her this was his first time in Australia and first international trip.

"Yes, a couple other times in the last few years."

She now knew. This man was not sent by Josef. What to do? Her mind raced. She couldn't call the police because that would involve Stan Malton. She had Ken Barnes' card. She'd call him. But first she had to get Benno safely out of danger.

"Steven. I've been a very poor host. Would you like something to drink? Tea? Water?"

Stump had been watching her carefully. He could see her doubts, but wasn't sure. "A glass of water, thanks."

"I'll get it and put Benjamin down at the same time. You don't mind, do you?"

"Not at all." Stump played along. But he was going to watch her. Susan got up and took Benno to his room. She thought about making a run for it. No, she knew she couldn't outrun him carrying Benno. She put Benno down in his crib. She needed to call Barnes. She needed help from someone. She went to the kitchen and turned the tap on. Then she went to the phone, which was on the wall by the kitchen table. She took Barnes' card out and started to dial the number as quietly as she could. She didn't get far. Stump pushed down on the receiver forcefully.

"You aren't going to call anyone," he said in a deep growl.

"What! I just needed to call a doctor. How dare you…" She was trying.

Stump pulled the card out of her hand and looked at it. "Ken Barnes is not a doctor." He grabbed her hand and yanked the receiver from her and hung up the phone. Still holding her hand hard he dragged her back into the living room. She started to cry. "Shut up. Keep your fucking mouth shut."

He threw her on to the sofa and stood over her. "Here is how this is going play out. I need certain information and you're going to give it to me. I need to know where Rebecca Thornton is? Where is she?" His voice was low, threatening, harsh.

Susan was terrified. "I don't know. I don't know. I told Manne that as well."

Stump was angry. He bellowed, "Wrong answer. Don't lie to me. You don't want to get hurt and you don't want your little boy to get hurt, do you? Because if you don't start telling me what I need to know this is what I'm going to do. I'm going to take little Benjamin and break one of his little arms. Easy to do. And I'm going to ask you again. And, if you don't tell me the truth, I'm going to take little Benjamin and drop him on his head. He'll either be brain dead or might as well be. Then I'm going to take you and pour some of that Bundaberg rum you have sitting on top of the cupboard in the kitchen down your throat and all over you. Drunkard mom kills, maims baby. And you'll have to live with that." Stump was heated, his voice was a menacing growl. "Now tell me, you fucking bitch!"

Susan stopped thinking. She had to save her son. She couldn't have him hurt Benno. "Alright, alright. All I know is Rebecca is in the Gold Coast hinterland. That's all I know. That's where Mr. Manne went."

"What address? Give me an address? Give me a fucking address."

"I, I don't have an address. I don't have an address. She's on the run from the police here. She's on the run."

"Not good enough, not bloody good enough," shouted Stump. "You know more." Benno had woken up, and was crying. "Hear that? He's going to get worse. You know more. Tell me."

Susan was now sobbing. "All I know is she sells paintings at markets on the Gold Coast. That's all I know. I'm telling you the truth. That's all I know. She sent a gift from Coolangatta market. That's what I told Mr. Manne. That's all I know. Believe me. God, please believe me."

Stump looked down at her. She was broken. He knew that. She would have given him an address if she had one. He had his information. Just one more thing to do. He grabbed her by the hair and pulled her head up. "Look at me. Look at me. You don't tell anyone about this. You don't say a word. Because if you do, I'll be back. Back not to hurt you, but to hurt your son. You say nothing. Nothing. Hear? I'm going to leave now. Walk away. I don't want to come back. But I will. Do you understand?" His words were cruel, spoken with venom and intended to terrorize. He let go of Susan's hair. She nodded, yes. Stump turned. Went to the kitchen. Poured a glass of water and drank it. He then wiped the glass and water container clean with a dish towel, wiped the phone and wiped the door knob. Finished, he threw the dish towel on to the floor beside Susan. He left out the front door walking nonchalantly away.

Susan remained on the floor shaking, crying. As soon as she was certain he was gone, she got up and ran to Benno, lifted him out of the crib and held him tight, so tight. She comforted him and he her. What to do? She could not go to the police. Talk to her husband. She had to talk to someone. Phone Mr. Barnes? She just didn't know. She knew Josef wasn't involved with Conway, or whatever his name was, she had already given him the same information about Rebecca. It meant Rebecca was now in danger and probably Josef as well. What to do? She could not let anything happen to Benno.

CHAPTER 12

Friday, June 9

Josef was up early, eager to plunge into the ocean. He soon found swimming was a challenge. Although a good swimmer, he had never swum in the ocean. He got beaten up by the heavy surf. After a few minutes he retreated to shore, to rest and recover. He struck up a conversation with a young surfer, who stood surveying the waves. The surfer, Pete, was the quintessential Aussie beach bum, long bleached blonde hair, laid back, tanned. He explained to Josef he was looking for rips, where the incoming water moves back out to sea, and how the waves were moving. He pointed to a line of breaking waves about 75 yards off-shore, which was a sandbar. He explained a gutter of deeper, calmer water was on the shore side of the sandbar. Today, he said, the waves were not rolling in, but were dumping, which meant they collapsed into the sand, slamming swimmers into the sandy bottom. Josef now knew why he'd gotten so battered by the waves. Better to wait until low tide was Pete's advice, which was in a few hours' time.

"Where are you from? America?" he asked.

"Canada."

"That explains it," said Pete, "only Kiwis and tourists go swimming this time of year. Too cold for us Aussies. Surfing yes, but swimming, no. Canada, must be cold there."

Josef told him the water was warm for him, especially since the ice just melted on the lakes where he came from. He knew this would blow Pete's mind. And it did.

For the rest of the morning he played part tourist and part sleuth. He began by exploring Burleigh town. The main shopping area, James Street, was a collage of small shops, quaint and from a bygone era in Canada. He drove to Coolangatta about five miles south, which was located at the border between Queensland and New South Wales. He drove to the top of Point Danger, which the tour book said was the perfect spot to see migrating whales. No whales, however, the view looking north towards the bulk of the Gold Coast was sensational: golden sand beaches, green headlands, transparent turquoise ocean and brilliant blue sky painted a scene a prairie boy could only dream about. In Coolangatta town, he confirmed there was an artisan market held every Saturday morning at the park. The market was on for tomorrow.

He returned to Burleigh Beach. It was low tide and the beach had grown 50 to 100 yards wider. The waves seemed friendlier. He had a refreshing swim, less battered by the waves, and went for a long walk along the beach. The hard sand at low tide was perfect for walking. He went from the Surf Club at Burleigh Heads north to Little Burleigh probably a distance of a mile or mile and a half. He soaked in the full sun, clear water, and constant rhythm of the waves. It was paradise. On his way back, a call interrupted his repose.

"Hey, Canadian? Over here?"

It was Pete waving. He and five or six other surfers were seated in the shade of a Norfolk Pine. Josef went over. Each had a beer in hand and Pete offered Josef one, which he readily accepted. Introductions all round. They were interested in Canada and he in Australia. Stories were swapped. They were terrified of bears and he was terrified of snakes. It was a draw.

Josef gleaned they all lived on the coast and worked odd jobs leaving them plenty of time to surf. Surfing was their prime purpose in life. He estimated they all were in their early 20's and he felt old.

Talk soon turned to the Vietnam War. Opinions were strong. Everyone was against the war. Josef didn't know Australia sent troops to fight. And the Aussies, in turn, were surprised to hear Canada had not. Opinion was fixed, get out of Vietnam.

Josef surveyed the scene, everyone was easy going. Yes, they worked, but not in high paying pressured jobs; they simply earned a few bucks in order to surf. Life was simple and cares were few. They'd found their passion and lived it. For how long? They didn't worry about that; they lived the moment. He envied them. Josef's life was dominated, consumed by work and responsibilities. Was life passing him by? He was 28. Were his best years behind him? Was work his addiction? It was enjoyable and he was good at it, but it definitely was not his passion. All too depressing. He bid farewell to his free-spirited surfers and walked back to his hotel.

Saturday, June 10

Josef arrived at Coolangatta just after 9:00. He was lucky to get a parking spot not far from the market. There were about 100 make-shift stalls lined up in two parallel rows on the grass. The day was somewhat cooler and there was a threat of rain. Josef slowly began walking down the first row. Creative people with an inspiring array of talent were selling their wares: knitters, glass blowers, gemologists, silversmiths, wood carvers, bakers, painters, photographers. Many were definitely hippies from the hills. He did not see Rebecca Thornton.

His hopes were dimming as he started down the second row. Towards the end was a painter's stall. He approached slowly. The vendor, a woman, had her back to him. She turned. It was a middle-aged woman. His hopes were dashed. He continued on, but paused by a nearby booth. He looked back at the painter's stall and examined the paintings more carefully from afar, many were of horses, and scenes of the outback; something Rebecca would paint. Then he saw her. She spoke to the middle-aged woman, who left. Obviously, the woman had relieved Rebecca for a spell. Josef stared, following her closely. She was in blue jeans, boots, a thick cotton shirt and woollen vest. You could not take the outback out of the woman. Josef returned to her stall. She was talking to a couple customers, but glanced at him with a welcoming smile. He smiled back and began to look more closely at the paintings. They were signed 'Rose Foster'; yes, her middle name and 'Foster' as in the Foster Ranch. He knew he had to be careful so as not to spook her. He looked at some of the other paintings. They were very good. They weren't usual landscapes, rather there were ghostly images within each painting. A ghost of a man, woman, or child would be looking

Old Bill's Last Will and Testament

back at you through the landscape or that of a horse, koala, kangaroo or emu. The ghosts gave the paintings a soul. Finally, the other customers left. He and she were alone. Josef decided the best approach was honesty.

"See anything you like?" she asked.

"They are wonderful. You are very talented. I especially like the ghosting. It seems to give each painting a deeper meaning." Josef replied.

"You're not from here?"

"No, I'm not."

"Don't tell me. Let me guess."

"You are very white, little tan. But I see you have a good case of sunburn on your nose. So, my guess is you are Canadian. Am I right?"

"I'm impressed. You are correct. I arrived in Australia just a week ago. My name is Josef Manne, and I'm a lawyer from Prince Albert, Saskatchewan. And I need to be honest with you Rebecca." He paused for effect. "I came to Australia in search of you and I am so happy I have found you." The blood in her face drained, her smile vanished. She gave him a piercing look. He continued quickly. "You and your mother have been left a large estate by a former Canadian soldier, who was with your father, Charles, in a prisoner of war camp in Japan. He thought so much of your father he left you and your mother his entire estate. I know about the Maltons, and why you had to run. Roberta at The Vic in Goondiwindi told me. She told me how her husband helped you to get out of town after Rupert Malton attacked you. Susan Blake told me to look here. Please, I know this is shocking, but I need to talk to you and show you some things."

Rebecca stood silent. Thinking. Flee, fight or listen? She was listening. He continued rapid fire, "Your paintings are signed Rose Foster. Rose is your middle name and Foster is probably taken from the Foster Ranch. I visited Ethel Foster, a wonderful woman. She sends her love and asked me if I ever found you to tell you to give her a call. I know your mother, Connie, passed away a few years ago, which now leaves you as the sole beneficiary under the will. Here is my card. I am who I say I am. Please. I know this is a surprise; however, we need to talk. Here is a second business card for Ken Barnes, a solicitor in Goondiwindi. He has been helping me."

Her eyes were fixed on Josef. How could she believe this stranger? She said not a word looking carefully at his business card and then at Barnes' card. Next, she asked him a question he had never expected, "You say you are from Saskatchewan. Tell me what is the name of the CFL football team from Saskatchewan?" She studied him in steely silence.

Josef laughed. "Well, it is the Saskatchewan Roughriders. Quarterbacked by Ron Lancaster with George Reed running back. Their uniform is field green. Do I pass?"

Rebecca nodded. "Yes, you pass."

"Tell me how do you know the Roughriders?"

In a matter of fact way, she said, "I spent a summer working at the Banff Springs Hotel and every weekend there'd be Canadian football on television."

"Can we talk?"

"Yes. But I do need to make money selling paintings. We can talk after the market closes at noon."

"Do I need to stick around until then? I really don't want you skipping out on me."

"I promise I won't, but if you're worried, pull up a chair." She turned to take care of a customer; her mind churning. His story was too unbelievable to be true. Was he really a lawyer?

Josef picked up a folding chair leaning against the tent pole, found a nearby tree, plopped down and watched her. She stood straight and tall, much like Ethel Foster. Her dark brown hair was cut fairly short, practical. Her face was tanned by the sun, but was still fresh and a few freckles survived. She had a strong chin, high cheek bones and a beautiful smile. Her eyes were an intense deep brown. Slight dimples appeared when her smile turned into a laugh.

She sold five paintings whilst he watched. Shortly before noon the stall owners started taking down their tents. Josef went over to help Rebecca. She packed the paintings in plastic and he tackled the stall tent. He told her he had a Ute nearby and offered to drive her home. He knew she had no car. She hesitated. Could she trust him? "And I'll throw in lunch," he pleaded.

"You are persistent, aren't you?" She gave him a resigned look. "Alright, I'll just tell my ride I'll be going with you." She walked over to a psychedelic Kombi van. Spoke with the driver and gave them a wave.

"Okay, where is your Ute?"

Josef pointed. Rebecca then hoisted the stall tent on her shoulder and carried it to the Ute. She was independent and strong. Josef followed carting the box of paintings. Once loaded, Rebecca simply said, "I know a place. It is in Currumbin. I'll direct." No light conversation. The café was right on the beach and looked out to Elephant Rock. When they sat down all she said was, "This café is known for its seafood."

She was guarded, careful, which Josef could understand. He brought out his file folder and gave her a copy of the letter Old Bill gave to him and a copy of the will. She read the two slowly, when finished, she turned to Josef and asked, "Why did Mr. Jones give us his estate? Do you know why?"

"I don't know. All we know is he was a prisoner with your father at the Niigata prisoner of war camp." She had yet to ask about the size of the estate. Josef gave her Gabe's one-page valuation.

After reading the valuation, she looked up and said, "This is a lot of money, an awful lot of money. More than I need or deserve. I don't even know Mr. Jones. I don't imagine his family will be too happy, but they are family, wouldn't it be the right thing to give them half?"

Josef replied, "Old Bill wanted to do this. He must have had his reasons. I can tell you from what I know of his brother and his family they are not good people. You could negotiate with them. That's your decision. However, I think it premature. There is a will, I am executor and I suggest we move forward to probate and see what happens."

The food arrived. It was a cue to change the conversation. He asked her about growing up on the Foster Ranch. She loosened up. She talked about her mother and about being the only girl on the ranch. In turn, she asked Josef about his family and growing up in Blue River. She wanted to know about Old Bill. She wanted to know about the wars, the Morrisons. Time flew by. They became more comfortable with each other; however, the fact was they were strangers and Josef knew he could not rush her. He had to earn her trust.

They stayed at the café until after 2:00 pm and had to go if Josef was to get up and down the mountain before dark. Rebecca navigated. Their destination was Springbrook, which was perched on the edge of an extinct volcanic caldera, some 20 or so miles inland in the hinterland. The Springbrook road followed the contour of the land with no exceptions. The road, a single lane of bitumen, winded its way ever upward. Switchbacks were common as were single lane bridges. No wonder Rebecca wanted Josef off the mountain before dark. The drive took an hour. They made it to the plateau and continuing along the caldera Rebecca told him to turn into a no address gravel driveway. She was home.

Josef turned the Ute off. "Phew, that was some drive."

"You get used to it. Let me show you the cabin, before we unload." She led him to the gate. There was a flimsy wire mesh fence surrounding a wooden, unpainted small cabin, built on cut timber piles, with a veranda along its front. As soon as she opened the gate, a screeching racket enveloped them.

"This is my alarm. Guinea fowl. They'll start chirping whenever someone enters the yard and, I've been told, they keep snakes away as well."

"Chirping, that's not chirping, that's squawking," Josef countered.

Once in the cabin the guinea fowl stopped. The cabin was cozy. There was a fireplace along one wall and a small kitchen, one bedroom and the back door opened on to another veranda looking out over a grassed area and then into nothingness. The cabin was located right at the cliff face of the caldera. Rebecca led Josef down a path to the rim. In the distance you could see the ocean. Looking down, Josef estimated the drop was over 300 feet, straight down. The path from the cabin intersected with another path that ran parallel along the cliff top. "You can follow it back to town." Rebecca pointed to a crevasse in the cliff face. "That's my hideout if someone comes," she said flatly, "I slip down the crevasse to a narrow ledge and follow it 20 to 30 feet to an overhang where there is a cave in the cliff wall. There I hide." In a quiet voice she said, "I am so tired of hiding." Rebecca turned to look at Josef, sadness in her eyes. That was the first time she showed any emotion and it passed quickly. She snapped out of her melancholy. "Come on, let's unload the Ute and I'll make you a cup of tea. It's the least I can do to fortify you for the trip down. You do realize most mountain climbers die on the way down a mountain. Most drivers too." She laughed. Josef didn't.

He sat in a rocking chair by the fireplace while Rebecca boiled water for tea. The cabin had a feminine touch. Flowers on the table and plants in the kitchen window. Everything was neat and tidy. Rebecca had closed the door to the bedroom. A wash area occupied an alcove by the bedroom, with a ceramic water pitcher and wash bowl. There was no indoor plumbing. An outhouse was off to the side of the cabin in the bushes. It was primitive, yet homey. A thick board resting by the front door caught his eye; the board was there to fit into iron brackets on either side of the door. This was home and a prison cell at the same time.

Rebecca explained how she found the place. "One of my artist friends lives on the mountain and when I first arrived I needed a cheap place to stay. In the last few years most families have left the area. The school closed. The farmer, who owns the cabin, was looking to rent it out to shearers working in the area. Well the sheep have gone and he was just happy to have someone live in it. I got it very cheap. I've come to love the place."

"Aren't you lonely? You're here all alone."

"Well, maybe at times, but there is a community on the mountain and I do go into town each and every weekend. Lots of time to paint." She didn't sound convincing.

A rumble of thunder echoed. The wind started to get up. "Storm coming," said Rebecca, "You'd better get going." Josef nodded yes. They agreed to meet back on the Gold Coast tomorrow for the market in Southport and he got directions. At that time, he'd have an affidavit for her to sign. She was to bring with her, her birth certificate, passport, and any other documents to confirm her identity. They'd get them photocopied and he would attach them to the affidavit. He'd see her again just before noon when the market closed.

She walked him to the Ute. He rolled down the window. She tapped the Ute's door and simply said, "Thank you for finding me." No time for anything else; the wind was getting up.

* * *

Stump drove hard to get to the Gold Coast. It was familiar territory. With money in his pocket he took a room in an upscale Surfer's Paradise hotel. He phoned Jimbo, who told him, "for fuck sake get it done." After hanging up on Jimbo, Stump phoned his mates and invited them over. They partied through the night and well into the morning. Friday was a wasted day for

Stump; more drinking, more partying. Saturday morning, head heavy, he went to Coolangatta Park. He sat for a time on the hillside overlooking the market. He had to be sure the woman in Goondiwindi hadn't gone to the police. No police. He then walked down to the market and saw Manne, who led him right to her. He waited. No good trying anything with all these people around and with Manne standing guard. Patience. He had plenty of time and money. He watched them load the Ute. They left the market. He followed. He watched through their lunch. He knew Manne would probably take her home and he'd have to leave her at some point. He followed them at a distance to Springbrook staying well behind because of the switchbacks. He saw the parked Ute, drove past and turned the motorcycle into an overgrown laneway further up the road. This was perfect, isolated, few if any people nearby and as far as he knew she lived alone. It was time. He took his .38 revolver out of the motorcycle bag. Checked it was loaded and slid the weapon into an ankle holster and strapped it on. He was ready and found a rock clearing in the bush where he hunkered down. He could see the Ute and waited for Manne to leave.

CHAPTER 13

Stump heard the rolling thunder. He hated to ride in the rain, but a storm would provide cover for what he was about to do. Come on lawyer, get going. What if he was going to stay? Kill them both? No. Too messy. He'd come back. He was nervous. Jittery. How to do it without getting caught? A conscience, he had none. Any regret about killing another human being? No. It was a job; it was money. He'd hurt people before, albeit never a woman. Above all he needed to show everyone that he, Stump, could do it and he was a man to be reckoned with. He popped a couple 'pick-me up' pills. Waited. Wind gusts sent shivers through the trees. Come on. Come on. A few drops of rain fell; a precursor of more to fall. Stump left his hiding spot and went to his bike, where he got his leather riding jacket and put it on. Returning to his spot, he saw the Ute back up and head down the mountain. He waited. The storm slammed into the mountain. The wind howled and the drops of rain turned into a torrent pushed sideways by the wind. He sought cover within the gnarled roots of an ancient Antarctic Beech tree. Its wide base stood as a formidable wall against the southeasterly wind and rain. The tree had weathered centuries of storms; this would be no different. The sky was dark. Flashes of lightning burst through the darkness followed by powerful cracks of thunder, echoing through the valley. The rain fell harder. The wind became cyclonic. Stump hugged the tree. There was an explosion of lightning and thunder, a last barrage. The storm passed; the wind subsided, as quickly as it had risen. Rays of sunlight fought through the darkness. The rain was now a light drizzle. Stump left the safety of the tree.

He walked to the laneway. Waited. Had she left in the Ute? No. He saw a dim light in the cabin. It moved, probably a kerosene lamp. Stump smiled to himself, good, the power is off. Dusk would soon turn into darkness. He needed to get this done before total darkness. He sneaked closer to the cabin. The rickety wire fence was too high and too fragile to climb over. He gently opened the gate. The screeching began at once, a cascade of squawking. The alarm was sounded.

Rebecca blew out the lamp; turning the cabin into semi darkness. She looked out and saw someone at the gate. Josef? Did he come back? She had neither heard nor seen the Ute. No, it was someone else. She picked up the thick board by the door and slipped it into the brackets and then she turned and ran out the back door of the cabin.

Stump stood frozen for a moment, then he saw the lamp go out. He knew she had seen him. Stealth was out. He charged at the door and flung his 200 lbs at it on the run. It didn't crash open; instead he was knocked back. He gave it a kick with his boot. The door held fast. He ran across the verandah to the side of the cabin and ran towards the back. He had his .38 in hand and slowed, worried she might be armed; most country folk had a shotgun. He stopped at the corner of the cabin and looked around the back. No one was there. The back door was open. He checked the cabin; she wasn't there. He saw a path leading towards a clearing. He followed the path. He couldn't lose her. If he did she'd disappear again. He walked carefully down the path, still thinking she might be armed. Then, in the faltering sunlight, he saw the cliff edge. There was another path, this time running parallel along the cliff edge. Which way did she go? He looked at the path carefully; there were no tracks in the wet mud of the path in either direction. If she had taken the path there would be tracks because of the recent rain. He examined the area more closely. He went to the crevasse and there, right at the rim of the crevasse was a foot print, and at the rim the mud had been further disturbed. He looked, there was a ledge below the rim. Stump knew he had found her. He put the .38 into his jacket pocket and turned backwards shimmying himself down to the ledge below. Once on the ledge, he could see it acted as a narrow trail on the cliff face. Don't look down. He critically examined the trail. It seemed to end about 30 feet along the cliff wall. He stood watching. Nothing, then a burst of sheet lightning revealed a gap in the wall, where the trail ended. He was sure she was there. He now had a new plan. Throw her off the cliff and no one would suspect anything other than an accident or suicide. He'd have to remember to go and unlock that front door. He started shuffling along the trail, facing the cliff, holding on with his hands to any gaps in the granite wall. He didn't like this one bit. After he had moved five to six paces he saw her. She moved to the ledge of the cave and threw a rock that ricocheted off the cliff wall above him. She threw another. This one found its mark and hit him in the side. Shit, he couldn't take the trail with her throwing rocks at him. He needed his gun, but it was in his left-hand pocket, Stump was left handed. He couldn't get hold of it without changing his position and he sure wasn't going to do that on the narrow ledge. He retreated to the crevasse entrance, put the .38 into his right hand and started again. This time he had his gun at the ready and he moved with more confidence.

Rebecca saw him coming and went to the cave edge to throw another rock. This time, a shot rang out; the bullet hit the stone near her face. She fled back into the cave. What to do? If she exposed herself in order to throw a rock, she'd be shot, especially when he got closer. She looked for anything in the cave she could use to defend herself. There was nothing other than the broken rocks. She took a careful look around the corner, he was slowly coming towards the cave. She picked up a jagged rock. She was not going to die without a fight.

Then she heard a voice, calling her name, "Rebecca, Rebecca, where are you?" It was Josef.

"I'm here. In the hideout," she yelled.

* * *

The rain engulfed Josef just after he passed the first one-way bridge. He was blinded by the deluge. The Ute's windshield wipers couldn't handle the water. Carefully he pulled over to the shoulder, which fortunately was on the mountain side of the road. He couldn't go any further up or down until the rain lessened. The storm continued with more intensity. The cracks of lightning and the booms of thunder shook the mountain around him. The gully beside the road grew into a rushing river. Josef had never been in such a storm. All he could do was wait it out. In minutes the storm cell moved on up the mountain towards Rebecca's cabin. He could see again and there was still some daylight left. He drove The Beast back onto the road and continued down, going very slowly. He hadn't travelled more than five minutes when he came to a particularly steep portion of the road and there, halfway down the grade, he saw a large gum tree had fallen blocking the road. He got out and walked to the debris. The trunk of the tree was at least four feet in diameter and some of the branches were two to three feet round. There was no moving this tree without a chainsaw. He also saw the tree had brought down some boulders. This was not a safe place to stop. Josef returned to the Ute and backed it cautiously up the grade to a wider part of the road, where he could turn around safely. And he headed back to Rebecca. There might be another road off the mountain.

The light continued to fade. Josef was having difficulty in finding the cabin. He went too far and needed to turn around. An overgrown lane was ahead, he turned into it and there he saw the motorcycle. Who would leave a motorcycle there? The answer came instantaneously, a biker. Roberta, in Goondiwindi, had warned him a biker had been looking for Rebecca. Christ, he had led the biker to her. What an idiot. He hadn't kept an eye out. He hadn't done anything except lead the biker to Rebecca. He recalled hearing a motorcycle earlier in day, when he and Rebecca first arrived. He hadn't thought anything about it. He turned back and found Rebecca's cabin about 200 yards down the road.

The gate was open. The guinea fowl were squawking. He ran to the door, it wouldn't open. She had barred the door. He ran to the back; the door was open. No Rebecca. He remembered her hideout and followed the path to the cliff edge. He had to be careful. Where was the biker? Nothing. Then he heard a gunshot. The shot had come from below the cliff edge. Caution be damned, he called out and heard Rebecca's call in return. She was still alive!

Stump was eight feet below Josef on the narrow trail. He had heard Josef's call and tried to move his head back to get a clear view, but couldn't without losing his balance. He needed to hold on to the cliff wall, or a root, lean back and fire. He steadied himself. The lawyer appeared and Stump fired. Damn, he was no good with this right hand. Josef jumped back. Stump couldn't switch hands. He decided to move back to the crevasse and take care of the lawyer first. He had no choice. He didn't get far. At that moment a powerful lightning strike landed near and the resounding thunder boom shook the mountain like an earthquake. Stump was in the process of turning his face and body to his left. When he planted his left foot he slipped, the smooth leather soles on his boots had no grip. He frantically tried to grab on to something, but his right hand still held the .38. Stump fell. As he fell, he tried to grab the rock face. All he grabbed was air. He careened off the rocks over 250 feet below and fell a further 20-25 feet onto a massive rock plateau overlooking the creek at the base of the cliff. Dead.

Josef saw Stump fall. He called out to Rebecca, "Rebecca are you hurt. He's gone. He fell. We need to get you off this cliff. Another storm is coming. Rebecca?"

"I'm not hurt, but give me a moment." Her voice was wooden, guarded. She closed her eyes. She needed to think. Is Josef really who he says he is? Was he hired by Rupert to find and kill me? He insisted on driving me home. Was he working with the killer? Why was he back? Did he return to make sure I was dead? Will he kill me now? No, this is crazy, the man shot at him. She just did not know. She gathered herself. "Okay, I'm ready. I'm coming back."

"Be careful, it's slippery," yelled Josef to be heard over the strengthening wind.

Rebecca slowly made her way on the trail to the crevasse and climbed up, taking his hand in support. She was wet and muddy. Josef didn't know what to do, whether to hold her or not. He moved to help steady her. She moved away from him saying, "I'm fine." She did not want holding. She was confused.

"Why did you come back?" It was part question, part accusation.

"A tree fell and blocked the road. Just past the first one-way bridge. I had no choice." He went on to tell her about seeing the motorcycle and realizing it was he who had led the biker to her. He felt so sorry that he had put her in danger. He told her when he saw the barred front door he thought he was too late. They walked back to the cabin together. The storm gathered for another attack on the mountain.

CHAPTER 14

Once at the cabin, Rebecca lit a kerosene lamp and candles. Josef started a fire in the fireplace. Rebecca washed and changed into dry clothes. She brought over a cast iron pot to heat water for tea. Neither said a word. They watched the water boil. Saying nothing. Finally, the water was ready and the tea was made. Rebecca wrapped herself in a blanket and sat on a small stool leaning in towards the fire holding her cup of tea in two hands.

"What do we do now?" she asked, not moving her eyes from the fire.

Josef had been pondering that same question. "First, we did absolutely nothing wrong. Second, we did not cause his death. He fell. Rebecca, we have to report his death."

"And when we report it, the police will ask about Goondiwindi and Malton will find out. There might be a warrant out for my arrest. I could give them my artist name, Rose Foster." She was fearful her cover would be exposed.

"Rebecca, don't give the police a false name. As soon as you do, you become a suspect."

"I'll be a suspect anyway. You too."

"Yes, but if we tell the police the truth nothing will happen. As I've told you, we did nothing wrong. Give them your correct name. Tell them what happened. No more. No less."

Rebecca digested what Josef had said, and sipped her tea. "You know there is a path down to where he is. It's a bit steep, and I wouldn't recommend trying it until the rain stops, but we could go down and at least check that he is dead. I feel strange sitting here knowing he's lying there."

"It is strange. But there's nothing to be gained in our doing that. We both know no one could survive that fall. Let the police retrieve the body. However, we do have to report it first thing."

"Who do you think hired him, Rupert Malton?"

Josef had been thinking about this as well. "I don't know. We know Rupert hated you, was fixated on you. However, certain things make no sense. Why hire a biker to pay for information? Malton could have done that himself. It also would have made more sense to hire the biker to follow me, once I arrived and started asking about you. Except, it's likely the biker was hired before I arrived. It just doesn't add up. There is one other thing, from what I know of a guy like Malton, he would want to hurt you in person. Have the satisfaction of killing you with his own hands. He's consumed by hate. Those guys don't give that pleasure to someone else. But, having said all this, Malton is still the number one suspect. Is there anyone else who wants you dead?"

Rebecca shook her head no.

"Rebecca, I have to ask you this, because the police will." Josef took his time. "Bikers are usually involved with drugs. Are you involved with drugs?"

She turned and looked hard at him; there was a flash of anger. "No, I don't use drugs. Never have. Just because I live in the hinterland, doesn't make me a hippie pothead."

Josef had crossed a line and apologized. "Sorry, it's the lawyer in me." He moved on. "Is there any other road off the mountain?"

Rebecca calmed down. "There is, but it is two miles or so further down from where you say the road is blocked. We have to wait out the storm. Emergency services are pretty good at clearing the road."

"Is there a phone on the mountain?"

"Yes, at the general store in Purling Brook Falls, back about two miles. But there won't be phone service until power is restored; the two go hand in hand."

"Then we wait."

"Yes, I have cheese, bread and some cold meat for sandwiches. Interested?"

"I'm starved. That would be great."

Rebecca got up and moved to the kitchen. The storm continued. They ate the sandwiches and both felt rejuvenated. They talked some more. Josef had Rebecca collect all the necessary documents they needed to take into town tomorrow. He knew they'd have to make a trip to the police station.

Josef saw she had a photo album and he asked her if he could look through it. Rebecca hesitated for a moment, then agreed. Soon she was seated beside him at the table describing the who, what, when and where of each photograph. She seemed happy to talk about her childhood, especially the time spent at the Foster Ranch. She was quite the tomboy. Still no power. Still raining. Rebecca brought some blankets into the living room. It was getting chilly on the mountain, although the rain helped to moderate the cold.

Josef didn't sleep well. He was trying to plan out tomorrow. So much would depend on the attitude of the police. He also couldn't stop thinking about Rebecca. A person had tried to kill her, yet she was so calm, which wasn't what he expected. Hysterics? No, that was for Hollywood. Rebecca was a strong person, a survivor. He admired her strength. His mind roamed to the killer. Why, and why now? Could it have something to do with the will? She was the only remaining beneficiary. Too far-fetched? Yes, he thought, too far-fetched.

Rebecca too got little sleep. Josef, was he really a lawyer from Canada? The story seemed so implausible. Yet, he was so convincing. She wanted to trust him, but could she? There were lingering doubts. Just in case, she placed a chair behind the closed bedroom door and hid a butcher knife in the night table. She just didn't know.

Sunday, June 11

The next morning was sunny and cold. Josef woke to Rebecca re-lighting the fire. It was 6:00 am. She was happy to report power was back on. The general store opened at 7:00 am and they could drive down to phone. Water was boiling in a kettle for coffee and Rebecca made eggs and toast for breakfast. Josef went outside to the cliff edge. The panorama of Springbrook National Park was breathtaking, with a light mist hovering over the caldera. He stood in silence and had to look down. The body was still there. Rebecca came and stood beside him. A flock of birds were flying in the distance. "Cockatoos," she said. "It is so peaceful up here, or was. Come, breakfast is ready."

Right after breakfast they drove to the general store, wanting to arrive at opening time. They exchanged pleasantries with the owner and his wife. The word was the road would be open shortly. A crew was already cutting up the tree. Rebecca and Josef went to the public phone and called the Mudgeeraba Police Station. Josef did the talking. He reported a man falling off the cliff. Yes, dead. It happened last night. No. No phone and the road was blocked. Suggest they bring a recovery team. He gave his name. How soon would the police arrive? They'd meet at the general store.

Rebecca and Josef sat on the store verandah to wait. The police convoy arrived about 40 minutes later, two patrol cars and the fire and rescue people. Josef and Rebecca stood up as the convoy pulled in front of the store. An older officer got out of the first vehicle, obviously in command. He was in his forties, tall, heavy set, a little over-weight, with a military bearing. He took charge immediately.

"You called in that a man fell to his death?"

Josef took the lead. "Yes."

"Senior Constable MacPherson and with me is Constable Kirby. And you are?"

"My name is Josef Manne, and I am visiting from Canada. This is Rebecca Thornton, whose cabin is up the road, where the man fell. We can take you, it's just up the road a few miles."

"Okay, do you know the man's name?"

"No, but I think he left a motorcycle near Miss Thornton's place, you should be able to trace the licence plate."

"When did this happen?"

"Last night at about 5:00 pm."

"And you just called us this morning?"

"As you know, there was a storm, the phones were out and the road down to Mudgeeraba was blocked. We called as soon as we could."

MacPherson nodded his head. "Fair enough, we saw them clearing the road when we came up. Take us to the spot."

Josef and Rebecca got into the Ute and led the way. "That was easy enough," said Rebecca.

"Don't be fooled, he's sizing us up. He'll probably want to talk to us separately. Remember, tell the truth, everything, and all will be just fine."

They arrived at the cabin. MacPherson and Kirby accompanied Josef and Rebecca, the other two police officers and rescue people stayed at their vehicles. Walking through the front yard the officers were greeted by the guinea fowl. Rebecca and Josef led them to the cliff edge. Josef said, "You can see him down there." The officers carefully moved to the edge and looked down.

"Did you go down to see if he was alive?" MacPherson asked, still peering down.

"No," said Josef, "we thought about it, but with the rain all night and the steep path down, it was too dangerous. He fell over 200 feet. You don't survive a fall like that."

MacPherson nodded his head. "So, there's a way down?" He kept looking over the edge.

Rebecca answered, "Yes, it's back down the road about a quarter of a mile. Pretty steep."

"How did he fall?" Macpherson asked, now looking at Josef and Rebecca.

Josef answered, "He was trying to kill Miss Thornton. He was on a ledge below us here. Come to this crevasse and you'll see the ledge." Everyone moved to the crevasse. "Miss Thornton had a hiding spot along that ledge and he found her. He shot at her. I heard the shot and came. He fired at me. And then there was a massive crack of lightning and thunder and he fell before he could kill either of us." MacPherson gave Josef an intense look with his light blue eyes, eyes that no doubt had coaxed many a confession out of many an accused. He didn't say anything for a few seconds, processing what Josef told him.

"So, the gun, it fell with him?"

"I imagine so, yes." Josef answered.

"Alright, Miss Thornton, you said there is a way down, would you please go with Constable Kirby and show the rescue team the path?" MacPherson spoke with Kirby privately and beckoned the remaining officer to come over; Josef was asked to repeat where the motorcycle was to be found.

MacPherson issued some orders to the officer, who left. Once everyone was gone, MacPherson turned to Josef. "Beautiful morning, shall we sit on the back verandah. I need more information." They went to the back verandah, where the sun provided a respite from the chilly morning air, and took a couple seats.

"First, tell me how you know Miss Thornton."

"It is a long story officer." Josef reached into his wallet and took out one of his business cards, giving it to MacPherson. "I'm a lawyer in Prince Albert, Canada and I only met Miss Thornton yesterday. She is the beneficiary under a will and I am the executor of that will."

MacPherson interrupted him, "This card says you are a criminal lawyer."

"Yes, it does and I am. This will probably be my first and last will case. Do you mind, I'll get a couple of documents for you, which will explain things? They're in a folder in the cabin." MacPherson gave a 'go ahead' expression. Josef retrieved the folder and showed MacPherson copies of the letter from Old Bill and the will.

Josef then recounted his travel to Australia and search for Rebecca Thornton. He told MacPherson about Rupert Malton and that Rupert's brother was a Senior Constable in Goondiwindi. "Officer, this woman feared for her life. You heard the damn guinea fowl in the front yard. They are her alarm. And just look at the front door, and the wood bar. And the hiding place on the cliff face." MacPherson didn't say a word, although he took it all in.

Josef continued, "It's my fault. I was obviously followed and led the biker to her. I was told in Goondiwindi a biker had been offering money for information about Rebecca. I should have been more careful. I wasn't and I led him to her." Josef then recounted how the biker died.

"So, you only know he's a biker?"

"I don't even know if he is a biker. All I know is he rides a motorcycle."

"Let's take a walk to the cliff edge." MacPherson got up and went to the crevasse. He lowered himself down to the ledge and bent down to follow the trail along the cliff face. He stood upright and asked Josef, "Where was he and where were you when he fell?"

Josef re-enacted as best he could.

"So, you were pretty well directly above him?"

"Yes, maybe I was slightly to his right, if he was facing the cliff."

"When did he shoot at you?"

"Right there. When I first arrived at the cliff."

"How many shots did he fire?"

"Two that I heard. I heard a shot and went to the cliff, looked down, saw him, he saw me, and he fired. He may have fired more shots before I came."

MacPherson pulled himself out of the crevasse. "When you were almost directly above him, what did you do?"

"I looked for something to throw at him, a tree branch, a rock anything. But he fell before I could do that."

"Why were you going to throw those things at him?"

"I heard Miss Thornton's, Rebecca's, call. She said she was in the hideout. She had shown it to me earlier in the day. He had a gun. I heard a shot. He shot at me. I was pretty damn sure he was intent on killing her. I wanted to stop him."

"Did you throw anything at him to make him fall?" MacPherson gave Josef that intense look.

"No. If I had found something I would have, but I didn't. He fell of his own accord and because of the storm."

MacPherson continued to look at Josef and said, "Thank you Mr. Manne. I'd appreciate it if you could come down to the station to make a formal statement. A man has died and from what you have told me, he was out to kill you and Miss Thornton."

Against all his better judgment as a lawyer, Josef answered, "Yes, I'd be happy to." He was of the view cooperation was the best route out. This was not a time to be defensive or uncooperative.

"Oh, just one other thing," MacPherson asked innocently, "last evening and night did you talk with Miss Thornton about what occurred?"

It was not an innocent question, but one designed to catch them in a lie, "Yes, we did. What we most discussed was who had hired the biker to kill her."

MacPherson gave an understanding nod and turned back to look down the cliff. The police and rescue people had reached the body. One police officer, probably Kirby, went over to it, and could be seen bending over,

Old Bill's Last Will and Testament

no doubt checking for life. He then stepped back. Another officer started taking photographs.

Rebecca arrived back. MacPherson turned to her. "Thank you for showing us the path down. Do you mind, I have a few questions to ask you in private?" Josef begged off and went into the cabin to gather his things. It was now Rebecca's turn. She and MacPherson sat on the back verandah. Rebecca followed Josef's advice and told the truth.

MacPherson ended his interview asking her the same question he had asked Josef, "Bye the bye, last evening and night did you talk with Mr. Manne about what occurred?"

"Of course we did. A man died trying to kill me." Rebecca replied, with a degree of anger. MacPherson gave a forgiving smile. The interview was over. He thanked Rebecca and she too was willing to give a statement at the police station. Rebecca came into the cabin and put the kettle on to make a pot of tea. MacPherson excused himself, to speak to the officer who had gone to find the motorcycle.

MacPherson returned and sat down at the kitchen table. He'd carefully surveyed the cabin, saw the front door bar, noticed the blankets and pillow in the main room, they hadn't slept together. Rebecca offered him a cup of tea and he graciously accepted. He took a sip and spoke, "The motorcycle is registered to a Sidney Hooper, who lives in Toowoomba. I can tell you that Sidney Hooper is known to us." Translation, thought Josef, Hooper had a criminal record.

MacPherson asked Rebecca to come with him to the police station and Josef was to follow in the Ute. Keeping them separate. Josef started to feel uncomfortable. He had already seen the Queensland Police in action with Senior Constable Malton and was wondering whether MacPherson was of the same nature. When they got to the station, he'd call Ken Barnes in Goondiwindi.

At the station, Josef asked MacPherson if he could make a long-distance phone call to Goondiwindi to speak to a lawyer. MacPherson gave Josef a sharp look but agreed, which was a good sign. Josef phoned Barnes' house. He was relieved when he heard Barnes' voice.

"Ken, Josef here."

"Thank God!" said Barnes excitedly, "I've been worried sick about you. Are you okay mate?"

"Whoa, why have you been worried?" Josef asked.

"Susan Blake called me yesterday. You know she was Rebecca's friend."

"Yes, I know her."

"A man visited her the day you left, said he was working for you, which she saw through. He threatened to hurt her and her baby. The bastard. She was terrified. She told him, what she told you. Can't blame her. I was worried he'd do something to you. Did you find Rebecca Thornton?"

"Yes, I did. And we're okay, but Ken, I'm calling from the Mudgeeraba Police Station. Long story short, a biker tried to kill Rebecca and me. I led him to her, just as I must have led him to Susan. We're cooperating with the police, but I'm not sure it's the right call. I just don't trust the police here. That's why I called you. Would you be willing to talk to the investigating officer and tell him what you've just told me? It might help. But we can't bring Susan into this because Malton will become involved."

"Understood. Let's give it a go. What's his name?"

"Senior Constable MacPherson. I'll get him. Hold on."

Josef called MacPherson over. "I am talking to Ken Barnes, who is a solicitor in Goondiwindi, you can verify that. Mr. Barnes has something to tell you, which is related to your investigation. Will you speak with him?"

MacPherson nodded yes, took the receiver and identified himself. Josef moved away, giving him privacy. Josef noticed MacPherson said little. He listened, taking some cryptic notes and hung up.

He turned to Josef. "What Mr. Barnes told me fits with what we know and what you have told me. You know, I've been a policeman for twenty years and I've got to tell you I thought your story was crap. Now, I don't think it is, which makes your statement all the more important."

Josef spent an hour in an interview room writing out a formal statement. Rebecca did the same in an adjoining room. Once completed, they met again with MacPherson. This time in his office. Constable Kirby stood listening in the corner.

MacPherson started, "I'd like to fill you in on our investigation. There are a few things I can tell you. First, Constable Kirby did find a .38 calibre revolver near the body. Two bullets were discharged. Four live rounds were still in the revolver. We also recovered six more .38 bullets from the deceased's pockets. Identification was found on him and the driver licence is in the name of Sidney Hooper. He had a considerable amount of cash, and what appear to be amphetamine pills in a small baggie. There are a couple other things I'd like to show you. Please look at this."

He pushed a photocopy across his desk. It was the yearbook picture of Rebecca and Susan. Josef was stunned. "I went to St. Mary's and made copies of some of Rebecca's yearbook photos. I made multiple copies. This must be one of those. How did you get it?"

"We found it in Hooper's motorcycle bag. Do you have any idea how he got a hold of it?"

Josef was still rattled. "I have no idea. No idea. I had the photocopies in my folder."

"Well, I might help you out," said MacPherson. "You mentioned to me you had stayed at The Victoria Hotel in Goondiwindi. Constable Kirby contacted the hotel. Their records show you checked in to the hotel on June 4. On June 6, a Sidney Hooper took a room at the hotel. You checked out early on June 8; he checked out later that same morning."

"So, he was the biker in Goondiwindi."

"Appears so, and it is likely he was the man who threatened that woman Barnes told us about." MacPherson paused, "We need her name to verify."

Rebecca was confused. "What woman? What threat?"

Josef explained, "I called Ken Barnes, the lawyer in Goondiwindi this morning. He was worried. Susan called him, a man who said he worked for me, came to see her and ended up threatening to hurt her or her baby if she didn't tell him what she told me. That man was likely Hooper."

"Was she hurt? Was Benjamin hurt?" Rebecca was frantic.

"No, scared, but not hurt. Thankfully," Josef continued, "Rebecca, we need to tell the police her name and details. We need to."

"But Malton will find out."

MacPherson interjected, "Sorry, Miss Thornton, I should have mentioned this sooner, I did some checking and just so you know, there is no arrest warrant out for you from Goondiwindi. So, no charges, but I appreciate your concerns. I know the Senior Constable stationed in Inglewood and I am sure he would make a trip to Goondiwindi on the quiet to meet with her."

Josef looked at Rebecca. Silence hung in the air. It was her call. She finally spoke, "Her name is Susan Blake. I'll write down her address and phone number for you, but I'd better speak with her first. She will need to know the name of the officer." MacPherson nodded.

He then pushed over an evidence bag towards Rebecca and Josef. "This was found in Hooper's wallet." The bag contained a small piece of paper. Written on the note was the following:

Rebecca Rose Thornton 8-10-43 <u>BEFORE</u> June 24

"Miss Thornton, Rebecca, that is your birth date, but why is June 24th of any significance?"

"I don't know," said Rebecca in a puzzled tone. "June 24 is not an anniversary or anything."

Josef knew. "I can tell you what that date means." He had everyone's attention. "William Jones, who gave his entire estate to Rebecca and her mother, died on May 10, 1972. June 24 is 45 days after his death. Any beneficiary under the will must live for 45 days in order to collect their inheritance. Rebecca's mother, Connie, died a few years ago, which leaves just Rebecca. If she died before June 24, the will lapses and William Jones' estate goes to his surviving family members. Senior Constable MacPherson, the estate is worth at least a half million dollars, enough money to kill for."

CHAPTER 15

There was a commotion outside the office. A big man, wearing leather, a bikie, was demanding to see MacPherson. A couple police officers were intervening. MacPherson gestured to Kirby to see what this was all about. Kirby went out, spoke to the man, and you could see Kirby point to a nearby bench and motioned for the man to calm down. The man reluctantly sat down on the bench. Kirby came back and whispered in MacPherson's ear. "Christ" is all MacPherson said and got up. "You two stay put, please." As he was walking out of the office, he asked Kirby, "Who the hell called the Toowoomba station?"

Josef and Rebecca watched as MacPherson spoke with the big man; MacPherson was showing him to an adjoining room. The big man stood and looked into MacPherson's office, looked at Rebecca and Josef. He pointed at them, asking something. MacPherson tried again to move him along. The big man resisted. Josef was surprised at MacPherson's restraint. Eventually the man went with MacPherson

Kirby came back to the office. "Come with me, please." It sounded urgent. Josef and Rebecca followed to a conference room removed from the front reception area. "Would you mind waiting here for a few minutes? We'll explain shortly." Josef and Rebecca shrugged. What real choice did they have? By now it was late in the day.

As soon as Kirby closed the door, Rebecca pounced. "You never told me about Susan." She was not happy.

"I'm sorry, I didn't have time. I called Barnes because, in all honesty, I wasn't comfortable with how things were unfolding. Us being questioned and all. When I called Barnes, he told me Susan called him. I gave her his business card. I feel terrible, I led Hooper to her as well as you."

"You feel terrible, my God I'm the one she was protecting. If anything happened to little Benjamin." Her voice became quiet, "I have to call her."

They waited for MacPherson.

Josef went to the window, which overlooked the town square. He saw why they'd been escorted out of MacPherson's office. There, parked in the square, on an otherwise quiet Sunday, were at least ten motorcycles with bikies standing nearby.

"Rebecca, come look!"

"Shit," was all she said.

"Well, at least we know Hooper was indeed a bikie."

MacPherson entered the room. He saw them at the window. "So, you see them. We need to talk."

"How did they know to come here? You just recovered Hooper's body." Josef wanted an answer.

"It's our fault. Protocol is relatives of a deceased are to be informed as soon as possible, unless there is a reason to hold back the information. In this case, I intended to hold back, because it looks like Hooper was involved in a contract killing. Unfortunately, in communicating with the duty officer here, when he was advised of the identification found on the body, he assumed it was important to inform the family. The officer called the Toowoomba police and informed them of the death of Sidney Hooper and asked that officers go to the address and inform the family. Under protocol we do this in person. The Toowoomba police went to the house and Hooper's mother answered the door. The officers informed her of her son's death. I'm sorry. It's on me, I should have clearly advised the duty officer to hold back informing the family."

"So, who are all these bikies?" asked Josef.

MacPherson looked sheepish, "There's more. I spoke with the Sergeant at Toowoomba. Sidney Hooper, also known as Stump, was a member of the Taipan motorcycle club. The Taipans operate out of Toowoomba, primarily moving drugs from Brisbane to the west." He paused. "The big man you saw in the outer office is Jim Hooper, Stump's older brother. Jim Hooper, known as Jimbo, is the head of the Taipans. And there is more. The sergeant told me Mrs. Hooper, is tough and mean. She will want revenge, as will Jimbo. You can see why I tolerated him this afternoon. Constable Kirby took him to the morgue to identify the body."

All was quiet. Josef spoke first. "No doubt Stump was sent by his brother to kill Rebecca. They had the contract, which means they still have the contract, and they'll want to kill her even more."

MacPherson added, "And you. I think Jim Hooper knows the two of you were involved in his brother's death. He grilled me on that as I was getting him out of the office." He looked out the window, it had started to rain again. The bikies were scrambling for cover.

"What now? We can't leave here with them out there."

"Miss Thornton, you certainly cannot go back to your cabin. It's too isolated. You'd be an easy target. Mr. Manne, do you have a place?"

"I'm staying at the Gold Coast Hotel in Burleigh Heads."

"Good, that isn't in Surfers, where they'd expect you to stay. I can get you out of here, and if you can stay there for the night, we'll work on a plan tomorrow morning. Where did you park?"

Josef pointed to the main parking lot in front of the station near the gathered Taipans. MacPherson took command. "Alright, one of my officers will go down and drive your Ute to a parking lot further down the road. Another officer and I will hide you in a police van and drive to your Ute and you can head off to your hotel. One other thing, here is my home phone number and my direct line at the station. You are only to contact me and only speak with me. Understood?" He wrote the numbers down and gave them to Josef.

Josef looked at Rebecca and she at him. They had little choice. MacPherson left to make the arrangements. When he returned, he had two other officers. He took down Josef's room number at the hotel. They agreed to meet with him the next afternoon at 2:00 pm in the hotel restaurant. He'd have more for them then. They watched as one of the officers drove The Beast away. They waited five minutes, took the stairs to the underground parkade. There was the police vehicle waiting, a paddy wagon.

The box on the back had a small door and miniscule window for the drunks. The interior reeked of vomit and medicinal cleaner. They climbed in. The door was slammed shut and locked. What the hell was happening?

Soon they were moving, jostled about like stones in a shaking can. Lucky for them the ride was short.

The van stopped. The back door opened. They relished the fresh air. The Beast was waiting for them. They drove off in the opposite direction from the Taipans.

* * *

Jimbo Hooper nodded for the attendant to lift the sheet off the corpse. Stump's body was bloated and broken. Rigor mortis had set in. His arms were misshapen; broken ribs protruded through his chest. Jimbo had seen enough. The attendant covered the body. Jimbo was told that he could not touch the body, pending an autopsy. Constable Kirby asked him if the deceased was his brother. Jimbo said yes, turned and walked away. He didn't want to speak. It was too hard to speak. His little brother, his best mate, was dead. Jimbo was his protector and had failed. With grief came rage. His mother had told him, "Get the bastards who did this." He would. He had to. He couldn't let Stump die without avenging his death. Someone hurts you, you hurt them twice as bad. To do otherwise shows weakness. What would the Rebels think? Fuck, couldn't even take out a woman. He'd be a laughing stock. Wasn't going to happen. This was personal. He told Kirby to take him back to the Police Station. Told, didn't ask. Fuckin' bozos these cops. He wanted to talk to that fuckin' Senior Constable and find out how Stump died. It wasn't a fuckin' accident that's for sure. The woman and the lawyer, who Stump told him about, they did this.

* * *

MacPherson plunked down into his chair in the office. He was drained. He finally got rid of Jimbo Hooper. He had to tell him where his brother had died. Jimbo hadn't accepted it was an accident. When MacPherson would not reveal the names of witnesses, Jimbo became right pissed. The meeting ended with him stomping out of the station, after calling MacPherson a 'fuckin' dickhead'. Comes with the territory being a police officer. MacPherson had a thick skin, hardened by twenty years as a police officer and five years in the army. He rarely lost his temper; for him loss of control was a sign of weakness. He admired officers who remained calm amidst chaos. Perhaps that was in part why he rarely swore. The worst you would get from him was a 'Christ' or 'Hell' unlike so many other officers whose foul vocabulary could make a seaman blush.

MacPherson, however, was troubled. He didn't trust Constable Brosnan, the duty officer who called Toowoomba. True, it was according to protocol, but normally you'd wait for the officer in charge to give the okay. Why the rush? Brosnan called without clearance. MacPherson knew corruption was part of the Queensland Police culture. Hell, over his twenty years he accepted gifts of appreciation, but never a bribe. He knew Brosnan was Irish Catholic, part of the 'green mafia' within the police force, where patronage was bestowed based on religion and, more importantly, fealty to the group. The green mafia held sway for decades. Now the Masons, English protestants, were on the rise and the green mafia weren't happy. Bloody tribalism within the Queensland Police. MacPherson road the fence. Did his job and progressed through the ranks. Did Brosnan make the call knowing Hooper was a Taipan? Was he on their payroll? About a year ago, a bikie was arrested for drug trafficking. The case collapsed when the drugs disappeared from the evidence room. Was Brosnan responsible? MacPherson didn't know. He'd need to deal with Brosnan eventually; no good having a cop you can't trust. Bring charges? No. No evidence, and you never bring charges against fellow cops. Cops cover-up for fellow cops. Couldn't fire him either. The police union would fight any termination, even if there was cause. Besides, he would then be blackballed within the force. No, he'd watch Brosnan, and see about a transfer down the road. MacPherson knew how to play the game. Meanwhile, he needed to protect Miss Thornton and the Canadian lawyer. Christ, they were in a real pickle. He knew Jimbo Hooper would have to act and try to take them out. First thing Monday, he'd call Brisbane. The new Queensland Police Commissioner, an outsider, was a good man and honest. He had recently set up a Crime Intelligence Unit to combat corruption and organized crime. MacPherson knew one of the officers in that unit, who might have info on the Taipans.

* * *

Josef parked the Ute behind the Gold Coast Hotel, he knew to be more careful and vigilant. There were no other rooms available. Burleigh was booming, tradies occupied most of the rooms, and it was also a long weekend. Monday was the Queen's Birthday. He and Rebecca would have to share a room; fortunately, he had one of the deluxe rooms with a sofa. "Sorry," he said to Rebecca, "You take the bed and I'll take the sofa."

"Don't be sorry," she replied, "And by the way, I've slept out camp with drovers many times. I think I can handle a lawyer." It was said as a good-natured jibe, with a message, 'Don't try anything.' With that, she picked up her bag heading for the room. She called Susan. Josef gave her privacy and went walkabout. He scouted escape routes. Checked out the clientele. No bikies. He returned to the room. Rebecca was off the phone and having a bath. Josef flopped on the sofa and closed his eyes. He awoke to Rebecca's shaking.

"Come on, we need to eat."

She was right. They decided to go to the bowls club nearby, figuring bikers would be unlikely to go there. The club was packed. Without a doubt, the bowls club was the social hub for the town and Sunday was roast night. The two were famished, Rebecca had the roast beef and Josef the roast lamb.

Little was said. Rebecca was pensive.

"How is Susan?" he asked, probing to see what was on her mind.

"She's fine. Susan is a very tough person. She told John, her husband, who is a great guy. They talked it over and both were worried about me. Imagine that. They had Benjamin to worry about. Anyway, they mulled it over and called Mr. Barnes the next day. Evidently, he was great." She changed the topic, "When is your flight home?"

"It's on the 22nd from Sydney."

"You can go home earlier, get out of the country and be safe. Why not return home? You found me. I'll be okay." She was earnest.

"After what I've gotten you into. No way. I almost got you killed and there's a motorcycle gang out to finish the job. No way am I going until I know you're safe." Josef was equally adamant.

"I've been hiding for two years. I'm used to it. I will move on after tomorrow. I'll disappear again and I'll keep in contact with you."

"How?"

"Mr. Barnes. He's the perfect go between." Rebecca had thought matters through. "I have his card, I'll make regular contact through him."

Josef knew Rebecca was probably right. Even though he had to concede she was perfectly capable of taking care of herself, he still felt responsible and wanted to ensure her safety. Yes, she was strong and independent, but he wanted to help her. "We'll discuss it more tomorrow. I have to prepare an affidavit and have you sign it. Just to confirm to the world you are, who you say you are." They returned to the hotel; Josef on the sofa; Rebecca in the bed.

CHAPTER 16

Monday, June 12

Jimbo was angry. The cop told him Senior Constable MacPherson had secreted the woman and lawyer out of the station when he was at the morgue. The cop was not to be trusted; what a weasel. He knew Stump was his brother, so he upped the ante for information about the woman and lawyer, and wanted $300. Fuck, he had only paid him $300 a year or so before to make the drugs disappear, when one of his couriers got arrested and the cop kept the fucking drugs! Jimbo paid the $300. The cop had him over a barrel, but he'd remember that. Fuckin' cops. What did he get? Names: Rebecca Thornton, he knew, and the lawyer, Josef Manne, and he got the licence plate number of the white Ford XY Ute. Only good thing it had Northern Territory plates. The cop was sure they were staying on the Gold Coast, MacPherson had told him that much, but not where. The Taipans were out searching for the Ute – starting with Surfers Paradise and working north and south along the coast. They'd find them.

* * *

Rebecca was up early; Queenslanders are like that, creatures of habit, get up early before it gets too hot. Josef dressed when she was in the bathroom. She came out wearing a light long sleeve shirt, her sleeping shirt, which covered her to mid-thigh. Josef noticed. She had an athletic healthy build, slim, but not too slim, muscled and toned. Josef re-focused and headed to the bathroom. When he came out, she was dressed in her regular attire, blue jeans, boots and long-sleeved shirt.

They had breakfast in the restaurant. Rebecca wanted to leave immediately for the cabin to retrieve her personal belongings. Josef wanted to prepare and get the affidavit signed attesting to her identity. They compromised. Josef spoke with the hotel manager, who was most obliging. Josef was certain his Canadian accent paved the way. The manager provided him with a portable typewriter, paper and carbon paper and helped Josef photocopy Rebecca's identity papers. Josef would type up the affidavit when they returned from the cabin.

They left for Springbrook. It rained heavily overnight and the rain stopped just as they left the hotel parking lot. The radio announced flood warnings throughout the Gold Coast. On the way, they stopped in Broadbeach; Rebecca needed something from the chemist. Josef saw two bikies slowly cruising through the parking lot of a motel across the street. They were checking cars. Satisfied, they crossed the street to another motel and slowly cruised through its lot. Rebecca returned. Josef didn't say anything. Perhaps it was nothing. Were they even Taipans? And, if so, how could they know to look for his Ute? Whilst they were still in the motel parking lot, Josef pulled out on to the street. Watching in the rear-view mirror he saw the bikies turn on to the street behind him. Rebecca told him to turn right at the next light. Josef moved into the right turning lane. The bikies stayed in the through lane. Good, thought Josef. He waited for the light to turn. Holding his breath. The through lanes had green. Josef slouched in the driver seat. They drove by. Whew, he thought. Then it happened, one of the bikies turned and looked at the Ute, peering at the licence plate. The right turn signal came green, Josef turned. He saw the one bikie gesture for his partner to follow him. They were lost from view. Had they turned to follow him? Josef stared at the rear-view mirror. Seconds passed. No bikies. Then he saw two motorcycles in the distance, speeding towards him. Relief turned to fear.

"Rebecca," Josef said, trying to be calm, "we might have a problem. Take a quick glance back. Do you see the two bikers?"

Rebecca took a look. "Are they Taipans?"

"I don't know, but they turned to follow after one of them gave the Ute and the licence plate a long look. They were going through at the last light and they turned back."

"But how would they know our plate number?" asked Rebecca in a raised voice.

Josef slowed down and the bikies slowed down; they seemed content to follow and nothing else. Rebecca told Josef to take a round-about and the third exit. He did. The bikies followed. He made another turn; they followed.

"Damn," said Josef, "they're following us. We could drive to the police station?"

"Yes, and what good will that do us? They must have gotten the number from the police in the first place. How else?"

Josef couldn't disagree.

"I have another idea," said Rebecca, "continue down this road toward Mudgeeraba." The bikies followed. Just before getting to the town, Rebecca told Josef to take Bonogin Road. The bikies followed. "Take Hardy Road," she ordered. The bikies followed. Josef was wondering what she was doing; they were driving into more remote country leaving the security of people. At the top of the crest of a hill, below Josef saw a creek in flood 50-60 feet wide. He slowed and without hesitation, Rebecca urged him on, "Don't slow. Go through the flood water. See the flood markers on either side, they are showing the water is at the two-foot mark. We can get through. The road here is flat and wide. Just drive, drive using the markers."

Josef did as he was told. He steadied The Beast and entered the flood water. He knew he could not stop. He had to keep forward momentum. The Ute fought the sideway push of the surging water. The water was over the wheels. The engine was revving, fighting against the water. The Ute held fast to the road. The water rose up the door, rising to the window on the passenger side. Still The Beast moved strong. Ten feet to go. 'Don't fail me now' thought Josef. The Ute didn't. They made it through. Without stopping Josef drove to the top of the hill on the other side of the creek from the bikies. He stopped and they both looked back. The bikies were circling, talking, pointing at the water. Would they risk their beloved Harleys by taking on the flood? One bikie waved his partner off, and slowly entered the creek. Too slowly. He tried to pick up speed. Too late. The motorcycle, even though it was a heavy machine, was no match for the power of the creek in flood. The bike soon was pushed downstream. The bike and bikie were swept off the road and immediately disappeared into the murky, brown, deeper water. The bikie popped up twenty or thirty feet downstream. With arms flailing, he struggled to grab on to tree branches as he bobbed and drifted down the creek. He could swim; the motorcycle could not. The second bikie left his bike and ran downstream. He wasn't going to risk his motorcycle trying to cross the creek.

Josef had to laugh. He shook his head and looked at Rebecca. "How did you know the creek would be in flood?"

Rebecca, very proud of herself, replied, "Oh, it always floods with the least amount of rain. I was pretty sure it would be in flood and your Ute could get through it." She smiled. "Although, I wasn't so sure my novice Canadian driver would get us through. You done good, mate."

"Frankly, I wasn't too sure either." Josef put the Ute in gear. "Where to now?"

"This road joins Springbrook Road in a mile or two. Just drive straight."

The sky cleared and the sun shone bright above the evaporating mist. The road to Springbrook was still wet and slick and The Beast growled up the volcanic mountain. As they drove, Rebecca and Josef discussed what to do next. Was MacPherson to be trusted? They concluded if he was responsible for the leak he would have told the Taipans they were staying at the Gold Coast Hotel. So, it wasn't him. Someone in his office? At Purling Brook Falls Josef stopped at the general store. He telephoned MacPherson, his direct line.

"Senior Constable MacPherson."

Josef bluntly and directly replied, "Josef Manne, here. Senior Constable do you mind telling me how the Taipans found out what vehicle I was driving and the plate number?"

"Christ, what!"

Josef went on to tell him about what had occurred. They both laughed about the lost motorcycle. MacPherson was apologetic and apoplectic; he'd get to the bottom of any leak. MacPherson cautioned Josef about being at the cabin. "Remember Jim Hooper knows where his brother died and may well head up to the cabin. Don't stick around too long. See you at 2:00 pm."

"We won't be long," Josef assured him. "But if we don't make the 2:00 pm meeting send the cavalry."

* * *

After hanging up, MacPherson was both angry and disturbed. His suspicion pointed to Brosnan. He immediately phoned Sergeant Bruce Taylor of the Criminal Intelligence Unit. MacPherson and Taylor had risen through the ranks together. They had spoken earlier in the morning, and Taylor filled MacPherson in on the Taipans. Interestingly, he wanted to come with MacPherson for the 2:00 pm meeting and they agreed to meet in advance at the station at 12:30 pm. MacPherson called Taylor hoping he had not yet left Brisbane. Fortunately, Taylor was still in his office. MacPherson changed the meeting to a café on the Gold Coast Highway. All he said was, "I'll tell you why when I see you."

MacPherson pulled the file on the bikie case that collapsed when the drugs disappeared and, in the file, there was a notation, 'known associate with Taipan MC'. Coincidence? MacPherson thought not. He also realized with Kirby taking Hooper to the morgue, and he along with the two other officers moving Thornton and Manne, that left Brosnan minding the station. Civilian staff didn't work on weekends. He would be there alone. MacPherson had left the Hooper death file on his desk. MacPherson looked through the file to ensure there wasn't any other vital information that could have been leaked. Only the 2:00 pm meeting. He checked he still had the paper where Manne wrote down where he was staying. Thank God it wasn't in the file or they'd be dead.

* * *

Jimbo was not happy. The woman and lawyer would know their vehicle had been identified. Fuck, they'd probably change vehicles or disappear. Fuckin' idiots, they should have followed at a safe distance; instead they drove up the fuckin' rear of the Ute and were spotted. Then they tell him

Old Bill's Last Will and Testament

one lost his bike in the creek. Fuckin' idiot. He looked at the map. Where were they going? This happened on Hardy Road, Mudgeeraba, which connected to Springbrook Road. Fuck, they were heading to her place in Springbrook. He fuckin' knew that. He gathered five of the Taipans. They needed to get to Springbrook.

* * *

Rebecca and Josef arrived at the cabin to be greeted by the guinea fowl, who were even more boisterous; they hadn't been fed. Rebecca got some grain and Josef spread it around. Rebecca packed. Josef loaded a number of her paintings into the Ute. Her possessions were few. She travelled light. She ended up with one suitcase leaving behind a number of summer clothes. All she said was, "It's winter and I have no need for them. I'm heading south. The girls up here can have them." She put on a low rider oilskin duster and an Akubra hat, "These I'll need." She was ready. Josef took the suitcase. With her photo album in one hand she closed the door with her free hand and didn't look back.

"What about the food and guinea fowls?" asked Josef.

"Oh, I'll tell Mr. Giles, who owns the cabin."

They left. Rebecca navigated them down a number of narrow laneways to Mr. Giles' farm. They stopped the Ute and got out. Giles emerged from a dilapidated old barn leaning with the prevailing winds. Giles looked like an old farmer thought Josef. He shaved sporadically, wore overalls, plaid shirt, rubber boots and a wide brimmed hat which had to be decades old. Probably more comfortable with animals than people. Rebecca introduced him to Josef.

"Pleased ta meet yah," and he nodded his head. Then turned to Rebecca. "I heard about the fella who died. You okay Rose?"

She never corrected him as to her real name. "Yes, I'm fine Mr. Giles, but I have to leave. I'm so sorry. No notice and all."

"Don't you worry. Every day you been in the cabin has been a bonus for me. You're paid up to the end of the week. And you kept it right good."

"There's food left, which you should get and the guinea fowl need tending."

He laughed. "Tending? Or eating. They is mighty fine tasting you know. Damn things make such a ruckus, although I think they scare the snakes away. We'll see." Then with a mischievous grin he asked, "Did you leave any of your canned beets?"

"I sure did, four or five jars I reckon," replied Rebecca smiling at him. She had him wrapped around her little finger. Josef doubted Giles had much female company.

"Good, I'll get down there in a couple of days and rescue the food and damn fowl. You take care of yourself young lady." He turned to Josef. "And you see to it she's cared for."

Rebecca gave him a quick hug, which embarrassed the grizzled old man.

Next stop was the home of the psychedelic Kombi van. The owner's name was Vincent, who was a true chilled out hippie. He took Rebecca's paintings, paying $10 a piece. He would resell them for three or four times that amount. Goddamn capitalist hippie thought Josef. Rebecca wasn't in a position, or mind, to quibble. She needed getaway money. She told a couple of the girls present to visit the cabin and take whatever clothes they wanted. They seemed excited.

With the deeds done, they got back into the Ute to head down the mountain. Rebecca suggested they take the north road back to the Gold Coast; it was not as direct as Springbrook Road, but they'd be less likely to run into any Taipans on that route. Having travelled about five minutes down the road they both heard the sound of motorcycles on the road ahead. They looked at each other, a measure of panic on their faces. What to do?

Rebecca quickly reacted. "Drive fast, hurry, straight ahead. Only a mile or so ahead is the divide in the highway. Remember? It's where the up-mountain lane follows the mountain ridge and the down-mountain lane goes inland, round a rock face. If you can get there before they get through the ridge they'll never see us. Hurry." Josef remembered the divide and gassed The Beast. The sounds of the motorcycles echoed along the valley. There were a number of bikes. How many? They didn't know, but too many for sure. The roaring became louder resonating off the rock. The Ute was almost at the divide. Josef saw the divide sign and one-way sign to his right. They made the divide and drove around a bend, where Josef slammed on the brakes and stopped hidden from view. They heard the bikes roar past, now producing a different noise, less intimidating.

Perspiration dotted their foreheads and they let out a collective sigh of relief. They were certain the bikes were ridden by Jim Hooper and the Taipans. Rebecca, perhaps unthinkingly, perhaps deliberately, put her hand on Josef's arm and gave it a squeeze. The sound of the motorcycles faded up the mountain. There was silence. Without a word, Josef started down the mountain once again. Rebecca had him turn on to the north road. They didn't say anything to each other. There was nothing to say; they were oh so lucky not to have driven right into the Taipans.

They returned to the Gold Coast Hotel. Josef dropped Rebecca off. He took care to park the Ute away from the hotel on a residential street. They adjourned to the hotel restaurant, took a private corner table, ordered some meat pies and waited for MacPherson.

* * *

Jimbo checked out the cabin. He had been told by MacPherson it was about two miles up the road from Purling Brook Falls. They found it easy enough; lots of tire tracks marked the spot. Fuckin' fowl erupted in the front. Jimbo motioned for his boys to walk around to the back. The fowl didn't make a sound. Note taken. The cliff face wasn't far from the back door. Jimbo went there and looked down. It was a hell of a fall. He went into the cabin. The doors weren't locked. Food was still in the cupboards and in the refrigerator, and clothes were still hung in the bedroom. Good. A sign she hadn't left. The place was isolated. If they could catch her here the kill would be easy. He wanted to make her suffer a bit before the killing. No, be smart, kill her clean and simple; if the lawyer is present, do the same. He'd seen enough. They rode back down the mountain.

CHAPTER 17

MacPherson and Taylor arrived at the Gold Coast Hotel Restaurant right at 2:00 pm. They sat down at the table. Introductions were made. First off, MacPherson wanted to know how the bikies identified them. Josef told the whole story in detail. Both MacPherson and Taylor agreed the bikies had to be Taipans and there had been a leak. Josef filled them in on their escape off the mountain.

"It's on me," MacPherson said, "I told Jimbo Hooper where his brother died. I'd do that for any family member. Sorry, had no choice. I figured he'd drive up there."

Taylor interjected, "What will they find in the cabin? You said you got Miss Thornton's personal things."

Rebecca told him she travelled light. Taylor was interested at what was left behind. And she told him.

After quizzing her, he concluded, "The cabin would still look lived in, would you say?"

"Yes," replied Rebecca.

"Good," said MacPherson, "I'd like Sergeant Taylor to tell you about what he knows about the Taipans."

Taylor began, "We are just starting to see motorcycle gangs, like in America. No Hells Angels, but a lot of wannabe bikers. There are some more established clubs, but the Taipans are fairly new on the scene. They work out of Toowoomba and mostly move drugs from the coast to the interior. Also, they do some prostitution. The total number of members is about fifteen, give or take a few hangers-on. The leader is Jimbo Hooper. I believe you know him. Sidney Hooper, Stump, was his brother. The bad news for you is they were very close. Jimbo protected his younger brother.

Their father, who was a petty thief and drunkard, abused them and their mother. He was found dead some 10 or so years ago, beaten to death. No arrests made. Rumour is Jimbo killed his father, perhaps with the help of his mother. She is a tough lady. No criminal record, but she is definitely a crime family mum. Sorry to tell you this, but Jimbo will not hesitate to kill you. Our information is he was involved in two murders, both bikers from a rival gang. Senior Constable MacPherson explained to me Stump fell because of the lightning and thunder storm, but that will mean nothing to Jimbo. Further, from what I've been told this seems to be a contract hit. Stump would not have gotten the contract on his own; it had to come through Jimbo and the Taipans. This is not good for you, because it means Jimbo will probably pick up the contract. Miss Thornton, you are in grave danger. Mr. Manne, I'd say Jimbo will hold you responsible as well. You both are in danger."

He paused, allowing the information to sink in. Much of which Josef and Rebecca knew; however, the depth of Jimbo's revenge and willingness to kill was chilling.

"What about witness protection for Miss Thornton?" Josef asked.

MacPherson answered, "I looked into it. Doesn't apply, because Miss Thornton, Rebecca, is not giving any evidence to assist in an ongoing investigation. The crime committed was by Stump and he died. Afraid that door is shut."

"What about police protection, at least until the 24th?" Josef persisted.

"Yes, that's the date the contract sets for the hit to be made. But, as I mentioned, Jimbo will want to kill Rebecca regardless. The date will be meaningless to him. And we can't provide ongoing protection." Taylor answered.

"There's something else," MacPherson said in a quiet, frustrated voice, "I'm afraid there is a leak at my station and until that leak is found I can't guarantee your security. The Taipans must have found out about your vehicle from someone in the station. And, right now, I'm investigating."

"I'll disappear then, you've given me no choice." Rebecca finally spoke up.

"Yes, that's an option. Can't deny that." MacPherson acknowledged, "But Sergeant Taylor has another option, which may well make both of you safe and uncover the leak in my station. I'll let Sergeant Taylor explain."

"I'm part of a special unit, The Criminal Intelligence Unit, stationed in Brisbane. It was set up to combat corruption and organized crime in the state. We are a small unit composed of carefully selected police officers. Motorcycle gangs are organized crime. We'd like to put the Taipans out of business and you do that by cutting off the snake's head, in this case Jimbo Hooper. With him gone the Taipans will disintegrate. We know Jimbo has a real hate on for the two of you. He will want to kill you. Our plan, if you agree, is to give him that chance."

Josef mumbled, "we're the bait."

"Yes." Taylor went on, "If he thought Rebecca returned to her cabin, perhaps including you, Mr. Manne, he would seize that opportunity to kill you both. The cabin is isolated. From what you've told us, he will have scouted out the cabin. It is still lived in. So, he may well accept Rebecca would return there."

"You want Rebecca, or the two of us to go back to an isolated cabin. We'd be sitting ducks." Josef sounded incredulous.

MacPherson responded, "No, no we don't want you to be there. But we want Jimbo to think you are there. Big difference. We drop word at the station the two of you have insisted on returning to the cabin. We'll target who we suspect is the snitch. Sergeant Taylor and his team will place the cabin under surveillance and will be waiting for Jimbo in the cabin. If we are right, we get the snitch and Jimbo."

"So, we won't be in the cabin?" asked Rebecca.

"No, you stay hidden. Thus far, I've kept you hidden. No one knows where you're staying. Christ, I haven't even told Sergeant Taylor."

"But this could take days, weeks," observed Josef.

MacPherson smiled. "Not if we do it right. First, I spoke with the coroner this morning and asked him to hold Stump's body for release to the family pending toxicology results. That will keep Jimbo in town for a few days. Second, we leak you both are only staying at the cabin for one night, tomorrow night, then you will be leaving. Mr. Manne, you are leaving for Canada, in fact, both of you are leaving for Canada. This will force Jimbo's hand. He'll have to take the bait or lose the chance."

"Unless he pays for a hit in Canada." Josef was playing devil's advocate.

Taylor responded, "Jimbo will want to kill you by his own hand. Believe me he wants his revenge."

MacPherson continued, "Sergeant Taylor will need time to get his team together. They are to be trusted. I'll make a scene at the station because you two are ignoring my order and returning to the cabin. If the leak bites, we are confident Jimbo will act. One of our officers will drive the Ute to the cabin. It will look like you are there. Jimbo enters, we assume he will be armed, and he and any accomplices will be arrested."

Josef was dubious. "And how long will you put him away for? A year or two, that's it. You'll have a firearm charge, big deal, and not much more."

"We think we can charge him with attempt murder," replied Taylor. "If he turns up at the cabin, breaks into the cabin, which is B & E, and is armed then, given the motive, I think we can go with an attempt murder."

"Even if we aren't there?" asked Rebecca.

"Yes, you can have an attempt, even if it is impossible to commit the crime." Josef's mind was going through the law on attempts. "For example, you set a bomb to go off and the target isn't even in the building. It could still be an attempt murder; provided you can prove strong motive. Here we have strong motive. At least that's Canadian law."

"Same in Australia," confirmed MacPherson.

"And if he doesn't take the bait?" Josef queried.

"Then your option is to disappear. All we are asking for is a day, to get this together. And we aren't asking, or wanting you to be placed in danger. If he does take the bait, he will be put away for a long time. And we'll have identified the leak." Taylor was making a strong case. "I wish you had more time to think about it, but we don't have time. We need to know your answer and we need to know it this afternoon."

There was silence. Rebecca spoke up, "I'll do it. I'm tired of running and it only means a day. I'll do it."

Josef immediately followed, "I'm in too. We'll give it a day."

MacPherson and Taylor looked at the two, and nodded in satisfaction. They had their plan. MacPherson would send Kirby, whom he trusted, by tomorrow afternoon at 2:00 pm to pick up the Ute and drive it to the cabin.

CHAPTER 18

Tuesday, June 13

They rose early for a walk on the beach at low tide and managed to walk around Little Burleigh to the beach at Miami. The day was calm. They stopped at the surf club overlooking Burleigh Beach for breakfast. Josef thought, 'life doesn't get much better'. Rebecca went into Burleigh town to do a quick shop and Josef returned to the hotel to see about photocopying the affidavit. Time was going slowly as they waited for the plan to evolve.

At 2:00 pm Josef met Kirby in the hotel lobby. He guided the officer down a residential street to where The Beast was parked and gave him the keys.

"Take good care of her," he told Kirby.

"Oh, I will mate, I will," replied Kirby and he asked, "What's your room number just in case I need to drop off the keys at the Hotel?"

"Room number 7; it's under my name."

"Only one room?" Kirby gave Josef a lecherous look.

"Yeah, one room. I'm on the sofa," replied Josef. "Good luck." Kirby got in and drove off. The plan was starting.

Josef, walked back to the hotel. Rebecca returned and they decided to walk the Burleigh Headland. There was a path around the headland to Tallebudgera Creek Bridge. The Headland is a remnant of the Mount Warning volcano composed of black basalt rock and stands as a bastion against the ocean. On the ocean side of the Headland, the vegetation is beaten down to scrub grass, clinging to the steep side of the Headland in the face of fierce southerly winds and storms. Looking up, one sees the black basalt obelisks literally perched on the top of the Headland waiting to join fallen rocks at the base of the hill. The shoreline is all black, rounded, weathered basalt and the ocean relentlessly smashes into the shore.

They stopped on the ocean side, near a sign, 'Beware falling rock. DO NOT STOP'. Josef asked Rebecca, "Did you see the movie Swiss Family Robinson? It was out a few years ago." Rebecca hadn't. "Well, in the movie the family is marooned on a tropical island and they have to fight off pirates. There is a scene where they are on top of a hill fighting the pirates. They throw exploding coconuts, unleash boulders and palm tree logs are rolled down the steep hillside. Rebecca, this is that hillside, I swear. I can just see those boulders coming down."

She laughed. "In that case we'd better move on." As an aside, she said, "The Family Robinson had to deal with pirates; we have bikies. Did they beat the pirates?"

"Of course, it's a Disney movie."

They moved along Tallebudgera Creek to the Gold Coast Highway and found themselves back at the hotel. It was past 4:00 pm and the sun was low in the sky. The trap would be set. Time moved slowly. They had supper, returned to the hotel room and tried to watch television. Their minds were on the cabin in Springbrook. Had the trap worked? They went for a short walk to the beach. When they got back to the hotel it was after 11:00 pm and reception was closed, which meant no phone calls; all calls came through reception. They'd find out in the morning.

* * *

Jimbo was frustrated. He had been told by the coroner his brother's body could not be released until toxicology tests were complete, which could take days. He didn't mind that so much because he wasn't going anywhere until he had found the woman and the lawyer. But his men hadn't found them, even though he was assured by the cop they were still on the Gold Coast. MacPherson had stashed them away. Then he received a call from the cop to meet him back of this gas station on the road to Mudgeeraba at 2:30 pm and, in his words, "bring lots of money, he had something." Where was the fuckin' cop? A Ute pulled up. Fuck it was the Ute they were looking for. The cop got out.

Jimbo came over. "Where'd you get their Ute? Fuck you know where they are?"

"Don't worry about where I got the Ute. Yeah, I do know where they are and I know something else, but it's going to cost you. I want $800."

"$800! You got to be kidding." Jimbo was pissed. It was a shake down and he didn't like that one bit.

"Hear me out. It's worth it. Worth every dollar. I'll tell you part of it. Then I want the money and I'll tell you the rest." Kirby paused. "First, the Crime Intelligence Unit has set a trap for you at the cabin on Springbrook. They know you were there yesterday. They also know there is a snitch, and the snitch would tell you the woman and the lawyer are at the cabin for tonight only, then they are taking off. They figured if you heard the woman and lawyer were at the cabin you'd be sure to try and take them out. Right?"

Jimbo nodded. He was listening. "Go on."

"Well, I suggest you send a couple of your boys up to Springbrook, at around 12:30 tonight. Have them go just past the general store at Purling Brook Falls. Got that. And have them turn around and return to the Gold Coast."

"Why should we do that?" Jimbo asked.

"To make it look like you were coming up to the cabin, but got spooked. I and another cop are to be stationed at the general store to give advance warning to the team at the cabin. This way they will still believe the snitch passed the information on to you and somehow you saw the trap and took off." Kirby was grinning. "Smart, hey." He then turned serious. "Now I want $800. I can tell you exactly where the woman and lawyer are and you need to do the hit at about the same time as when your boys are at Springbrook. Gives you a fuckin alibi man—so long as they can't make out who's riding the bikes. Obviously, I'll say I'm certain it was you. Hell, you could have one of them ride your bike up there."

Jimbo was thinking; it was fuckin' good. The cops would verify his alibi. "Alright, $800. But I need to know where the fuck are they. I want an address. Don't fuck with me."

Kirby shot back, "How about a hotel room number, good enough? Give me the $800. I got to get this Ute up to Springbrook. Part of the trap set for you."

Jimbo counted out $800, in $50 bills, and handed them to Kirby. Then all he said was, "Where?"

"Room number seven The Gold Coast Hotel in Burleigh Heads, on the Gold Coast Highway at the turn by the bowls club. Both of them are in the same room, number 7. I got to get going."

* * *

MacPherson was nervous. He came back to the office after the station closed. He sure wasn't going to be in bed whilst one of his men and the Crime Intelligence Unit were carrying out this dangerous trap. How would Jimbo react? Would he shoot or allow himself to be arrested peacefully? It was 50/50.

He thought back to earlier in the day. He briefed Kirby in the morning. Brosnan was in the outer office at reception. After giving Kirby the rundown they waited. Taylor phoned at 11:30 am, as arranged. Kirby was then to walk to the door and open it. MacPherson slammed the receiver down and feigned rage, "Do you know what they want to do now? Do you?" MacPherson yelled. Kirby meekly shook his head 'no'. "They want to. No, they insist on going back to stay at the cabin tonight. Miss Thornton insists. She wants to get her personal belongings and stay one last night at the cabin. And Manne agrees. Tells me I can't stop her. Christ, let them go. We can't protect them there. Let them go. I don't believe it. Then they're leaving the country, going to Canada. I should arrest them for something. I should." Kirby left and MacPherson slammed the door. It was a good act. Brosnan would hear every word and his lunch break started at noon. He'd go and call Jim Hooper from outside the station.

Taylor had five men. One would be with Kirby, look-outs near the general store. They'd radio the team at the cabin when Hooper arrived. One man would be in the bush in front of the cabin. Two would be in the back and Taylor with one man would be in the cabin. Manne's Ute would be parked outside the cabin in the driveway. It was a good trap. Once Hooper was arrested, Taylor would arrest Brosnan. Had to be done.

As the night wore on, MacPherson thought things through again and again. He was pretty sure Brosnan was the leak. Pretty sure? Is that good enough? Who else? It had to be Brosnan. Why would he have called Toowoomba about Stump? A mistake? Doubtful. And it was Brosnan's notation in the missing drug case file referring to an association with the Taipans. That was troubling? Why would he do that if he was going to feed information to them? Stupid. Better to have left the drug courier as 'unaffiliated'. It was right at the end of the file. Had Brosnan just obtained some information and included it in the file? Who was the arresting officer? MacPherson hadn't checked. Probably Brosnan. No! No! It was Kirby, Kirby was the arresting officer.

MacPherson sat back. He trusted Kirby. But Kirby could have called Hooper once he was off the mountain. Perhaps Hooper already knew Stump was dead, before he was told by his mother? Kirby is the one who accompanied Hooper to the morgue. He had lots of contact with Hooper. He could have told Hooper about the Ute and its licence plate. Kirby knew the plate number and make. He also knew they were staying on the Gold Coast. MacPherson never told him where they were staying, until today. He sent Kirby to pick up the Ute at the hotel. Kirby now knew the hotel. Did he mention the room number? No, he hadn't. Good. Christ. It could be Kirby. He just bought a new Holden sedan. Said he got some money from his grandfather. Coincidence? Kirby? What if he was wrong about Brosnan? If he was wrong, he had just set up Thornton and Manne to be killed. Doubts were growing in his mind.

MacPherson phoned the Gold Coast Hotel. It was almost midnight. No answer. Uncertainty gnawed at him. Christ, he had to go and check. He couldn't just stay at the station twiddling his thumbs. MacPherson got his cap and headed to his cruiser.

* * *

Jimbo scouted the Gold Coast Hotel. There was good cover back of the hotel and up the hill. He could park there and come and go with little

Old Bill's Last Will and Testament

chance of being seen. The hotel had a reception, but it closed at 11:00 pm. That would leave free access to the hotel rooms. He didn't stay long because he didn't want to be seen by staff or by the woman and the lawyer.

He decided to send two of his boys up to Springbrook. No way was one of them going to ride his machine, but he did pick a rider whose machine was the same model as his. They had their orders. They were to ride up to and just past the general store at Purling Brook Falls and to be there at 12:30 am. Look around and then beat a hasty retreat down the mountain.

He was oiling his M1911 .45 caliber Colt Government handgun; it was a staple of the US army. He'd had it for a few years. Seven bullets plus one in the chamber. He had two loaded magazines and a silencer. The silencer wasn't silent; however, the sound of the rounds being fired would definitely be deadened. He wanted a clean hit. The .45 cartridges packed a good wallop. Two bullets in each; one in the head for sure. Probably in bed together. He thought about bringing some of the boys along, but no. Some jobs needed to done alone. Fewer mouths to talk that way. Besides, this was personal. He wanted revenge for Stump. "Little Brother, I'll take care of them." No one needed to know except him and his mum. He shoved a loaded magazine into the M1911, chambered one cartridge and pocketed the silencer; it was easier to attach the silencer when there. He was ready. He wore a nondescript black jacket, blue jeans, and an army bush cap.

CHAPTER 19

Jimbo arrived at the Gold Coast Hotel just after midnight. Driving slowly around the hotel he saw nothing untoward. All was quiet. He parked his car back of the hotel, on the hill and sat watching. Nothing. He got out of the car and gently closed the door. Stopped. Listened. Nothing. The Colt was holstered, an extra magazine in his right pocket and the silencer in his inside chest pocket. He took a position by a tree, hiding in the darkness overlooking the hotel and town. He waited, watching. There was nothing to see. No police. He slowly, carefully made his way down to the brush that ringed the hotel's parking lot. He stopped, looked, listened. Nothing. Deciding it was safe, he made his way to the rear door of the hotel, which wasn't locked. The hotel keepers were trusting souls he thought. He entered the hotel. All was quiet. Reception was closed, as he knew it would be. He climbed the stairs silently sneaking up to the first floor, where the rooms were located. At the top of the landing, he checked. No one was about. He went to the vending machine alcove and there he took out the Colt and the silencer. He slowly screwed the silencer on to the nozzle of the M1911. Then he heard a noise down the hall. A man, bare legged, slightly staggering, scratched his ass as he walked to the communal washroom at the end of the hall. Jimbo waited. The man must have a non-bathroom room. A minute or so later, the man emerged and staggered back to his room, no doubt to collapse on his bed. Jimbo waited. He was in no hurry. He wanted to do this right, a clean kill. The hall lights were dimmed. Good, less light in the room when he opened the door. He took a plastic card out of his wallet and slipped the Colt into his belt. He put on thin leather gloves and moved down the hall, ever so quietly. If interrupted he'd go to the washroom and wait. Nothing stirred.

Room number 7 faced the street, with a beach view. He stood at the door and tried the door knob; ever so gently, quietly. It was locked. He knew it would be. He held on to the knob and took out a credit card, running it down the side of the door. He felt the resistance when the card hit the slant latch. He now pushed the card against the slant latch and leaned hard against the door, turning and pulling the knob to the hinge side of the door. He felt the latch move in and the card slipped inward ever deeper. The door unlocked. He took the Colt out, checked once more up and down the hall. Nothing.

* * *

Josef was lying on the sofa. He couldn't get to sleep. The sofa was on the west wall of the room, behind the room door. He heard a noise, a gentle turn of the door knob. He saw shadows blocking the hallway light through the gap between the door and the floor. Someone was there. This was not good. He whispered to Rebecca, "Rebecca, get up. Someone is at the door. Wake up." He heard no response. She was in the bed near the north wall overlooking the beach. He heard more, a sliding and gentle push on the door. Damn, there was no chain. Josef got up and pressed himself against the door wall, hidden by the door if it were to open. He wasn't dreaming, someone was outside.

Ever so slowly, the door opened towards him, and he saw through the crack on the hinge side a man and a gun. With the door three quarters open the man stepped forward, slowly, gun leading the way. Josef reacted.

He shoved the door hard into the man and at the same time grabbed the gun barrel. The gun had a long barrel. He heard a dull thud. It didn't sound like a gunshot, but he felt the heat on the barrel and recoil. The man had pulled the trigger! Josef yelled, "Rebecca run! Rebecca run!" He threw himself at the intruder. It was Jimbo. He knew.

Jimbo was surprised by the attack. He had expected Josef to be in the bed, which he could see straight ahead. Surprise turned to anger and then turned to rage. He fired a shot, which was an unthinking reaction. Josef held on to the barrel. Jimbo couldn't aim the Colt. He struck out with his left hand and hit Josef in the side. Hit him again and again. Josef released his right hand and hit Jimbo hard in the gut. Jimbo turned and pushed Josef back. He kicked at him, Josef moved and took the kick on the side of his thigh. Josef realized he couldn't give Jimbo any space. He drove himself into Jimbo's body, always holding on to the barrel with his left hand, preventing him from aiming the gun, and tucking his head into Jimbo's right side. With his right hand he could fend off any blows. He kept screaming, "Rebecca Run! Rebecca run!"

Rebecca didn't run. Instead she joined the fight. She ran at Jimbo and punched him on the side of his head. Jimbo hardly flinched. He was preoccupied with Josef. Rebecca grabbed an iron from the closet and tried to land a crushing blow to Jimbo's head. Jimbo saw it coming and partially dodged the iron. It sliced a glancing blow to the side of his head. She was now in his range and as she lifted the iron to strike again Jimbo struck out with a vicious backhand fist with his left arm. It caught Rebecca, just above her temple and she crumpled. Her head struck the wooden bedpost with a sickening smack and she fell to the floor, where she lay not moving.

Jimbo could now concentrate on Josef, who held on to the barrel and had his head dug into Jimbo's chest so he couldn't land a powerful blow with his left hand. Jimbo needed to push Josef back and free the gun to finish him off. With his left hand he grabbed Josef's hair and yanked his head back. Jimbo tried to head butt him, but couldn't, Josef kept his bear hug. Jimbo moved his left hand down to Josef's throat, grabbed it and pressed. Josef struggled to free himself with his right hand. Jimbo kept pressing. Josef then jerked his head up hard catching Jimbo's chin and you could hear the crunching of teeth. This enraged Jimbo more. He released Josef's throat, took another swing at his head and grabbed his head again and pivoted so that Josef was slammed against the door frame of the bathroom. Jimbo began pounding Josef's head into the door frame. Pulling his hair and ramming his head again and again into the door frame. Blood sprayed from a puncture wound to the head. Still Josef hung on to the barrel. Jimbo pulled and jerked his right hand, the gun hand, he turned the gun towards Josef and pulled the trigger. Josef pushed the barrel away just in time. Jimbo's strength and size were proving too much for Josef,

Old Bill's Last Will and Testament

who was tiring. Jimbo threw him around like a rag doll. Still Josef hung on to the gun barrel, which was now searing hot; it was close to burning his hand, but he couldn't let go.

Josef knew he was fighting for his life. Adrenalin giving him strength. They continued to wrestle and fell over Rebecca, who remained lifeless on the floor. Jimbo got up. Pulling his gun hand up. Josef hung on. Josef could see Jimbo was going to stomp on Rebecca; he'd kill her that way. Jimbo tried to kick Rebecca; Josef pushed Jimbo back but in so doing he opened up space between them. Jimbo was no longer caught in a bear hug and he kicked Josef hard in the stomach. This time he connected. Josef was now fighting for breath. Jimbo with his free hand hit Josef hard in the face; blood gushed from his nose. Jimbo hit him again. Josef tried to defend himself, tried to ward off the blows, but was too weak. Jimbo kicked him again in the stomach. Pain pulsated through his body. Jimbo gave Josef an elbow smash to the top of his head. Josef's grip on the barrel finally gave way. As he was falling to the floor he heard a yell. It seemed distant. And he heard two loud gunshots. That was the last he heard before he fell to the floor stunned.

MacPherson arrived at the hotel at about 12:20 am. All was quiet outside. When he entered the hotel, he heard noise from the first floor and without hesitating ran up the stairs taking out his revolver at the same time. When he reached the first floor, he heard thuds and blows coming from an open door down the hall. It was room number 7. He ran, cocking the revolver. At the door he saw Jimbo standing, gun in hand aimed at Manne and Miss Thornton lying at his feet on the floor. MacPherson yelled, "Drop the gun, hands up. Drop the gun. Police." Jimbo looked at MacPherson, eyes filled with rage and anger; he didn't drop the gun. MacPherson couldn't wait. He fired two shots aimed at Jimbo's chest. Both struck their mark, one in the heart and one in his left lung. Jimbo fell back against the wall. The Colt M1911 fell out of his dead hand.

Doors opened. Heads peeked out. MacPherson turned and ordered a man in room 5, "Call 000, tell the operator shots fired. Move man, move." As the man was leaving to make the call, MacPherson yelled, "And we need an ambulance. Hurry."

MacPherson kicked Jimbo's gun away from him, and checked for a pulse. There was none. He then turned to Rebecca. He felt a pulse. He checked for any gunshot wounds; couldn't see any. He turned to Josef, who was a bloody mess. He, at least was conscious. A lady came, dressed in a house coat, and said, "I'm a nurse. Move over." MacPherson gave way.

It took a few moments for Josef to fully recover. He had difficulty breathing, but had not been shot. At least he didn't think so. Rebecca remained unconscious. "Is she okay? Has she been shot?" Josef wheezed.

The nurse replied, "She's still unconscious. We'll just let her rest. Best not to move her."

MacPherson bent down by Josef and told him, "Jimbo is dead. You take it easy. We'll get you to hospital. We'll take care of Miss Thornton. I don't think she's been shot."

Josef looked at MacPherson. "Did you shoot him?" MacPherson nodded his head, yes. "Thanks," said Josef.

"I almost cost you both your lives. I'm sorry, I read things wrong," replied MacPherson. He paused and then continued, "I have one question, when Constable Kirby picked up your Ute, did you tell him your room number?"

Josef thought for a moment. "Well yes. He asked for it in case he needed to drop the keys off."

Sirens could now be heard in the distance. Police and ambulance soon arrived. Rebecca had not regained consciousness. She lay on the floor, eyes closed, unmoving, the side of her head swollen and red, dried blood trickled from her ear. Josef could see the concern on the faces of the paramedics, who carefully prepared her for transport to the Gold Coast Hospital.

MacPherson spoke to the officer in charge in the hallway, told him he had shot the deceased, and told him to call homicide. He surrendered his firearm to the officer, as is protocol when there is a police shooting.

He then went to his patrol car and radioed Taylor. As soon as Taylor got on the line he told MacPherson two bikers arrived at Purling Brook Falls at around 12:30 am, just a few minutes before, but turned and raced back down the mountain. Taylor felt they must have spotted something. MacPherson told Taylor to call off the operation that Jimbo was dead and had tried to kill Miss Thornton and Manne. MacPherson went on

Old Bill's Last Will and Testament

to outline his suspicions about Constable Kirby. Taylor and MacPherson agreed to the following: the Crime Intelligence Unit was to arrest Kirby and hold him as a party to attempt murder, and at the same time search the Ute and his person for money. They would then obtain a search warrant to search Kirby's home. MacPherson would meet them at the Gold Coast police headquarters.

Josef could not focus. He couldn't shake the vision of Rebecca. He wanted to go to the hospital, not for treatment, but to check on her. However, he was a captive of the police. The homicide detectives needed to question him. He gave a detailed oral statement, once completed, a police officer took Josef to the hospital.

At the hospital a triage nurse insisted Josef be seen by a doctor, who pronounced him battered, cut and bruised, but otherwise fit; nothing was broken and no internal injuries. One cut to his head took six stitches. The police officer stayed with him and eased the way to see Rebecca. She was in the intensive care unit. A formidable head nurse wasn't about to let any worse for wear stranger, battered and bruised, see her. "Family only," she said "and you aren't family, are you?" She asked Josef this, with an accusatorial tone. Argument would do no good. Deceit was the best answer.

"Yes, I am. I'm her fiancé and I travelled all the way from Canada to be with her. I want to be with her." Josef lied.

The head nurse looked at him unconvinced. She queried him about Rebecca's background: age, next of kin, address, occupation. Josef had answers for each. He ended, "She has no family. I am all she has and I want to be with her."

The police officer interceded: "Head Nurse Minsk," referring to her name tag, "this man and woman were attacked and almost killed tonight. And my orders are to remain outside this room to see both are safe."

The head nurse folded. She showed him to Rebecca's room. Rebecca was connected to an intravenous drip and monitors recorded her vital signs. Josef stood at the foot of her bed. His throat tightened. He swallowed hard and managed to whisper, "Rebecca you're strong. Fight. Keep on fighting."

A young nurse came in. She had a blanket and pillow for him and pointed at a leather lounge chair in the corner. With a sympathetic smile she said, "Try to get some sleep. Head nurse's order."

A doctor turned up a few minutes later. He introduced himself and said, "I understand you are her fiancé." Josef's little lie was growing. The doctor explained he suspected Rebecca had a brain contusion and there were concerns about swelling and bleeding on the brain. Fortunately, there was no skull fracture or broken bones as a result of the blow. Her vital signs were good. They had given her a mild sedative via the IV, essentially to allow the brain to rest and reduce the chance of swelling. She would be monitored closely during the night and the effects of the sedative would dissipate by late morning. Hopefully then she would regain consciousness.

Josef stayed with her, sleeping little. Nurses continually came in and out. He managed to nod off a few times, but very few. His mind was a chaotic mess.

CHAPTER 20

Wednesday, June 14

MacPherson had a long, albeit, rewarding night. Perhaps 'rewarding' was not the right word; however, he was able to resolve two open cases. Miss Thornton and Mr. Manne were safe and their would-be hitman dead. MacPherson did not feel badly about killing Jimbo; it was done to save the lives of two innocent people. He thought back to his youth. As a young nineteen-year-old soldier in Korea he had fought and killed; that was war. He felt badly, but his platoon leader, who saw him mulling over the killing, told him 'MacPherson you're a soldier, you kill the enemy, that is what soldiers do. Better him dead than you.' MacPherson moved on.

He was disappointed in Kirby and, in himself, for not being more careful and observant. In searching him, Taylor's men found $800 in cash. The money was carefully secured in an evidence bag. Fingerprint analysis would tell the tale. Taylor was already on it, and the results would come back quickly from the forensic lab. Any latent prints would be compared against Jimbo's (on file in the criminal data base), Kirby's from his personal file, and from Manne's taken in the investigation of Stump's death. In the execution of the search warrant on Kirby's home, 100 grams of cocaine and $1200 cash was found stashed in Kirby's gun locker. He would now be charged with possession of the cocaine, probably trafficking. MacPherson had also spoken with Brosnan first thing in the morning about the notation in the biker drug case. Brosnan recalled writing the notation. The reason was simple, he was the duty officer responsible for forwarding the file on to the court officer who would be handling the biker's bail hearing. Brosnan thought it made sense to contact the Toowoomba station to see if the biker had any gang association, which might make it more difficult for the biker to get bail. Brosnan got the word from Toowoomba and noted it in the file. In short, Brosnan was doing his job, being thorough. Normally you'd expect the arresting officer, Constable Kirby, to have made those type of inquiries. He did not for obvious reasons. MacPherson missed all this. Lesson learned. MacPherson needed to be more careful in trusting and in not trusting his personnel.

Kirby was still being held at headquarters and had contacted his union rep. For the time being he was suspended. MacPherson was realistic, party to an attempt murder would be a tough case to win. Yet, MacPherson was confident fingerprints on the money would link Kirby to Jimbo, and would be very difficult for Kirby to explain away. In any event, they had him for the cocaine, and if that cocaine could be traced back to drugs stolen from evidence lockers Kirby could well be looking at prison time. Bare minimum, Constable Kirby would be forced to resign from the Queensland Police Force. One bad cop removed.

* * *

It was late morning and the hospital was a buzz of activity. Sleep was now impossible. Rebecca was still unconscious. Josef found his way to the cafeteria for a hospital breakfast. When he returned to the room, it was standing room only. The doctor and an entourage of interns crowded around Rebecca's bed. She was conscious! The doctor was asking her a series of questions and seemed satisfied by her responses. When the doctor saw Josef, he motioned for him to come in, "Make some room, this is her fiancé."

Rebecca gave Josef a confused look, but didn't say anything. He went to her side and took her hand, "Good to have you back with us." The doctor continued his examination, conducting a battery of physical tests checking her hearing, vision, balance, reflexes, strength and sensation and then he turned to cognitive questions. Rebecca remembered everything up to being hit by Jimbo. The doctor was satisfied, but wanted her to remain at the hospital for one more day to be monitored. Then he was off with his entourage.

Rebecca and Josef were alone. As soon as they were gone, Rebecca asked, "Fiancé, hey. I don't remember that."

Josef blushed, "Sorry, it was the only way I could stay with you overnight. The battle axe nurse would have kicked me out otherwise."

"You stayed with me?"

"Yes, actually the leather lounge is quite comfortable."

She turned serious. "Thank you. You saved my life. I remember you telling me to run."

"And you didn't."

"No, I didn't. What happened?"

"MacPherson arrived just in time. Jimbo was going to shoot us. I was certain. Then I heard two shots. MacPherson shot him." Josef took a deep breath and continued, "Rebecca, I am so sorry, I'm responsible."

Rebecca squeezed his arm. "Don't blame yourself. We're survivors." Then to change the subject, "I guess the engagement is off?"

"Not quite," replied Josef, "Head Nurse Minsk must not find out. So, we remain engaged until tomorrow. Should I call you dear?"

"No, this is Australia, call me 'darling.'" Rebecca laughed and winced at the same time. She looked at Josef and said, "You're a real mess and should be in hospital, not me. Are you okay? You took quite a beating."

"I'm okay, cuts and bruises nothing broken."

MacPherson arrived. He thought Rebecca looked pretty darn good considering she was on the losing end of a fist; in turn, Josef looked awful. The bruising around his one eye had turned into a purple reddish welt, cuts to the forehead were bandaged, and stitches marked a cut to the side of his head.

MacPherson was much relieved to hear Rebecca was going to be okay. He filled them in on the police investigations. Taylor cleared the way for Josef to leave the jurisdiction, and a homicide detective would come by later in the afternoon to take a statement from Rebecca. MacPherson suggested to Josef they drive to police headquarters and retrieve the Ute and leave Rebecca in peace.

When they got to police headquarters, Sergeant Taylor dropped down to thank Josef personally. Taylor told Josef his unit conducted raids on Taipan houses in Toowoomba and on the Gold Coast. The club was in disarray. They had cut off the head of the snake and he didn't think the Taipans represented an ongoing threat to him or to Rebecca. Why the police officer at the hospital? Just a precaution.

Taylor wished Josef well, "Good luck, and for a lawyer you happen to be one hell of a fighter."

MacPherson said he'd drop by the hospital tomorrow morning before Rebecca was discharged. Josef drove away. Next stop was the Gold Coast Hotel. The forensic team had finished its work and Josef could pick up his and Rebecca's belongings. The manager greeted him, apologizing profusely. Josef retrieved their belongings and the manager did not seem concerned at all about the damage to the room: two bullet holes, one in the wall and one in the floor, not to mention blood stains on the carpet and on the wall. No doubt the manager feared a lawsuit, especially when one of the injured guests is a lawyer. After all, the intruder gained access to the rooms precisely because the rear door was not locked at night. Josef smiled to himself, ah the fear of litigation.

Driving back towards the hospital he decided to splurge and take a room at Lennons Hotel, which was right on the beach in Broadbeach. They had a large room with two double beds — no sofa, no lounge for him tonight. He returned to the hospital with a change of clothes for Rebecca and her night bag. She was sleeping. Josef didn't want to wake her, and headed back to the hotel. He needed to make some telephone calls. First to Straun McNeil, who deserved an abridged update. Straun was concerned and became even more concerned when Josef told him the police thought it was a contract hit. "Some holiday," he said.

Next call was to Ken Barnes, news of the police shooting on the Gold Coast was a big story and had reached Goondiwindi. Both Rebecca and Josef's names were mentioned. The reporter alluded to possible motorcycle gang involvement. "Both victims were injured, with Rebecca Thornton still recovering in the Gold Coast Hospital." Great, thought Josef, now everyone in Goondiwindi knows where she is. When Josef went into the details, Ken was flabbergasted. "Mate, you've really stirred up a hornet's nest. How yah doing?"

"Battered and bruised. Rebecca was knocked unconscious. I really thought we were going to be killed and then MacPherson, the police officer you talked to, arrived and saved the day."

"Bloody hell, is there anything I can do?"

"As a matter of fact, yes. Rebecca is going back into hiding. Probably happy to get rid of me, but we need to keep in contact. Would you be willing to act as a go between? We don't want to endanger Susan Blake again."

"Of course, I agree, not a problem. You have my details and we can go from there."

Josef knew he could rely on Ken.

CHAPTER 21

Rupert sat in front of the television fixated, watching the news, sipping his morning coffee. He didn't move. Old hate welled up in him. No one messed with a Malton. That was the family creed. Old man Malton hammered that into his boys. If someone wronged you, you made them pay. As his father said, 'The weak get beat; the strong do the beating.'

So, the bitch was in the Gold Coast. The reporter said she was in hospital. If he was to act, he had to do so before she disappeared again. The news also mentioned the guy killed, a motorcycle gang member, evidently tried to kill them both. Good, any subsequent killing would be laid on them. Be patient and be smart. Why not disappear wild pig hunting out west? No one would suspect a thing. He did that occasionally throughout the year. Who'd know the difference? The police sure couldn't prove otherwise.

He loaded his Ute, as he would for hunting: binoculars, sleeping bag, ground sheet, food, water, an esky filled with bottles of coke, few limes and a bottle of Bundaberg Rum for medicinal purposes. He'd need to get ice, a few changes of clothes and his trusty 12-gauge Winchester model 1200 pump action shotgun. It was his favorite, holding five shells, snub nosed, slightly shorter than most shotguns, light and easy to handle. It stopped full grown charging wild pigs in their tracks and would make a real mess of a person at close range. That is what he wanted; he wanted to see the fear in their eyes before they died. He threw a box of #4 buckshot shells into the cab of the Ute.

Rupert was methodical. He called the foreman at the ranch and told him since things were slow he was going out west to do some pig hunting. Not a problem. Rupert took the highway west out of town and stopped at the Shell station for gas, sandwiches, ice and snacks. He made a point of talking to the attendant telling him he was heading west pig hunting. Once out of town, Rupert took some side roads back to the highway heading east. He was on the hunt and it felt good.

He drove straight through, sipping on his mug of Bundy, coke and lime on ice, which gave him a nice buzz as he drove. His mind focused on planning his kill. He arrived on the Gold Coast just before 6:00 pm, made a quick stop at a grocery store, grabbing junk food, drinks and a bouquet of flowers. First stop, the Gold Coast Hospital, a relatively new, 1960s concrete box oozing functionality and lacking aesthetics. He put on his best outback country charm and went to the information counter.

The elderly lady sitting at the desk saw him coming and was eager to assist, probably a slow day. "And how can I help you?" she asked, as Rupert got to the desk.

"G'day, I heard that an old friend of mine was in the hospital and just wanted to drop some flowers off. To make her feel better."

"What a nice idea. What's her name?"

"Rebecca, Rebecca Thornton."

The lady looked through a ledger. "Oh yes. Here she is. Yes, Rebecca Thornton. She was brought in last night." She paused. "Oh, but I'm sorry she is in a restricted ward on level five. Unauthorized visitors are not allowed."

"Gosh, I bought these flowers and all. Could I just drop them off on the 5th floor?" Rupert had no intention of doing so, but figured he better continue with the charade.

"Nooo, sorry".

"Well, I'll drop them off at her place then. You don't happen to know when she might be discharged? No point leaving the flowers at her door, if she won't be back there for days."

The lady looked back at her ledger. "It does show she is marked for discharge tomorrow. But all depends on the doctor giving the okay."

"Thank you. I'll drop the flowers off at her home then and take the chance."

"My pleasure," the lady smiled up at him, "and you might want to put the flowers in water just in case."

Rupert nodded, turned and walked away. Once out of her sight he threw the flowers into a garbage bin, and found a spot in the main floor waiting room where he could watch the elevators and hospital entrance. He was a satisfied man. He'd gotten all the information he wanted; she was still in the hospital to be discharged tomorrow and he felt certain Manne would likely be close by. Rupert found a corner lounge chair from where he could keep surveillance until visiting hours ended.

Rupert didn't have to wait long, there was Manne coming out of the elevator heading outside. Rupert got up and followed. Manne went to the parking lot, and got into his Ute. By now it was dark, easy for Rupert to remain unseen. He took a good look at the Ute, Northern Territory plates. Easy. His vehicle wasn't parked too far away. He jogged over to it, intent on following. The traffic wasn't heavy and he could easily keep Manne in sight. After driving through Surfer's Paradise, Manne entered Broadbeach. He turned east at Lennons Hotel. Rupert followed remaining well back. He watched him park and walk into the hotel. Lennons was a high-end hotel, five stories. Typical, thought Rupert, lawyers always stay at the best digs; leeches as they are.

Satisfied Manne was staying at Lennons, Rupert decided to scout the surrounds. He was enjoying this; there was excitement in the hunt. Surprisingly, Lennons was like an oasis on the sandy beach. The beach was a short distance away, a path leading to it. A band of sand dunes ran north and south. The dunes were topped with a short crop of diehard shrubs and beach grasses. Lennons had a big outdoor pool, a beach club and tennis courts. Rupert took this all in. What surprised him was the hotel's isolation, nothing to the south and just a few small beach shacks to the north. The parking lot wasn't large and Rupert parked on the adjoining street, where he had a clear view to the hotel and Manne's Ute. No trees for shade, and Rupert wasn't about to hide in the dunes, bloody snake pits. He walked to the beach, which stretched for golden miles. It was dark and he was alone. The stars formed a sparkling canopy. Beautiful, but he had things to do.

Manne wasn't going anywhere. Rupert returned to his Ute and drove back to Surfer's Paradise, where he paid cash for a room in a small ubiquitous motel. One night only. He wanted to keep on the move. He stayed in his room. The fewer people who saw him the better. His dinner was takeout meat pies and more Bundy. His mind churned as he ate and drank.

Killing them in the hotel was too messy. Too many people would be about and there were limited exits. The parking lot was better, cleaner. He could drive up, shoot and be gone. Definitely an option. He decided he'd do them at the same time. Tomorrow. He was confident Manne would pick her up from the hospital. If all goes well, he'll be back at the ranch in a few days.

CHAPTER 22

Thursday, June 15

Manne woke at 8:00 am, his body rested, but sore everywhere. Getting out of bed was a challenge. He went for a swim in the hotel's pool, which helped.

After breakfast the next stop was the hospital. When Josef arrived at Rebecca's room, a police officer was still on guard. Rebecca was dressed in her favorite blue jeans and shirt. The swelling on the side of her head had mostly disappeared.

"Thanks for bringing my stuff. It felt so good to get out of my hospital gown," Rebecca was re-energized and ready to get out of the hospital. They waited. A nurse took her vitals and her doctor finally turned up, and did a quick examination. Satisfied he agreed to her release, prescribing rest and relaxation.

MacPherson arrived and the officer on guard was dismissed. He suggested they have a coffee, his shout. Josef thought he looked tired. His face was gaunt and drawn. Rebecca gently asked him, "Are you okay?"

MacPherson gave her a wane smile, "Thank you for asking Miss Thornton. I'm bushed. It has been a hectic few days and I'm frustrated and disappointed in Kirby. I trusted him. It hurts. Do I regret shooting Jim Hooper? Honestly, no, it was the right thing to do. He was going to kill you both and it was my job to protect you."

"Thank you again," replied Rebecca.

MacPherson turned back to business, "So, what are the two of you going to do?"

"I'm going to disappear, again," Rebecca answered quickly.

"I'll be heading back to Canada on the 22nd," said Josef.

"Well look, I need to know how to contact you Miss Thornton. The Taipans are under surveillance, but are still a factor. Then there is Mother Hooper. She is a dangerous woman; hard to know how she'll react. There also may be questions arising from the shooting. I've been cleared by an internal panel, but, once again, who knows."

Josef had an answer, "How about this, I'll need to keep in contact with Rebecca. You can call me. Does that work for you?"

MacPherson nodded. He was going to ask Rebecca where she might be going, but changed his mind. Better not to know. He finished his coffee. "Got to go." Rebecca and Josef got up. Josef shook his hand. Rebecca gave him a heartfelt hug. MacPherson was touched. Days like today were special. This was why he was a cop.

Josef and Rebecca went to Lennons Hotel. In the early afternoon, they had lunch in the hotel restaurant and the conversation became more serious and personal.

Josef had ordered a local beer and a ginger ale, 'Canada Dry', for Rebecca. "Is there a reason you don't drink alcohol, or just a matter of personal preference?"

Rebecca took a sip of her drink and replied, "Truthfully, I don't really like the taste, but there is more to it." She took another sip and went on, "When I was sixteen, I was at Foster Station for the summer holiday. It was New Year's and everyone was celebrating. One of the transient workers took a shine to me and plied me with gin. I was young and foolish. I had too much and began acting silly. Fortunately for me, my mother was ever watchful. She found me and dragged me from the group of men. Boy, she gave them a blast. Beware a mother protecting her child. I got sick a couple times on the way home. Mum put me to bed. The next morning, early, Mum woke me up and forced me to the kitchen, where she placed a bottle of gin on the table and offered it to me. It was the last thing I wanted. 'C'mon, c'mon,' she said, 'have a drink, get drunk, have a good time. Isn't that what you want? Because you know what, that is exactly what the men want. They want you drunk and helpless, so they can get what they want. You need to be in control. Never let drink control you.' Mum, was right. I vowed off alcohol then and haven't missed it since. I was lucky, very lucky.

But you don't drink much either, I bet you'll nurse that beer through lunch. Any reason?"

"My reason is not nearly so meaningful as yours. At a post football party there was plenty of alcohol, and I got wasted. I blacked-out. My best friend brought me home. He told me I was a real idiot. I couldn't recall anything, which scared me. I had lost control, just like your mother said. And, after that, I decided never again. Drink to moderation. So, I do."

They talked about their families. Rebecca missed having no brothers or sisters. It was just her and her mother. She asked him about his sister.

Josef rarely talked about his sister, it was a painful a memory. "My sister, Alexis, was an addict and drugs killed her. She got involved with the wrong crowd in high school and never escaped the drugs. For years she dragged the entire family through hell. My parents tried everything. Nothing worked. They worried every time she'd go out. Would she come back? Would she be high? Would she even be alive? She couldn't live at home. Frankly she didn't want to; she wanted her freedom. She wanted her drugs. Tough love. My parents kicked her out; they had no choice. Alexis was like a poison killing us all. She left for Vancouver, following the drugs. I never saw her again. One day my mother received a call from the Vancouver police, Alexis had died of an overdose. She was only 23. My parents, I think, always blamed themselves."

Rebecca could see his pain. She changed topic. "Is there a girl back home?" Her brown eyes watching him closely.

Josef blushed a bit red and stammered out, "No, no, I never seem to keep a relationship. Look at us. In the last six days we've been together we've been chased, shot at, attacked, beaten and tomorrow it will be over. Story of my life."

Rebecca whispered, "Maybe, maybe not."

What did she mean by 'maybe'? He should follow it up. But he couldn't. She'd been hurt by men and distrusted them. He knew he was attracted to her, but was too afraid to tell her. In his torn state of indecision, he bailed. "Where will you go tomorrow?"

Rebecca took her time. "I'd like to go south of Sydney. I want to be by the ocean. I've had enough of dust. I'll head south."

"South, I could give you a ride. I can drop the Ute off at Sydney airport and you could be my guide as we drive down the coast. I don't leave for Canada until the 22nd." Josef was excited and hopeful.

Rebecca didn't put up an argument. She replied softly, "I'd like that. I'd like that very much."

Pristine clear blue sky, a warm sun, and calm conditions made for a perfect day. They spent the rest of the afternoon lounging around the hotel pool. They said little, but enjoyed each other. The cloud of fear was lifted, although they both remained alert and wary.

* * *

Rupert tailed Manne to the hospital. He found a spot to park in the shade under a Moreton Bay Fig. He waited. He watched one cop arrive and another cop leave. He waited anxiously. Time moved slowly. Then he saw them: Manne, Rebecca and a cop come out of the hospital. Rupert thought about killing them here; however, no way, not with a cop on site. Manne and Rebecca went to the Ute. She looked the same – bitch. He'd shoot her in the face. The blast would leave nothing but raw meat.

Manne pulled out and headed south. Rupert was sure his destination was Lennons. He followed at a safe distance. Depending on where they parked at Lennons and whether there were witnesses about he might be able to do the killing as soon as they arrived. The Winchester was loaded, lying hidden under a blanket behind his seat. Soon, it could be soon. His hands became clammy; his mouth dry. He took a swig of Bundy, straight up. The fire of the rum gave him a shot of courage and calmness.

Manne turned into Lennons. Rupert followed closer. Damn, there was a spot right in front of the hotel. Manne took it. Fuck. Fuck. And there was a bus loading a bunch of ladies. Too goddamn many people. Fuck. He slammed his palm into the steering wheel. Patience. Don't let them see you. Rupert drove through the parking lot, pulled a U-turn and parked on the adjoining street. Manne and Rebecca got out and went into the hotel. Shit. He was going to have to sit and wait. The sun was blazing. It may be winter in Queensland, but the sun is strong any time of year. The

Ute became a roaster. There was no shade; no place to hide. Patience. He needed patience. He waited and drank warm Bundy and coke.

* * *

The sun was setting. There was now a chill in the air. Enough lounging. Rebecca got up, restless, and said, "C'mon, let's go for a walk on the beach." They stopped by the front entrance and Josef went to the Ute to get a jacket. They then took the path leading to the beach.

Rupert saw them at the entrance. He was hot and Bundy lubricated. They caught him by surprise. He grabbed for the shotgun, only to relax when he saw they turned to walk towards the beach. In seconds, his plan changed. Killing them on the beach was ideal. In all likelihood the beach would be deserted and it was getting dark. He scrambled to retrieve his three-quarter length coat, old Akubra Snowy River hat and shotgun. With the shotgun, he pumped a shell into the firing chamber, safety on, attached the strap and slung it barrel down in front over his right shoulder and put on his coat. The snub-nosed shotgun was completely hidden by the coat and his hands were free. He grabbed a few more shells, put them in his pocket and got out of the Ute. He headed for the beach, following a trail through the dunes.

Rupert was on the hunt. The path they'd taken was dug through the dunes and was hidden from view. Just before going over the crest of the last dune, Rupert laid low and looked down the beach. In the gathering dusk he saw no one. Fuck. Had they turned around and gone back? Where were they? Then he saw them emerge from the path. They were probably 200 yards to the north of him. He held his breath. Would they turn and walk his way? Or go north away from him? Or turn around and go back? He waited. 'Come on, come to me,' he whispered to himself. They didn't. They turned north at a diagonal heading to the ocean surf and hard packed sand of low tide. They struggled through the deep loose sand and finally made it to the shoreline.

Josef and Rebecca stopped to admire the surf. They stood looking out to the Coral Sea taking in the moment. Rebecca led the way north. The sun set and a new moon took its place. They watched. The moon cast a silver

OLD BILL'S LAST WILL AND TESTAMENT

path over the dark ocean. Lorikeets could be heard in the distance, calling out that the day had ended. All was peaceful.

Rupert pushed himself up. He slowly made his way to the hard-packed sand by the ocean's edge, ever keeping an eye on Manne and Rebecca. They were 250 or more yards down the beach, moved to higher ground and sat down. Rupert stopped, turned his face away, looking out to the ocean. He thought they might intend to make out right there on the beach. Wouldn't that be great? To kill them in the throes of passion. But that wasn't what they were doing. They took their shoes off, rolled up their pant legs to walk barefoot into the surf. They continued walking north leaving their shoes behind. Obviously, they intended to come back this way. Rupert slowly walked north and found a spot in the dunes 50 to 60 yards away from where the shoes were stashed. He'd lie in wait for them to return and when putting their shoes back on he'd kill them. All was good! The beach was deserted, the surf would muffle any shotgun blasts and it was dark, yet the moon provided enough light. Rupert was excited. He sat down and watched them walking away. He thought about what he might do or say before shooting them. He didn't want a quick surprise hit. He wanted them to know it was him and this was his revenge. Rupert waited in anticipation and took another swig of Bundy.

Josef and Rebecca were in no hurry to end their walk. The beach scene was too spectacular and the day was too special. They were more comfortable with each other. As the moon rose higher in the sky, the night grew colder; it was time to get back.

They returned to their shoes. Josef sat down, feet in the air, knocking the sand off. He used his socks to clean his feet. Rebecca knelt beside him gathering up her Redback leather slip-on boots. She noticed then for the first time a person, a man, down the beach stand and walk towards them. There was something about him. He was silhouetted by the moon. The way he walked. He wasn't a beach walker. He was wearing a long oilskin duster. Odd. Through the moonlight she saw the hat. That hat! She recognized that hat.

She whispered urgently to Josef, "That man, coming towards us. It's Rupert Malton. We have to get out of here fast." Josef didn't say anything.

Nor did he argue. He took a quick look. The man was walking slowly towards them. Josef left his shoes and turned his body to spring up and run.

Rupert eyed them carefully. He'd keep the shotgun hidden, until he was very close, then unstrap the barrel and take it out ready to fire. What fun! What a surprise! He wasn't in a hurry. Let them get one shoe on, one shoe off. He was now only about 30-40 yards away. The range of the shotgun, with luck, was about 40 yards. Better to get closer. He continued to walk nonchalantly forward.

Then Rebecca and Josef jumped up and started running. Rebecca was in the lead; Manne followed behind. By instinct, Rupert fired. There was the loud bang of the shotgun; followed by an immediate pump of the shotgun as the second shotgun shell was chambered. He fired again. This time his aim was more relaxed, more controlled. Josef cried out and tumbled forward falling. Rebecca stopped to help. "No, Rebecca run. Go, get help. Go."

Rebecca ignored him. She helped him up. They limped further away. Josef could feel the burning shot in his right thigh, calf, knee and lower leg. He reached down and could feel the warm blood, squirting out with each heart-beat. "Go, please go," he said again.

Through gritted teeth, Rebecca said, "I am not leaving you. Now come with me." She started dragging, pulling him into the surf.

"What are you doing?" Josef asked.

"We can't outrun him, but we can hide in the ocean."

Josef understood. He put all his energy into struggling through the surf. At waist height they both dived into a breaking wave. Rupert fired again, but the shot was both out of range and dissipated by the water. They continued to swim out to sea. There was a deep gutter about 30 yards out, once through it a sandbank allowed them to stand, keeping their heads, just above the waves.

They could see Rupert standing on the shore. He didn't enter the water. They saw him raise the shotgun. They dived under the water. None of the buckshot reached them. They were safe. Once they came to the surface, Rebecca asked, "Where are you hit?"

"My right leg, it took a number of shots. The one in my lower calf, I think the shot severed an artery. I'm holding it. But I can feel the blood squirting out."

Josef started to pull his belt off, with his left hand. "We need to make a tourniquet." Rebecca helped him. It wasn't easy. They were pummeled by the surf. The waves were powerful and unrelenting. They had to brace themselves as the surf was intent on pushing them into shore or dumping them into the sand. Finally, Rebecca looped the belt and slipped it over his right leg and pulled it as tight as she could just above the knee. Next, she removed her jacket and shirt and ripped the shirt, as best she could, into strips of cloth. Working under water against the surf she wrapped the make-shift bandages around his leg from thigh to ankle.; tying each as best she could. Was it doing any good? She didn't know. She just had to do something. She pulled the last bandage tight below the knee. In so doing, she felt the pulsating squirt of blood. She didn't say anything, but it wasn't good. With each wave trough they looked for Rupert. He hadn't moved. Nor had he tried to shoot again.

"Why doesn't he come into the water and force us out? He's just standing there." Josef shouted above the rage of the water.

Rebecca replied crisply, "He can't swim."

"He can't swim?"

"No, he's an outback kid and he can't swim. I was told that by a couple of ranch hands, who worked with him."

The water was not cold, still probably mid to high 60s, but how long could they stay in the water? Malton seemed content to stay put and wait. The biggest danger was the severed artery. They both knew that. Josef could well bleed out.

"Rebecca, you need to go and get help."

"No, I'm not going to leave you."

"Well if you don't, then you'll be staying with a dead man. I'm losing blood. You need to get help."

"And how am I supposed to do that with Rupert waiting on shore?"

"He can only see our heads. Give me your jacket." Josef took the floating jacket and rolled it up. "In the darkness, this jacket will be your head. You move behind me. That way he'll have a tough time seeing you. There is a current, a rip, pushing to the south. You dive under and swim with that rip. It will take you down the beach towards Lennons. Once you are far enough, slip on to shore and get help. I'll stay here, with your rolled-up jacket."

Rebecca gave Josef a long look, much like she had days ago when they first met. She knew this was the only hope and she began taking her blue jeans off. She dipped her head under the waves and disappeared. Josef made sure Rupert could still see him, he allowed a wave to lift him up. So long as Rupert did not see Rebecca leave there was hope.

The rip was powerful, angling somewhat out to sea. Rebecca was a strong swimmer and gently broke the water surface for breaths of air. Otherwise she swam under water. In the surf and darkness, she would be difficult to see. How long did Josef have? She didn't know. But she knew this was his only chance to survive. She took a peek and could still see Rupert standing by the surf. She didn't think he had moved. She was over 100 yards to the south of him and needed at least another 100 yards. She went under the water again, frog kicked and let the rip take her. Frog kick, glide. Frog kick, glide. She didn't know for how long. Too long she feared. But she could see the lights of Lennons, like a lighthouse beacon. She saw the path to the hotel and started to work her way into shore fighting out of the rip. She took a look and saw Rupert, a faint sentinel in the distance. She surfed in on a breaking wave, which pushed her to the shore. She didn't move. She dared to look north. Rupert was still there. She crawled on her elbows through the surf, until the surf died. She rested a moment. The moon disappeared behind a bank of clouds. Now! Rebecca rose to a crouch and ran to the path. Rupert had not moved.

Rupert was confused and befuddled. His prey were right there. So close, yet so far. Just out of shotgun range. He couldn't swim out to them, and wading in would accomplish little; they'd just swim further out. Should he leave? Indecision driven by hate. No. He was so close. He wasn't going to leave just yet. They'd go to the police. Did they see his face? He thought not, but why did they run? Must have. He did have his alibi. No, he'd wait. He had time. It was getting colder. They wouldn't be able to stay in the water much longer, especially since he knew he had wounded Manne. He had time. Patience. How had she known? How? He cursed letting them get away. But it wasn't over. He'd wait. He took a swig of Bundy.

Josef was feeling faint. He could actually feel the oozing blood with each pulse. The bandages and tourniquet were tight, but they weren't stemming the flow of the blood. The water wasn't cold for him. He thought of the many times he swam in the cold Northern Saskatchewan lakes. His mind meandered. He recalled swimming in Waskesiu Lake one May long weekend with ice still on parts of the lake. He survived. He thought of Rebecca. Thoughts of her brought him a renewed will to live. He couldn't see her. He held Rebecca's jacket above the water. Then his mind turned to sharks. Pete, his surfer friend, had regaled him with tales of shark attacks, right here on the Gold Coast. Sharks are attracted to blood. He had read Great White Sharks can smell blood from three miles away. If a shark came, would it be better to swim in and let Rupert shoot him? To be shot or to be eaten that was the question. Josef decided he would rather be shot. He lost feeling in his right leg. Had it fallen off? Shark bite already? He shook his head, back to reality. Must keep his head above the water. Hang on. Don't give in. He could feel his life blood flowing out. He was getting so tired. His strength was going. So tired.

Rebecca ran like she had never run before. Her feet were bruised and battered, but she didn't care. She made it to the hotel. It was quiet. She ran to the front foyer. The young man at reception looked wide-eyed at the disheveled young woman, wearing nothing more than a bra and panties, mauled by the ocean, barefoot and bleeding. Rebecca shouted at him, "Call the police, call for an ambulance. A man has been shot on the beach. Hurry, hurry."

To his credit, the young man moved into action. Immediately he called the police and ambulance. He also called for backup. The matronly manager of the restaurant arrived. A blanket was found for Rebecca. A cup of tea was brought. The police arrived. They too were young. The officer in charge began an interrogation of Rebecca. Name. Address. Who was with her? Who was the shooter? Were there others? Where? Rebecca lost it. Time was of the essence. She gave her questioner a spray, "There is a man standing on the bloody beach with a loaded shotgun. I told you where. He has shot my friend, who is wounded, probably bleeding to death in the water. You need to get your ass down to the goddamn beach! Now! And if you won't then get me a police officer who will. Call Senior Constable

MacPherson from the Mudgeeraba police station. He knows me and he knows what's going on."

It then clicked with one of the police officers, "Were you the lady he saved the other day?"

"Yes," she spit out.

The police galvanized into action. They moved out on the run, one officer remaining with Rebecca, just in case Malton turned up. Other police arrived. An ambulance arrived. The paramedics wanted to treat Rebecca. She wouldn't have it. She told them to get to the beach and explained that her friend's artery in the leg had been severed. She saw in their faces; it was not good. They tried to get a time line as to how long ago he had been shot. She wasn't sure. But guessed it must be around 30 minutes or more.

Rupert heard sirens in the distance, but didn't react. Then he saw men approaching. There were at least four. They had flashlights. They were cops. He was befuddled. Who called them? He didn't know what to do. It was too late to escape. He stood in paralyzed indecision. He could still see Manne and Rebecca out in the water. Soon the cops were within shouting distance. "Police, put your hands in the air and drop any weapon. Hands in the air." Rupert could see their weapons were drawn. He didn't drop the shotgun. He didn't put his hands up. He was beaten. He knew that. He had failed. However, he could not let Manne and Rebecca be the victors. That could not happen.

"Put your hands up. Drop your weapon. Put your hands up." The command was closer and shriller. Rupert held his shotgun at his hip. Pointed it towards Manne and Rebecca and fired. He started walking into the surf, pumped the shotgun and fired again. He continued into the surf. The four officers fired. Rupert fell dead into the surf. The officers ran forward and two shone their flashlights into the water. Josef was sighted, and they swam out and dragged him in from the surf.

The paramedics arrived and took over. Josef was limp. The makeshift tourniquet belt was removed and a weak squirt of blood shot out of the wound. A proper tourniquet was applied. He was alive but unresponsive.

CHAPTER 23

Rebecca was numb. Her elbows rested on her knees in a fetal position. She cradled the cup of tea in both of her hands, sitting on a bench, the blanket wrapped around her shoulders. She was cold and shivering, tremors moved through her arms and legs. She felt so helpless. Her thoughts were scattered. Why Josef and not her? Malton was her problem. She wondered, had Josef deliberately shielded her from Malton. He hadn't run beside her, instead he followed right behind. Was he protecting her back?

She quietly prayed. She closed her eyes and her mind strayed back to when she was a little girl. She and her mother would kneel by her bed in prayer each night. Their prayers always included a word for her father and assurance he was watching from above, looking after them, and her little girl had done him proud that given day. As she grew older, the prayers faded and eventually stopped. Rebecca hadn't prayed for many years. After her mother died, her heart wasn't in it. God had not saved her mother from cancer no matter how much she prayed. But, now she prayed once more, this time for Josef. He was a good man. She knew she was certainly attracted to him. He was so kind, so brave, so quiet, so respectful and so, so handsome. She wasn't used to being treated as an equal. She'd grown up in a man's world and knew men expected little of her; all looks and little substance. She knew what they wanted. Independent women, like her, scared men. Not Josef. He respected her. Yes, he was special. She knew that and she prayed.

"Rebecca, Miss Thornton," a familiar voice interrupted her thoughts. Rebecca looked up, it was Senior Constable MacPherson. "Are you okay? Are you hurt?"

Rebecca managed a halting answer, "No, no, I'm not hurt. Josef, he's been shot. Is he okay?"

MacPherson replied in a soft succinct manner, "The paramedics have him. He is alive. They'll take him to the hospital."

"I need to go. I need to be there." Rebecca pleaded.

"I know and I will take you there, but first I want you to go up to your room and have a hot shower. You look like you're freezing. Get some clothes on, come back down, and one of the detectives will need to take a short statement from you, and then, I promise, I'll personally take you to the hospital."

MacPherson paused and gestured for a police woman to come. "This is Constable Beattie, she has your room key and she'll help you. Okay?"

Rebecca nodded then asked, "What happened to Rupert Malton?"

"The officers had to shoot him. He's dead."

Rebecca didn't respond to that news. No shock. No remorse. No joy. Constable Beattie helped her up from the bench. She was unsteady on her feet and Constable Beattie put her arm around Rebecca, giving her support, and guided her to the elevator.

Once in the room, Rebecca had a hot lingering shower. As the warm water soothed her body, her thoughts turned to Malton. After he had tried to rape her, she had taken a long shower, trying to cleanse herself of Malton's vileness. Her mind flashed back to the attack; a moment and image she never forgot. She could feel the grab of her hair when she unlocked her door that night, him dragging her inside. Her scream for help muted by a punch to her face and him putting his hand around her throat. The whispered threat in her ear, "cry out again and that will be the last thing you do, bitch". He threw her to the floor in the living room. She hit her head on the coffee table. Malton didn't care. He was on her. Pawing her. Tearing open her blouse, fighting with her bra, feeling her. He lay on her grinding his pelvis. Grunting at her, "take your pants off", "open up". Spittle oozed from his mouth. His breath was foul, smelling of dried beer and greasy food. Sweat sprayed off his dirty unwashed body. But it was his eyes that were most frightening: dark, uncaring, cruel. The attack wasn't about sex or passion; it was about violence. He had been rejected. No one did that to him. He wanted her to see his power. He was intent on hurting her, breaking her, destroying her. Rape was his ultimate weapon. He was in a frenzy of hate. Rebecca remembered she was about to give up, let him have his rape and move on, but she couldn't. She was a fighter. Her mother instilled that in her. And she fought back. An empty coke bottle had fallen off the coffee table. It lay by her right hand. She grabbed it by the neck and swung as hard as she could. The base of the bottle smashed into the side of his head. He was stunned. Rebecca knew this wasn't enough, holding the shard neck, she rammed the broken glass into his face and kneed him in the groin at the same time. Pushing him off. He erupted in a savage cry, holding his face and eye, blood pouring out, writhing on the floor. She rolled away from him and ran. She'd been running ever since. No more.

She turned the shower off. It was as though Malton was washed out of her life. She was free again. Ready to move on. Her shivers were gone. She had new strength. She did a quick dry of her hair, got dressed and returned to the foyer with Constable Beattie.

Senior Constable MacPherson met her and provided a quick update. Josef had lost a great deal of blood, and was on his way to the hospital. He introduced her to Senior Detective Nash, who asked if she could provide him with a short statement. He promised he would not keep her for more than 10 or 15 minutes and then Senior Constable MacPherson would take her to the hospital. The Senior Detective was soft spoken. He asked Rebecca to tell him about what happened on the beach. He let Rebecca tell her story with little interruption, only occasional questions of clarification. His focus was on the beach. No doubt he had been filled in by MacPherson about the history. Only at the end did he ask about Malton's motive. Remembering Josef's advice, she told the truth about Malton's attempted rape, her glassing of him and her being on the run. In his final question he turned back to the beach, "I'm curious, how was it you knew by going into the water you'd be out of range and safe?"

Rebecca replied, "Every girl born and raised on a farm knows the sound of a shotgun from a rifle and knows shotguns have a limited range." Nash smiled and closed his notebook. True to his word the statement was taken in about 15 minutes. He thanked her and handed her over to MacPherson.

On the way to the hospital they discussed how Rupert Malton happened to turn up on the Gold Coast. Rebecca suspected Stan Malton. MacPherson thought not. Rather, he blamed the media coverage for naming both Rebecca and Josef in their reporting of Jimbo Hooper's death. "You know, in a sense Australia is one big small town; a murder in Victoria makes news in Queensland. So it was that a police killing on the Gold Coast made its way to Goondiwindi and to Rupert Malton."

They arrived at the hospital. It was good to have MacPherson with her. He cleared the way. Josef was in surgery and they were shown to a waiting room. Head Nurse Minsk arrived, her tough demeanour replaced by obliging assistance. Rebecca feared this change was prompted by Josef's dire condition. Nurse Minsk assured her the surgeon, Dr. Hartley, was the hospital's best. "He served three tours of duty in Vietnam and knows everything there is to know about gunshot wounds."

MacPherson stayed with her. They waited. Two hours passed ever so slowly. Finally, a tall doctor approached, late 40's, premature grey, military bearing. Nurse Minsk was with him. Rebecca thought this an ominous sign. Both she and MacPherson stood up. In seeing them the doctor smiled. The smile spoke volumes; Rebecca knew the news was good. Dr. Thomas Hartley introduced himself, "I understand Mr. Manne is your fiancé?" Rebecca kept up the ruse.

Dr. Hartley got right to the point. "He lost a great deal of blood. We've stopped the bleeding and have given him intravenous transfusions. He's now stable, but needs close monitoring for the next 24 hours. He is sedated to allow his body to heal. He'll be moved to intensive care shortly and you can stay with him."

Rebecca was relieved. Josef was alive! He had survived!

Dr. Hartley had a calm reassuring demeanour. "Please have a seat. I'll explain." Once seated he turned and spoke directly to Rebecca. "We removed three shots from his right leg. A fourth shot entered and exited the leg. One of the shots cut the femoral artery in his lower leg. Fortunately, the artery was not completely severed, and some blood continued to circulate, but he lost a large amount. I'd estimate, more than 40% of his blood, which usually is fatal. When he arrived, he was in hypovolemic shock, from the loss of blood. Frankly, given the timeline it's a miracle he's still alive. I understand you put a tourniquet on the leg, Miss Thornton."

"Yes, but please call me Rebecca. We used his belt."

"Well Rebecca, that belt may well have saved his life, combined with being in the cold water and him being strong and fit. We also must not forget the fantastic job the paramedics did. As I said, it is a miracle, a real miracle. If that shot had severed the artery he most certainly would have died. He is a very lucky man." Dr. Hartley paused collecting his thoughts. "Regarding his leg, none of the shots struck bone, which is good. There was muscle tearing and, of course, the cut artery, but the wounds mostly caused tissue damage. The leg should be fine. No gangrene, given there was some blood flow to the foot. The leg is the least of our concerns. Our concern now is his internal organs may have been compromised in particular his kidneys, liver, heart and brain. We'll know more in the morning when he wakes up. At present he's stable. You get some sleep. I'll be back in the morning to check on him."

You could see his military training, just facts, no sugar coating. He got up to leave and stopped at the door fishing a small container out of his pocket. "I almost forgot," shaking the container, "here is the shot we took out of the leg. Officer, I assume you may want them." MacPherson took them and Dr. Hartley was off.

Nurse Minsk escorted them to Josef's room. A blanket and pillow were already in a neat pile on the lounge chair. MacPherson took his leave, winking at Rebecca, "Fiancé, hey." Rebecca went over to Josef. He looked pasty white. His forehead was cold to touch. But he was breathing; he was alive. The monitors showed a constant rhythm. Rebecca curled up in the lounge chair exhausted.

Friday, June 16

Sleep was intermittent. An orderly arrived with breakfast for her, courtesy of Nurse Minsk. Rebecca was surprisingly hungry and even the hospital food tasted good. She was sipping her coffee when she heard a croaking, "smells good". Josef was awake!

She went to him. His eyes were open and when he saw her, there was a big smile.

"Hi," he whispered.

"Hi," Rebecca smiled back, "good to see you awake."

"Good to be awake," he licked dry lips, "could I get some water?" Rebecca bent down lifted his head a bit so he could have a drink of water through a straw.

He rested his head back not taking his eyes off Rebecca, "You look wonderful."

"You are a liar; I must be a complete mess," Rebecca rebuked him.

"Not to me," Josef swallowed and licked his lips. "Are you hurt?"

"No, just some sore feet."

"You saved me."

"And you saved me. You took the shot aimed at me, didn't you?"

Josef didn't answer. "What happened to Malton?"

"He's dead. The police had to shoot him."

Josef nodded.

Rebecca went to the nurse's station and announced that Josef was awake. A nurse came back with her to check Josef's vital signs. She raised the bed so that he could sit up. With that he felt a little faint, woozy. Breakfast was brought and he managed to nibble on the offerings. They didn't say much to one another.

Dr. Hartley arrived next. He told Josef much of what he had told Rebecca earlier. Then he spent a number of minutes examining his patient. For each wound he explained the damage done by the shot, the repair operation and recovery. He was pleased with what he found and was confident the leg would heal well. It just needed a little tender care for a few days; the sutures were not to be burst. He prescribed crutches for a week.

What the doctor was more concerned about was internal organ damage given the blood loss. He listened intently to Josef's heart and lungs, then quizzed him on his recall and reasoning. Josef passed. Blood tests and monitoring were still required looking for kidney and liver damage.

To conclude, he pronounced Josef a "living miracle".

"When can I be released?" Josef immediately asked.

Dr. Hartley laughed. "Hang on mate, you just got here. You know a few hours ago you almost died. Hell, you should be dead. Your body has been through much. It needs rest and we want to keep an eye on you for a day or two."

Josef understood. "Next question, my flight to Canada leaves on the 22nd. Can I fly?"

Dr. Hartley took a moment before answering. "You know there are blood clotting worries associated with flying, but when I was in Vietnam we fixed up plenty of our boys and many flew out within days back to Australia. It's your call. If you do return to Canada, you'll need to have a doctor remove the sutures in two weeks' time. But I'm surprised you want to leave Oz, given our hospitality." With that he laughed, patted Josef on the shoulder and left.

A nurse arrived to take blood, which was Rebecca's cue to leave. She was exhausted and desperately wanted to have an uninterrupted sleep. She gave Josef a squeeze of the hand and left for the hotel.

On the way out of the hospital a scrum of reporters descended on her at the entrance. She was taken aback. Reporters from the various news outlets fired questions at her; cameras clicked and microphones were jammed in her face for comment. She fled to a waiting taxi. One police shooting is news; two police shootings in a few days involving the same victims was big news. The media followed in pursuit of her to the hotel. Rebecca ran to the sanctuary of their room and the comfort of the bed where she fell asleep.

In the early afternoon MacPherson paid a visit. Nothing official, he just wanted to check-up on Josef. They had a nice chat. It was obvious MacPherson wasn't overly confident Kirby would be facing much justice other than losing his job. The police union was too strong and the Crown prosecutors were too weak. The easiest course was to have him agree to resign, ruffling few police feathers. He already was out on bail. The powers that be were not looking forward to exposing corruption within the ranks. Better to cover things up. Josef could sense his frustration. He also knew it was out of MacPherson's hands; the higher ups were calling the shots. MacPherson warned Josef about the media, who were swarming. Two police shootings were a media event. His parting words, "Tread carefully; those reporters have a mean bite."

Josef was allowed to get up and walk with a physio attendant, who wanted to train Josef in using crutches. They walked to the ward lounge. A television was on and the headline was the "most recent police shooting on the Gold Coast". Josef and Rebecca were named as the "targets". The channel ran a video of Rebecca leaving the hospital. The reporter ended the segment, "Not much is known about either of the targets, or the reasons behind the attacks. What is known is one of the shooters had gang affiliations and was involved in illicit drugs. Was this a drug deal gone wrong? We don't know."

Josef was outraged, the innuendo was clear, these were drug related hits.

CHAPTER 24

Rebecca returned mid-afternoon running the media gauntlet, once again. She'd seen the television reports and was fuming. "We're made out to be a couple of drug runners!"

She was interrupted by a knock on the room door. "Mind if we come in?" Ken and Ruth Barnes had journeyed from Goondiwindi.

"Man, am I happy to see you," said Josef from his bed. "Rebecca, meet Ken Barnes and his wife, Ruth."

Ruth hugged Rebecca.

Ken said, "When we heard about the second shooting and you had been shot, I said to Ruth, 'I've got to check on my Canadian friend'. And Ruth said, 'I'm coming.' And here we are."

Once assured Josef was on the mend and out of danger they chatted. Without being asked, Rebecca and Josef opened up about the three attacks. They wanted to tell their story. It had been bottled up inside them. The conversation turned to the media.

Ken's view was simple and direct. "Saw the reports. They're doing a job on you, mate. They can be cruel."

Josef vented. "I'm so damn frustrated, we're not portrayed as victims but as suspected drug traffickers, or drug users saved by the police from a drug hit. And the Queensland Police would be happy to leave these as drug related shootings. Senior Constable MacPherson, came to see me earlier today and he was down. It's obvious Queensland Police want to bury news of the corrupt cop who fed us to the Taipans."

"Fight back," replied Ken, "tell your story as you told it to Ruth and me. That's the real story. But you need to do it soon, before the media lemmings all jump onto the bandwagon against you."

Ruth agreed, "In an information vacuum the media in this country will make up their own story, regardless of the truth."

"How do we do this? I have no idea," said Josef.

"Well, I've had a few media cases," Ken answered. "First thing, find a reporter or publisher you trust to tell your story. Second, you cannot take any money for the interview. No money. Blows your credibility. Third, has to be the absolute truth."

"Who can we trust?" asked Rebecca.

There was a pause, then Ken spoke, "A classmate of mine in law school is a journalist. I stuck to law and he became a journo. Writes for the Courier Mail in Brisbane. Does crime reporting, corruption stuff. I've helped him out a few times over the years. Name's Ted Norton. He's a straight shooter, honest. And the Courier Mail is always after the government about corruption. I trust him and can give him a call, if you want."

Rebecca, who hadn't said much, responded, "Let's do this. I'm tired of running, tired of being bullied and tired of corrupt cops. I want to fight back. I want the truth to come out." Josef nodded his head.

Ken clapped his hands. "I love a good fight. I'll call him. But may I make a suggestion. We need to plant the seed, now, not tomorrow or next week. It is perfect timing, Rebecca you should make a short statement to the media I saw waiting outside when we came in; it will make the 6'oclock news."

"What would you have me say?" asked Rebecca.

"The truth," replied Ken.

"Ken, I think you should act on our behalf and lead the way. Be our agent. It's better you make the contacts than us. Rebecca, you okay with that?"

"Completely."

Ken was thrilled to play his part. They began prepping Rebecca. Some people are terrified of public speaking. Not Rebecca. She was a natural. A short statement was prepared. After a few run-throughs she was ready. Ken and Ruth would accompany her and then escort her to their car.

It was time. The three of them left. Sure enough, the media were waiting outside like vultures. Ken had the three of them stand for a minute inside the hospital before exiting the doors. This allowed the media time to get the cameras rolling. The three then went outside.

Old Bill's Last Will and Testament

The media converged, as they had before, firing questions. Ken took control. "Oi, Oi, wait up, quiet." He yelled, "Miss Thornton has a short statement to make. Give her some room."

Rebecca moved forward to the top of the stairs, where she stood tall. She waited for them to quiet then spoke with a strong voice, clear and distinct: "My name is Rebecca Thornton and I want to set a few matters straight." She had notes, but wasn't bothering with them. She looked directly at the media scrum. "Within the last week there have been three attempts on my life and the life of Mr. Josef Manne, who is lawyer from Canada. Last night we were walking on the beach here on the Gold Coast and we were ambushed by a man named Rupert Malton, who I know from Goondiwindi, Queensland. Rupert Malton tried to rape me almost two years ago. I fought off the attack and glassed him. He has been hunting me ever since. I did not go to the police in Goondiwindi to report the attack for good reason; because Rupert's brother, Stan Malton, is the Senior Constable stationed at Goondiwindi. Rupert Malton shot Mr. Manne, who I am so relieved to tell you is recovering."

She paused and looking over the media continued, "A week ago a man tried to kill me on Springbrook Mountain where I live. The attacker, who fell to his death in the attempt, was a member of the Taipan biker gang. And I am advised by Mr. Manne and by the Queensland Police this was a suspected contract killing related to a will in Canada. It turns out I am the sole beneficiary under a will made by a Canadian soldier, who knew my father in a POW camp in Japan in World War II. Mr. Manne is the executor of that will and he travelled to Australia in search of me. Three days ago, the head of the Taipans, who also happens to be the older brother of the biker who died on Springbrook Mountain, tried to kill both Mr. Manne and me at the Gold Coast Hotel in Burleigh Heads. We were saved by the bravery of Senior Constable MacPherson of the Queensland Police. At the time we were in hiding from the Taipans. The Taipans found our location because a corrupt police officer with Queensland Police gave them our location. Simply put, he gave us up so we could be killed."

She paused and when she continued there was an edge in her voice. "I want to make something clear, the Taipans may be involved in drugs and contract killing. Mr. Manne and I are not. It is also my view that

Rupert Malton, who hunted me for almost two years, found me because of you – the media. You reported our names three days ago. You told Rupert Malton where he could find me." She stopped, looked at them and forcefully ended, "I hope you will have the courtesy of setting the record straight. Thank you."

Ken took over and bulldozed Rebecca and Ruth through to the car. The media was left madly contacting their respective news outlets.

Once in the car, Ken turned back to Rebecca. "You were sensational. Outback girl tells it straight. BEAUTIFUL!"

Rebecca's hospital statement aired on all the networks. Only portions were broadcast, but the import was the same, Rebecca and Josef were now taking the offensive.

Ken telephoned the Courier Mail newspaper from the hotel room and finally was put through to Ted Norton. "Ted? Ken here. Have you heard about the Gold Coast police shootings? Did you see Rebecca Thornton's statement? Yes." Ken was in his element. "Do you want an interview? There's a story here. You know that. You don't have time to think about it? Other networks are in the wings. They'd love to get this scoop. No, they aren't looking for anything from you other than a fair go. Look, Mr. Manne has a flight back to Canada on the 22nd; you can't dither. Our one and only request is a fair interview. Agreed? When can you get here? See you tomorrow morning."

Saturday, June 17

Josef was running a fever and there was no way Dr. Hartley was going to release him from the hospital. Josef knew it was the right call; he was still pretty weak. Rebecca turned up in the morning joining him for breakfast. She was excited, but at the same time somewhat nervous about meeting Ted Norton. Josef felt very confident for her.

Ken played agent and saw to it all ran smoothly. He met Ted and escorted him to Rebecca's room. Ted was a smallish man, slim. There was an intensity about him. He was an earnest, serious sort, soft spoken and perceptive.

For the next two hours he and Rebecca talked. She told her story. He listened. The conversation was recorded and occasionally he'd jot down a note. Mostly, he wanted to get a better understanding of Rebecca and details of what happened. They took a break for lunch. After lunch, he asked her to take him to the various places where she was attacked. Ken was the chauffeur.

At the end of the day she begged off having dinner with Ted, Ken and Ruth. She wanted to see Josef. When she got to the hospital, the media scrum had disappeared, perhaps Saturdays were not work days. Josef was sitting up in bed. His colour looked better, but he was weak. She felt his forehead. The fever had gone. She told him all about the interview. He felt good about what they were doing and felt confident he would be released from the hospital tomorrow. Dr. Hartley promised to see him first thing. The two of them were alone; the hospital was quiet. They talked. Much was said and much was left unsaid.

Rebecca didn't know what she was going to do. Her cover was blown. People would now know who she was, yet, on the other hand, there was no need to stay in hiding. Josef urged her to give Ethel Foster a call. "You are the daughter she never had you know?" Rebecca silently knew that was true. For Josef, he had mixed feelings about returning to Canada. He wanted Rebecca to come with him, but was too afraid to tell her so.

He was fading. It was time to go. Rebecca gave him a peck on the cheek, a smile, a wave and left.

Sunday, June 18

Dr. Hartley was true to his word and turned up at 8:00 am. Josef was washed, ready for inspection. The good doctor took his time. Josef failed inspection. He still had a slight fever, tired easily and one of his wounds showed signs of infection. Dr. Hartley was gentle, but firm. "Young man you were close to death, very close to death. Your body needs time." Josef knew in his heart he was right and was resigned to staying in the hospital.

Ted Norton visited Josef at the hospital. Josef too was impressed by him and his soft-spoken style. They spoke for almost two hours. Josef knowing full well everything said was on the record. Norton was most interested in the will and Old Bill. The bequest to the wife and daughter of the RAAF pilot provided a tantalizing mystery. The conversation turned to the search for Rebecca and the attempts on her life. Josef was tiring. Norton saw that and left.

Ken gave Norton the names of people to talk to in Goondiwindi about Rupert Malton. Things were falling into place, sources and information were verified. Norton already had put the paper on notice he wanted a sequenced three-part series telling Rebecca's story, beginning with the Monday paper. The focus was police corruption, but at the same time extolling the heroism of honest cops out there. The mysterious inheritance was an inviting enticement for the readers. Ken was right, this was a story worth telling.

Monday, June 19

Dr. Hartley checked on Josef early in the morning. The antibiotics had done their work and Josef's fever had subsided, along with the threat of infection. This time he passed inspection and was to be discharged. He thanked Dr. Hartley profusely. Somewhat humbly and sadly the good doctor replied, "I am always happy to see my patients leave the hospital; I've seen too many young men who didn't." And he was gone.

Ken and Rebecca received the word and picked him up at the hospital. They had copies of the Courier Mail. Rebecca was front page news. Josef cringed where he was quoted as saying, "The Queensland Police sure aren't the Royal Canadian Mounted Police"; it was not a compliment. The article was a good read, with a promise of more to come. The radio and television media picked up the chorus, the Queensland Police needed cleaning up.

That evening Rebecca, Josef, Ken and Ruth had a grand supper. Ken regaled all with his never-ending repository of hilarious stories, whether it be the time he swears in taking a pee in wintery Saskatchewan he suffered frostbite to you know what; or the time he took payment from a client in camels and brought them home to Ruth. Josef would miss them. They were intent on getting up and being on the road early. Ken figured they'd have breakfast in Toowoomba. Ruth insisted, "You two don't get up for us.

You've been through a lot." She hugged them both and whispered in Josef's ear, "She's a keeper," giving him a telling look in the eye.

Josef and Rebecca retired to their room. They were truly exhausted and fell asleep in separate beds.

Tuesday, June 20 and Wednesday, June 21

They stayed at Lennons for two days.

Romance? Hardly. Josef's wounds needed tending; Rebecca was his nurse. Was she more? Nothing was said. Safer for them to avoid the topic. Feelings for each other smouldered without catching fire. They slept in the same room, but not in the same bed. Neither made the first move.

On Wednesday they drove north to Brisbane to be nearer to the airport for Josef's early morning flight to Sydney, then on to Los Angeles and eventually on to Canada. They said little as they drove to Brisbane.

CHAPTER 25

Airport goodbyes are awkward. They stood at the departure gate. His flight was called. Looking at Josef, with a weak smile, Rebecca said, "Well, I guess the engagement truly is off."

Josef didn't know what to say. So, he stood mute. Instead, he gave her a tight hug, as best he could with his crutches. Rebecca responded, coming to him, resting her head in his chest. They kissed, a lingering tender kiss goodbye.

Then the embrace was broken. "I'll miss you," he said and was off. What does that mean? Hardly a statement of deep affection.

They were going back to their separate lives. Rebecca had called Ethel Foster a few days before. They had talked for a long time and Rebecca was invited to stay and work on the Foster Ranch. She'd live in her old house. As Rebecca said, "I want to go home for a time." Josef was returning to his career. He rationalized it was the right thing to do. She needed her space. So, he told himself.

Josef settled into his seat for the flight to Sydney and closed his eyes. His inner voice said, "Get off this plane and go to her! Don't blow this! Follow your heart man!" Too late. The plane powered off the runway forcing its way into the sky. He sighed and chastised himself; once more he was too timid and chose the safe, sensible choice. He should have said to her, "I love you." But he hadn't.

* * *

Upon his return, Josef poured himself into his work, which provided a respite from pining for Rebecca. Old Bill's estate file was his main focus.

Gabe prepared the paperwork for probate. In Gabe's detailed itemization, the estate was worth $535,500.00. Josef, Gabe and Straun held a strategy meeting.

Usually an Application for Grant of Probate was filed within 60 days of death, which would be July 9 at the latest. Gabe diarized Friday, July 7 for filing. The ninth was a Sunday. The application, which would be public, would include a copy of the will and itemization of property.

"Do we have to advise regarding the status of the beneficiaries?" asked Josef.

"You mean, do we tell the world Rebecca is alive?" replied Gabe.

"Exactly."

"Nope, no need at this stage. Obviously, down the road Bill's brother will find out."

"Yes, but I think it's worth left hanging for a bit," Josef went on, "What do you expect Bruce Jones to do?"

Gabe thought before answering. "If I was acting for him I would have already filed a caveat in the court to freeze the estate. I'm surprised he hasn't. Rest assured, when he finds out the estate is worth half a million he'll file a caveat or a motion contesting the will. In either case the estate is frozen."

Josef commented, "He probably didn't file a caveat or motion because he was confident Rebecca would be dead. If she was dead, he'd want the will to be probated, and he'd recover as next of kin. He'll file as soon as he finds out Rebecca is alive. That old bastard."

Straun agreed and asked Gabe, "What do you foresee as the issues in contesting the will and what do we need to do to defend against them?"

Gabe went into soliloquy mode. "They'll attack testamentary capacity. The problem with a holograph will is there are no witnesses to the making and signing of the will. They'll argue Bill didn't know what he was doing. They'll say he was suffering from loss of memory and loss of mind as he receded into the past. Won't be hard to get an expert neurologist to testify to that effect. Next, the will is very vague. Did Bill even know what property he had? There is no reference to specific property. A testator needs to show an understanding of what his estate includes. But, what is most troubling, is why he left everything to two people he never knew, never met. Raises a suspicion of senility. I can see the family making an arguable case to overturn the will."

Gabe's answer cast a sobering pall over the meeting. Josef broke the silence, "How do we defend the will?"

"We get affidavits from everyone who had contact with Bill in the days surrounding the making of the will. That is our starting point and hopefully all will say Bill was completely competent."

"I'll get on that," said Josef, "the operative date is March 26. I'll contact people in Blue River, the doctor in Saskatoon, and the Morrisons as well, they saw Bill around that time."

Straun was quiet, taking in the advice, finally he spoke, "Fellas, I think we need to be more proactive. Take the offensive. Stop worrying so much about what the opposing side will do. In other words, let's start building a damn good case to support the will – Bruce Jones be damned. What can we do to bury him?"

It was good to hear Straun's fighting spirit and he was right; they were too worried about the opposing side's case. Josef took his lead. "You know something has been bothering me. I think we assume, without proof, Bruce Jones was behind the contract hit on Rebecca. But why? Why bother killing her if the estate was nothing more than Bill's old shack and a few sections of scrub bush? We now know the estate is worth half a million, but Bruce wouldn't know that. Nobody knew. It is the Morrison stock that makes the estate worth over half a million. We're missing something."

Gabe broke in, "Must be the two sections of land. Remember, Bruce Jones searched those parcels of land a few months before Bill's death."

"My thoughts exactly," said Josef. "He wants those parcels. Why? We need to find out."

Gabe answered, "I have a friend, who I've used a few times in searching mine claims. I could have him do a quick survey of those parcels. Then at least we'll know if there is buried treasure."

"Let's do it," said Josef, "but there is more. Bear with me. If we assume Bruce was prepared to kill Rebecca in order to get the parcels, then why not kill Old Bill in the first place? Bruce was the only surviving relative and who would have thought Old Bill would have a will. Kill Bill and the parcels would be his. I can tell you Bruce was plenty shocked when I told him about Old Bill's will. I think I'll have a chat with the investigating RCMP officer in Blue River. He and the doctor probably just assumed Old Bill fell and died. End of story. I'd like to check it out."

"Yes, and a wrongdoer cannot receive under a will. Murderers can't profit from their killing." Gabe added.

"Worth looking into," concurred Straun, "anything else?"

"The will. That's the key problem. Why give his estate to the wife and daughter of the Australian airman? Sorry, that speaks to an unstable mind. We need to find the reason why." Gabe unfortunately was quite correct.

Josef responded, "I've been thinking about that as well and I think the answer lies with John Morrison. He has the connections. We need to track down some prisoners of war who were at Niigata. I'll be seeing the Morrisons to take affidavits from them and I'll raise that with him."

Straun clapped his hands. "Fellas that's more like it. Let's get to it."

* * *

Sebastian Wright had been chasing Josef about whether the beneficiaries had been located. He wrote a letter to Josef on June 24. No response. He followed up about filing for probate. Still no response. Then on Monday, July 10 he received a terse letter advising him William Jones' estate filed application for probate on July 7 in the Court of Queen's Bench in Prince Albert. Wright was thrilled when he saw the probate application. The estate was worth over a half million dollars! Billable hours! Wright phoned Bruce Jones with the good news. Bruce was surprised at the size of the estate and pushed Wright about any news as to whether the daughter was alive. 'Nothing to report' was not an answer Bruce wanted to hear.

Wright's euphoria was short lived. Two days later he received a call from Graham Sinclair Q.C. of the Saskatoon law firm, Sinclair and Schmidt. Bruce Jones had fired Wright. In Sinclair's words, "he wanted a more experienced litigation firm to handle the file. You understand." Sinclair asked that all documentation on the file be forwarded to him. Wright was downright angry. His legal golden egg was scrambled.

* * *

On Friday, July 14 Josef received a letter from Graham Sinclair Q.C. informing him Bruce Jones had switched lawyers. Along with the letter was notice of a hearing set for Thursday, July 20 in the Court of Queen's Bench Prince Albert requesting: 1) a caveat be filed freezing the estate pending grant of probate; 2) particulars regarding whether the named beneficiaries are alive; 3) transfer of the action to Saskatoon and 4) other relief to be determined. Graham Sinclair Q.C. was firing the first legal salvo in the probate war.

Bruce, Gabe and Straun held a war council. Straun took the lead. He was relishing a civil tussle. He particularly liked that an out of town firm was now representing Bruce Jones and family. Josef asked him whether he knew Graham Sinclair. He did. Straun in his circumspect way said, "Some lawyers know the law, and some know people. Sinclair is the latter." Straun worked with Sinclair on a number of law society committees and he described Sinclair "as a lot of talk little work". Enough said. Josef concluded Straun, who generally had a good word to say about everyone, did not like Graham Sinclair.

"Who is the judge sitting during the summer on civil motions?" asked Josef.

Gabe piped in, "Justice Podorchuk, who is in from Battleford."

"Justice Podorchuk," said Straun with some glee, "I know him well."

"And?"

"All good." Straun moved into story mode. "He is from sound Ukrainian stock. Came to Canada, as a teenager, with his family after the First World War. No English. You'll see he still has a bit of an Eastern European accent. 'What' may come out as 'Vat'. The family had nothing. Settled in the bushland. Not good farming. He worked in lumber camps. With the start of World War II, he signed up first thing. Hell of a lot easier than working in the bush. He went in with the Canadians at Normandy and was wounded in the Falaise Gap. Terrible battle. He lost his index finger. His commanding officer evidently wanted to ship him home. No way. He showed the commander how he could fire his rifle with his middle finger. I'll tell you a story about that in a minute. Anyway, he finished out the war and went to university on a veteran's allowance, studied law and became a prosecutor. As a prosecutor, he was formidable in a courtroom. Only had a trial with him once, in Melfort Court. He had that country, homey approach, but what was most effective is he'd still point, without an index finger. This stub would be pointing at the witness or the jury and it mesmerized whoever was its target." Straun laughed. "I lost the case."

"He was appointed to the bench in the early 60's. He's a good judge. Doesn't like speeches. Likes to move things along." With a chirp in his voice, Straun went on, "And, more importantly, I know the Honourable Mr. Justice Podorchuk, hates high and mighty big south firms coming up here to show us northern hicks how to do things."

It was a good story, now back to the case at hand.

"Turning to the caveat," said Gabe, "there is no point us contesting that. It is normal for a caveat to be attached when a will may well be contested."

"Agreed," said Straun.

"Particulars regarding the fact Rebecca is alive, also no reason to contest," Gabe was going through the list.

"Agreed," replied Straun.

"Transfer of the action to Saskatoon. No, we should fight that."

All agreed.

"What does the request for other relief mean?" queried Josef.

Straun had the answer. "They are going to request the estate cover the legal expenses of Bruce and his family. It's a common motion. They're just being clever by not specifically naming it. I bet that's it and we need to be prepared, but at the same time appear surprised, if not shocked, by the request."

Straun went on, "Josef, I know you're a litigator, and damn good, however, I'd like to handle this hearing. But only if you are comfortable with me doing so. I know Justice Podorchuk and I don't think you've ever appeared before him. Is that right?"

"Straun, I'm happy for you to take the lead. You're right, I've never appeared before him."

"Oh, I'm not going to take the lead. I don't want to take the case from you. It's yours. You are still lead counsel, but for this hearing I might well have something to offer."

Josef smiled. "Agreed." He knew Straun had something up his sleeve and he thought there was something personal between Straun and Mr. Graham Sinclair Q.C.

CHAPTER 26

The Court of Queen's Bench sits on a hill overlooking Central Avenue and downtown PA. It is the most prominent building in the city, constructed in the 1920s when the city was touted as the gateway to the north. The Central Avenue viaduct, which traverses the railroad lines in the flat below, begins at the foot of the court house.

Straun and Josef decided to walk to court from their downtown office. It was a warm July afternoon, clear skies dappled with whiffs of non-threatening white cloud. As they strolled up the viaduct they discussed the hearing. When they reached the steps of the court they turned to take in the view. The court faced north, supposedly to where the city's future was to be. In the foreground was the North Saskatchewan River meeting the evergreen carpet in the background.

Straun broke the quiet reverie. "Josef, I'd like you sit in the gallery and not at the counsel table. Okay?"

Josef was surprised, but really didn't mind. He was curious, however, "Not a problem, but why?"

Straun looked at him, with a small grin. "My boy, you will see. You will see." They turned and walked up the steps. "Let's get on with it."

Courtroom four was one of the smaller courtrooms, designed for judge alone hearings as opposed to jury trials. The room was finished with oak, oak and more oak. Oak wall panels throughout, an ornate oak judge's desk, long oak benches in the gallery and large oak counsel tables. When Straun and Josef entered, already seated at one of the counsel tables were three lawyers. Josef now knew why Straun wanted him to sit in the gallery. Bruce and Ron Jones were seated a few benches back of their counsel. Straun dropped his briefcase on the counsel table and greeted Sinclair, welcoming him to Prince Albert. Straun introduced Josef. The other two lawyers with Sinclair were younger, probably a few years out, they were scrubbed clean, immaculately dressed in new suits, all spiffed up and looking very serious. Josef reckoned they had not done much trial work. Not surprising for civil litigators, who rarely get into court. He watched Sinclair, who looked summer smart in a grey suit, which had a folded dark blue handkerchief perfectly placed in his breast pocket. Sinclair was tall, a little on the heavy side, he had an engaging air, you could see he was a glad hander, a smoothie and a phoney. His thick wave of white grey hair complemented his suit. He was tanned, which always raised suspicion in Saskatchewan. Farmers were tanned of necessity from working long hours in the sun and wind, a city slicker tan spoke of indulgence. Yup, Sinclair and his juniors reeked of the city.

With introductions over, Straun went with Sinclair for a brief word in the hall. Josef took his seat in the gallery a few rows back from Straun. The lead lawyers returned and Straun glanced back to Josef and gave him a quick wink.

At precisely 2:00 pm the bailiff ordered, "All rise". The Honourable Mr. Justice Podorchuk entered the courtroom from a side anti-room. He was not a big man; somewhat curmudgeon-like with a face full of character, dominated by a rather large nose, Jimmy Durante-like, and small beady eyes that were not hostile but inquisitive. He wore horn rimmed glasses stationed half way down his nose. When he spoke, his voice was surprisingly deep and resonated unexpectantly from his small frame.

Counsel appearances were taken and Mr. Sinclair stood to begin. "My Lord, I act for Mr. Bruce Jones and his family, and today we come out of necessity seeking certain relief. A will, purporting to be that of William Jones, has been filed in this Court in application for probate." He got no further.

Justice Podorchuk interrupted in what sounded like a deep growl, "Mr. Sinclair, I have read the file. Get to what you want today and why."

Sinclair was not phased. "First, we want a caveat to freeze the estate property, such is …"

Cut-off again by Justice Podorchuk, "Mr. McNeil, what is your position regarding a caveat?"

Straun rose, "M'Lord, as I told Mr. Sinclair before court, we consent to a caveat being placed on the estate pending grant of probate."

"Caveat granted pending grant of probate. Next Mr. Sinclair."

Sinclair, still not getting the message, started speechmaking again. "My client, who is William Jones' only brother, was shocked to find he and indeed all of his family were cut out of his brother's will. They were even more surprised to find the estate was left to unknown persons in Australia. Mr. Sebastian Wright, who until recently acted for my client, wrote to the executor on June 24th seeking clarification as to whether the named beneficiaries in the will were even alive to receive under the will. Mr. Wright received no response. Therefore, ..."

Cut-off again, "You want to know if the beneficiaries are alive?"

"Yes, such would be common courtesy."

"Fair question. Mr. McNeil do you know the answer?" Justice Podorchuk looked over his glasses at Straun.

"Yes, as I told Mr. Sinclair before court, the beneficiary, Connie Thornton, is deceased. Rebecca Thornton, however, is alive."

Sinclair remained standing, and interjected, "Yes, I was told just before court. My point is simply, why wasn't my client made aware of this a month ago? It shows lack of courtesy and really points to why we had to come to court today in order to obtain this essential information."

Justice Podorchuk didn't like lawyer delay games, without saying a word, he gave Straun a charged look. "Any reason why you didn't tell counsel earlier? It is a simple request."

Straun responded, "M'Lord we had good reason." He paused to look towards Mr. Sinclair and back to Bruce and Ron Jones. "We did not inform Mr. Wright because Miss Thornton's life was in danger. It is a bit of a story, but I think the Court will see our concern."

Justice Podorchuk's interest was piqued; a boring estate battle had some bite. "You have the podium Mr. McNeil."

Straun carried on, "This past June three attempts were made to kill Miss Thornton."

He had the rapt attention of Justice Podorchuk. "Three attempts you say."

Straun went on to tell the story of the first attempt. He concluded, "Now you might ask, what does this have to do with our case. Well the

Queensland Police were of the view it was a contract killing. A note was found in the attacker's wallet, which read, 'Rebecca Rose Thornton, 8-10-43', which is her birth date, 'BEFORE,' in capital letters and <u>underline</u>d, 'June 24'. Interesting date, which as your Lordship has already heard, was the same day Mr. Wright wrote to the estate to find out if the beneficiaries were alive. Coincidence?" He shrugged and continued, "The significance of that date is under the will there is a 45-day survivorship period. William Jones died on May 10. June 24 is the 45th day."

Straun is a great storyteller and he had all present engrossed in the tale. He went on to tell the story of the second attempt.

Josef watched Bruce and Ron Jones closely. They moved not a muscle, no expression, rigidly still. They were not enthralled at all with the story unfolding; rather they sat frozen hoping no one was looking their way.

Straun went on to tell the story of the third attempt. "Three attacks. Three deaths. That was our concern and is why we did not tell Mr. Sinclair until today that Miss Thornton is alive, and more importantly, is in a safe place."

Silence. Mr. Justice Podorchuk nodded his head, and said, "Seems you had reason to withhold the information. I am not saying what you've told us shows a connection to the case before the court, only it would provide you with a possible basis for concern. Mr. Sinclair, you've got your answer; let's move on. Your next motion."

Sinclair needed to gather himself. "We next request this action be transferred to the Court of Queen's Bench in Saskatoon."

Josef was galled by the arrogance of the Sinclair and Schmidt firm. Obviously, they wanted the transfer for their own convenience, pure and simple. The message: 'we're an important law firm and your small firm is not'.

Sinclair couched the transfer request as a matter of practicality. "We anticipate a number of experts may be called upon to testify and some may be from Saskatoon or able to travel more readily to Saskatoon than to Prince Albert. Convenience dictates…"

Justice Podorchuk interrupted, "Mr. Sinclair, experts are paid witnesses. They will be well paid for their time. What about the regular witnesses from Blue River, who will likely be called? They will have to travel four hours to Saskatoon, won't they?" His Lordship did not expect an answer. "Do you have a compelling reason for this transfer other than the fact you and your firm are in Saskatoon?"

"It is, as mentioned, primarily a matter of convenience."

"Yes, but whose?" Retorted Justice Podorchuk. "Mr. McNeil, what is your position?"

"We oppose any transfer out of this Court. Blue River is within the Prince Albert Judicial District. Litigants deserve to have matters dealt with by their local courts and not to be transferred to benefit counsel. There has to be valid reasons to transfer an action and, with respect, here there is not."

Justice Podorchuk did not wait for any further submissions from Mr. Sinclair. "Motion to transfer the action to the Court of Queen's Bench in Saskatoon denied. Anything else Mr. Sinclair or have we concluded for the day?"

"One last matter. As is customary, we move to have the reasonable legal fees, which will no doubt arise in our contesting of the will, be covered from the estate proceeds. This is a long-standing practice in Saskatchewan. It allows for those, such as my clients, close relatives of the testator, to test and insure a will is valid. Otherwise many worthy claims will not be pursued, because of the costs involved."

"Mr. McNeil," said Justice Podorchuk.

"We are definitely opposed. William Jones made his desires known clearly and concisely in his will. He specifically cut his brother, Bruce Jones and family, out of the will. Now, through a side door they wish to receive payment to contest William Jones' specific instructions. Mr. Sinclair says such payments are, in his words, 'customary'. They no longer are. Two years ago, the Court of Appeal addressed this very issue in the case of *Oman v. Oman*, and the Court ruled payments for intervenors in estate cases was entirely discretionary and, of more import, the Court stated the normal cost rulings should apply. Meaning successful litigants get their costs; unsuccessful litigants do not. The Court was prompted to make this change because estate matters were becoming a lawyer's windfall, depleting, if not exhausting the money in many an estate. Look today. I stand before your Lordship alone. Across the table sit three lawyers. Three. They all travelled here from Saskatoon. Two hours here. Two hours back. Four billable hours per lawyer. Twelve lawyer hours and another three hours in court. And William Jones' estate will be asked to pay for that! The one exception the Court of Appeal noted was for impecunious claimants. I suggest Mr. Bruce Jones, the majority shareholder and CEO of Jones Trucking, is not impecunious. The bottom line is this, if Mr. Jones has a valid claim against the will, let him succeed at trial and he will get his legal expenses from the estate. Not before. Those are my submissions."

Mr. Sinclair rose to counter. Justice Podorchuk waved him to remain seated. "Motion for the estate to cover the claimant's legal expenses is denied."

"If there is nothing further, we are adjourned."

Graham Sinclair Q.C. dared not raise anything else.

Round one, a knockout, to Straun, a legal maestro who played on the hubris of Graham Sinclair Q.C.

CHAPTER 27

A few days after the hearing Josef was pleasantly surprised to receive a telephone call from Ken Barnes, "Canuck, how are you doing, my friend?"

Barnes was happy to report the series of articles in the Courier Mail about Rebecca had an impact. The Queensland Police could not hide the corruption and Barnes had interesting news. Constable Kirby had been charged with criminal offences: obstruction of justice, breach of trust, theft, possession of narcotics, and trafficking in narcotics. No attempted murder, but criminal offences nevertheless. It seemed even the Police Union couldn't save Kirby. And there was more. Stan Malton was transferred out of Goondiwindi. "Good riddance to him," said Barnes. He thought Malton was sent to a small station north of Cairns on the Cape York Peninsula. The last news involved the Taipans. Evidently, according to the Courier Mail, they had disbanded and a number of the members had joined the Rebel bikie gang working out of Brisbane. 'Rebel', Josef took note; Saskatchewan also had a Rebel motorcycle club.

Barnes asked about Rebecca. "She's a good one, she is." All Josef could say was she was safe. He didn't want to tell him her exact whereabouts.

"How's the will battle going?" Josef told him about Straun's handling of Sinclair at the first hearing.

"We get the same. Brisbane lawyers come out, know-it-alls. Generally, they get their butts kicked and head back home."

It was good to talk to Barnes. After Josef hung-up, he checked the time in Queensland and decided to give Rebecca a call. He had sent her a few letters: part law business, part personal, but had not spoken with her. Impulse took over from his normally cautious nature. He called the

Foster Ranch. Ethel Foster answered, as Josef expected, it was wonderful to hear her lazy Queensland drawl. Rebecca wasn't at the Ranch; she was off mustering a flock of sheep. Josef made a comment about the fact Rebecca would enjoy riding horses again.

Ethel laughed. "What do you take us for, a bunch of cowboys? The Man from Snowy River is long dead. No horses. We muster using motorcycles. Faster than horses and far cheaper."

Josef passed on the news from Barnes. Ethel was particularly happy to hear about Stan Malton moving on. In her words he was, "A real mean mongrel. Won't be missed." Ethel asked about Josef, his wounds, his work and she took a moment to get to the heart of what she wanted to say. "Josef, I'm going to say this straight out," she paused, "you know Rebecca means a great deal to me. I see her moping. I see her waiting for the mail and when she gets a letter from you, well you've made her day. But she deserves more than a pen pal. She has feelings for you, I know. Now I don't know what your feelings are for her, but damn it, let her know. She deserves to know, one way or the other. I've had my say."

There was silence. Josef was paralyzed by his emotions. He'd just heard what he so wanted to hear, but was too afraid to know. Rebecca had feelings for him! He managed a mumbled reply, "I promise to write her."

Ethel's words echoed in his ear. "You tell her you hear. You tell her."

After he hung up, Josef took pen in hand and wrote a letter to Rebecca. Would he have the courage to send it?

* * *

Trying to meet with witnesses and get affidavits signed concerning Old Bill's testamentary capacity was not an easy task in the middle of the all too short Canadian summer. Josef did much of the interviewing via telephone, then prepared the affidavits and set up a time to have the affidavits witnessed and signed. The easier group of witnesses were the Blue River folks.

Mr. Wallace, the banker, saw Old Bill on March 27 and again on March 29 and Old Bill had "full capacity", he "gave instructions" on opening certain bank accounts, and showed "full understanding" as to what he was doing.

Minister Knox had known Old Bill as a "semi-regular" member of his church congregation. He recalled on the last Sunday in March, which was the 26th, Old Bill attended and wanted to speak with the Minister for a few minutes after the service. It was then that Bill gave the Minister a cheque for $5000 to cover anticipated funeral expenses. Minister Knox had kept the hand-written list of requests attached to the cheque: simple pine casket, closed at the service, playing of last post, honour guard provided by the Legion, burial at Blue River Cemetery, reception at Legion to follow, open bar. Old Bill said he'd provide further instructions on a eulogy and he did.

Mrs. Maggie Cameron had known Old Bill for over 30 years and, as next-door neighbours, she saw him most every day. His mind was always "sharp", he kept up with the news via CBC radio and helped her when needed. Old Bill had slowed down a bit in the last few years, they both had, but his mind "never slowed".

However, Josef's prize witness was Marv Polanski. Josef knew Old Bill travelled to Saskatoon and he had contacted the Saskatchewan Bus Line office in Blue River. They didn't have a passenger list, but they put a driver, Marv Polanski, on the phone. "Bill Jones, sure I know him. Known him all my life. Did I drive him to Saskatoon? Yup. Let me check my rotation. Yup. Here it is March 22 to March 25. I recall I took him down on March 22. First day of my four-day rota. Bill sat in the front seat. He returned on March 25, last day of my rota. Sat in the front seat again. I remember a young, long-haired hippie tried to sit in the front seat and I told him it was reserved for seniors. How did Bill seem? Just fine. I only talked to him during the rest stop in PA. About hockey; he's a Boston fan and Toronto is my team." Marv was an important witness. First, he was independent. Second, he established Old Bill was away from Blue River from March 22 to March 25. Josef anticipated Graham Sinclair Q.C. would march in a whole raft of locals attesting to Old Bill's mental incapacity. None would be able to say anything about Old Bill's mental state during those critical few days and Josef had his Saskatoon witnesses who would.

Josef drove up to Blue River in the morning. He managed to get all the affidavits witnessed and signed by lunch time. Mrs. Cameron insisted he come by and have a quick lunch. Josef didn't mind. He moseyed over to Old Bill's place. Nothing missing from the shack. He walked the path down to the river. The boat was still tied up to the dock, as were the two logs. The boat needed bailing and Josef obliged. It was a tranquil summer day. Josef kicked himself; he hadn't brought his fishing rod nor his swim trunks. Next time.

After lunch, Josef had a meeting with Constable Richard Feeney at the Blue River RCMP detachment office. Constable Feeney was about Josef's age; he was born and raised in Northern Ontario, Thunder Bay, but as is the practice of the RCMP he was stationed elsewhere in Canada. He was tall and gangly and had an easy manner, which was well suited to a rural posting. Josef liked him immediately. Over the phone Josef had outlined he was executor of Bill's estate and was wondering whether he could have a look at the autopsy report. Constable Feeney had it on his desk at the ready.

Before handing it over, the Constable had a few questions. "I'm just wondering why the executor of an estate needs to look at the autopsy report." He gave Josef a quizzical look.

Josef decided to be truthful. "Fair question. It might be my criminal law background. Suspicious of everything, but here is the thing. I knew Old Bill for years. He was always fit and, believe me, has rescued wayward logs from the river for decades. I just couldn't see him falling. A heart attack or stroke yes. But there is more, I recently travelled to Australia to find the lone surviving beneficiary of Old Bill's estate. She had two attempts on her life, and the Queensland Police thought a contract may have been put on her life related to the estate. You see, if she is dead, then Old Bill's brother and family get the estate. I'd like to tie up this loose end and be satisfied he indeed died of natural causes."

Constable Feeney was leaning back in his wooden swivel chair listening. "Does raise some questions. His brother is Bruce Jones. I know him. Take a look. Want a coffee?" He pushed the file across the table.

"Love one, thanks. Milk and sugar."

The autopsy report form was pretty cursory. Estimated time of death was fairly inconclusive, put at between 5:00 pm May 9 and 8:00 am May 10. What was interesting is Old Bill had two injuries to his head: one to his front forehead and the fatal one to his right temple. Shattered skull fragments were driven into the brain leading to almost immediate death. No water was in the lungs. Old Bill died from the blow to the head, presumably after a fall. There were a number of photographs. One was taken of the logs tied up to the dock, where a close up caught a small pool of blood. There was also a small evidence bag, which contained a wood splinter removed from Old Bill's right temple. No sign of stroke or heart attack. Lungs were in advanced state of cancer and traces of cancer were found in the liver. Not much else.

Constable Feeney returned with mugs of coffee, handing one to Josef. All he said was, "Well?"

Josef sat back and took a sip of the coffee, which was typical police coffee, heavy on caffeine, light on taste. Josef took his time. He could say nothing; however, there were interesting findings, and he felt that if he wanted any cooperation with the police better to be forthright. "Old Bill didn't drown. Looks like he fell on the logs tied to the dock, but did you look for any signs of struggle elsewhere on the property?"

Feeney didn't take offence, or at least he didn't show it. "I did check the cabin on the property and woodshed and did a walk around the property. Nothing pointed to an altercation or robbery. Why? Do you think he was killed somewhere else and dumped in the river?"

It was a serious question. Feeney wasn't joking. He seemed to have a genuine interest. Josef replied, "Here's the thing. There were two blows, which would mean Old Bill must have fallen once. That would be face first and hit his forehead. Then he got up, must have been standing because he'd have to fall pretty hard to shatter his skull the way he did when he fell the second and fatal time."

Feeney took a sip of his coffee. "Could have been dazed from the first fall. Got up. Unsteady and fell again."

"True, but twice? And if he did fall, wouldn't he have just rolled over on to the dock, steadied himself and then gotten up. He wouldn't have tried to stand up again on the logs. Makes no sense."

Josef continued, "There's more. The splinter in the exhibit bag, taken from Old Bill's temple, is smooth. Not like a splinter off some uncut log. Has it been tested?"

"What do you mean tested?"

"I had a case a few years back that involved glass. A forensic expert from the RCMP lab in Winnipeg examined the glass and matched it to my

Old Bill's Last Will and Testament

client. I imagine they have wood experts as well. If the splinter comes from spruce then it's a match to the logs tied up to the dock. If not, this may not have been an accident."

Feeney sat comfortably in his chair sipping his coffee. He looked out the window and said, "Tell me about the estate, the beneficiary and the contract on her life."

"That might take a while," smiled Josef.

Feeney replied, "I've got the time and coffee."

Josef had his opening and told the full story. He provided the constable with copies of Old Bill's letter, the will and the evaluation of the estate.

Twenty minutes later, when Josef was done, Feeney simply said, "The forensic people might take some time. Summer and all. But I'll send it to the Winnipeg lab. I do hope it comes back 'spruce'. Much easier that way. But let's see for sure. I'll get back to you with the results. Confidentially of course."

"Understood," said Josef, "thank you officer."

"My pleasure counsellor."

A few days later Josef set off for Saskatoon. He had already contacted Margaret and John Morrison. They wanted to help in any way they could and insisted Josef stay for lunch. The gist of their evidence as to Old Bill's testamentary capacity was that Bill had full faculties. He spent the afternoon and evening of March 24 at the Morrison's. Margaret put it well, "He was determined to put his affairs in order." Following supper, John and Bill adjourned to the study sharing a brandy and a good Cuban cigar, much to Margaret's chagrin. Bill told her, "At this stage one cigar is not going to make a bit of difference." She couldn't disagree. John and Bill reminisced. They'd been through much together. In John Morrison's words, "Bill was not fixated on the past. He was still Bill Jones: stubborn, good natured and level headed."

Lunch with the Morrisons was a delight. Margaret made it all: freshly made rolls, a chilled cucumber soup, a light orange, almond and iceberg lettuce salad, and cold pieces of fried chicken followed by the highlight – Saskatoon berry pie and vanilla ice cream. As John said, "She was looking forward to spoiling you."

Josef was called upon to tell them all about his search for Rebecca. They were enthralled. With the story ended, Margaret from across the table gave a knowing smile. "It certainly seems you and she had quite the adventures. Do you happen to have a picture of her? I'd like to see what she looks like."

Josef did. He had a polaroid photo of her taken on the Gold Coast. He took it out of his wallet and showed it to Margaret.

Margaret looked carefully at the photo, taking her time. "She's a very attractive young woman and look at those eyes. Brown?"

"Yes, a deep brown."

"There is a confidence and strength about her." Margaret passed the photo to John. He simply smiled and nodded.

Margaret with a playful grin teased Josef, "Unusual for a lawyer to keep a picture of a client in his wallet isn't it?"

John came to Josef's rescue. "Leave the boy be Maggie."

Josef blushed and changed topics. "When John was a prisoner of war it must have been very hard on you Margaret?"

"Yes, it was. First, there was relief he was alive. After the fall of Hong Kong, we had no idea. It was months before we got confirmation John was a prisoner of war. Then I'd write letters never knowing if any reached him. I'd prepare Red Cross boxes, never knowing if they ever arrived. I have no idea where the letters disappeared to."

John joined in, "I received only two letters from Margaret. But they meant the world to me. We weren't forgotten. It gave me a will to live."

"I never received a letter from John until after the Americans liberated the camp." Margaret said sadly.

"John, did you get any Red Cross packages?" asked Josef.

"Yes, a couple when imprisoned in Hong Kong, which were vandalized by the Japanese. At Niigata, never. We knew Red Cross packages including medical supplies occasionally arrived at the camp, but were confiscated by the Japanese."

Josef turned to the crux of what he wanted. "John, I know Niigata is a painful memory for you, but I need your help. The biggest problem I have is the will itself. Why would Old Bill give his entire estate to the family of this Australian POW? Without a reason, it smacks of the whimsical decision of a senile old man. Can you put me in contact with other POW's who would have known Bill and who might help?"

John, without hesitation, replied, "I certainly can and will. There is an association of Hong Kong War Veterans and I still have contacts with the Winnipeg Grenadiers. Let me make some phone calls. One of the difficulties is we officers were separate from the enlisted men. They worked; we didn't. And to be honest in the winter of 1944-45 I was pretty sick. Leave it with me. I'll treat it as a high priority. From what you have told me of this young Rebecca Thornton, I want to see Bill's bequest is honoured. The least I can do for him."

After lunch it was on to the University Hospital. Old Bill's oncologist, Dr. James Schurr, was most cooperative. Usually doctors and lawyers do not mix well. However, once Josef explained the purpose of the call, the good doctor understood the importance of his evidence. Referring to Bill's file, he examined Bill on March 23rd and met him for a consultation the morning of March 24th. Dr. Schurr described Old Bill as a well preserved, physically fit man of 88 years. He recalled Old Bill fully understood the terminal nature of his illness, listened to the various options, most which were highly invasive with little realistic chance of success. Bill chose to do nothing: no radiation, chemotherapy or surgery. He was given 6 months to live, give or take. Dr. Schurr termed Bill as "stoic", "soldier like", "brave". The good doctor was of the opinion Old Bill had full cognitive understanding.

Josef didn't want to take up much of Dr. Schurr's time, however, he had a couple follow-up questions. "Would the onset of the lung cancer cause dizziness or stability issues?"

Dr. Schurr considered the question and replied, "No, only in the last stages, when Bill would have been in a weakened state."

"What about prompting a seizure or unconsciousness?"

"No, the cancer was primarily located in the lungs, spreading to other internal organs, such as the liver. I doubt it would gravitate to the brain. What one could expect, as the disease progressed, would be severe coughing fits as the lungs filled with the cancer."

Josef, mulling over what he'd learned, while driving back to Prince Albert, was confident he had a strong case to present on Old Bill's testamentary capacity. Yet, he worried as to what Graham Sinclair Q.C. might come up with.

CHAPTER 28

Graham Sinclair Q.C.'s reply came approximately a week later. A thick envelope from Sinclair and Schmidt was delivered to Josef's office. The package contained sworn affidavits from eight Blue River residents, including Bruce Jones and his wife, Mary. Bruce described how close he was to his older brother, that is until the last six months when Bill seemed confused and retreated into himself. 'Retreated into himself' is what a lawyer would say not Bruce Jones. Mary described the family Christmas dinners and how the family so looked forward to seeing "Uncle Bill". That changed. Bill changed. He became forgetful, remote and tied to the past. She recalled one instance, a few months before his death, at the local grocery store when Old Bill did not remember her at all. Josef thought "oh sure". In the box of cards kept by Old Bill not one was from the Bruce Jones' family. Six other folks from Blue River swore to the same. The picture they painted was of a lonely, senile old man. Most hurtful were the affidavits from two veterans, who described seeing Old Bill at the local Legion, on Saturday evening March 25. Old Bill evidently was watching Hockey Night in Canada; Toronto was at home playing the Los Angeles Kings. Old Bill sat alone at a table next to them. They described Old Bill as "feeble", "spilling more beer than he drank", "talking to himself throughout the game", "rambling on about war and battles long past". Sinclair needed witnesses to give evidence close to March 26 when the will was written and he dug up these two. Josef was incensed. He'd talk to the Legion bartender and started by calling Mrs. Cameron; she'd know the scoop on these vets.

"Those two! No good drunks. Spend all their time at the Legion. Alcoholics both. Probably arrived at opening time that day and never saw the sun. They'd sell their souls for a free beer." She was similarly scathing about the other affidavit providers. All seemed to be living tough and in need of money. She was disappointed in Mary Jones. "I thought she'd have more backbone."

"Don't be too hard on her," Josef replied, "there's a lot of money at stake"

"I suppose," said Mrs. Cameron, "but the more I know people; the more I love my dog."

The package of materials from Sinclair and Schmidt also included two expert reports. One was from Dr. Horace McIver, a psychologist, with loads of letters after his name, and countless certificates and academic degrees. Josef thought he was trying too hard. Dr. McIver, without having examined Old Bill, diagnosed him as a "classic retrograde geriatric". He based this diagnosis on the affidavits and an overview of the file. A retrograde geriatric suffers from short term memory loss and recedes into the past. The present is too overwhelming; there is comfort and familiarity in the past. In this case Old Bill receded back to his wartime adventures. Certain events would come to dominate his mind and he would be prone to fantasies. Ultimately, he'd become divorced from present reality and, in the doctor's opinion, that is exactly what happened here.

Dr. Horace McIver had a twelve-page curriculum vitae. Single spaced. He included trials where he had been accepted as an expert witness. Josef would check each of the trials and contact the lawyers on the other side. They'd tell him all he needed to know about the good doctor. He'd also have the firm's summer student do a research check for the cases Dr. McIver did not include on the C.V. and obtain his listed publications. Josef regarded Dr. McIver as an expert for hire, who would tell the court whatever the lawyer wanted and would pay for.

The second expert, Dr. Peter Cook, was the Head of Neurosurgery at the University of Saskatchewan. His report was more benign, Dr. Cook spoke generally about degenerative brain function typically found in geriatric patients. He did state that a person well into his 80s and living a secluded, isolated lifestyle was more likely to exhibit signs of dementia than individuals more socially active.

Josef put the estate file aside, still fuming. He had court that afternoon. After completing his matter, he saw Corporal Gerry Rolston. Rolston was assigned to the RCMP's gang unit in Prince Albert. Josef in his dealings with Rolston always found him reasonable. Josef caught up with him. "Corporal Rolston, got a minute?"

Rolston turned, and upon seeing Josef smiled. "I heard you got shot in Australia."

"Yes, I did. Other than that, a great place to visit. Can I buy you a coffee? I'd like to pick your brain about something."

"A defence counsel buying a cop coffee. That I cannot refuse."

They walked the short distance to the court house coffee shop, which was an afterthought stuffed into the basement. Coffee in hand they found a vacant table in the corner. Josef gave Rolston an abridged summary of his Australian adventures. He then tied it into what he wanted. "Queensland Police think it was a contract hit on her taken up by the Taipan motorcycle gang. I just found out recently that a number of the Taipans signed on with the Rebel motorcycle gang in Brisbane. I know the Rebels have a club in Saskatchewan. Here's my question, are the various Rebel clubs linked?"

Rolston pondered the question. "What you're really asking is whether the Rebels here could contact the Rebels in Australia to make the hit?"

"Yes."

"The Rebels are still pretty loosely linked. Not like the Hell's Angels, who are far better connected. If my memory serves me correct, there are some major Rebel clubs in Colorado, Montana and Los Angeles. Do they communicate with one another? Yes. In fact, they have occasional gatherings. I assume the Rebels in Brisbane would be part of this loose network. In terms of linking a hit from Saskatchewan to Australia through this network forget it. Too difficult to trace."

"No, I wasn't thinking about trying to trace the contract hit. I just wanted to know if there could possibly be a link."

"More than possible, if Mel Laxon, head of the Rebels here, wanted a hit he'd probably go through the Rebels. Makes sense. Do you have any information connecting him to the estate you're working on?"

"None. I was just trying to piece together why a motorcycle gang would get the contract."

"I think you've been watching too much television. Most contract killers aren't the cool, silent types. Often they are complete idiots, simply needing some money, which may apply to your two gang killers."

Old Bill's Last Will and Testament

"But these were Taipan members, not Rebels?"

"I imagine the Taipans are affiliated with the Rebels. Junior members, Rebel wannabees if you like. It's quite common for senior clubs to pass more unsavory tasks on to underling clubs." Rolston finished his coffee. "Look, if you find out a connection between your estate action and the Rebels, let me know."

They walked out of the court house together, stopping at Josef's car, Rolston looked at it with a practiced eye. "Very nice wheels."

"This was my dad's car. He loved Merc's. It has a great ride."

Rolston nodded his approval. He hesitated, there was something more he wanted to say. "Josef, I just want to give you a heads up. Laxon is unpredictable and dangerous. There are a few killings we think he was involved with, but can't prove it. Be careful."

"Great, this was going to be a simple estate file," said Josef.

"Stick to criminal law, it's safer," laughed Rolston.

* * *

Three days after receiving the package from Sinclair and Schmidt Josef received a telephone call from the man himself, Graham Sinclair Q.C. "Got our package?" Without waiting for an answer, he continued, "Interesting isn't it."

Josef was leery, best to say little. "Yes, we received it."

"Seems like the testator was not all there. You're going to have a tough time proving the will. No witnesses to the execution and all."

"We'll see."

"You've seen the expert reports. Pretty damaging I'd say."

"So, just why are you calling Mr. Sinclair?"

"Cut to the chase. I like that. I have an offer to present to Miss Thornton and you are the only person I know who has contact with her."

"You do know I act for the estate and do not represent Miss Thornton."

"All a formality, all a formality. Here is our offer. Mr. Jones is prepared to have her receive $100,000 under the estate. The remainder goes to the Jones' family. Quite generous of him. Better than nothing I'd say. She'd have to sign a release to Mr. Jones of the remainder of the estate, in exchange for her getting the $100,000. You, of course, proceed to probate with no opposition from us. We all save everyone the lawyer bills. You forward that offer on to her. We'll give you a week to get back to us. If she doesn't agree, then we'll be putting this matter down for a hearing seeking a trial requiring you to prove the will in solemn form. And, given what we have found, I don't think there is a court in the land that would find the testator had the necessary testamentary capacity."

There was no point arguing the case with Sinclair. "I'll try and contact her and get back to you, as I said to you, I'm not her lawyer."

Sinclair laughed. "Whatever you say. It's a good offer. Christ she'll be getting a $100,000 gift. Good talking to you."

After hanging up, Josef knew this was the first gambit; they'd go higher. $100,000 was but a starting point.

Scott Munroe, the firm's summer student, was waiting at his door. Scott was somewhat shy and far too deferential. He needed that kicked out of him if he was to succeed in law. "What can I do for you Scott?" Josef asked.

Scott had a copy of Dr. McIver's curriculum vitae in his hand. "Oh, sorry to bother you Mr. Manne."

Josef put his pen down, leaned back in his chair and smiled. "Scott, how many times have I told you to call me Josef. Mr. Manne makes me feel old."

"Er, sorry, it is about the research on Dr. McIver. All of his publications are in psychological journals, which we don't have. I was wondering whether the firm would cover my expenses if I travelled to Saskatoon and went to the U of S library. My undergrad was in psychology and I know my way around the library."

"Scott, sounds like a great idea. We'll cover your travel costs, meals and if you need to overnight in a hotel room, but not at the Bessborough Hotel."

"Oh, thank you. I can go in the next day or two, if that works for you."

"Do that, research into Dr. McIver is a high priority. Just let Mr. McNeil know in case he had something planned for you to do." Josef paused. "Now Mr. McNeil is old enough to be a 'Mr.'"

"Got ya."

* * *

Josef put off phoning Rebecca. He really didn't know why he was procrastinating. On the one hand he really wanted to talk to her, hear her voice. On the other hand, he was afraid. He didn't know what to say to her about them. Finally, he found the courage to call. He went into the office on a Saturday, knowing it was Sunday in Australia and knowing no one would hear his side of the conversation. He dialed the number. Ethel Foster answered. She was happy to hear from him and went to get Rebecca.

Then he heard Rebecca's voice. They talked about all manner of unimportant things. Josef turned to the offer. He emphasized the estate was worth roughly $535,000 and Bruce Jones was wanting to buy her off with $100,000. She thought Josef had to get the will approved first. He confirmed he did, and he was prepared to defend the will, but as the sole beneficiary she could enter into a side deal with Bruce Jones. What Jones was giving up was a legal challenge to the will, which could tie the estate up for years. Josef told her he thought Jones would put more money on the table. Then she asked him, what Josef knew she would ask: "What do you recommend?"

Josef had his pat lawyer answer. "Rebecca, I don't act for you. I act for the estate. What I can say is in my opinion it is early."

"Will you win if it goes to trial?" she pressed.

"I think we have a good case. The one problem is why Old Bill would give his entire estate to your mother and you. It seems crazy."

"If I accept the money, Bruce Jones wins, doesn't he?"

"Yes, yes he does," conceded Josef.

"Does he deserve to win?" Rebecca asked this question with a determined sound in her voice.

"No, no he doesn't Rebecca. Old Bill was right about his brother. He's not a nice person."

"That's what I wanted to hear you say. If we go to trial and lose, I will have gained nothing, but I also will have lost nothing. If I take the money I will have lost much, my self-respect. I'm tired of being bullied. Say no to the deal."

"Good on you Rebecca. I'll be happy to pass that on to Mr. Sinclair."

"You could also tell him the Aussie girl tells him to get stuffed."

"That would be my real pleasure."

They said their goodbyes; all was very businesslike. Josef berated himself, he still had not summoned the courage to tell Rebecca his strong feelings for her, but he resolved to send her his letter. He took it out of his briefcase, already stamped, and he walked down to the Central post office and mailed it.

CHAPTER 29

Straun, clearing his desk before leaving for three weeks of holiday at his lake cabin, set a Monday morning meeting first thing with Gabe and Josef to discuss Old Bill's estate. Josef asked Scott to sit in.

Straun started, "Okay, where are we at? I understand we have a court hearing set for this Wednesday."

Josef took the lead. "Well, first Sinclair put an offer on the table. Bruce Jones would give Rebecca $100,000 in exchange for her signing over the rest of the estate to him. I have discussed it with Rebecca. Her answer, was an emphatic no. In her words, I was to tell Sinclair 'to get stuffed.'"

"Good on her. I like that gal," said Straun.

Josef continued, "Our witness affidavits regarding Bill's testamentary capacity are ready to be filed and will be delivered to Sinclair today. I think we make out a strong case. Most importantly all our witnesses saw Old Bill shortly before he wrote the will. Regarding the affidavits filed by Sinclair, I have done some digging and I'd say almost all are shaky."

"The affidavits from Bruce Jones and Mary Jones are obviously biased, and do not talk specifically about Bill's state of mind around March 26. Four of the other Blue River witnesses are struggling, facing financial difficulties. None saw Bill within a few days of the will writing. Two veteran witnesses say they saw Bill the Saturday night before, but to be blunt their evidence is dodgy."

Josef had their attention. "I did a little probing. I spoke with the bartender on duty at the Legion Hall that night. The two veterans arrived, as was their routine, before noon and stayed all day and night. Drunks. The bartender did see Old Bill that evening; he came in late carrying his kit bag and sat alone at a table, had a beer and listened to the news then left. According to the bartender, Bill was not there for long and was certainly not watching the hockey game, as stated by the two. Their evidence is shaky."

"What about Sinclair's two experts?" Straun asked.

"The doctor from the U of S is sound, but his opinion really doesn't help them much. The key expert is Dr. Horace McIver." Josef turned to Scott. "I asked Scott to be here because he spent a few days at the U of S library in Saskatoon and uncovered some interesting findings. Scott tell Straun and Gabe what you found."

Scott was a little nervous. "Mr. Manne, asked me to check out Dr. McIver's publications. Since they were all in psychology journals I went to the University of Saskatchewan main library. I'm a psychology major. Dr. McIver listed ten publications. Five are published in newsletters, local magazines, rather than peer reviewed journals. Not much there. I then tracked the five peer reviewed articles. What I found was three were published in the Indian Journal of Psychology, which is a pretty new and obscure journal printed in New Delhi. The first article titled "Recognizing Sudden Fright Syndrome", was published in 1963. What caught my attention is the article was referring to traumatic incidents such as murders and armed robberies, which had occurred in 1959. I found that odd, not current at all. So, I started to search using those incidents. What I found was an article written in 1960, which was titled, "Eye-Witness Evidence Affected by Trauma". This article was published in the University of Wichita Psychology Journal. I have copies of both articles. Should I pass them around?" Scott looked at Josef, who nodded to go ahead.

With the articles passed around, Scott came to the point. "He plagiarized the article. His article is identical to the 1960 article, except he changed the title substantially." Scott was now getting excited. "It's identical. He changed nothing. Read the first paragraph in each, you'll see."

They read the first paragraph. Sure enough, it was word for word the same.

Josef was pleased for Scott and Straun burst in, "Well done Scott! Well done young man! Our doctor is a fraud!"

"But there is more," Scott interjected. "I checked the other two Indian articles. He plagiarized those as well. What he does is change the titles markedly, but nothing else. For example, his article "Convicting the Innocent" was from an article titled, "The Frailties of Eye-Witnesses Identifications". In the third article, "Recollection and Memory in Seniors", was plagiarized from an article titled, "Aged Witness Testimony Under Scrutiny". I have copies of all the articles. They are identical."

Josef added, "Scott also has an interesting theory about the articles selected."

"Well, I kind of wondered why he hasn't been caught. A couple things come to mind. First, the articles are from pretty minor psychology journals in different countries. But I thought the original authors might at least have discovered that their work was copied. Then I found a common denominator in the three. Each was authored by a Master's student and I could not find any other articles written by them. So, my theory is that a Master's student is just happy to get something published and they move on. They never bother checking or reading up on their article. Just a theory."

"But a good one," Josef backed him up. "I can also tell you I am almost finished going through the list of cases Dr. McIver provided where he testified as an expert witness and I have spoken with a number of the lawyers who faced him in court. They describe Dr. McIver as: a fraud, hired gun, arrogant ass and a few other choice words. I think it safe to say we have a great deal of ammunition to use against Dr. McIver."

"Sounds good," commented Straun, "Gabe, what about a survey of the two sections of land? Where are we at?"

"Still nothing. I called my surveyor last week and stressed we needed the survey."

"How much are we paying him?" asked Straun.

"$500."

"Well, here is what I suggest. Up the ante to $800, but we need the report by next Monday. If not, we go elsewhere. We need the survey. We're flying blind right now. Okay."

Gabe wasn't too pleased. He was always tight with money, but replied, "Can't be Monday, it's the banking holiday, make it Tuesday. I'll contact him and put it to him."

"Good," Straun continued, "I too have some information. I had a corporation search done on Jones Trucking Ltd. What it showed was two years ago there was a shareholder change. Bruce Jones used to control 75% of the shares. Now he has 51%, his wife has 5%, his son, Ronald, 15%, and a few other relatives have another 4%; however, the big change was that a new shareholder got control of 25% of the company. The shareholder is a numbered company. We tracked it down. The numbered company's sole shareholder is Marlene Ducharme. Mean anything to you?" Straun looked around the room. "No, well we checked her home address. She lives common law and her partner is Mel Laxon. Name mean anything to you?"

"Head of the Rebel motorcycle club in Saskatchewan," Josef answered.

"Correct, it seems the Rebels are now linked with Bruce Jones."

"I can provide some further input," said Josef. "I spoke with the RCMP officer in PA who deals with gangs. He advised me the local Rebel club could connect to international Rebel clubs and yes that could be how a contract hit found its way from Saskatchewan to Australia. The possible links are there, but difficult to trace. He also told me Mel Laxon is dangerous. Thought I'd throw that into the mix."

"Alright, Gabe, we have a motion set for Wednesday, where Sinclair will move to set the matter down for a contested hearing arguing Bruce Jones has a genuine issue requiring a trial on Bill's testamentary capacity. The hearing will probably be in September. What are your thoughts?"

Gabe took his time. "In my view, notwithstanding some of the problems with the affidavits, the hearing judge is not to rule on credibility. Therefore, the affidavits are accepted at face value. With that in mind, I think Sinclair has presented enough to raise questions about Bill's testamentary capacity."

Josef replied, "I agree with Gabe's assessment, as it now stands. Sinclair has three key witnesses: the two veterans and Dr. McIver. However, I do think all of these witnesses are suspect and could well have their credibility destroyed at trial. But why wait until then? Why not move to cross-examine these witnesses on their affidavits before the hearing to determine if we go to trial? Their evidence contradicts our witness affidavits. In a normal proceeding I could move to cross-examine the witnesses on their affidavits to try and clarify these contradictions. If one witness says X and another witness says Y, courts allow us to clarify that contradiction through cross-examination of the witnesses. I understand in estate actions normally cross-examinations on affidavits are not done, but that does not mean such cross-examinations cannot be done. Especially if we don't ask to delay the hearing on whether a genuine issue exists. So, my proposal is simple, let's go after these witnesses now and not wait until trial."

Straun took a moment. He was thinking. Finally he replied, "Why not? And I think Justice Podorchuk is intrigued enough by the case he'd approve the cross-examinations. Josef, it will be on you. I'm on holidays. Gabe?"

Gabe, naturally cautious, was keen. "Why not indeed. Josef, give it a try. Can't hurt."

"I'd like to. Since I have to call Sinclair to tell him to get stuffed, I'll advise him we are agreeable to an early hearing date in September on genuine issue."

"Good. Anything else? Scott good work on that research. Folks I'm going on holidays." Meeting adjourned.

* * *

The Wednesday hearing was again in Courtroom Four. This time only one lawyer turned up from Sinclair and Schmidt. His name was Jonathan Westcott and he had been part of the threesome from the previous court appearance. Courtroom Four was filled with lawyers coming and going. This was motions' day and the docket was full. As is custom, matters are not called by number, but according to the seniority of counsel. The rule is simple, more senior lawyers do not have to wait, juniors do. There is logic in the tradition, in that the more senior the lawyer the more valuable his or her time. Josef and Jonathan waited their turn. Mr. Justice Podorchuk was his rascally self. Lawyers caught unprepared wished they were, delay and dalliance were not tolerated. The cases moved along. Soon the matter of 'Application for Probate of William Maurice Jones' was called.

Young Mr. Westcott made his request to have the matter put down for hearing on whether a genuine issue exists challenging Mr. Jones' Will, which if successful, would require the executor of the estate to prove the will in solemn form at a trial. He requested an early hearing date in the fall session. Justice Podorchuk turned to Josef. "Your position Mr. Manne."

"We agree, M'Lord and are in favour of an early hearing date in the fall." Josef knew to be brief and to the point.

"Very well," Justice Podorchuk had his calendar out, "contested hearing gentlemen?" He asked looking over his glasses.

Both counsel agreed.

"After reviewing the affidavits, seems like much contested evidence. How long do you need?"

Josef could see young Mr. Westcott was adrift. He stepped up to the podium. "We'd estimate two days."

Justice Podorchuk, without looking up, said, "Nope, too long, I'll set it down for one. The affidavits will be in, only oral argument. One day is plenty, no more. Let's have this set down for 10:00 am Friday, September 8, for one day. That way you'll have incentive to be done before the weekend. Anything else?"

Josef was already standing and replied, "Yes, M'Lord we request an order to cross-examine certain of the witnesses on their affidavits, namely: Henry Hartman, Phillip Pruitt and Dr. Horace McIver. Our request is limited to these witnesses and is prompted by the contradictory evidence they give in contrast to our witnesses…"

Justice Podorchuk interrupted, "It is quite unusual to cross-examine on affidavit evidence in probate matters Mr. Manne."

"Unusual yes, but not prohibited. Your Lordship has read the affidavits and commented on there being "much contested evidence". Surely to find a genuine issue for trial we need an opportunity to challenge the genuineness of these witnesses' affidavits. Ours is a limited request and we do not seek to delay the ultimate hearing set for September 8."

Justice Podorchuk had a slight smile. "Mr. Westcott, what is your position?"

Poor young Westcott, he was like a deer in headlights. He was not prepared for this. He had driven up to PA simply to set a hearing date. "My Lord, I'm sorry I do not have any instructions concerning cross-examination on the affidavits."

"I didn't ask you about instructions. What is your position?" Justice Podorchuk wasn't going to let the young lawyer off pleading no authority.

Young Westcott, to his credit came up with an argument. He argued the order was unfair in that Mr. Manne would have an unfair advantage in cross-examining their witnesses, but they, in turn, were not allowed to cross-examine Mr. Manne's witnesses. And if such widespread cross-examination were to occur, they may as well move to a trial of the case.

"Mr. Manne," growled Justice Podorchuk.

"First, there is nothing to stop Mr. Westcott and his firm from cross-examining any of our witnesses. They are available. However, that probably won't happen because there is nothing to cross-examine them on. We, on the other hand, see an imperative need to cross-examine these three witnesses on the genuineness of their affidavits. Second, as mentioned, we are only seeking to cross-examine a limited number of witnesses. This is not wide-spread cross-examination."

Justice Podorchuk, after hearing the submissions, paused. The courtroom waited. "It is an unusual request brought by counsel for the estate. However, I have reviewed the various affidavits submitted by both sides and there are significant contradictions in that evidence. The Court of Queen's Bench is a court of equity; there to see justice is done. A hearing on whether a genuine challenge to a will merits a trial is an important safeguard, weeding out frivolous claims from those with merit. Therefore, I see 'genuineness' lies at the heart of any such hearing and evidence bearing on that issue is worthy of being received. Accordingly, I will allow the Executor's request to cross-examine the witnesses named on the following conditions: 1) all witnesses will receive the prescribed fees and travel expenses; 2) counsel for Mr. Bruce Jones may cross-examine any of the affidavit witnesses on contradictory evidence filed by the Executor; 3) all cross-examinations are to be completed before September 6, 1972 and 4) there will be no adjournment of the September 8 hearing date arising from the cross-examinations. Thank you counsel."

* * *

On Thursday, August 3, Mel Laxon and Bruce Jones took a table in the far corner of the Debden Hotel Bar. The bar was dingy, drab and dark. Everything needed paint or replacing. It was a place to drink, nothing else.

Having said that, it was a perfect place to meet, if one desired privacy and did not want to be seen. Laxon and Jones wanted both.

They got their beer and turned to business. Bruce started. "You never told me the ten thousand was to pay for a hit on the girl. I put the money up to find her that's all."

"Bullshit," Laxon replied crisply, "what did you expect for ten thousand? If they'd done the job, you'd be in it for a further $15,000. Look on the fuckin' bright side you saved yourself $15,000. Now what is happening with the lawsuit?"

"I was just told there's going to be fuckin' cross-examination of some of our witnesses. More lawyer fees. Bloody lawyer on the other side is a pain in the ass."

"Lawyers are like that. So, what you're telling me is you aren't getting anywhere?"

"Well we have a hearing set for September 8, where we show we have a case to go to trial."

"Yeah, and if it goes to trial when will that be for fuck sake? We need this thing wrapped up. Have you made an offer to the girl?"

"Yes, we offered her $100,000 to walk away and she turned it down."

"Up the fuckin' ante. What's the estate worth?"

"Half a million."

"Offer her half, $250,000. She'd be silly not to accept."

"Easy for you to say, it's my $250,000." Bruce was defensive; money was precious to him.

"Yeah, well if we don't get the land and can't start mining with access to Alberta we lose millions. Remember, this is my pipeline into Alberta and the oil camps. Who else is blocking us?"

"The lawyer, Josef Manne, as I said he's a pain in the ass."

"Well, I'll look into him. Maybe we need to persuade him to pressure the little girl to agree to our deal."

"I don't want nothing to do with that. You hear," said Bruce.

"Getting a bit squeamish, are we? Too late for that my friend. We got too much on the line." Laxon gave Bruce a long stare. "We okay." It wasn't a question.

Bruce nodded, downed his beer and left.

Laxon sat sipping his beer. He was soon joined by a man, who had been sitting near the front door of the bar throughout. The man was solid, brush cut, looked like a logger or a trucker except upon closer inspection one would see that his hands were soft. Not the hands of a manual labourer. And his clothes were selected with care. The golf shirt was new and clean and the pants were pressed. No blue jeans. The man took a chair opposite Laxon. He didn't say anything.

"Nevada, got to get this thing moving, too much money is at stake. I want you to dig up whatever you can on the lawyer fighting us. Name is Josef Manne, check him out. Tail him. Find out his weak spot."

Nevada merely asked, "When do you need it by?"

"Soon. The Aussie girl turned down $100,000. I told Jones to up it to $250,000. If she doesn't accept that then we know she's not going to settle. This lawyer might be the problem. Maybe she's following his tune."

Laxon took a long pull on his beer. "I don't like obstacles and these two are becoming obstacles." He then leaned in and whispered to Nevada, "We might need to get rid of him. You think about that. But it would have to look like an accident. Nothing messy that could come back to bite us. We don't need the cops to start looking into our dealings with Jones. You start thinking about that. An accident."

Nevada merely nodded.

They finished their beers and left.

* * *

Nevada had no qualms about killing. He'd killed before. Business was business and if Laxon gave the order he'd do the kill. He kind of enjoyed the challenge, the excitement and, yes, the rush in taking another person's life. He felt no remorse, no empathy. It was a job and he was good at it. The 'why' didn't worry him. If Laxon wanted somebody dead, so be it.

He turned his mind to the how. A normal hit was easy. Pick your target, wait for a good time and do the kill. Easy, kill and run. Sure, careful planning was needed because the most important thing was not to get caught. Nevada learned from youthful mistakes that put him in prison. He now was far more careful and meticulous, more professional. The result was unblemished success over the last ten years. How many kills? He had to think, four.

To make a killing look like an accident is hard. Various ideas percolated in his mind. A gas line explosion at Manne's home was rejected, too complicated and would need to involve too many others. Suicide was another thought, but didn't fit the profile for Manne. Successful lawyers don't kill themselves. The police would be sure to smell a rat. No, the easiest and best option was an automobile accident. Faulty brakes were an option, but not a good one. First, there were few dangerous roads in the area where failed brakes would result in a fatal accident. Second, cut brake lines were very obvious. This did not rule out an automobile accident, only a different type.

Nevada focused on a collision. Car accidents were routine. Nevada thought and the more he thought the more things fell into place. The idea of a head on collision germinated. Of course, a head on collision would be suicide for the other driver. Or would it? It would not be suicide if the other vehicle was a truck, the bigger the better. Truck drivers invariably survived; car drivers did not. Nevada had a truck and driver in mind.

Derek Ford owned a beat-up old gravel truck and, in the winter, he used it to plow snow. The truck was a real monster, with the reinforced metal front frame for plowing, it would be lethal in a head on collision. And Derek Ford was perfect as the driver. He was a heroin addict, who was in over his head with the Rebels, owing them over $15,000. The debt kept growing and growing and there was little chance Derek could ever pay it off. In past years Derek had been in debt before and he had done a few jobs for the Rebels to pay them off. This time the debt was much higher and the job would require a much higher payback.

Would Derek take the job? Most likely. Two things Nevada knew: first it was his only way out; he was too addicted on heroin to quit. Second, Derek would keep his mouth shut; he had in the past. But, Nevada smiled to himself, he'd make sure of Derek's silence. After the accident, Nevada would see that Derek died of an overdose. He'd provide Derek with a gift of high-grade heroin laced to kill – and it would. Yes, he'd have a little talk with Derek.

CHAPTER 30

The long weekend in August sees most city folks escaping to their favorite camping spots or cottages. Josef stayed in town. His baseball team was entered in a weekend tournament. The teams were mixed and for most of the players it was social fun, of course, there were the odd players who took the games far too seriously. His team, the Lawlots, was composed mostly of lawyers, law staff and partners. Josef was one of the more experienced players. He actually played baseball as a kid. Others on the team were novices.

The weekend weather was superb, no rain, a fresh breeze and balmy temperatures. During the team's first game, Josef sat relaxing on the bench waiting his turn to take the field. He was still resting his right leg and didn't want to overdo it. He leaned back and looked around the various baseball diamonds. Four games were on the go. He caught the eye of a man sitting by himself in the stands at an adjoining game. The man quickly turned away. Strange. Sure, there were a few fans about, mostly family and kids running around and assorted members from teams waiting to play. But this guy wasn't dressed to play ball. Why waste a long weekend to sit in the sun watching sandlot baseball?

His game ended. The Lawlots won. Josef actually hit a triple, should have been a homer if he had a good leg. Josef looked for the man; he was gone. The team only had 90 minutes before their next game and Josef was sent for a beer run. He hopped into the Parklane and headed to the nearest beer vendor. As he drove, he checked his rear-view mirror. A black car pulled out and was following, or so he thought. Josef parked at the vendor and he glimpsed the black car, an Impala, driving past. Probably nothing. Josef returned to the team with the beer. He never saw the man again.

That evening the team had a barbeque. When Josef returned home he was not followed.

Once at home, he felt uneasy. Was his mind playing games? He checked the doors and windows. All were locked. Everything seemed to be in its place. Josef was a neat bachelor. He surveyed his den carefully. Nothing was amiss and he scolded himself for his paranoia. Yet, the next morning before leaving for baseball, he left a small piece of paper wedged in the front door; if the door was opened the paper would harmlessly fall to the floor. More paranoia?

Another glorious day perfect for ball. No man seen. Josef started to doubt himself. That night he drove a team member home, she lived across the city on the flat. On his way he saw the black Impala; he was sure. Turning into her cul-de-sac, the Impala had no choice but to drive right around before exiting. Two men were in the car. After dropping her off, Josef returned to the main thoroughfare, no Impala. Ever watchful, Josef returned home. He left the Parklane in the driveway and entered the house through the garage door. Inspecting the house, he checked the front door. There lying on the floor was the small piece of paper. The door had been opened. Upon inspection he found nothing out of order, but that didn't make Josef feel any more secure. He went into the basement, to the cold cellar and went to a crate, which was usually filled with potatoes, and in the false base he took out his father's prized World War II relic, a German Luger. Josef carefully unfolded the oiled wrap. The handgun was there as was the box of 9mm bullets and two magazines, each capable of holding eight bullets. His father had taught Josef how to care for the gun; how to dismantle, clean, load and most importantly how to respect the weapon. Josef had an antique permit for the Luger, but he had not taken it out for years. Now he sat down in the basement, cleaned and oiled the handgun, opened the bullet box and loaded the two magazines. He was torn. He didn't want to take the gun, yet he had to admit he felt more safe and secure. He took out the holster, which fitted on to a belt and put the Luger into the holster, not loading the magazines into the weapon. He returned upstairs. That night he slept with the Luger in his night table with magazines nearby.

* * *

Nevada reported back to Laxon. He had done a thorough background on Manne. "Nothing. He is single. No family. Sister died a few years ago of an overdose. Parents both dead. He lives in the parent's home. He's a clean freak. Fuckin' house is as neat as can be. No girlfriend or boyfriend. He's not a bad ball player. Couldn't find any debts. Owns everything outright."

Laxon listened and replied, "Alright, get one of the boys, and have a word with him. Nothing too much. Just pass on the word he needs to convince the Aussie girl to do what is best for everyone. Phrase it like that. Nothing more. You know what to do. No headlines. Be persuasive but don't get carried away."

* * *

On the holiday Monday Josef was looking forward to a day of fishing. He was going to drive up to Blue River and fish off Old Bill's dock, perhaps take the row boat out. He packed a lunch, loaded the fishing gear into the trunk and debated: gun or no gun? He went back inside and returned with the Luger and magazines. He was on high alert and it wasn't long before he saw the black Impala. What to do? He made up his mind.

Travelling over the North Saskatchewan bridge he took the road west. The Impala followed at a safe distance. North on to a gravel road, dust billowing behind obscured his stalkers. They'd have no trouble following him. West on to a narrow track, no more than a logging trail. The dust was gone, as he rose to the top of a hill he caught a glimpse of the Impala, still tracking him. Lost Lake was about a mile distant. Really it wasn't much of a lake; it was more like a clear water slough, plenty of tiny hand size perch but not much else. The lake was surrounded by scrub bush mostly mangy poplars and a smattering of black spruce. It was deserted. Josef parked the Parklane in the small circular grass parking lot. A path led down to the lake. He took the holstered Luger and magazines out of the glove compartment and popped the trunk. Taking the Luger out, he loaded the magazine and took a fishing rod out leaning it against the car and waited for his stalkers to arrive.

The black Impala slowly pulled into the lot and parked 30-40 feet back of Josef's car. Josef looked at the car. There were two men. He recognized the man from baseball, who was in the passenger seat. They sat in the car. Finally, the driver got out and went to the trunk of his car and the baseball guy got out. The driver had retrieved a baseball bat. Pretty hard to fish with a baseball bat thought Josef. Their intentions were clear. The driver smacked the head of the bat into his free hand. They were confident, cocky.

Baseball guy closed his door and spoke, "We'd like to talk to you." The voice was assertive, demanding.

Josef looked at him and replied, "And if I don't want to talk to you?"

Baseball guy smirked, "We can be pretty persuasive lawyer man." The two advanced towards Josef.

Josef turned and calmly waited until they were about twenty feet from him then he lifted his right hand from the trunk and aimed the Luger at baseball guy. The two men stopped.

"Whoa, we just want to talk," said baseball guy, "settle down."

Josef was pissed, really pissed. He was tired of being stalked, hunted and hurt by thugs. "Like I said, I don't want to talk." Aiming at the driver. "You, drop the baseball bat". The driver looked at baseball man, bat still in hand.

"Don't look at him. Look at me. I said drop the bat or I'll shoot you right now. No qualms at all. I said drop it." The driver did.

"Good, now hands up. Both of you. Hands up."

Baseball guy spoke again, "Mr. Manne, you're not going to shoot us." He gave a mock laugh.

Josef replied in a low, cold voice, "Damn right I will. You see no one is around. It would be your word against mine. I bet both of you have criminal records. I don't. And I've been attacked and shot at in the last two months by bikers. I assume you two are bikers. So, we have two bikers who follow me to a fishing hole and I defend myself. No one would believe otherwise. Fact is I have a free card to shoot you both. Damned right I'll shoot. So just give me a reason to shoot. Hell, I don't even need a reason."

Baseball guy was not so confident anymore. The reality of their situation set in. They were trapped by their prey.

"Now, I want you both to loosen your belts and drop your pants."

"I'm not going to drop my pants for nobody," fired back the driver.

"Where do you want the bullet? Which leg?" Josef aimed and asked.

"Drop your pants," the baseball guy told the driver. They did.

"Good, now down on the ground and put your hands behind your back." Both did.

Josef moved forward. "Don't try anything. Safety's off and this gun is a might sensitive at times. I'm going to reach in and take your wallets out of your back pockets." Josef carefully leaned over the driver first and got his wallet. Then moved to baseball guy, who whispered as Josef was getting the wallet, "You don't know who you're messing with. You have no idea."

Josef whispered back, "Oh, but I do."

With the wallets in hand, Josef went through them and took out their driver's licences. He read out their names: baseball guy was Calvin Gold, and the driver was Mike Lahosky. Josef kept the licences and threw the wallets on to the grass near the two.

"Don't move boys," Josef went to the Impala and opened the driver's door. He kept the Luger aimed at the two of them. He took the keys out of the ignition, popped the hood and moved to the front of the Impala, lifting the hood he seized the distributor cap wires and ripped them out. Then he leaned back on the front of the Impala and spoke to baseball guy. "Calvin, what is it you want to talk to me about? You had something important to tell me?"

Calvin had moved his face to the side to look at Josef, he didn't reply immediately. "Simple message, talk to the Aussie girl and convince her to do what's best for everyone. That's all."

"That's it," said Josef, "you didn't need a baseball bat for that did you." Josef moved to the back of the Impala, keeping both in view. He opened the trunk and there he found a sawed-off double-barrelled shotgun. He was thankful that Mike had opted for the baseball bat and not the shotgun. He breached the shotgun and saw it was loaded. He emptied the weapon, allowing the shells to drop to the ground. He then took hold of the barrel and slammed the stock into the trunk of a hereby poplar. The stock shattered. Josef threw the rest of the shotgun into the woods. He walked around the car, checked the front and back seats for other weapons and opened the glove compartment. No other weapons.

Josef turned back to the two. "You tell your boss to back off. You tell Laxon that." Josef moved to the Parklane. "Now, I'm going to leave you here. A few miles back there's a gas station and phone. Nice day for a walk. Don't get up until I'm gone."

In the rear-view mirror Josef saw the two scrambling up. He smiled to himself. How did he feel? Euphoric, but that would only last as long as the adrenalin was flowing. What had he just done? Would he have shot them? He honestly didn't know. Fortunately, they didn't know either. What he did know was that he was now a target and would need to be very careful, very, very careful.

What to do? He was on the main highway, left was Prince Albert, right was Blue River. He turned right. A day of fishing and reflection was needed.

CHAPTER 31

Josef arranged to meet Corporal Rolston at RCMP headquarters in Prince Albert first thing Tuesday morning. He informed Rolston of Darlene Marchand's interest in Jones Trucking. Both were on the same wavelength, with the new highway going to Alberta this would be a perfect conduit to move drugs to Northern Alberta.

Josef handed over the driver's licences. That got Rolston's attention. When he looked at Calvin Gold's licence all he said was "Nevada". Rolston went on to fill Josef in. Nevada was the so-called sergeant-at-arms for the Rebels motorcycle club in Saskatchewan. In other words, he was the force behind the throne. He kept law and order within the club and meted out punishment when warranted. He had a violent criminal history, but was clean for the last ten years. "Clean" did not imply law abiding; he simply had not gotten caught. In sum, Nevada was dangerous and smart, not a person to mess with. Rolston asked the inevitable question, "How did you get the licences?"

Josef told the story. Rolston was both bemused and concerned. Bemused because he knew Nevada was a fastidious dresser and visualizing him lying on the ground, dirtying his top of the line clothes made Rolston laugh. Then, when Josef told him he had them drop their pants, Rolston lost it. After Josef finished, Rolston shook his head. "And you survived? You have just made an enemy of the worst kind."

Rolston became serious, Josef had stirred up a hornet's nest. He needed protection, which the RCMP couldn't provide, but he did have an alternative. "You know handguns in the west have had to be licenced since the 1930s, and cannot be carried without reasonable cause. We, of course, regulate the registration. Give me a moment, do you have the existing handgun permit with you?" Josef handed it over. Rolston left and returned about twenty minutes later. He handed Josef a new permit. "This authorizes you to carry a handgun based on reasonable cause. At least you can arm yourself."

"Thanks, but you don't sound too optimistic about my chances of living to old age."

"Who knows, maybe Nevada has developed a sense of humour. Just be careful. Be on the lookout. You might want to put your law firm on notice, just a precaution. Without more, our hands are tied. You mentioned the message for you was about the Australian woman, which is consistent with the contract on her life. But why all this trouble? What is the connection? The estate, even at half a million, isn't worth this effort. If you find out; let me know. By the way, where's the Luger?"

Josef sheepishly said, "At home."

"Doesn't do you much good there," replied Rolston.

Josef headed to the office. He would call Straun, Rolston was right, the law firm should know of this potential danger. As soon as he got to his desk, Gabe barged in, waving a report in hand. "We got the geology report. We know why Jones wants the parcels of land."

"Why?" asked Josef.

"The sand. The sandstone cliffs are high grade, very high grade, silica sand, which is prized in the oil and gas industry and guess where the new highway is going? To the Alberta oil fields."

Josef was caught up in Gabe's excitement. "How much? What are we talking about?"

"Millions, the sand could be open pit mined, and with the Alberta market a fortune awaits."

Josef finished where Gabe was going. "Especially for a trucking company. So, Bruce Jones really only cares about the two sections of land. What about other deposits around there?"

"My guy thinks it highly unlikely there are other viable deposits. Not with the same purity as found at the Sand Cliffs."

"I'll call Straun, sit in," said Josef. He let Gabe tell him the news and then Josef told both about the incident on Monday. Straun suggested a quiet memo and a discrete word to the staff about suspicious parcels received or unauthorized people poking about, an 'alert' but not an 'alarm'. Josef would take care of it.

After Gabe left, Josef read the report in detail. He had no idea how valuable sand could be. The report was unequivocal, this was an incredibly valuable silica deposit – if developed. His thoughts were interrupted by a call from Graham Sinclair, who was not his jovial self. He didn't like to have his junior lawyer "ambushed" about the cross-examinations on the affidavits. He accused Josef of unprofessional dealings. In all of his years of practice he had never before witnessed such "unethical conduct". Josef let Sinclair blow and bluster. "Look if you have a complaint, file it with the Law Society."

Sinclair moved on. Against his advice, Bruce Jones was now willing to split the inheritance with Miss Thornton. He was prepared to offer her $250,000 in exchange for her transferring the estate to Bruce Jones. "A generous offer", "one she could not refuse", and it was "final". Sinclair ended the call, "Put it to her and get back to me by the 15th of the month. Good bye."

Things were moving. $250,000 was a far more reasonable offer, given the estimated estate value of $500,000. But it was an unreasonable offer, given the estate's true value was millions. No point informing Sinclair of that fact.

Josef called Corporal Rolston, left a message. Rolston got back to him late in the day. Josef filled him in on what he had just found out. The silica sand made all fall into place. Laxon's 25% stake in Jones Trucking would be worth millions and Jones' trucks hauling the sand would be a wonderful conduit for drugs to make their way to the wealthy oil camps of Northern Alberta. It all fit. Rolston appreciated the information. He finished the call by saying, "This also makes Laxon more dangerous. Take care."

Josef ended the day. He inspected the Parklane before getting in and starting it. His heart missed a beat as he turned the ignition. No explosion. He knew he should never have gone to see The Godfather movie. Once at home, he checked all doors and windows and retrieved the Luger. If this was his new life, it sucked.

On Wednesday he had a full day trial. His client, a regular, was charged with break and enter. The client was adamant he was innocent. Yes, he was in the vicinity of the warehouse broken into; yes, he ran when he saw the police (he always runs when he sees the police); but no, he didn't do it. Josef tended to believe him because in the past he'd take his punishment for his crimes. The police officers testified they followed his client's footprints in the freshly fallen snow to the scene of the crime. The trial judge found footprints in the snow raised a suspicion, but did not prove guilt beyond a reasonable doubt. Josef's client was acquitted.

As Josef left the courtroom a familiar voice said, "Good job lawyer man." It was Nevada, dressed in a blue blazer and grey pants.

Josef looked at him and replied, "Thank you Nevada. Here to shoot me?"

Nevada laughed. "No, shooting here is too messy and too noisy. If I were going to kill you it would be a shiv in the back, silent and quick. I was in the neighbourhood and saw you had a trial and decided to say hello." He walked with Josef. "You know my nickname."

"Yes, as soon as I showed the RCMP your licence they said 'Nevada'. You seem to be well known there."

"I bet," he asked, "Am I to expect a visit about our little incident the other day?"

"No, I told them it was a misunderstanding. You wanted to talk to me and I didn't want to talk to you." Josef turned to go down the stairs, "Just like right now."

Nevada said these parting words, "Remember what's best for the Aussie girl. See you lawyer man."

Josef knew Nevada's visit was not a coincidence. He wanted Josef to know even in the halls of justice there was no safe haven. It was a power play by Nevada. Josef's mind churned, Laxon must know of Sinclair's latest offer, which was to expire on August 15. Why not buy himself some time and protection? He'd tell Sinclair Rebecca was out rounding up cattle and could not be reached until the end of August. They don't know what he'll advise her to do about the offer; however, so long as they think there's a chance he'd persuade her to accept they'll not act. He'd first call Rebecca and put the offer to her. If she accepts then everything is over, but somehow, he didn't think she would. If she rejects the offer, he'd call Sinclair and get the extension until the end of the month. Of course, he couldn't tell Rebecca about the threats because she might accept the deal for all the wrong reasons. He'd call her on Friday, Saturday Queensland time.

The next day he received a telephone call from Constable Feeney in Blue River, who started the conversation by saying, "It's hickory wood." Nothing more needed to be said. The blow to Old Bill's head was not inflicted by a spruce log; he had been clubbed. Feeney asked Josef if, as executor of the estate, he would authorize the RCMP to search Bill's property. Constable Fenney didn't want to go through the paperwork of getting a search warrant. Josef gave him permission adding, "The key to Old Bill's shack is under the iron dog boot scraper." Josef then suggested Constable Feeney might want to contact Corporal Rolston, RCMP in PA, as there was a gang connection that might interest him.

Later in the day he received an even more interesting call, this time from John Morrison. After exchanging greetings, John got right to the point. "I have some names for you. First, there is Dr. Walter Trott. He was a doctor at Niigata Prisoner of War Camp." John provided his address in Winnipeg. "He's retired now, but his mind is sharp. I spoke with him and he expects a call from you."

The second name was that of Teddy Branagan. "He was a private. I don't know him. He wasn't in my unit, but I'm told he was close to Bill. He's at the Deer Lodge Veteran's Hospital in Winnipeg. I'm afraid he came out of the war pretty scarred physically and mentally. Tread softly. I have spoken to the head of the hospital and he will assist. I hope these men can give you the answers you need."

Josef was energized. Things were happening quickly. He contacted Dr. Trott, who had a quiet, English accent. He'd be available on Monday, August 14. Concerning Teddy Branagan, the head of the hospital recommended a Sunday visit, when the hospital was most open to visitors. Teddy Branagan didn't have many visitors and the head was sure he'd be happy to meet him. Josef decided to drive to Winnipeg on Saturday, which would take 10-12 hours.

Friday came. He made his call to Rebecca. He was nervous. Had Rebecca received his letter? Should he ask? What could he say? He heard the Australian double rings on the line, answered by Ethel. They chatted for a minute or two then Ethel said, "You don't want to waste your money on me. I'll get Rebecca, she'll be delighted to speak to you. Hang on." At least Ethel was positive, thought Josef.

He heard Rebecca's soft voice. "Hello Josef."

His heart was pounding, blood racing through his veins. "Good to hear your voice Rebecca."

"Josef, I have something to say to you." Oh God, thought Josef, I'm being dumped, right off the top, she's going to ream me out. "Josef, I'm just going to say it, I miss you so much; I care for you deeply."

Josef could breathe again. Did he hear her right? He managed to say, "You got my letter?"

"Yes, it arrived yesterday. I only wish you said it to me at Brisbane Airport. I thought it was all over between us, and the kiss was our first and last – a kiss goodbye."

"Rebecca, I was a fool; there was so much I wanted to say but didn't. I never had the courage to say those things to you directly."

There was a distant "yes" over the line followed by a 'click'. The Foster Ranch party line had been breached. Rebecca and Josef both laughed.

The ice was broken between the two. They talked anew. More personal, more meaningfully. Eventually, Josef turned the conversation to Old Bill's estate. He informed her of Sinclair's new offer.

"$250,000 is a lot of money," said Rebecca.

"Yes, basically half the value of the estate, but you need to know the estate is actually worth far more." Josef went on to tell her about the silica deposit and the new road going to the oil fields of Alberta.

"So, they are offering me a pittance."

"Yes."

"Cheap bastards," Rebecca laughed.

"Yup. All they want are the two parcels of land at the Sand Cliffs. They could offer you the entire estate minus the parcels."

"What do you recommend?"

"Well, let's look at where we stand. First, I think we have a strong case to support the will. If you reject their latest offer in all likelihood we go to the hearing on September 8. If we win, frankly I think they are toast. The estate will be yours. They may appeal, but Gabe tells me such appeals rarely succeed. Second, worst case scenario, we lose the September 8 hearing. In that case the matter will be set down for trial to prove the validity of the will. It just means there is a trial. Negotiations continue. I'd imagine they'd want to settle without a trial. We're in a good position."

Rebecca summarized the situation. "If we win, we win. If we lose, we fight another day."

"Exactly."

Rebecca made up her mind. "Reject the offer. Thank Mr. Sinclair, but still tell him to get stuffed." She laughed and continued, "I'd like to come to Prince Albert for the hearing. Would that be okay?"

Josef's heart skipped a beat. He'd love to see her. Would she be safe? Josef needed to tell her. "Rebecca I'd love to have you here, but I do need to tell you more. Bruce Jones has tied himself up with a local motorcycle gang, The Rebels. There is a Rebel chapter in Brisbane. The original contract to kill you probably came via the Rebel connections, which we can't prove. The bottom line is there are millions at stake and these people are dangerous and desperate. There is also evidence Old Bill's death was not an accident; he may have been murdered."

"Oh, that poor man."

"Yes, they may have murdered an old man who had terminal cancer. By the by, have you got a will?"

"You'll be happy to know I do. The Foster Ranch lawyer did one up for me. So, I should be safe."

"I should also tell you I'm driving to Winnipeg tomorrow to track down some soldiers who were with Old Bill and your father at Niigata Camp. I'll keep you posted."

"That is exciting. You sound so busy. Do you really want me to come?"

"Rebecca, I'd love for you to come, but I don't want to put you in danger."

"I'm tired of running scared, I want to stand up to these bastards and give them what for."

"Alright, give me possible dates and I'll make the arrangements. It also buys us time. I'll call Sinclair, tell him you are intending to come for the hearing and he can talk to you directly about the latest offer."

"Dates, are easy. Any time around the end of month. You make the reservations and I'm available."

"Miss you."

"Miss you too."

The words carried far more feeling now.

Josef's final call of the day was to Graham Sinclair. Josef informed him Rebecca was out mustering cattle and would not be available until the end of the month. Sinclair huffed and buffed. Josef let him go on. He then told him she intended to come for the hearing and if Sinclair wanted to talk to her in person that was the time. Josef played to his ego. "I've told her in the past about settlement and your latest offer is generous, but she doesn't listen to me. You're probably more persuasive." Sinclair seemed pacified.

CHAPTER 32

The Parklane purred east on the Yellowhead Highway towards Winnipeg. Josef felt free, alive and happy. The rolling Saskatchewan parkland gave way to the rich flat Manitoba soil, once glacial Lake Agassiz. The crops of wheat and barley were thick, high and waiting harvest. The day breezed by and he arrived in Winnipeg, where he found a motel on Portage Avenue, near to Assiniboine Park and to Deer Lodge Hospital. He had made good time and went for an evening stroll, buying an ice cream and walking leisurely across the footbridge over the Assiniboine River to the park.

Sunday, he was ready for his visit to Deer Lodge. The woman at reception was young, fresh, rosy cheeked with flaming red hair. She radiated positive vibes.

As Josef approached, she eyed him and immediately asked, "How yuh doin today?"

It caught Josef off guard. He smiled. "I am just wonderful, and you?"

In a heavy Irish brogue, she said, "I'm grand."

"Don't tell me. I know your accent…"

She interrupted him, "Now don't you go about; if you say I'm English I'll knock your block off."

"No, I was going to say Scottish."

"Get on with you."

"I'm looking to see a patient; his name is Teddy Branagan."

"Ah Teddy, room 432, I'll write this down for you, Dieppe Wing on the fourth floor." She gave Josef the room details and directions.

"Thank you so much."

"My pleasure, Teddy doesn't get many visitors, you might go for a walk outside. He'd like that."

Josef gave the young woman, Darla was her name, an endearing look. She cared. "I just might do that."

The hospital smells grew stronger and stronger. Josef found room 432, the door was ajar and Josef gave a quiet knock. "Come in. Come in. Been expecting you." A squeaking voice called out from inside the room.

Teddy Branagan was a tiny man. He was stooped, frail, washed out; it was as though he had just been liberated from the POW camp and was emaciated. He had wisps of straggly grey hair. His face was wrinkled and his eyes were a dull bluish grey. He had difficulty moving. Pain seemed to shoot through his body.

"Head came to see me. Says you want to know about Bill Jones."

"Yes, Bill was a friend of mine. He died a few months ago and I'm executor of his estate. Do you remember Bill from Niigata Prisoner of War Camp?"

Teddy sat back in his chair. "Yeah, hell of a place."

There was a wheel chair in the corner, Josef asked, "Would you like to go outside? It's a beautiful day."

Teddy brightened. "Love to. Did Darla put you up to that? She's a sweetheart."

Josef replied, "I can't lie, she did suggest it."

Josef got the wheelchair, helped Teddy up and followed his instructions on getting him into the chair. As Josef wheeled him by reception, Teddy waved to Darla and she blew him a kiss.

Teddy gave Josef a quick tour of the grounds and they found a secluded spot with a bench under the shade of a willow tree. Josef found out Teddy was 50. He looked 70. He was a 'lifer' at Deer Lodge, couldn't hold down a job, too broken to work, too much pain from arthritis. He blamed that on the years in POW camps. Bones were brittle was the way he put it. Brings back bad memories. The Japs were cruel, inhuman. He sat in silence. Josef wanted to direct the interview. Did he mind if he recorded it? No, easier that way.

"How did you know Bill Jones?"

Old Bill's Last Will and Testament

"Bill was older you know. I was so young. Barely 20 when the fighting started in Hong Kong. God, I was scared. I thought for sure they were going to kill us. Our unit surrendered but that didn't mean much to them. Beat us. I was shit scared. At the camp, Bill came over to me. I think he could tell I was terrified, shaking and all. He told me the story of the Great War and waiting to over the top into battle and how scared he was; thought he was going to shit himself. But he went over all the same and survived, didn't know how. He told me there was no shame in being afraid, because we all were. It was like my dad talkin' to me. Saved me. He asked me if I'd take his back, and I said I would if he'd do mine. From that day forward, we was partners."

"Niigata, hell on earth, cold, black, gloomy. Bill and I stuck together. I think the Japs respected Bill because of his age, and how he carried himself. He was a soldier: head held high, shoulders back, brisk walk. Bill was a batman for a Captain and he'd go between the officer quarters and enlisted men. He worked in the hospital, and got me a spot there as well. Probably saved my life. I couldn't have handled carrying coal down at the docks. There were metal dumpsters the men had to push up and down the ramp; the men were skin and bone, weak and they'd fall and be crushed to death. The guards didn't care. Bill saved me."

"Did you know an Australian Officer; his name was Charles Thornton?" Josef waited afraid to breathe.

Teddy retreated inwardly. "Yes, always Lieutenant Thornton to me. He was a brave man, brave man."

"Can you tell me about him? I understand he died on January 31, 1945." Josef waited.

"It was cold, so cold that winter. The men who worked at the coal docks brought back a bit of coal and we made stoves out of old oil drums. But we were always cold. The snow was high and wet; it would freeze and rot your feet. So cold." Teddy lapsed into silence and then continued, "I first saw Lieutenant Thornton when he came to be with an injured American flyer, who was the Lieutenant's navigator and was in a bad way. I think he had been injured when their plane was shot down. The Lieutenant cared for him. I remember he told Bill and I that was what Aussie mates do; they care for each other. The navigator hung on for about a week and the Lieutenant was there by his side. He wasn't going to let his navigator die alone. After that, the Lieutenant kept coming back to help at the hospital. He didn't have to you know, officers didn't have to work, like us enlisted, but he did. Cleaned out bed pans, changed bandages, washed men when they soiled themselves, most of those officer pricks did nothing. Good man. He was alone you know, no other Aussies or New Zealanders. Bill and I became his friends; even though he was an officer and all he never pulled rank."

Teddy chuckled. "You know those Australians don't like authority much."

"How did he die?"

"Japs murdered him." Teddy replied. "They tied him to a pole in the muster yard, bloody cold, they stripped him down to his undershorts. There he died. Nobody could survive the cold. Bill and me, we took him down, carried him away to be cremated. Cremated us they did. No burials, didn't want to have us contaminate their land I guess. Bill, I remember, he stood his ground and insisted the Lieutenant be dressed in uniform for cremation. He went toe to toe with the guards. I thought they was going to kill Bill then and there. But they knew deep down Bill was right."

Teddy was fading. "Need a drink? A rest? Something to eat?" asked Josef.

"A lemonade would be grand."

Josef left to get one from the cafeteria. When he returned Teddy was fast asleep. Josef went back to the cafeteria and got a bag of ice. He wanted Teddy to have a cold drink. About 45 minutes went by and Teddy shook himself awake. Josef had the cold drink ready. He took a deep sip; you could see the joy of that drink pulsating through him. He picked up from where he left off.

"It was towards the end of January and a Red Cross shipment meant for us arrived at the camp. We could see from the hospital there were Red Cross medical supplies. Problem was we never got the Red Cross packages. The Japs took them. We might get a few worthless odds and ends, but no medical supplies for sure. The supplies were stored in a barrack outside our camp. In the past the Japs quickly moved the supplies out, usually the next day. We knew that. Bill was beside himself, his Captain was in a bad way. Pneumonia I think. He cared for him like a doting nurse. Bill told us he was going to steal some of the Red Cross medical supplies. We both told him if he got caught he'd be beaten for sure or killed, but he'd made up his mind. Next thing yah know the Lieutenant says he's in. Said he was tired of seeing men dying and wanted to do something, fight back. That left me, and I couldn't let them down. I was in too."

"Bill was clever. He'd been thinking about this for a while. You see at that time in the war there were regular air raids and all the lights would go out and the moon was waning and it was snowing; all good for us. The guards were mostly useless, bored and drunk. You see, nowhere for us to go. We'd stand out like a fox in a hen house. Bill had thought things through. There was a drainage trench running parallel along the fence line then it turned to run through the compound where the supplies were stored. Bill had already cut some of the wire gauge fencing near the ground, now covered by the snow and it had never been repaired. We could follow the drainage trench, go under the fencing, get underneath the barrack block and break in. Simple."

"That day we took a few surgical gowns from the hospital. One of the doctors caught us and asked us what we were doing. Bill simply told him, "You don't want to know", and the doctor turned a blind eye. That night after roll call and supper, slop would be a better word, the air raid siren went, which was our signal. We met at the hospital, all wearing white. It was still snowing, which was good cover for us, and we crawled and kneed our way along the trench. The sirens stopped and we lay low for a time, another air raid and the siren blew again. By this time, we were at the fence and sure enough we pushed the snow aside and there was the hole. We prodded a few of the fence wires up and slid under slick as can be. We crawled fast to a point where we were only fifteen or so feet from the supply barrack. From there we ran for it and crawled under the barrack. Bill had with him a metal lever, like a crowbar, and pried up three of the boards, enough for me to get through. I was the smallest. Bill told me we needed medical supplies, particularly sulfa tablets. I had a small candle. Didn't take me long to find the boxes, which were about two feet by two feet and a foot deep. Not too heavy. I showed one to Bill and he nodded that I had the right one. I went back and got two others and wiped the floor down. We put the flooring back, and tied it down in a makeshift way and were ready to go back."

Teddy had finished his lemonade. He licked his lips. Josef put some broken pieces of ice in his glass. Teddy sucked and chewed on the ice. When he was ready he continued. "The second air raid was over and the lights were back on. We waited. No other raid. But the snow was coming down harder and there was no moon with all the cloud. It was bloody dark. We decided to chance it. I was the first to the trench. Keep in mind we each had a box. Bill followed me. We crawled along the trench towards the fence. Lieutenant followed. As soon as he landed in the trench we heard a Jap call out. It was a guard walking towards us from the other side of the compound. I was right beside Bill and I could sense him getting ready to stand up and give himself up. But the Lieutenant beat him to it. He stood up, having covered the box with the surgical gown. He put his hands up and walked towards the guard. I thought the guard might shoot him. He didn't. He hit him with the rifle butt and shoved him towards the compound gate. I crawled like a badger to the fence. Bill did the same. He went back and got the Lieutenant's box. We rammed the boxes under the fencing, crawled through and continued toward the hospital. Bill talked to one of the doctors, who took control of the boxes. We left the gowns and returned to our hut."

Teddy took a long suck on a piece of ice, "The next day the Lieutenant was carried out and tied to the post, naked but for his underwear. He'd been beaten. We watched from the hospital. It was so cold. He sat there. Not saying a word. His head was bowed. Some of the Jap guards in walking by would kick him, punch him. He never made a sound. I think it was his message to them. He'd die in silence. And he did. The doctor went out in the late afternoon with Bill and me. He was dead." Tears welled up in Teddy's eyes and flowed down his cheeks. He choked out, "He was a brave man. We owe our lives to him."

Josef could hardly speak. His throat was tight and dry, "How did Bill take it?"

Teddy gathered himself, "Oh, he took it hard. I remember Bill insisted on going through the Lieutenant's kit. You know the dog tags, any last letters and stuff. I sat on a bed nearby. Bill was going through some of the Lieutenant's personals when he let out a wail and buried his face in his hands and sobbed. Never saw him cry before. I didn't know what he had found. Then he showed me; it was a photograph of a pretty woman holding a little baby girl. That's when it hit; they'd never see him again. Never." Teddy was crying.

He couldn't go on, and they both needed a break, so Josef went and got more lemonade. When he returned they sipped their drinks in silence. Eventually, Josef asked, "Did the medical supplies save lives?"

"You bet they did. The doctors were thrilled to finally have something to give the men. Bill's Captain was saved. You know we never spoke again about that night. Never. But I could never forget." Teddy looked at Josef sadly and said, "You know they forgot about us. Everybody."

"You're not forgotten. Private Branagan, you're not forgotten." Josef wheeled him back to his room. Once settled, Josef explained to him why he was interested in what happened at Niigata. Teddy was tired, but would be up to sign an affidavit tomorrow late afternoon.

As Josef was leaving the hospital he saw Darla, he walked over to her and simply whispered, "You take good care of Teddy."

Without saying a word, she put her hand over his and gave it a pat. He left. It had been a good day, but emotionally draining.

The next morning, he drove across the Assiniboine River to a part of the city called River Heights. The streets were lined by tall elms whose spreading limbs made a cathedral canopy. The houses, mostly 1930's or 40's vintage, were solid, tasteful stucco and brick. Josef found Dr. Trott's street. His home was a sturdy 1930s two story, winged roof and front veranda. An elderly gentleman was tending a flower garden in the front. Josef parked just down the street and walked towards the house. The man stood up from his tending and stretched his back. He watched Josef approach and spoke, "Mr. Manne, I presume." He took off his garden glove to shake Josef's hand.

"Dr. Trott, good of you to see me."

Dr. Trott, with a twinkle in his eye, replied, "One doesn't turn down John Morrison too often. Come, good timing, I have finished my gardening for the day. Shall we sit on the veranda; it is a lovely day. Take the chair, the rocker is my throne and may disintegrate in any moment. I'm going to get myself an iced tea, like one?"

"That would be nice, thank you."

"Oh, don't thank me yet, you haven't tasted it. My Merle used to make the best iced tea. She passed away a few years ago. I try, but it is not the same." He retired inside the house. Josef admired the comfort of the veranda. Newspapers, books and magazines adorned the coffee table. Dr. Trott probably spent many hours in the worn wicker rocker. He returned with two tall crystal glasses filled with ice, a pitcher of iced tea and a platter of Dad's oatmeal cookies. Dr. Trott poured the iced tea. Josef took a sip; it was superb, not too sweet, more tea tasting than sweet. He complimented the doctor, "You made this from scratch, didn't you? This isn't a pre-mix."

"Iced tea from a mix is an American abomination," Dr. Trott replied. "John told me you have some questions about Bill Jones. Sorry to hear that he passed. He was a good man. Had a good life though. What is it you want to know?"

"First, do you mind me taping this conversation. My note taking is a bit slow." Dr. Trott waved his approval. With the recorder on and checked, Josef continued, "Actually, I am primarily interested in knowing about an Australian Airforce Officer, Lieutenant Charles Thornton. He died at Niigata in January 1945."

Dr. Trott took a sip of his iced tea, a cloud passed over his gentle face. You could see he was a kind man, whose caring and emotion lived close to the surface. "You are asking about a time that even after all these years is raw for me. I do not know if I have fully healed from my time at Niigata. I know many of the men carry with them far worse scars than mine." He put a closed fist to his mouth, rubbing his nose, and lips. His kindly green eyes, hidden partially by thick, busy eyebrows, kept focused on the ground.

"That young man, Lieutenant Thornton, did not deserve to die the way he did. He was trying to help all of us and the Japanese tortured him and killed him. I pronounced him dead. Did you know that?" He finally looked at Josef, who shook his head no.

"I don't know for sure, but I think he was one of the soldiers who broke into the Red Cross supplies and stole medicine for our men. I do not know that for sure. I do know Bill Jones brought the medicine to me the night before Lieutenant Thornton was killed. Bill had with him a young private, I forget his name…"

"Teddy Branagan," Josef offered.

Old Bill's Last Will and Testament

"Yes, a little whiff of a man. Bill and he worked at the hospital. Bill kind of took the young man under his wing. I was on night duty and the two of them arrived in surgical gowns, carrying boxes of medicine. Bill gave them to me and said something along the lines of 'don't ask'. I took and hid them in our various stash hideouts so the Japanese wouldn't find them. They returned the gowns. Oh, one other thing, Bill asked me to take care of Captain Morrison."

He paused, took a cookie and munched on it. "You know how painful it is for a doctor to see people die, who you could save, if you only had medicine or equipment. During my time at Niigata I was largely a caring mortician. There was little I could do for most of the men. They were being starved and worked to death; every prisoner was skin and bone. Dysentery swept through the camp, lice, bed bugs fueled infections, broken bones couldn't be properly set. I had no medical weapons to work with. The medicine Bill and private Branagan brought saved lives; it certainly saved the life of Captain Morrison. It also cost, I believe, Lieutenant Thornton his life."

Dr. Trott, took a moment, Josef could see the emotion within him rising as he remembered. "The next morning at roll call, Lieutenant Thornton was brought out from the guard house. He had been beaten and was naked except for his underwear. Two guards dragged him to a post in the yard and tied him to it. The Commandant had done that before. The day was cold. It was end of January and a wicked wind blew in from the north across the Sea of Japan. There they left him. Throughout the day guards in passing would kick him, hit him with their rifle butts, slap or punch him. He never responded. Never called out. It was as though he was in a self-induced trance. I could see the Japanese were befuddled, why wasn't he pleading for help, pleading for salvation? He was left there until after evening roll call. I was then allowed to go to him. Bill and Private Branagan came with me. Lieutenant Thornton was dead. No doubt hypothermia."

"You know the Japanese really did not know what to do with us. Prisoners weren't taken by the Japanese and their samurai code saw dishonour in surrender. For a Japanese soldier surrender was not a practical option; it was no option. You'd fight to the death and, if you did not, you were a coward not worthy of being a soldier. That is how they saw us, unworthy human beings. That did not justify what they did. Humanity, common decency, must prevail and they should have been held accountable. Kato, the commandant, was a cruel, psychotic man. He was responsible. I filed a war crimes report about the death of Lieutenant Thornton. Not much came of it; cold war politics. Kato spend a few years in prison and was released. We needed the Japanese on our side against the communists. The Canadian government, in particular, did nothing. What is the saying, 'The surest way for evil to prevail is for good men to do nothing'? Edmund Burke, I think. Canada did nothing." He was quiet.

"Do you recall how Bill reacted to Lieutenant Thornton's death?"

"No, not really. There was so much death you see. We were all working hard to survive. Sorry, can't help you much there. What I can say is Bill and he were friends. Unusual, Bill wasn't an officer and the Lieutenant was an Australian. But I think the Lieutenant enjoyed doing something, helping out at the hospital. I watched as he nursed an American flyer. He was so tender, hardly left his side. The Lieutenant was different, independent, not by the book. Bill was the same."

He quietly added, "At Niigata, I witnessed the best of men and the worst."

The interview over, it was only as Josef was leaving that Dr. Trott asked, "What does Lieutenant Thornton's death have to do with Bill Jones?"

Josef smiled and told him, "Bill left his entire estate to Lieutenant Thornton's widow and daughter. The estate is valued at over half a million dollars."

Dr. Trott beamed. "Good for Bill and you needed to know why he'd do that?"

"Yes," Josef replied.

With the affidavits prepared and signed, Josef was eager to return to Prince Albert. He decided to drive part of the way back that evening, stopping at Yorkton, Saskatchewan. The sun wouldn't be setting until about 8:30 pm. He'd finish the drive the following day going through Saskatoon. Josef felt John Morrison deserved to hear in person what had happened at Niigata.

CHAPTER 33

After receiving the forensic report on the wood splinter, and speaking with Manne, Constable Feeney did call Corporal Rolston at RCMP Headquarters in Prince Albert. They had a long and productive conversation. The RCMP Major Crimes Unit North was contacted and a meeting was immediately set up in Prince Albert.

Constable Feeney was excited. He had not been involved in many homicide cases. At the meeting Feeney was tasked with much of the ground work at Blue River. Two additional Major Crime Unit officers were assigned to him. They'd start with a thorough search of the property and canvas of the area. Feeney would be in charge of both. He wasn't optimistic: the time of death was broad from late in the day on May 9 to the early morning of May 10; the crime scene had been compromised in the interim; Manne himself tidied the old man's house when in town for the funeral; and whether anything was taken in a robbery wasn't known. There was not much to go on.

Feeney and the officers began their search of the property. Their primary interest was the murder weapon. A scuba team was on call, to search the river, if needed. One of the officers entered Old Bill's shack, which was tidy and organized. The most lethal wood weapon found was a large wooden spoon. The rest of the acreage was similarly in order. Mrs. Cameron had a local boy cut the grass. The officers slowly walked the acreage looking for signs of disturbance. Fenney concentrated on the path down towards the lake. There had been a number of heavy thunderstorms in the past month, which would have washed away much evidence.

He entered the woodshed. Even Bill's discarded mess had order. There was a lifetime of rusting tools, not to be thrown out: an assortment of splitting axes, hoes, shovels, sledge hammers, iron wedges, manual drills and bits, all manner of cutting saws and a semi-new chain saw. What caught his eye was a spare axe handle leaning against the wall near the doorway. He called one of the officers over to take photographs, carefully bagged the axe handle, closed the door to the shed and put police tape across it. A forensic team was requested, both to examine the woodshed and the dock for blood residue; they'd be on site the next day.

The axe handle was brought to Prince Albert, where a fingerprint expert dusted for any prints. No prints at all, which meant the axe was either wiped clean or its users always wore gloves. Either was possible. The axe handle was sent to the forensic lab in Winnipeg for comparison to the splinter and for more thorough examination for blood.

The forensic team arrived the next day and had double frustration. The woodshed revealed nothing. It was ruled out as the scene of the attack. The dock was another story; blood was everywhere. However, the blood was not human, but fish.

The canvas turned up some leads. A pick-up truck was observed driving on the highway in the early evening of May 9. Mrs. Cameron was no help for that evening, because Tuesday night was bingo night at the local recreation centre. She never missed it. Feeney wondered if the killer knew that.

Feeney and the officers interviewed friends and relatives. The officers didn't say much, other than they were looking into Bill's death. The Jones family was targeted. They were an uncooperative bunch. Monosyllable answers were the norm. Bruce, Mary and his daughter's family were at the family farm. Never left. Except Mary and the daughter went to bingo on Tuesday night in Blue River. Ron was with his family as well. Tyler and Alex were fishing at Dore Lake. Left Tuesday early afternoon and returned home early evening on May 10. Could anyone verify that? No. Ron vouched for them returning on May 10, with a good number of walleye cheeks on ice. How'd they get to Dore? Drove in Tyler's pick-up, 1963 Ford, black.

Feeney and his team were suspicious. The officers went to work recanvassing Blue River. Had anyone seen Tyler's truck the night of May 9, morning of May 10? A farmer living south of town on the highway leading to Prince Albert recalled seeing, what he thought was Tyler's truck parked at an abandoned gas station just south of town. He knew Tyler's truck, all black. Remembered because no reason to be parked there. Figured he might have been with a girl. That was it. Not enough to do anything with.

Tyler and Alex were prime suspects. Alex, of course, because he was a member of the Rebels. They had motive, or at least their father, grandfather and Mel Laxon did. Feeney was certain the boys would never turn on each other but Tyler was the weaker of the two. Feeney and his team decided to keep Tyler under a loose surveillance and find out as much as they could about him, his beefs, desires, relationships.

The forensic analysis came back from Winnipeg much faster than the earlier report on the splinter, which had taken weeks. Homicide cases are given priority. The splinter was matched to the axe handle. They had the murder weapon. A small trace of human blood, was absorbed into the handle where the splinter had broken off. It was type O, same as Bill Jones.

Feeney met with Sergeant Frost of the Major Crimes Unit and Corporal Rolston at Prince Albert Headquarters. They brainstormed. They had a murder weapon. Odd, the weapon was from the property. One would assume the murderer would have brought his or her own weapon. Had it been a break and enter gone wrong and the killer just grabbed whatever was available? But if that were the case, why put it back? Why fake an accident? Thieves, who get caught, panic and run. No, dumping the body by the logs was deliberately intended to look like an accident. If it were an intended killing the Jones boys were prime targets, especially Alex. Assuming the value of the silica find, Bruce Jones and Mel Laxon had strong motive. Kill Bill Jones and Bruce would assume he'd get his brother's estate. The will was a surprise, which explains why the surviving beneficiary under the will, Miss Thornton, was targeted. How to prove it? They were at an impasse.

Corporal Rolston, who had been quiet through much of the brainstorming, now spoke, "Remember the cartoon a few years back, Rocky and Bullwinkle." Both Feeney and Sergeant Frost looked at him quizzically. "The arch villain in the cartoon was Mr. Big. I know you're wondering where this is going, well last year I know a unit in Major Crimes South pulled what they called a 'Mr. Big' sting. One of my friends was involved. It was a murder case. Young woman disappeared. Ex-boyfriend was the prime suspect. He wasn't talking. Case was stalled. A Mr. Big sting was tried. A couple undercover cops, from narcotics, befriended the boyfriend. Invited him to join their criminal organization. I think they simulated some drug deals. Not sure of the details. In any event the boyfriend was interested; however, in order for him to become a member he had to meet Mr. Big, who would demand absolute loyalty. They'd heard about the cops sniffing about concerning his ex-girlfriend. Mr. Big might help. He had influence with the police. A meeting was arranged in a swank hotel. Mr. Big interviewed the boyfriend, demanded absolute truth, he needed to know everything from the boyfriend. Mr. Big didn't want any surprises. You know what, the boyfriend confessed he killed his girlfriend. What did he do with the body? I'm told he laughed, said he buried her atop a freshly dug grave. Pretty smart hey. Except, the confession to Mr. Big was all recorded. The boyfriend was arrested on the spot and the young woman's body was found in the grave yard exactly where the boyfriend said it would be. Why don't we do a 'Mr. Big' on Tyler?"

Sergeant Frost was the first to speak. "I've heard about that case. I think Major Crime South has been trying to keep it out of the media for obvious reasons. No entrapment, because what is being uncovered is a past crime and not entrapping an accused to commit a new crime."

"I don't think a Mr. Big would take much time with Tyler. If we are wrong, and don't get anything, then it absolves Tyler. If he confesses like the boyfriend, we solve a murder and maybe, just maybe can get those who put Tyler up to the killing. Richard your thoughts?"

Feeney liked it, "We are at a dead end. This is like a cold case. Tyler seems to be our best bet. He's a loner, works pumping gas, odd jobs at a gas station. Not bright, passed grade 12, but that was it. Doesn't have much of a future. Joining a criminal organization could be his ticket. The one problem is Alex already is a Rebel and if we assume Tyler was involved with Alex in the killing then he's already tied to the Rebels."

"I've thought about that. What if our undercover boys pretend the Hells Angels are looking to move into Northern Saskatchewan and they are in secret discussions with the Rebels; taking over the Rebels. But the Hells Angels want their own people. Hence a Hells Angels scout and recruiter arrives in Blue River. Trust me these narcotic undercover boys are very believable."

Old Bill's Last Will and Testament

Sergeant Frost interjected, "Except the Hells Angels aren't in Canada yet."

"True," replied Rolston, "but Tyler doesn't know that."

Sergeant Frost nodded and asked, "What is the cost in manpower and time?"

"I can put you through to the officer, who was involved in the boyfriend scheme. He'll be able to put you on to his officer in charge. But I don't think we need to be too elaborate and aim for a two week or so sting. I also think there is a bigger picture here; if we can link the killing of Bill Jones to the higher ups in the Rebels we gain a great deal."

Sergeant Frost looked at both Feeney and Rolston, "I'll get the wheels moving. Gerry contact your friend ASAP."

Mr. Big was in motion.

* * *

In mid-August, Nevada dropped by to see Derek Ford, who lived in a decrepit one room trailer north of the river. The trailer was propped up by assorted timbers, but it still had a noticeable lean. No plumbing, there was an outhouse nearby, which leaned even more than the trailer and its door hung on one hinge. The yard was strewn with junk, an old Chevy truck was stripped down in front of the trailer; its engine block sitting on the ground nearby gathering rust. Derek's monster truck was parked next to the trailer and the plow lay beside it covered by weeds.

Nevada stepped carefully on to the wooden steps; the second step was broken. He knocked and stepped back. No way was he going to cross the threshold into that cesspool of a trailer. There was movement in the trailer.

"Yah, who the fuck's there?"

"Derek, it's me, Nevada, we need to talk."

Silence.

"Come on Derek, I only want to talk. I have a business proposition for you."

The trailer door creaked open and a dishevelled Derek Ford emerged. He was gaunt and unhealthy looking, had pasty pockmarked skin and facial fuzz trying to form a goatee. Even though it was mid-day, it looked like Derek was just waking up.

"Come on Derek, move it. I haven't got all day." Nevada walked away from the trailer to his car. Derek was tall and lanky and had a lazy hunched over saunter, arms moving out of synch with his legs. He was wearing a sweat stained T-shirt and pants brown from dirt, but may have started out as blue jeans, and his boots were Salvation Army rejects.

Nevada began, "Derek, my man, you got yourself into a $15,000 hole." Derek started mumbling about making payments. Nevada cut him off. "Stop. Think I'm a fool. You know damn well, there isn't a hope in hell you'll ever be able to pay that money off. But I have a way out for you. Listen." Nevada outlined what he wanted him to do. Derek listened, but baulked. His old truck was all he owned and he wasn't keen on sacrificing it in a head-on collision. Nevada explained his insurance would cover any accident. He also told him accidents happen all the time when deer jump out in front of a car or truck. That would be his story, a deer spooked both drivers and they swerved into one another. They missed the deer but not each other. Derek needed little convincing, a drug addict's cravings usually take precedence over everything else in life.

"Details to follow. Don't tell nobody. Understand?"

"Yah. Who am I going to hit?"

"Better you not know. Does it matter?"

"No, not really."

Nevada gave Derek a few hits of heroin as a down payment and left.

CHAPTER 34

Rebecca's flights were booked; she'd be arriving in Saskatoon on September 1. Josef was nervous and anxious to see her. His focus now, however, was on the cross-examinations of the Blue River witnesses. The examinations would be conducted in McNeil's board room. No judge would preside, only a court reporter to transcribe the evidence and the lawyers were to police themselves.

The day arrived, Thursday August 24. Josef had deliberately suggested a 1:00 pm start time, ostensibly so that Sinclair and the witnesses could travel to Prince Albert and return home on the same day; his real reason was it gave both Hartman and Pruitt time to have a few drinks. Upon arrival, Scott showed them to a waiting area. He then joined Josef in the boardroom and whispered in his ear, "they've had a liquid lunch".

Josef called Hartman first; he had been told by Mrs. Cameron that he was the ring leader, Pruitt the follower. He started gently, establishing Hartman had served in the Canadian Army in the liberation of the Netherlands. Manne then confirmed what Hartman had said in his affidavit. Cross-examination is like stacking cards; you need to build up the stack before you knock it down. The examination went as follows:

Manne: You and Mr. Pruitt were at the Blue River Legion on March 25 of this year, correct?
Hartman: Yes.
Manne: According to your affidavit you were watching the hockey game between Toronto and Los Angeles?
Hartman: Yes.
Manne: You also say Bill Jones was there also watching the game?

Hartman: Yes, he was mumbling to himself.

Manne: And according to your affidavit he did that throughout the game. That is what you say?

Hartman: Yes.

Manne: I just want to be clear, your evidence is that Bill Jones was at the Legion on March 25 from the start of the game to the finish?

Hartman: Yes.

Manne: The game started at 6:00 pm?

Hartman: Yes.

Manne: It ended at about 9:00 pm?

Hartman: Yes.

Manne: You and Pruitt arrived at the Legion that day about noon, correct?

Hartman: I guess.

Manne: You stayed there all day?

Hartman: Yah, it's a second home for us.

Manne: And, of course, you had a few drinks throughout the day?

Hartman: A few.

Manne: Now a few months later, a lawyer from Mr. Sinclair's firm came to the Legion, didn't he?

Hartman: Yes.

Manne: He asked about whether anyone had seen or talked to Bill Jones, in late March, something like that?

Hartman: Yes.

Manne: You and Pruitt put up your hand, right?

Hartman: Yes.

Manne: And it would be fair to say he told you he was acting for Mr. Bruce Jones looking into Bill's mental capacity?

Hartman: Something like that.

Manne: Asked you whether he seemed crazy, forgetful?

Hartman: Things like that.

Manne: And to be hospitable, no doubt, he bought you and Pruitt a beer?

Hartman: Yah.

Manne: Maybe more than one?
Hartman: Don't recall.
Manne: Anyway, that is when you told him your story about March 25?
Hartman: Not a story, we told him what happened.
Manne: I just want to be clear, so there is no mistake, on March 25, at the Legion, you saw Bill Jones watch the hockey game between the Leafs and the Kings from start to finish. Correct?
Hartman: All correct.
Manne: Both you and Pruitt together gave your statements?
Hartman: Yah.
Manne: You made these statements together?
Hartman: Yah.

Josef was now ready to shift gears, and attack. Calling a witness a liar is a chancy thing to do, as a cross-examiner, no one likes a lawyer who throws mud, unless it sticks. In this case he had the proof.

Manne: Mr. Hartman, I want you to listen very carefully to my next question because I'm going to give you a chance to come clean. Mr. Hartman, what you said about Bill Jones on March 25 in your affidavit is not true, is it?

Hartman looked uncomfortable. He was looking for a lifeline. Sinclair couldn't help him. He chose indignation and slurred out his answer spittle flying from his mouth.

Hartman: No. How dare you call me a liar!
Manne: I have spoken to the bartender. He tells me Bill Jones arrived after the game. The bartender is mistaken?
Hartman: He's not mistaken, he's lying.
Manne: The bartender also told me Bill was carrying his kit bag and only stayed to have one beer. He's mistaken about that?
Hartman: Lying.

Manne: Well, we also know Bill Jones was in Saskatoon on Saturday March 25 and returned to Blue River by bus. You don't know when the Saskatchewan Bus Lines bus arrives at Blue River do you?

Hartman: No.

Manne: I'll tell you; it arrives at 10:00 pm. Except on that day, March 25, the bus driver told us it arrived at 9:55 pm. Bill Jones was a passenger on that bus. He could not have been watching the hockey when you say he was?

Hartman: I know what I saw.

Manne: Mr. Hartman you told the lawyer what he wanted to hear. You made all of this up?

Hartman: No.

Manne: No? You and Mr. Pruitt together for a few beers didn't make all of this up?

Hartman: No.

Josef ended his examination. Hartman's denials were running hollow indeed. Sinclair and his junior slunk down in their seats. No eye contact with Hartman; no reassurance. Defeat. They asked for a short adjournment. Josef agreed, but also reminded them and Mr. Hartman there was to be no communication with Mr. Pruitt about the evidence just given. Sinclair shot Josef a vicious look, but said nothing. Scott took a seat in the waiting room across from Pruitt, just in case.

The examination re-convened and Pruitt was called. Pruitt had served in the Royal Canadian Navy in World War II; he was on a tribal destroyer, the HMCS Haida. Funny, thought Josef, how many prairie lads enlisted in the navy. Pruitt was nervous. Josef was gentler, but firm. Pruitt was less argumentative than Hartman; he feigned memory loss. The result was the same. After being confronted with the fact Bill was not there for the game. Pruitt took refuge in loss of memory:

Manne: Bill Jones wasn't there watching the game, was he?

Pruitt: I don't recall too much now, I don't know.

Manne: You don't recall, or you don't want to recall?

Pruitt: I don't know. I got problems with my memory.
Manne: Problems because of drinking too much?
Pruitt: Suppose.
Manne: So, when you made your statement to the lawyer, you simply repeated what Hartman had said. That is what you're telling us?
Pruitt: Pretty much.
Manne: Your affidavit is based on what Hartman said?
Pruitt: Yes.
Manne: You have no independent recollection?
Pruitt: No.
Manne: No further questions. Thank you, Mr. Pruitt.

With the cross-examinations concluded, Josef hand delivered to Sinclair the completed affidavits from Dr. Trott, Teddy Branagan, the bartender and an addendum to Marv Polanski's affidavit, this time including the information that the bus with Bill Jones on it arrived in Blue River on March 25 at 9:55 pm. Sinclair took them without a word. He and his junior were rushing out, wanting out of McNeil's office, wanting out of Prince Albert.

Josef called Rebecca. Of course, he got Ethel first. Upon hearing his voice, she said, "You told her! Glad you did. She's one happy girl. You keep it that way. I'll get her." Trust Ethel: blunt, to the point and full of heart. Rebecca's voice sung with cheer. She was busy packing. What to wear? Josef was honest, September in Saskatchewan could be summer hot to winter cold. Bring clothing layers. No swimsuit. The lakes would be too cold for an Aussie. He filled her in on the cross-examinations. She was pleased, but did feel a tad sorry for the vets.

CHAPTER 35

Late August

Murray Knecht looked like a quintessential biker. He went by the moniker Rocky, was a big man; former football linebacker and his broken nose provided ferocity. He wore his hair shoulder length, was unshaven, and looked tough. It was all bravado. He was a gregarious person, had he not been an RCMP officer he would have been a used car salesman. He could read people; perhaps that was why he was so good at undercover work.

He and his team had been briefed. He had the file on Tyler and interviewed Feeney about what to expect at Blue River. Rolston provided background on the Rebels, particularly concerning Alex. Rocky's role was to play a scout for the Hells Angels looking to expand into Northern Saskatchewan and take advantage of the new highway to Northern Alberta. What Rocky and the team were not given was any information about the investigation into Bill Jones' death. All they were told is he had been killed. Period. Any information was to come from Tyler and not from cross-contamination. Their time-line was approximately two weeks.

At precisely 12:10 Rocky road into Blue River on his new 1971 Harley Davidson FX Super Glide and pulled into the gas station where Tyler worked. The owner would be on his one-hour lunch break. Tyler was working in the garage changing a tire.

"Hi, fill her up," said Rocky as he pulled up to the pump.

Tyler admired the bike. "Beauty," is all he said as he came to the pump. "New?"

"1971, FX Super Glide, bought in the winter, just breaking her in," replied Rocky, "You into bikes?"

"Yah man, I wish. How much power?"

"57.5 horse power, 1207 CC. It'll move out I tell ya. What you driving?"

"Oh, I got that F-100 over there." Tyler pointed to his parked pickup.

"Hey man, love the Raven Black paint, don't see that often. Mean lookin truck," said Rocky. "What ya got in it the V-6 or V-8?"

"V-8, 292 CC," replied Tyler.

Rocky walked over to the pickup. "You take good care of her. Love the short box stepside, truly unique. Chrome wheels and oversize tires, great. Three speed manual?"

"Yah, goes good. But you'd wipe my ass in a race."

"True," laughed Rocky and stuck out his hand, "name's Rocky."

"Tyler, pleased to meet you."

Rocky leaned against a pole, "I hear the fishing is good on the river."

"Not this time of year. Mostly Jack, you'll catch lots of them, but the Walleye are hiding out in the deep water."

"Jack no good to eat?"

"Nah, not now. Okay in the spring, when the meat is fresh. Now late in the summer, the meat tastes weedy and is soft."

"Oh well, I usually just catch and throw them back. The fun is in the catching, not the cleaning. Know what I'm saying?" said Rocky.

"Sure do."

"You ride?"

"My brother has a '65 Harley Davidson Electra Glide and I've taken it out a few times," said Tyler.

"Whoa, that is a beast of a bike. Heavy damn thing. That's what I like about my FX, lighter, and more horsepower. Electra Glide would eat my dust." Gas was filled, and Tyler led them back into the store. Rocky picked out a few snacks.

"Need a fishing licence?" asked Tyler.

Rocky laughed. "Never."

Tyler then asked, "You part of the 1 percent?"

"Got that right," replied Rocky, "and with the best. The best."

"Holy shit," said Tyler, "my brother is with the Rebels. I didn't know the Angels were looking to come this way."

Rocky took on a more serious demeanour. "And right now, we want to keep everything secret. Got that." Giving Tyler an intense look. "Can I trust you?"

"Yah, I keep things to myself."

Rocky lightened up. "Why aren't you riding with the Rebels? You're a big guy, look like you can handle yourself. Beats pumping gas."

"I don't know. I've done a few odd jobs for them; that's it."

"Odd jobs hey, sounds like they're stringing you along. As far as we're concerned, you are either in or you're not." Rocky paused. "You got a break coming up?"

"Yah at one," replied Tyler.

"Here's the deal, you show me a good fishing hole, and I'll let you try out the FX. Deal?"

Tyler was excited. "You got yourself a deal. I'll meet you down by the dam. Go into Blue River, as the highway goes down to the river, turn left, not right. The highway goes to the right. Turn left, and the dam is about a mile down the road."

"Good, see you then a little after one. Great day for a ride." Rocky cranked the FX and was off.

Tyler saw the bike parked as he drove up, just a few minutes after one. Rocky was lying in the grass soaking in the sun. With a baseball cap resting over his eyes, all he said was, "Punctuality is a virtue. Right on time." He got up and showed Tyler the various controls for the FX. He cranked it up and gave the bike to Tyler. "Try a few laps around here. Get the feel. Riding a bike is like riding a horse; it's all feel."

Tyler had a few false starts and jerky gear changes, but soon got the hang of it. "You know my brother has no patience, never gives me a chance."

Rocky replied, "People got to learn and they learn best through their minor mistakes. Now don't go and do anything stupid. Take it for a ride. I'm going to have a nap."

Off Tyler went. He was thrilled as he went down the gravel road. He got it into high gear on a straight stretch of road, but didn't want to crash. He was gone for 15 minutes and loved the ride. When he returned Rocky was lying on the grass again and never got up. All he said was, "How was it?"

"Great, man. Great."

"Bike and rider both in one piece."

"Sure are."

Rocky sat up stretched his arms and back, "Now where is that fishing hole?"

Tyler smiled. "Right here. Try just below the dam. Best spot on the river."

Rocky looked at his watch, "You got to be back at work in a few minutes. Pain isn't it punching the clock. I like you Tyler. I got a good feel about you. We could use a guy like you. I'm going to tell you something, that's just between you and me. Got that?" Tyler nodded. "We're looking to take over the Rebels. Discussions are already taking place, on the quiet. But what we want are some of our own people along the highway heading to Alberta. Not that we don't trust the Rebels, but we don't. I'm a scout and a recruiter. Does that interest you?"

Tyler didn't know what to say. He wasn't used to having anyone interested in him. Alex had little time for him and his father and grandfather both thought him too stupid to do anything. Pumping gas was a life he hated. He dreamed of being somebody, of having some respect. This was all going through his mind and he hesitated.

Rocky continued, "I should mention, any Hell Angel has seniority over new members who we take over. You'd be senior over your brother. Thought you might like to hear that." Rocky knew he was dangling an enticing bait in front of Tyler.

Tyler still said nothing. Rocky took the lead. "I'm going to write a restaurant and address in Prince Albert, where I'm going to be this Friday night at 7:00 pm. I'll be at a table for two. If you're interested I'll see you then. If not, well Tyler nice talkin with you and I wish you the best."

Tyler's mind was racing. "Thanks, it's not that I'm not sure. It's just a surprise is all."

"I understand. It is a big decision. I'm not going to push you. The offer is there; just to talk. No guarantee of membership. That's down the road. You think on it."

"I will, thanks. And thanks for the ride. Man, that is a machine."

Tyler drove away. Rocky was certain he'd see him at the restaurant on Friday.

Rocky arranged a reservation at the best Steak House in Prince Albert. 7:00 pm came and so did Tyler. "Good to see you Tyler, take a seat. Best steak in the city. Enjoy." For the next hour they talked. Rocky got a better understanding of Tyler, his family and the family dynamics. Tyler was dominated by his brother, father and grandfather. It was a love hate relationship. They had a low estimation of Tyler and he was desperate to prove them wrong. They talked about hockey. Ever thus in Canada. Both agreed Team Canada was going to thump the Soviets, in the eight game summit series. Rocky predicted 7-1 for Canada, Tyler was 8-0 for Canada.

With the dinner over and the restaurant crowd thinning out the talk got more serious. Rocky played to Tyler's need for esteem. "You know to be a 1 percent, you got to be 1 percent. We want good people. Lots of money and fun in it for you if you cut the grade, and I kinda think you will. My job is to watch you, see how you act and react. Get to know you and if I think you are the right stuff I'll call in the boss for an interview. You okay with that?"

Tyler nodded yes and asked, "Do I need to give up my gas station job?"

"Nope, no need right now. You'll see that much of what we need to do is off hours in the night. Having a regular job is a great cover."

He continued, "You got a criminal record?"

"No."

"Good, means you can go over the border to the US easy. Got a passport?"

"No."

"Well you'll need to get one. Do drugs?" Rocky gave him a long stare.

Tyler hesitated then answered, "Just pot now and again. Nothing hard."

"Here's some advice: sellers sell; users use. Don't ever forget that. I've seen many a member who dips into the pool and nothing ever turns out well. Been involved in fights?"

"Yah, a few. Me and my brother fought all the time. He'd usually beat the crap out of me."

"He's older than you. To be expected. We got a few ex-military who can teach you some tricks." Rocky continued, "Tyler, we'll be doing some background on you. We have friends in the know, including the police. We got to check you out." Rocky looked at his watch. "I've got some business to do, as I said our days start late. How about we meet here same time next Friday, expect to stay overnight. Okay?"

"Sounds good. Thanks for the steak."

Rocky replied, "That's just the start."

Driving back to Blue River, Tyler was over the moon. He felt he had passed the first interview. He liked Rocky. God, how good would it be to be a Hells Angel, to ride a Harley. People would know who he was and who was behind him. Forget Alex. It was a dream come true.

Friday, September 1

The following Friday the entire country was waiting with expectation. The first game of the Canada-Russia series was to be played on Saturday in Montreal. Tyler arrived promptly again, and Rocky was at the same table. They spent much of the dinner talking about hockey. Neither changed their predictions. As before, talk turned to business. "We've done some checking on you, Tyler. All checks out. No criminal record. Not even a juvenile record. Good. There is just one concern, and I don't know if this is any worry. It's about your uncle, Bill Jones, I think is his name. He died last May and our information is the police are asking questions about his death. Have they talked to you?"

Rocky could see that Tyler's face flushed. "Yah, he's our uncle. Never saw him much. He fell into the river and died. The cops talked to all the family. Nothing to it."

"Good to hear. You know we got connections with the cops if needed." Rocky decided to change the topic. "Finish your drink, I've got a friend I'd like you to meet. He's over at the Sheraton lounge. We'll take my car."

The Sheraton Lounge was Prince Albert's ritziest drinking spot. Rocky knew Tyler would never have been there before, nor ever expect to be there. Rocky directed Tyler inside and led him to a red leather alcove booth, where a man was seated between two very pretty women. As they approached Rocky said, "Hi, Colin, ladies, this is the guy I was talking about, Tyler." Introductions all around, the ladies were Yvonne and Clare.

Rocky could see Tyler was tongue tied. Rocky motioned for Tyler to sit by Clare and Rocky took a seat on the opposite side of the U, beside Yvonne.

Colin was a clone of Rocky, big, long hair, fit, brash and outgoing. "Nice to meet you Tyler. Drinks?" Colin took the orders and motioned for the waitress. Clare took over, teasing, flirting and probing Tyler. He blushed and certainly enjoyed the attention. Stories and laughter were the order of the day. After about an hour, Colin said, "Well ladies. Time to work. The clientele awaits."

Clare pretend pouted, "I thought Tyler and I could have a little fun."

Colin replied, "Sorry, not tonight; he's not in the club yet. Off you go." Yvonne and Clare got up and went to the adjoining tavern. Tyler's mouth dropped. He had no idea they were hookers.

Colin could see the surprise on Tyler's face. "Those two are high-end and are worth a lot. I drop by to see they are safe. We've an arrangement with the management here, so long as the ladies are discreet and high-end, no problem, it's like a perk the hotel offers." Rocky left for the washroom and Colin moved closer to Tyler, and in a confidential tone said, "Rocky thinks very highly of you, he's got good judgment. Hope you don't let him down." And Colin gave Tyler a long riveting look. "Take care. Hope to see you again, got to keep an eye on the merchandise." He left for the tavern.

Tyler's head was swimming. This was a whole new world for him. It seemed like Rocky wanted him, and Clare. He'd never ever talked to such a beautiful woman and she seemed honestly interested in him, as far as a hooker would go.

Rocky returned and motioned for Tyler to leave with him. "We've got some work to do." When they got into the car, Rocky joked with Tyler; he thought Clare liked him. "She's a nice girl you know. Makes a mint of money. Don't know what she's saving it for." He explained they had to drop in to see one of their dealers. He'd shortchanged them in last month's payment. Rocky needed to fix that. All Tyler had to do was look tough, say nothing, and do as he was told. They drove into a new residential part of the city, Crescent Heights. Rocky pulled up to a house. From the glove compartment he took out a pistol. He pushed a clip into the handle. "I don't expect to be using this. It's all about intimidation. You see the people in there don't know that. Follow me."

They got out of the car, Rocky banged on the door, from inside they heard, "Fuck, hang on. Who is it?"

Rocky said, "Roger, open up, it's Rocky." The deadbolt on the door turned, and the doorknob lock was released. The door was opened a tiny bit. "Yah, what do you want?"

Rocky didn't take kindly to having to talk through the door, he shoved it open, pushed in and had his gun out pointing it at a slim, young male's head. "That's not a nice greeting Roger; Beth with you?"

"Yah."

"Get her ass in here now," said Rocky darkly and menacingly.

"Beth, get in here, it's Rocky."

Beth, a tall, skinny blonde hesitantly came into the room. Rocky keeping his eyes on Roger told Tyler, "Check the house. See if anyone else is here."

"Nobody else is here," said Roger.

"And why should I trust your word for anything?" spat back Rocky. "Sit on the sofa, Beth you too. We need to talk." Tyler checked the three bedrooms, basement, no one was found. He returned to the living room and gestured to Rocky all was ok.

Rocky took a seat in a lounge chair and lowered his gun. "You know why I'm here. You shortchanged us $3,000 last month."

Roger interrupted and in a whiny voice, "We were cheated by a couple regulars. They skipped town. It wasn't our fault."

Rocky wasn't going to accept that excuse. "How you deal with your clients is your problem, not ours. We supply, you pay. It is as simple as that. Now we've been doing business for about two years. No issues, until now. I told the boss to hold back, I'd come and talk to you. You let me down you know. What disappoints me is you never came to me in the first place and said, 'we've got a problem this month'. Instead you simply shortchanged us. That shows disrespect. I don't like disrespect. Got the money? I want the money now."

Roger started complaining, "That kind of money is not easy to come by. I'll need time."

"You need time? You had a couple weeks to call me. You didn't. You got no time. I need $3000 plus my expenses of $500 for this house call. You either pay me now, or you pay for a hospital visit." Rocky looked fierce.

Beth spoke up, "Christ, Roger give him the money for fuck sake."

Rocky looked at her. "At least someone has some brains. Beth go get the cash. Tyler go with her."

Beth got up and went to the master bedroom. Tyler followed. There she pulled out the bottom drawer of a chest of drawers, and in the base of the piece was a metal cash box, and baggies of drugs. She got the cash box out and was about to open it. Tyler told her "Stop". She shrugged and carried it back to the living room.

"Open it Beth."

She opened it, money nothing else.

"Count out $3,500," ordered Rocky. Roger didn't say a word. Beth counted the money and gave it to Tyler.

Rocky got up. "Don't make me come here again. This is your warning. You need to earn back my respect. Don't ever shortchange us again. You make good money. Don't get greedy. Roger, you thank Beth, she saved you a knee-capping. Let's go."

They left. Got into the car. Rocky took the magazine out of the pistol and put them back into the glove compartment. Driving away nothing was said. Rocky broke the silence. "Roger needed a scare. Don't have to do that often."

Tyler asked, "Would you have knee-capped him?"

Rocky replied, "What do you think?"

"I think you would have."

Rocky laughed. "No, he wasn't going to be knee-capped. You see, I knew he had money. Remember when I first asked about the money, he replied he'd need time. If he truly didn't have the money, Roger is the type of guy to whine his head off. He didn't. I knew he was simply playing for time. What I would have done is shoot a hole in his floor first. That would get his attention. You see, violence for the sake of violence is a waste. Yes, sometimes you need to resort to violence, but the art of intimidation is getting what you want without beating the crap out of somebody. Helps to keep everyone on good terms. I heard you say 'stop' in the bedroom. What was that all about?"

"She was going to open the cash box and I wasn't sure whether there was a gun or something inside."

Rocky looked over to Tyler. "Smart, you learn quick. Let's go back to the hotel and celebrate."

Tyler's room at the Sheraton was a suite. Upon their return, Tyler counted the money, $3,500. They sat down and went through the bar fridge. As the night progressed, Tyler's tongue became looser, and his mind less cautious. He asked Rocky, "Have you ever killed anyone?"

Rocky replied, "First, that is a question you never ask a member, ever. Walls have ears. But the answer is no and I'm thankful for that. What about you, kill anyone?"

Rocky noticed a hesitancy, a false start to his answer, when Tyler eventually said, "No, not me." Interesting answer thought Rocky. He decided it was not the time to pursue it. He called it a night.

"See you tomorrow at 12 noon. Meet at my car. Put everything on the room. Tyler, you done good tonight."

Rocky went back to his room and joined Colin with Clare and Yvonne, who were both RCMP officers from Calgary. Rocky congratulated them on their performance. "Clare, I think Tyler is in love with you."

She replied, "He seems like a nice kid; too bad he might be a murderer."

Clare and Yvonne were staying at another hotel, and were leaving for home first thing in the morning. They'd already prepared their reports on the evening interaction with Tyler. They wished Colin and Tyler good luck.

Colin and Rocky talked strategy. Colin asked how it went with Roger and Beth, both RCMP officers from Saskatoon. Rocky felt it went well. He told Colin, about Tyler's answer, "no not me".

Colin mulled it over. "Could mean nothing or mean, 'I was present but didn't do the killing'. Things are going well." Tomorrow, Rocky would make a couple money pick-ups, using the homes of RCMP officers in the city. They'd return to the hotel and have Tyler count the proceeds. This would give Tyler a glimpse of the money to be made. No money was to be given to Tyler. Rocky also thought about going out to the old gravel pit north of the city to do some shooting practice with the pistol. Provides a good sense of power. Everything had to be over before four o'clock. The first game of the Canada-Russia series would begin at 6:00 pm. As Colin said, "Can't miss that."

Saturday, September 2

Tyler was waiting at the car when Rocky arrived at noon. Rocky explained as they drove that he made monthly cash pickups from dealers they supplied around the city. They were in a nice neighbourhood, stopped in front of a well-kept bungalow. Rocky got out, went to the door, was invited in for no more than a minute or two and returned to the car. Once in the car, he reached into his breast pocket and pulled out a thick envelope handing it to Tyler. They drove to another part of the city, big house on an acreage. Same routine. Rocky handed the thick envelope to Tyler. That was it. Simple. They returned to Rocky's hotel room. Rocky cracked a couple beers and Tyler counted the money, $17,850. Tyler had never seen so much money. Rocky smiled. "And that is just two of our dealers, both good ones though." Rocky hid the money.

"Want to go and do some shooting?" asked Rocky.

"Shooting, what?"

"Mostly tin cans. Thought you might like to try shooting a pistol. Ever done so before?"

"No, never. That'd be neat."

"Let's go."

They drove outside the city limits. Why? Because the RCMP had jurisdiction outside of Prince Albert and if an RCMP officer happened to drop by, Rocky could explain the situation. They drove about ten miles north of town into a sandy pine treed area. Taking a rough two wheeled track they ended up at an abandoned gravel pit. The debris of busted beer bottles, bullet riddled cans and signs told Tyler they were at their destination.

Rocky took the pistol out of the glove compartment and went to the trunk where he got a box of bullets. They sat on a fallen tree trunk and Rocky showed Tyler the weapon, which was a standard Browning Hi-Power. Rocky explained the pistol had a 13-bullet magazine, twice that of most other handguns, hence its name 'Hi-Power'. He showed Tyler how to load the bullets into the magazine and how to load the magazine into the handle of the pistol. Once explained, he had Tyler do it. Tyler relished the learning. Next Rocky explained the safety, on and off, and how to break the weapon down. He had Tyler do it. Tyler was ready for the shooting lesson.

Rocky was an expert shooter. He patiently worked with Tyler to get his grip right. Strong arm was the trigger arm; other arm was for support. Forget one hand shooting to start with said Rocky, "You won't hit a damn thing. No accuracy." Having a correct grip, Rocky turned to line of sight alignment. He emphasized to Tyler he needed to line the front sight with the rear sight. Next trigger control. Rocky emphasized a smooth squeeze, "slow and easy" he kept repeating.

Finally, it was time to put instruction into action. They lined three cans at the base of the side wall of the gravel pit. Rocky paced off thirty feet. He fired three shots hitting a can three times as it flipped and moved on the ground. Show off. It was Tyler's turn. He slowly fired three shots at the remaining two cans. He managed to hit the gravel pit. They laughed. All three shots were low. Rocky explained to Tyler that he was flinching in expectation of the shot and the recoil. Forget the shot, think of the front sight only. Don't look at the target, look at the front sight.

Tyler re-loaded the magazine. He fired again. Closer. Again. Closer. On the third shot he actually sprayed the can with gravel. He was really close. Rocky kept whispering, "slow and easy". Tyler fired. The can went flying in the air. He emitted an excited "whoop". He turned to the last can, on his sixth shot he winged the can. They put up some other targets, sipped on a beer and shot. Tyler was definitely improving. They ran out of bullets. It was a grand day for Tyler. Rocky was like a mentor to him, a father or brother he never really had.

They drove back to the hotel, Rocky pulled the car into a parking space and shut off the engine. "Good day today?" he asked.

"It was a great day," replied Tyler.

"Well, every member needs to know how to shoot." Rocky gave Tyler a gentle pat on the shoulder. "Come on, I've got a few things to settle up with Colin." They went to Colin's room. Colin opened the door, turned and asked, "Beers?" Without waiting for a reply, he got one for each. They sat around and Rocky told Colin about the target practice at the gravel pit. According to Rocky, Tyler was a 'natural shot'.

Colin moved the conversation along. "Rocky, what do think? Does Tyler have what it takes?"

Rocky sipped his beer. "Yah, he does. Has lots to learn but he's cool under pressure." Tyler relished the praise. Growing up as a boy there was none. These guys appreciated him. They were his friends; friends he never had before. They were family.

"And that pickup of yours is a beauty, a black beauty." Rocky, patted Tyler on the knee.

Colin continued the conversation on Tyler. "Is he ready to see the Boss?"

Rocky reflected, took another swallow of his beer, looking at Tyler, he said, "Yah, I think he's ready."

Tyler was overjoyed. This was it. He burst out, "Oh man, I'm going to be so nervous."

Colin responded, "Don't be nervous, but boy you had better tell the Boss everything. No lies. He asks a question, you answer. No bullshit. No secrets. When I was interviewed by him, I'd beat a guy up pretty bad, almost killed the guy. I wasn't sure whether the guy was going to go to the cops. The Boss asked me if there were any troubles I might have, that's how he put it, 'troubles', man I was sweating. Should I tell him? I almost blew it. I told him everything. He then told me the Angels had connections; they could help. But, and this stuck with me, he said, 'we can't help you if you don't tell us'. Man, that stuck with me. He's scary though. Eyes will bore right through you."

Rocky added, "The Boss wants absolute loyalty, which means members be absolutely truthful and forthcoming, that's all. We are a family. No secrets. Tyler, you'll do just fine."

Tyler asked, "When will this be?"

Rocky took his time. "I know the Boss is in town next weekend. I'll try and line something up for Saturday or Sunday. Be good for you?"

"I'm free," gushed Tyler.

"Good man. I'll let you know." Rocky finished his beer. "Time to go." Rocky walked him back to his truck.

"Okay, once I know things I'll give you a call. Now you need to get a move on if you're going to get back to Blue River in time for the hockey game."

Tyler was off. Rocky went to his hotel room and filled in a report on the day's activity. He felt Tyler was ripe for Mr. Big. He showered and laid on the bed resting his eyes. He kinda liked Tyler and felt sorry for him. The kid had no prospects, no self-confidence, all had been beaten out of him by a dominating father, grandfather and brother. When you are told you are a nobody, you tend to become one. The Hells Angels was his way out, his chance at being a somebody. All would come to an end soon. If he confessed, he was going to prison and God only knows what would happen to him in there. If he says nothing, nada, zilch, then he's innocent, but we move on, no Hells Angels either way. Rocky hoped he was innocent and, if so, he resolved to let him down gently. He'd tell Tyler he had done good, had passed the interview; however, the Angels decided not to move into Northern Saskatchewan. Sorry. He'd also tell Tyler to get out of Blue River, find a passion, find a life. Yes, that's what he'd do, if Tyler was innocent.

CHAPTER 36

Friday, September 1

Josef was a bundle of nervous energy anxious to see Rebecca. He climbed the stairway to the observation deck at Saskatoon Airport. Waiting was torture. Time refused to speed up. The Air Canada DC-9 landed and taxied to the gate. He waited. The passengers came down the stairway to the tarmac. Where was she? Then he saw her. He ran to greet her at the gate. She saw him, waved and rushed into his arms. They kissed, a long-starved embrace. He held her tight. "God I've missed you." He whispered. They broke apart and he presented her with a bouquet of roses. She kissed him again.

He looked at her. She hadn't changed: hair pulled back into a pony tail, long sleeved shirt, leather jacket, blue jeans and her Aussie boots. They retrieved her bag. Yes, a single bag; she travelled light.

She was impressed with the Parklane and they headed north to Prince Albert. As they drove they exchanged news. Rebecca told Josef all about Ethel and her matchmaking. "She likes you, you know."

"What is it that you'd like to do when we arrive?" asked Josef.

She replied, "Go to bed" and with a flirtatious smile she added, "with you".

Josef blushed. "Well then, I'll step on the gas!"

Soon they arrived at Josef's home. He gave a quick tour. The tour ended in the bedroom, which is where they spent much of the remainder of the day. Josef prepared a light supper, but Rebecca succumbed to jet lag and fell asleep shortly after. He tucked her into bed.

Saturday, September 2

Rebecca woke, as one is prone to with jet lag, at about 1:00 am. She lay in bed, eyes open, mind racing. She was so happy. Finally, she dozed off again only to waken at 11:00 am. Josef was up and about. He had prepared a breakfast of pancakes for the guest of honour. Following breakfast, Rebecca had a walk around the yard and they went for a leisurely stroll through the neighbourhood.

Josef warned her Straun was putting on a 'Hockey Barbeque'; he explained to her the Canada-Russia Summit Series and the first game would be televised starting at 6:00 pm. The barbeque was a warm-up and everyone was curious to meet the Aussie girl.

"What should I wear?" she asked.

"Anything you want, you look good in anything."

"Oh, go on. Casual, comfortable?"

"A barbeque is not formal, especially when hockey is included. Your blue jean outfit is just fine."

She vetoed his suggestion and put on a flowered summer dress, and brushed her hair out. Josef thought she looked smashing.

Straun had a small acreage just east of the city. He actually had a few horses. His wife, Sue, was a farm girl, and a go-getter. Upon Josef and Rebecca's arrival, Sue whisked Rebecca off. The men congregated around the stone barbeque, where Straun was holding fort. Talk was hockey, hockey and more hockey. No one thought the Russians had much of a chance, but it would be fun to give the Russian bear a black eye. Straun had set up a couple televisions in a large rec room in the house. Everyone from the firm was there with families in tow. Josef barely had any time with Rebecca. She was the centre of attention, the Aussie jillaroo, lilting Queensland drawl and captivating brown eyes. Straun came up to Josef and said, "You know I just love to hear Rebecca talk."

Eating over. Drinks poured. All headed to the rec room for the game. Rebecca knew about hockey, but humoured a number of the men who were intent upon explaining the finer points of the game. The game started. Canada scored! Canada scored again! All was playing out as it should. Then the Russian skating and conditioning took over. The Russians won 7-3. Everyone in Canada was in shock. How could this be? The anticipated celebration became a wake. With the end of the game, the guests commiserated with one another and left a sombre group.

For Rebecca the day had been special. As she said, "A Canadian experience." For Josef it was nice to have Rebecca back. They laughed and shared stories of the evening. Rebecca was a novelty and she had enjoyed that, but what struck her the most was how down to earth everyone was, no pretenses, no airs about them. Reminded her of the outback. The forecast for Sunday was glorious, hot and sunny; it was a day not to be wasted and Rebecca was keen on going to Blue River. They decided to picnic there. Time for bed, and in Rebecca's words, "perhaps even a little sleep".

Sunday, September 3

Sunday morning Josef got up, smelling the bacon. It wasn't even 8:00 am. Rebecca was in the kitchen and had made a full breakfast. After cleaning up, Josef took Rebecca's hand and asked her sit down with him at the table; he had something to tell her. He was serious.

"Rebecca, there is no good time for this, but I wanted to tell you in person."

Rebecca's face was drained, worried.

"I found out a couple of weeks ago how your father died and thought you would want to know. I couldn't tell you over the phone."

Rebecca was stoic, not saying anything. Josef then told Rebecca about Teddy Branagan and Dr. Trott. He recounted their story to her. As he talked, she wiped away tears. He had to stop a number of times; it was not easy. When it was done, Rebecca was sobbing, deep painful sobs. She composed herself enough to ask, "Why? Why did he have to go? Why did he have to give himself up? He had a wife and daughter, a daughter he never saw." She started sobbing again.

Josef answered the best he could, "From talking with Teddy Branagan, Dr. Trott and Mr. Morrison it is clear to me that soldiers don't only fight for a cause. They fight for each other, for their mates. That is why Old Bill, Teddy and your dad risked their lives to get medical supplies. Their mates were dying. Old Bill was desperate to save Captain Morrison, and he did. Bill was ready to go alone, but Teddy and your dad knew the men needed medicine. They were soldiers again, not POWs. They were fighting back.

Their mission was to save lives and they did. Your father was an Aussie soldier, who gave himself up for his mates."

Rebecca nodded. "I don't blame my dad. I don't blame Bill. I'm just so angry at the loss, the price paid. I never saw my father. Were any of the guards prosecuted?"

"Dr. Trott filed a report on your father's murder. He doesn't think anything happened. Our governments were too concerned with the cold war and too prepared to let the atrocities be forgiven."

"I'm angry about that," she said and looked at Josef. "Thank you, thank you, it helps to close a chapter in my life. I'm only sorry my mother never knew. It hurts, but it helps." She took a deep breath. "I must look a mess".

"No, you don't," Josef gently replied. "If you don't feel up to going to Blue River, I understand. I may have raised it at the wrong time."

Rebecca gave him a pained look. "There'd never be a right time. Come on let's go see Old Bill, I want to thank him in person."

The day was indeed glorious, a last gasp of summer, a deep blue sky and warm sun. The poplar and birch trees were just starting to yellow, breaking up the solid green matt of the spruce forest. As they drove, both were in a reflective mood and little was said. The Blue River cemetery was just south of the town on the highway and was the first stop. On the way, they spotted a patch of daisies in the ditch and stopped to pick a bunch. Something to put on the grave. Old Bill would have liked that, a gesture from the heart. The grave was already under attack from weeds, a simple wooden cross was the temporary marker and a small Canadian flag stood in tribute to the dead soldier.

Josef engaged in a silent conversation with Old Bill, telling him all was well and he had done the right thing with his will. Rebecca knelt down, touched the wooden cross, picked up a small handful of soil and sifted it through her fingers over the grave. "Thank you, Old Bill. Rest in peace." She rose, went over to Josef and put her arm around his waist. He did the same to her and together they walked away.

Mrs. Cameron was thrilled to see Rebecca. Josef had warned Rebecca, that escaping Mrs. Cameron without staying for lunch or supper would be a challenge. They got away with a cup of tea and home-made chocolate chip cookies. They begged off, citing the day and that they wanted to drive up to the Sand Cliffs.

Josef showed Rebecca Old Bill's shack. She found it charming, a 'swagman's home'. Josef mentioned tearing it down, once the will was probated. Rebecca demurred, "no, it is a special home". They took the path down to the lake. Josef bailed out the row boat, and they went out on the water. It was so quiet, peaceful. Eagles called from a nest high in the trees and circled the river. A beaver was busy building for winter and was none too pleased to see them, twice slapping its tail on the water in disapproval. Josef was not a fan of beavers. "Destructive rodents" he told Rebecca.

After an hour of relaxing on the water they set off for the Sand Cliffs, which were about nine miles upriver. Josef found the unmarked trail, a two wheeled dirt, potholed track. A bumpy few minutes later, the track abruptly ended at the river. The Sand Cliffs were to the north and there was the beach, white bleached sand.

The water was crystal clear. They took off their shoes, rolled up their pants and waded through the water. Rebecca shivered in the cold water, or, at least, what she took to be cold water.

They put the blanket down, rolled up towels into pillows and lay sunbathing. It wasn't a Gold Coast beach, but was pretty darn nice. As they lay, they kissed and caressed each other; lunch could wait.

Lunch over, Rebecca surveyed the surrounds. "What a beautiful spot, and Bill's brother wants to destroy it?"

"If he ever gets the property," replied Josef.

"If I get it, could a mining company come in and develop it against my will?" she asked.

"Underground, yes, but here they'd probably want to have an open pit, which would mess up your property big time. They'd need your permission. I'll show you the geology report. It is worth millions."

Rebecca's reply was swift, "Money is not everything."

Josef started disrobing. "Come on, last swim of the year a skinny dip. Come on Aussie wimp." If there is one thing Josef had learned, is that Australians always take up a challenge.

"Who's a wimp," Rebecca yelled back, peeling off her top.

They ran into the fresh, cold water. Adrenaline kept them in the water for a minute, then they ran back to the blanket and towels.

CHAPTER 37

Monday, September 4

Monday was a holiday, Labour Day, but not for Josef, it was now less than a week before the hearing and he had a great deal to do including preparing for the cross-examination of Dr. McIver the next day. He and Rebecca spent the day at the office. She immersed herself in the case file reading all of the documents, affidavits and reports.

They returned home in time to watch the second game of the Canada Soviet series. She accused Canadians of being consumed about the hockey. Thank God Canada won the second game 4-1; the hockey world was now back to where it should be.

Tuesday, September 5

It had been difficult arranging Dr. McIver's cross-examination. He was very particular. The hotel where he was to stay had to be the Bessborough, agreed. His flight to Saskatoon had to be business class, not agreed. The only possible examination date was September 5, agreed. And the examination had to be held in Saskatoon at Sinclair and Schmidt's office, agreed. Josef and Rebecca drove down from Prince Albert. She was coming because Sinclair wanted a private meeting with her.

Josef was uncomfortable having her meet with Sinclair, without a lawyer.

"Sinclair is experienced and shifty. He is used to getting his way. I'd never allow a client of mine to meet with an opposing lawyer without me being present, never."

"Well you're not my lawyer, are you? On numerous occasions you told me you act for the estate." Retorted Rebecca.

"Look, my concern is you are going into his den. He has all the advantages; he'll threaten, cajole, misrepresent and no one will be there to act as a buffer."

"What you're really saying is no one will be there to protect me. Well you need to understand this, throughout my life I've had to deal with people like Sinclair. I can take care of myself. Rest assured, I have no intention of settling anything. I've read the file, we have a strong case, and I have confidence in you. You won't let me down and I won't let you down." There was fire in her eyes.

Josef gave in. "Okay, I surrender, you win."

Scott was back at law school in Saskatoon and he was eager to sit-in, to see the fruits of his research. Josef had booked the court reporter, not relying on Sinclair's "stalwart choice". Simply put, Josef did not trust Sinclair, and wanted to ensure that a transcript of the examination would be prepared and filed in time for the hearing in three days' time.

The office of Sinclair and Schmidt was located on the seventh floor of a newer high-rise. Rebecca went walkabout through the city downtown, to explore; she'd be back in two hours. Presumably the examination would be finished by then. Scott met Josef in the front foyer of the building and they went up to the office together. Plush carpeting, expensive detailing, luxurious leather furniture greeted potential clients. For corporate people, whose law bills were written off as business expenses, the office exuded success (at a cost); however, for the average Joe Shmoe this was a law firm to avoid. One of Sinclair's juniors showed them into the board room.

Scott and Josef took their seats. The court reporter was set-up already. They were made to wait. At 2:15 pm Sinclair, two juniors and Dr. Horace McIver entered. Josef looked at McIver closely. He wore a tweed jacket, leather elbow pads, tweed vest, and tartan tie, all very professorial. McIver was in his late 40's, prim, overweight, pale skin, balding, bulbous nose, a sign of a drinking problem Josef wondered, horn rimmed glasses, wispy mustache and goatee. Josef took an immediate dislike to the man. It was said if you call yourself an expert that was good enough for the courts. The result was too much expensive junk science being allowed to taint the courts; there would be a day of reckoning.

Josef was warned by other lawyers who had confronted Dr. McIver that he was prone to speech making and filibuster answers. Examining counsel needed to control through short, simple fact questions. Josef was prepared. He began:

Manne: Dr. McIver, your report is dated July 25, 1972, correct?
McIver: Yes.
Manne: And you relied, in part, on the affidavits provided to you by Mr. Sinclair?
McIver: Yes.
Manne: You've made no supplemental report?
McIver: No, I've not been asked to.
Manne: Your report, therefore, does not take into consideration affidavits from witnesses that we have filed?
McIver: No, it does not.

Josef was shocked. McIver and Sinclair were ignoring all contradictory evidence. Josef went through each of his affidavit witnesses and had McIver confirm he had not taken their evidence into consideration. Josef then turned to a more general line of inquiry:

Manne: Doctor, you'd agree with me that a person may be insane one day and sane the next, correct?
McIver: Yes, that is temporary insanity.
Manne: It would be fair to say, a person may be incompetent one day and competent the next?
McIver: Yes, if the state of incompetency is not permanent.
Manne: And a person may know what they are doing one day and not know the next?
McIver: Yes.
Manne: Bill Jones wrote his will on March 26, so it is fair to say that is the day we need to focus on?
McIver: Yes, it would be best to have had witnesses to the making of his will on that date. Unfortunately, we don't have any.

Manne: Better to have witnesses, who saw Bill Jones in the days surrounding his writing of the will, then weeks or months before?

McIver: Yes.

Manne: When I look at the affidavits you considered, the only two witnesses who saw Bill Jones within a week of writing of the will were Henry Hartman and Phillip Pruitt, correct?

McIver: That would appear to be the case.

Manne: Have you been shown a transcript of the cross-examinations on their affidavits conducted by me on August 24 of this year?

McIver: Yes, I have.

Manne: Does that cross-examination alter your opinion in any way?

McIver: No, it does not.

Manne: It doesn't? Not at all?

McIver: No.

Josef decided to leave it at that. Why argue with the witness? He'd make the point with Mr. Justice Podorchuk. It was time now to attack McIver's credentials.

Manne: You provided a list of cases, where you were recognized as an expert in the courts. However, there have been times when you have not been so recognized, correct?

McIver: Yes, a few times. Usually when I was being asked to testify on matters beyond my expertise.

Manne: You never listed those rejections on your c.v.?

McIver: No, I did not.

Manne: Kind of like a report card, where you only list your "A's" and not your "F's"?

McIver: I wouldn't say it was like a report card.

Manne: How many times have you been rejected?

McIver: I said, a few.

Manne: Perhaps, I can help you out, we've found 11 times in Canadian courts, you disagree?

McIver: If you say so.

Josef then proceeded to go through all 11 cases to underscore McIver's mixed record before the courts. Josef knew judges really frown upon being misled. Witnesses and counsel must be fair, bad comes in with the good; hiding of the bad is deception. Now it was time to show his true deception.

Manne: Dr. McIver, I have read over your c.v. and it is very impressive. If you don't mind I'd like to go through some of your publications. Let's start with your peer reviewed publications. In 1963 you published an article in the Indian Journal of Psychology entitled, "Recognizing Sudden Fright Syndrome", you wrote that?
McIver: Yes.
Manne: No co-author?
McIver: No, me alone.
Manne: You alone. I'm going to show you an article entitled, "Eye-Witnesses Evidence Affected by Trauma", published in the University of Wichita Psychology Journal in 1960, authored by James Landry. You're not James Landry, are you?
McIver: No.

Josef could see McIver was sweating profusely, looking for help from Sinclair, who, of course, did not know what was coming.

Manne: I have copies of the articles for you and Mr. Sinclair. Dr. McIver, you changed the title, but you plagiarized this 1960 article word for word. You never wrote the 1963 article, did you?

McIver didn't answer, Sinclair and his team were huddled reading and comparing the articles.

Manne: Dr. McIver, you stole this article and passed it off as your own. Didn't you?

McIver: I did not!

Manne: Word for bloody word. I invite you to read through the two articles. I'll give you and your counsel a few minutes if you wish to find one word that you changed in the body of the article. One word.

Sinclair objected that this was beyond the scope of the cross-examination. Josef responded by saying he intended to put on the record further fraud. Sinclair threatened to shut the examination down. Josef countered that a phone call to Mr. Justice Podorchuk would clarify whether his questions were within the scope of proper cross-examination. Josef looked across the table at Sinclair and said, "Fraud and deception are always proper areas of cross-examination. It lies at the heart of cross-examination."

Sinclair knew his protests would only highlight the wrongdoing. He withdrew his objection and left Dr. McIver to fend for himself. Josef went on to the two other articles. Exactly the same thing. Dr. McIver finally had been outed as an academic thief.

The examination was over. No professional handshakes. Josef turned to the court reporter and made sure the transcripts would be ready by tomorrow. Sinclair, his juniors and McIver left the boardroom without saying a word. Josef would have loved to have heard what Sinclair had to say to Dr. McIver. Josef congratulated Scott on his diligence; lesson learned about the value of thorough research.

One of Sinclair's juniors returned and asked Josef if he would meet with Sinclair in his office. Josef followed into the inner sanctum. Sinclair was looking out the window and didn't turn to speak, "Quite the show. I've decided to withdraw McIver's report from our materials. No need for you to file the cross-examination transcripts."

Josef laughed, which prompted Sinclair to turn to face him. "Forget that. I am filing the transcripts. McIver is a charlatan, a fraud, and I want Justice Podorchuk to see that and say so on the record. Then I'll file a complaint with the psychology association."

"I won't agree to that," replied Sinclair.

"Frankly I don't need your agreement, but if I was you I wouldn't try to defend McIver at all in front of Mr. Justice Podorchuk. Up to you. I'd play the victim, not the defender. You were fleeced by him as well. As I said, I don't really care what you do, but it's going on the record."

Sinclair was deflated, but not defeated. A good lawyer always keeps a poker face. "I'd like to cross-examine your two World War II witnesses. Seems fair that I'm allowed to do so. Therefore, I'll be requesting an adjournment of the hearing on September 8." Sinclair was now playing the delay game.

Josef's response was swift and categorical. "No. First, Justice Podorchuk's order allowing for cross-examination, specifically said you could cross-examine 'on contradictory evidence'. There is no contradictory evidence compared to your witnesses. You may not like what they said in the affidavits, but that is not a basis for cross-examination. Second, Justice Podorchuk was clear, no adjournments to allow for cross-examination. You've got a phone, go ahead and call right now. I have the number."

Sinclair didn't reply instead he said, "Is Miss Thornton here, I'd like to speak with her? There is a good offer on the table."

"She is here, but after today I'm not sure what is left of your case. I'm not her counsel, but I understand she is willing to talk to you. She should be in the waiting room."

Sinclair regained a measure of his arrogance. "I'd like to speak with her alone."

Josef replied, "Understood, see you in court on Friday. I know the way out." Josef turned and left.

Rebecca was in the waiting room, chatting with the receptionist. The topic of conversation was Australia, the receptionist always wanted to go there. Josef sat down beside Rebecca and simply said, "It went well." Rebecca knew all about Dr. McIver. A few minutes later Sinclair grandly came to get her, all Mr. Smooth. Rebecca went with him.

Once in his office, Sinclair showed her to a seat and he went to his desk chair, the power chair. He asked her about her trip, thoughts on Canada, the weather. He was all charm. Rebecca replied in kind; she was used to sizing up men and knew he was a viper in silk.

Sinclair got down to business. "My dear, there is a good offer on the table. $250,000 is a lot of money, especially since you did not know, nor, I'm sure, never expected to get any money from a World War II Canadian

Old Bill's Last Will and Testament

soldier. Quite a story. You see, and I'm sure Mr. Manne has told you this, trials are very unpredictable. I've been doing this a long time and am constantly surprised. Why not take the money and be on your way?"

Rebecca was seething inside at his patronizing tone. She held her tongue. "Thank you, Mr. Sinclair for your thoughts. It is a lot of money."

"It is half the estate, half the estate. You do know that."

"Yes, I can do the math. I also know Mr. Jones' wishes were that my mother and I were to inherit his estate." Rebecca smiled sweetly at Sinclair.

"True, but it appears Mr. Jones may not have been thinking too straight when he wrote his will. Too bad he didn't have the will properly prepared by a lawyer. And I have a number of witnesses who will say that he was, to be blunt, nuts."

"And you are ignoring all the witnesses who will be called by Mr. Manne, who will say, to be blunt, that he was not nuts."

"My point is this, if the will is not valid you get absolutely nothing. You do know that? Mr. Manne has told you that?"

Rebecca's temperature was rising. "Mr. Manne has fully and completely informed me of all my options. Of course, I am also well aware should the will be valid your client gets nothing. Seems to be a wash; doesn't it Mr. Sinclair."

"What will it take to convince you? What number?"

Wrong question for Rebecca. "It is not all about money. Mr. Jones wrote his brother, your client, out of the will for good reason and wrote me and my mother in. I admire Mr. Jones and those were his wishes."

Sinclair turned more aggressive and raised his voice. "Missy, don't give me that rot. Admire him. You never even met him. What is your price? I can write you a cheque today and you can be on your way. Or I can tie you up in legal knots for years to come and you won't get a cent."

Rebecca had been bullied before, wrong approach. She held his stare and replied in a calm soft voice, "I'm prepared to see what happens at trial."

Sinclair laughed. "Boy are you naïve. Only a fool gambles on a trial. Everyone has their price. What's your price?"

Rebecca was now seething. "You want my price? I'll tell you: ten million dollars. Now, I'm not saying I'd agree to that, but tis fair."

Sinclair laughed. "You got to be kidding. Doll, you truly have no idea."

A sexist, disparaging remark, not good. Rebecca rose out of her chair, leaned over the desk, glaring at Sinclair, she said, "Not even a roughneck drover is dumb enough to call me missy or doll to my face. I have no idea. You have no idea about the true value of the estate, do you? Your client hasn't told you? You pompous twit."

She turned and walked out of his office. Sinclair was left wide eyed with his mouth open in disbelief. Rebecca marched into the waiting room. "Meeting over, let's go." She turned to the receptionist. "Hope you make it to Australia; too bad you're working for such an ass." On that note Josef and Rebecca left.

Over drinks at the Bessborough they shared stories about the day's events. Josef couldn't stop chuckling. "You called him a pompous twit? A twit. Love it."

"Believe me, I let him off gently, I had a few choice words left in reserve." Rebecca sipped her drink and smiled.

CHAPTER 38

Wednesday, September 6

Mel Laxon wasn't happy. The girl had turned down the $250,000. Said she wanted ten million. Bruce told him Sinclair asked about the true value of the parcels of land. At least Bruce had the sense not to tell that candy ass. She must know. That means her lawyer knows. Bruce said Sinclair was still confident they would succeed at the hearing on the 8th. Laxon swore, Bruce should never have dumped Wright, he was a bulldog, knew how to street fight, this prima donna rich Saskatoon lawyer was full of bullshit. He didn't trust him at all. Laxon made up his mind, if they lost the hearing he'd take matters into his own hands.

Laxon called Nevada, they arranged to meet at a local park and went for a walk. Trees don't have ears. "Are you ready?" asked Laxon.

"Yah, just give me the word. I'll need a few days' notice to put it all together."

"There is a slight complication. The Aussie girl is in Canada. Staying with the lawyer I think. I want them both to have an accident. Is that a problem."

Nevada thought for a moment. So long as they were together he could kill both in the same accident. "No not a problem."

"Good, good. We hold off until the hearing on the 8th is over. Got that?"

Nevada nodded.

"Sebastian Wright is going to sit in at the hearing. He'll give me a full report. Who knows we might win, but I doubt it. Jones' lawyer is a fuck-up."

"I'll wait to hear from you. One thing, I need to know if John Morrison and his wife attend the hearing. Ask Wright about them; I assume he knows who they are."

"They the ones' in the grain business?"

"The same."

They ended their walk. Nevada phoned Derek Ford and told him to meet him that afternoon, at 2:00 pm at Fish Lake Park. The Fish Lake Road was to be the scene for the accident. Nevada picked the road with care. First, it was paved; the car would then be going at a higher rate of speed than on gravel. Second, the highway was little used – no witnesses. The road ran straight west up a gradual incline for about two miles, then at the summit the road descended to the lake a further one mile distant. The road itself had a narrow gravel shoulder and steep ditches; there'd be no escape for the unsuspecting driver. Furthermore, near the intersection with Highway 2 there was an entrance to an abandoned homestead, which was grown over by weeds and surrounded by scrub trees on the highway side. It was an ideal lookout, where Nevada could hide as spotter; he'd have a clear line of sight to the crest of the hill and any driver heading to Fish Lake late in the day would be driving right into the sun. Perfect. At Fish Lake there was a small parking lot, washrooms, a covered picnic hut and a little used beach. The park was generally deserted after the summer ended.

The old Fish Lake Lodge overlooked the parking lot, which the government had taken over and renovated. It was used for getaway conferences and day camps. Nevada checked and the lodge was closed for the season on September 1.

Derek arrived on time. Nevada told him "this is the road". They went through what would happen and scouted the road. The parking lot was gravel and Nevada told Derek if he was asked by the cops why he was there he could say he wanted to see if the lot needed a load or two of gravel.

They would communicate by CB radio. Nevada had driven out in one of the club's courier cars, a beat-up Chevy Nova, used for drug running. It had a CB radio. They agreed on a selected CB channel and their handles, Nevada was "Vegas" and Derek was "Goose Dog", why Derek chose that moniker he wouldn't say. They tested the CB's and reception was loud and clear. He was to keep the channel open and when he heard "watch for deer" he was to start driving. Derek knew what to do next. The two vehicles would make contact in a little over a minute.

Nevada told him to "standby". The "accident" could well be in the next few days. Derek was okay with that. The only thing he cared about was erasing his drug debt. They left separately. During the time they had been at the park not a single person was seen. Perfect.

The last piece in the puzzle was how to get Manne and the Aussie girl on that road at a specified time? This had taken some digging. Laxon had all the legal filings and Nevada read through them searching for a hook and he found it.

* * *

Game three of the Canada-Russia Summit on September 6 was held in Winnipeg. Rebecca and Josef were invited to join friends at a local bar. After Canada's win two days before the aura of confidence, if not superiority, returned to the crowd packed in the bar. Surely the game one loss was an isolated aberration. Canada took the lead; the Russians tied and that is how the game ended. Better than a loss.

Rebecca and Josef were leaving when at the entrance Nevada was arriving. "Hello lawyer man," he said with a wicked grin.

Josef looked at him. "You seem pleased Nevada." Josef had no intention of introducing Rebecca.

"I am. I put my money on the Soviets with great odds I might add." He boasted eying Rebecca.

"How patriotic of you," replied Josef sarcastically.

"Patriotism and betting do not mix. I figure the Russians are in better condition, better skaters than we are and without Orr and Hull, two of our best players, we aren't as strong as everybody thinks. So far so right." He was looking at Rebecca. "And this must be the Aussie girl. Welcome to Canada."

Rebecca had caught Josef's vibe and didn't say anything.

Nevada, without taking his eyes off her, left with a parting comment, "I'd take the deal if I were you. Not going to get better." Turning to Josef. "See you lawyer man."

Josef watched him go into the bar.

"Who was that?" Rebecca asked.

"That was Nevada, whose real name is Calvin Gold, he is the sergeant-at-arms for the Rebel motorcycle gang and he was one of the thugs who tried to ambush me at Lost Lake."

"Where you had them drop their pants?"

"Yes."

Rebecca squeezed his arm. "Had I known I would have said how good he looks wearing pants." She laughed.

Josef shook his head. "He's not the type to mess with. He's a killer."

"I know, but it is priceless what you did. He is a bit of a Dapper Dan isn't he."

Thursday, September 7

The day was cloudy, threatening rain, with strong winds blowing in from the north. It was a good day to work and Josef was busy with final preparation for the hearing. Just before 2:00 pm he received a delivery from Sinclair and Schmidt. This was not good. At this late hour it had to be bad news and it was. Sinclair, just that morning, had filed an affidavit from a Winnipeg Police Officer. The affidavit showed Teddy Branagan had a number of criminal convictions for fraud, theft, false pretenses, and drug possession. He had served a total of three years in jail and had been detained under a warrant at the Selkirk Mental Institution suffering from Paranoid Schizophrenia. Sinclair included a personal note: "Can we believe anything Mr. Branagan says?"

Josef was kicking himself, he had not checked for any criminal convictions, in fact, he hadn't even asked Teddy about any. He was sloppy and now Teddy's credibility was shot. No more mistakes. He needed to double check all. Rebecca was at home hunkered down, and he called, asking for a favour; could she go through the file box in his den where he kept Old Bill's assorted treasures. Mary Jones in her affidavit had mentioned sending and receiving Christmas cards from Old Bill. He wanted to double check there weren't any such cards found in Old Bill's possessions.

Old Bill's Last Will and Testament

Rebecca sat at Josef's desk and went through the file box. Halfway through the photo album she stopped. Staring at a photograph. It was of her mother holding her. She would have been only a few months old; Rebecca recognized the knitted baby jumper and cap her mother had made. It was one of the baby mementoes, a keepsake, which her mother passed on to her. This photograph was the only one on the page in the album. She took a deep breath and gently removed the photograph from the four corner tabs and turned it over to look at the back. There was written in block letters 'Charles Thornton Died January 31, 1945', and below those words in faded feminine hand 'Love Connie and Rebecca Return to Us Safe'. Tears flowed down her cheeks, rocking back and forth, lips trembling, emotion welling up inside her. Wiping her eyes, she examined the back of the photograph closely; there in the corner was a small stamp. She deciphered it, 'Goondiwindi Photos'. For a few minutes she sat unmoving, numb. Then she collected herself, sat upright, strong, carefully put the photograph back into the tabs and quickly finished going through the album and the remainder of the file box. No Christmas cards from the Jones' were found.

She changed her clothes, phoned for a cab and made her way to Josef's office. It was a busy place. Shirley greeted her with a harried look, but upon seeing how solemn Rebecca was, she stopped typing and asked, "Rebecca are you okay? You've been crying."

Rebecca's lip started quivering. "I need to see Josef. I know this is not a good time."

"Nonsense girl, I'll get him." Shirley got up and hurried to his office, knocking gently and entered. "Josef, Rebecca is here and you need to see her. Now."

Josef was alarmed. Without protest he followed Shirley out of his office. Rebecca was standing still holding the photo album into her chest. "I found something," was all she said. Josef gently took her arm leading into his office. Shirley followed with a glass of water and left. Rebecca sat down. Josef said not a word. Waiting for when Rebecca was ready. She took a sip of water, placed the glass on his desk and opened the album to the photograph. She turned it to him. "My mother is holding me. I recognize the outfit, my mother made it for me. Take the photo out and look at the back."

Josef carefully removed the photograph and read the back. "Oh, Rebecca, I am so sorry. I hadn't looked through the album. I should have."

"Old Bill must have taken the photograph, when he went through my father's personal things. Teddy Branagan, in his affidavit, mentioned him finding it."

"The fact Old Bill kept this photograph says so much; it collaborates what Teddy Branagan has told us. I need an affidavit from you and include the photograph as an exhibit. We can't file it today, the Court Office is closed, but maybe I can get Justice Podorchuk to accept it at the hearing. Are you up to doing this?"

"Of course, that's why I came down. What do I have to do?"

"I'm going to ask you some questions. All will be recorded and I'll quickly draft an affidavit. Shirley will type it up in a jiffy and I'll get you to sign it. Okay."

Rebecca nodded. "By the way, no Christmas cards from the Jones."

"I didn't think there would be."

Shirley stayed late and prepared the affidavit. Josef remained working at the office through the evening.

After signing the affidavit, Rebecca took a cab home. When she got home she flopped on the bed, cried a bit more and fell asleep.

CHAPTER 39

Friday, September 8

Courtroom four was full. On Josef's side of the aisle there was Rebecca, Straun, Sue McNeil, Gabe, Scott (skipping classes), Mrs. Cameron and the Morrisons seated at the back. On Sinclair's side was, of course, his two junior lawyers, Bruce Jones, Ron Jones and a family contingent. Curiously, Sebastian Wright watched from the back row.

All the evidence was in via the various affidavits, exhibits and cross-examination transcripts. Justice Podorchuk would have read all thoroughly. This hearing was limited to oral argument. Sinclair, as applicant, went first.

He spent his opening ten minutes 'reminding' the court as applicant he need only raise a genuine issue, give it, in his words, 'an air of reality', which would lead to a full trial.

Some judges let counsel drone on, not Justice Podorchuk. He'd had enough. "Mr. Sinclair, I want you to concentrate on the key issue at hand. Why say you that Mr. Jones lacked testamentary capacity on March 26, 1972?"

Sinclair spent much time summarizing the affidavits of his various Blue River witnesses. Justice Podorchuk wanted focus. "Mr. Sinclair, do you accept March 26 is the operative date?"

"Yes, but there needs to be context."

"Save your context, point me to the evidence, which shows Mr. Jones lacked capacity on March 26."

Justice Podorchuk was forcing Sinclair to the evidence of Henry Hartman and Phillip Pruitt. Sinclair tried to defend the indefensible.

Justice Podorchuk peppered him with questions:

"Was this evidence not fabricated?"

"It conflicts with the affidavit evidence of the bartender. What do I do with this conflict?"

"Doesn't the affidavit evidence of the bus driver, Mr. Polanski, conclusively show Mr. Jones could not have been at the legion to watch the hockey game as they say?"

"Didn't your own lawyer, in conducting the interviews, taint the evidence?"

Sinclair sang an awkward refrain: the witnesses may have 'exaggerated' and been 'mistaken' but the gist of their evidence was sound. "Maybe the bus driver lied. We don't know. And, most importantly, credibility issues are not a proper consideration for this hearing; that is for trial."

Justice Podorchuk responded, "But that does not mean I throw my common sense out the window."

"What about the evidence presented by the estate? In their affidavits these witnesses found Mr. Jones of sound mind, memory and understanding, did they not? And they saw Mr. Jones within days of March 26, some even on that day? You are not questioning the integrity of a bank manager, minister of the church, specialist doctor, respectable businessman and his wife?"

Sinclair fell back on the burden of proof. "It is not a question of accepting their evidence or not. The question is whether our evidence has raised an issue for trial."

Justice Podorchuk fired back, "Has it?"

Thus far Sinclair had not mentioned Dr. McIver. He couldn't hide him. Justice Podorchuk asked about the good doctor. "What do you have to say about the report of your expert, Dr. McIver?"

Sinclair should have voiced his own outrage at being duped by McIver. Instead he presented a weak defence. "At the end of the day, Dr. McIver did diagnose geriatric regression."

Justice Podorchuk pounced. "Is it not the case that Dr. McIver, in making that diagnosis, only looked to the affidavit evidence of your witnesses?"

"He never looked to the estate's evidence, did he?"

"Why hadn't the doctor considered the estate witnesses?"

"It comes down to the evidence of Mr. Hartman and Mr. Pruitt, doesn't it?"

"And, how much weight do we give Dr. McIver's opinion if the evidence of Hartman and Pruitt is fabricated?"

"What about the plagiarism?"

"Why should I give his evidence any credence?"

Sinclair had no acceptable answers.

Finally, Justice Podorchuk asked, "What else do you have Mr. Sinclair?"

Sinclair turned to Niigata. He attacked Teddy Branagan. "The Court cannot rely on the word of Teddy Branagan as to what happened. He is a broken man, broken both physically and mentally; his criminal and psychiatric history speaks to that. Without corroboration, Teddy Branagan's evidence is worthless. His evidence needs to be tested and that is why a trial is required."

In closing, Sinclair returned to Niigata. "We can all sympathize with the horrors that befell Bill Jones and the other prisoners of war at Niigata. But, this too, is precisely why it is understandable that Bill Jones, 88 years old, terminally ill may well regress back to that most traumatic time of his life. Be dominated by it. Cast aside the present. Cast aside his loving family. Recede into the past. Lose reality. That is why we say there is a real issue that Mr. Jones lacked testamentary capacity and we respectfully seek a trial."

Sinclair finished. He had been on his feet for over an hour and twenty minutes. Justice Podorchuk asked Josef if he wanted a short adjournment before he began his submissions.

Josef asked for a moment before adjourning. He picked up Rebecca's affidavit. "M'Lord, with the indulgence of the Court, at this time I would like to file the affidavit of Rebecca Thornton, who is the daughter of Lieutenant Thornton and the sole beneficiary under the will. She is present in court today seated in the first row. She only became aware of this new evidence late yesterday, as is explained in the affidavit, and that is why it was not filed earlier. I have copies for the Court and for Mr. Sinclair."

Sinclair, without even seeing the affidavit, objected, "All affidavits should have been filed in advance, as is the rule of the Court. This manufactured last-minute evidence should not be accepted; it smacks of ambush and unfair surprise."

Justice Podorchuk responded, "Surprise cuts both ways Mr. Sinclair. I note the affidavit of the Winnipeg Police Officer filed yesterday actually was prepared and signed on September 1. I take it Mr. Manne only received a copy of that affidavit yesterday as well. I'll look at the affidavit before ruling." Justice Podorchuk took his time. He eventually lifted his head and gave Rebecca a look over his eye glasses. "This new evidence, according to the affidavit was discovered late yesterday afternoon through happenstance. There is no attempt to surprise or ambush. Courts are here to see justice is done in a fair and just manner for all parties. Accordingly, I will accept the affidavit of Miss Thornton. We will have a short adjournment."

Mr. Justice Podorchuk returned to court. Josef rose, went to the podium and began. "M'Lord, this case is not about whether Bruce Jones and his family is loving, estranged or something in between. It is about the wishes of Bill Jones. Your Lordship has a copy of the letter Bill wrote to me on March 29 of this year, where he named me executor of his will. In that letter he wrote, 'I never had the courage to do what was right when I was alive. In death I hope to make things right.' I've puzzled over those words. They are not the words of a deranged person. They are thoughtful and, I confess, I didn't fully understand what they meant for a long time. I now do. Bill Jones was putting his affairs in order. Dr. Schurr told him he had lung cancer and only six months to live. Margaret and John Morrison urged him to prepare a will and in typical Bill fashion he wrote his own. He went to the bank, saw Mr. Wallace, put his financial affairs in order, and he went to see Reverend Knox, to pay for and plan his own funeral. These are the acts of a reasonable man, who knew he was going to die. They are not the acts of a person divorced from reality; rather they are the acts of one facing the reality of his own dying."

Josef paused to take a sip of water. Mr. Justice Podorchuk was not interrupting, listening intently.

Josef continued, "I have in my hands the photograph, which Rebecca Thornton found in Bill Jones' photo album just yesterday. This photograph is old and tattered. It literally has been through the wars. It is the photo of a young woman with long flowing dark hair; she is holding in her arms a

Old Bill's Last Will and Testament

baby girl. On the back of the photograph is the faded stamp 'Goondiwindi Photos'. It is a photograph of Lieutenant Charles Thornton's wife, Connie, holding their daughter, Rebecca." Josef's voice was cracking. He stopped to collect himself.

"This is the same photograph Private Teddy Branagan spoke about in his affidavit where he tells the story of Lieutenant Thornton's death at Niigata. Teddy Branagan told how he and Bill had cared for the Lieutenant after his death. The two of them were with Dr. Trott and it was they who took him from the post where he was tied. It was Bill who stood up to the guards and insisted that the Lieutenant be dressed in uniform for cremation. Bill was standing up for his friend, his mate. Teddy Branagan then described how Bill reacted when going through his friend's personal effects; he saw a photograph and wailed and sobbed. This is the photograph. Remember Teddy Branagan said "it was a photograph of a pretty woman holding a little baby girl." M'Lord, look on the back of the photograph, see the words, 'Love Connie and Rebecca Return to Us Safe'. Those words must have gutted Bill Jones. Lieutenant Thornton was not going to return to his wife and baby daughter. Bill kept that photograph all these years. Why? Because he blamed himself for Lieutenant Thornton's death."

"We know he wasn't to blame, but it was his idea to steal the medical supplies. Bill Jones was desperate to save his Captain, his friend, John Morrison, who also is here in court today. The doctors had nothing. Dr. Trott in his affidavit phrased it well; he said he was a 'caring mortician'. No supplies. They'd seen the Red Cross supplies arrive and they knew those same supplies would soon disappear, to be taken by the Japanese. Bill was going to act. Private Branagan and Lieutenant Thornton volunteered. These three were willing to risk their lives to save their mates. They'd seen so much suffering and they were determined to do something about it. So, they went out into the night to break into the supply barrack. It just so happened Lieutenant Thornton was the last man out. A Japanese guard saw them. Lieutenant Thornton stood up, put his hands up in the air and walked towards the guard, which allowed Bill and Teddy Branagan to escape with the supplies. In that moment Lieutenant Thornton sacrificed himself for them, and he was killed in a cruel, despicable way. Lives were saved because of his bravery."

The court room was completely silent. Josef paused and took another sip of water. "The mission was a success, but at what cost? Bill Jones, at least in his mind, felt he was responsible for the death of the husband of a young woman, and the death of the father of a daughter, whom he never would live to see. How do you compensate them for that loss? How do you face them? Bill couldn't in life. He decided to do so in death." Josef had to stop.

Once composed, he started again. "This is what Bill meant when he wrote to me, 'I never had the courage to do what was right when I was alive. In death I hope to make things right.' This was his burden; a chance to give back to the wife and daughter of the man, who Bill Jones felt responsible for killing. This is what he was doing. He was making amends through his last will and testament. Is it a rational decision? Yes. Is it understandable. Yes. And, M'Lord, with all due respect, no court in the land should deny William Maurice Jones this his final wish. Those are my submissions."

Josef sat down, emotionally drained. Silence. Justice Podorchuk said not a word. He was looking down. Not writing, just looking down. After a time, he looked up at the clock. "It is now five minutes before noon. We will adjourn until 2:00 pm when I will render an oral decision."

Bailiff, "All rise."

Once Justice Podorchuk left, Rebecca, who had tears streaming down her face grabbed Josef and held him tight. There was an emotional release by all those on Bill's side of the aisle. Margaret Morrison hugged him; Sue McNeil hugged him; Mrs. Cameron hugged him. The ladies then retreated to form a tight circle, sharing tissues. John Morrison came up to Josef. He couldn't speak, tears welled in his eyes, he shook Josef's hand and mouthed, 'thank you'.

Sue McNeil, ever the organizer, arranged a quick lunch of sandwiches, tea and coffee at the offices of McNeil and Associates. Rebecca and Josef did not stay long, they decided to walk back to the court house. In the surrounding gardens, they found a bench and sat down holding each other close, saying nothing.

At 2:00 pm, Justice Podorchuk rendered his decision. He was scathing in his examination, perhaps the better word would be 'destruction' of the applicant's case. He was thorough and precise. No weight could be given to the evidence of Hartman and Pruitt. The report of Dr. McIver was 'rubbish'. The evidence of the estate was overwhelming. "Disappointment by relatives left out of a will does not a genuine issue make." Justice Podorchuk was convinced at the 'highest level' of evidence that Bill Jones had testamentary capacity at the time of writing the will. The applicant's motion seeking a trial to contest the will was denied. Full costs of the hearing to the estate.

Victory! The decision was not well received, on the losing side. Bruce Jones swore and stomped out of the courtroom, with his scowling family following. Graham Sinclair Q.C. and his juniors simply wanted out of town. And Sebastian Wright, wearing an 'I told you so smirk', sneaked out.

The Morrisons and Mrs. Cameron were travelling home. Josef took time to thank them both. For Margaret and John, the hearing had been particularly poignant. Margaret and Rebecca huddled together talking for a long time, tears flowing. When it was time to say good bye, Rebecca gave John a long heartfelt hug.

Straun announced that celebratory drinks were to be had at McNeil and Associates; he kept a bottle of champagne on ice for just such occasions. It truly was a team effort; everyone contributed to the success. Straun and Sue insisted all adjourn to their place for Chinese food and to watch game four of the Canada-Russia series. Josef thought Rebecca was 'hockeyed' out, but she was game.

The game did not go as hoped. The Russians outplayed Team Canada and the Canadian players, in frustration, responded with lack of discipline and dirty play. They lost 5-3. With the series now heading to Russia, the Canadians were down in games 2-1 with one tie. Not good.

* * *

Sebastian Wright too was celebrating. Bruce Jones did not get what he paid for thought Wright. Teach him to dump me. Wright leaning back in his office chair, whiskey in hand happily called Mel Laxon with the news. According to Wright, Sinclair bungled the case from the get go. There was, in his view, no chance at all on appeal, which meant the will would go to probate. The Aussie girl gets the estate.

After hearing from Wright, Laxon phoned Nevada. They needed to talk; not over the phone. Laxon was in Saskatoon. Nevada was in Prince Albert. Laxon told Nevada to meet him at the Rebel's club house outside Rostern, which was halfway between the two cities; they'd watch the hockey game and talk.

"We lost." That was all Laxon initially said. Nevada waited.

"Wright tells me there is little hope on appeal. We'll not get anywhere with the Aussie girl and with Manne. We need to get rid of them both. She'll probably leave her estate to relatives in Australia and they'll just want a quick buck and run. We have no other choice. Are things lined up?"

Nevada gave a smile. "All is ready. I just needed the word. Did you ask Wright about the Morrisons?"

"Yah, they were in court. Why?"

"I have my reasons. Trust me."

"When?"

"I'll try for Sunday. If not, it will be soon."

"Look like an accident?"

"You bet it will."

CHAPTER 40

Saturday, September 9

Saturday morning, handkerchief over the mouthpiece and a wad of gum in his mouth, Nevada made his call from a pay phone in a quiet corner of a local hotel. He dialed the number:

"Hello, Josef speaking," a tired voice answered.

"Josef, Josef Manne, William Morrison calling from Saskatoon." He paused to let that sink in. Nevada had done his research. Laxon had all the court filings and in reviewing them he found the affidavits of John and Margaret Morrison. With further digging he found William Morrison and, over the phone, he played him as prim and proper, a bit formal. He assumed Manne had never met William, "Sorry to bother you. Must have been a big night with your court win yesterday. My parents were thrilled, absolutely over the moon by it all."

"Thank you, William, it was a good day and it was great to have your parents there. It meant a lot."

"It meant a great deal to both of them, especially my father." Nevada then got to the meat of his call. "I won't keep you, however, I have been remiss. We've been planning an anniversary surprise party for mom and dad. And I should have invited you, but I forgot. Yesterday after talking with my parents I realized I had not sent you an invite. I so wish you and Miss Thornton can attend the surprise party. I'll give you the details, it is tomorrow night at 7:00 pm, won't be too late. Can you make it?" Nevada held his breath.

Josef took a moment. Tomorrow was Sunday night, nothing on. "We'd be honoured. Where is it going to be held?"

Nevada was much relieved. "Wonderful. It is at the old Fish Lake Lodge on Fish Lake Road. We are asking all guests to get there for 7:00-7:15 pm. There is a parking lot right at the lake. Now I have favour. We've pulled a few strings to have the lodge kept open for us so we are asking all guests to keep that secret. We don't want allegations of government favoritism to mar the occasion. You understand."

"Understood." Josef replied.

"Perfect. Do you need directions to Fish Lake Lodge?"

"No, no I know it well. Just off highway 2."

"Yes, that's right, and one other thing. Absolutely no gifts, no cards, just bring yourselves. Dress is casual, which is what my parents would want."

"Sounds good. We'll just bring ourselves."

"Well, I apologize again for the late invite, but am so pleased you both will be coming. Remember 7:00 pm. Oh, don't come too early we want the day trippers to have gone before we arrive. That was part of our arrangement in getting the lodge. I look forward to meeting you. Thanks again, see you then."

After hanging up, strange thought Josef; he and William had met at Bill's funeral. He must have forgotten.

Nevada pumped his fist. They were hooked. Nevada next called Derek Ford and gave him his orders. He was to be at Fish Lake Provincial Park tomorrow at 6:15 pm. Nevada would make CB radio contact when he arrived.

* * *

It was to be a special supper, win, lose or draw at the hearing. Better that it was a win. Rebecca searched every butcher in Prince Albert for fresh lamb. She knew from Australia, lamb was a favorite for Josef. Finally, she was put on to a Hutterite Colony a few miles out of town and she had her lamb.

She prepared it using one of her mother's secret recipes. The lamb was served with creamy bacon bit mashed potatoes and steamed asparagus, broccoli and beans. For dessert she made sticky date pudding with caramel sauce. It was a traditional Aussie meal. She also bought a bottle of New Zealand Marlborough Sauvignon Blanc. She set the table using Josef's mother's finest china, fine linen tablecloth and candle light. She wanted everything to be just right.

She pulled her dark brown hair out of the bun, and brushed it so the hair fell in gentle waves over her shoulders. She dabbed on a touch of make-up and was wearing her summer dress.

Josef was barred from the kitchen. When all was ready she escorted him into the dining room. When he saw it, he pulled her to him and gave her a kiss. Exactly what Rebecca wanted. They had a leisurely meal, mostly talking about the hearing and the result. Josef teased Rebecca that she was now a wealthy heiress, and would likely take her inheritance and run. With a sly smile, Rebecca said in reply, "What will be, will be".

Rebecca refused to let Josef clean-up. "Not tonight. The dishes can wait." They retired to the living room and snuggled on the sofa. Little was said. They were happily wrapped together.

After a time, Rebecca wiggled free from Josef's arms and ordered him to "stay put". She returned to the kitchen.

When she came back she stood right in front of him. In her hand he noticed she held a small box. She was biting her lower lip, which she did when nervous. He was about to say how beautiful she looked, but she put up her hand for him to stop. Then she spoke, in a halting, nervous voice, "Josef Manne, I have something to tell you." She took a deep breath, composed herself, and continued, "You are the kindest most caring man I have ever known. You saved my life, twice." She was flushed, biting her lower lip again. "I never thought it possible to meet someone as special as you." Her voice breaking, "I love you with all of my heart."

She nervously fingered the box and took another deep breath, "Josef…"

Josef cut her off, "Stop". Her eyes went wide, startled. He stood up, took her hand. Then he knelt down on one knee, looking up at her, he said, "Rebecca Thornton, I love you. I knew the first time I saw you. I want to be with you forever. Rebecca, will you marry me?"

Her cheeks were flushed and she had trouble speaking, eventually she blurted out, "Yes, yes, of course, I'll marry you!" Josef rose, wiped a tear from her eye, and taking her face in his two hands gave her a long, tender, passionate kiss.

She put her head into his shoulder and then started hitting him gently with both fists, "Why did you stop me? I was going to ask you to marry me. I was so terrified when you said 'stop'. Why?"

Josef laughed. "Because I could never let you propose to me, never. I'd never live it down. Imagine having to tell everyone you did the proposing. Hearing that, every person would think I was a complete idiot. She had to ask him! No, I couldn't have that. Much better for me to do the proposing. Saves my self-respect."

She gave him a good-natured punch. They sat down on the sofa, holding each other. Rebecca showed him inside the box was her mother's engagement and wedding ring, which she hoped he would have made into a wedding band.

Josef had to ask, "Why did you decide to propose to me?"

Rebecca gave him a sideways look. "Because you tend to think too much. Look at how long it took you to tell me you loved me. You never told me at Brisbane airport. Remember I said to you, 'I guess the engagement is off'. I was waiting. You didn't say a word. Finally, I got a 'I'll miss you'. It was a long drive to Foster Ranch I can tell you. Then you had to tell me your feelings in a letter. You know my return flight to Australia is a little over a week away and I reckoned I needed to lead the dance."

She was right. Brisbane Airport was not Josef's finest hour.

They talked and talked. The wedding? Neither had family, nor were they religious. A justice of the peace was just fine. Keep it small and make it happen soon. Where to live? Move to Australia? If they did, it would have to be by the ocean. She was sick of dust and flies. In the end, they decided to give Saskatchewan a go for one year, finalize the estate and see if she could survive a Saskatchewan winter. How many children? More than one Rebecca insisted, she did not like being an only child. What will she do with the inheritance? Not sell Bill's place that is for sure. Sell the Sand Cliff parcels? She didn't know. The river frontage was so spectacular. She hated the thought of open pit mining. Could she sell it to the government to make a park? Josef cautioned her, "Government can be ruthless when they smell money, worse than criminals." They talked into the wee hours.

Life was very, very good.

CHAPTER 41

Tyler had been waiting for a call from Rocky and when it came he was excited. Rocky suggested Tyler come into PA Saturday evening. Go to the Sheraton. They'd have supper and they'd book a room for him. On Sunday he'd have his interview with the Boss. This was Tyler's big chance.

Tyler arrived right on time. Rocky saw him in the entrance to the restaurant and beckoned him over. Colin was there and two others (RCMP undercover from Saskatoon). Instructions were clear, tonight was to be social, friendly, no talk about the Boss, that was to be left to Rocky. The objective was simply to introduce Tyler to others in the Hells Angels family; show him what could await should he be accepted. He was put into one of the suite rooms, a deliberate taste of luxury.

Rocky walked Tyler to his room. "Get a good night's sleep, order in room service, all on us. Sleep in. I'll drop by and get you at five minutes to 12 noon and take you to the Boss. You ready?"

Tyler said, "A little nervous."

Rocky patted him on the back. "A few nerves are good. Means you want it. Just don't try to bullshit him. He'll see right through you. Good night."

Rocky went up to his room on the fourth floor, which was adjacent to Mr. Big's suite. The undercover officers were there. Surveillance cameras and hidden audio microphones were in place and being tested. Mr. Big had been briefed. All was in readiness.

Sunday, September 10

Rocky knocked on Tyler's room door exactly at 11:55 am. Tyler was dressed and spruced up as best he could. Nothing was said. They took the elevator to the top floor. Mr. Big's room was one of the VIP suites. Rocky knocked. They waited. The door opened, a tall, big man, dark complexion, slicked back black hair, very Italian looking, opened the door. He nodded to Rocky, who left and turned his gaze to Tyler. "Come in." Tyler was literally trembling in his boots. The Boss directed him to sit in a wing back chair; he sat down opposite. It was the man's eyes, they were a cool blue grey, and were so out of place with his dark features, kind of like blue-eyed malamute huskies. The eyes were penetrating and to Tyler totally terrifying.

The Boss had done this before. Establishing a presence, the aura was the thing. He needed to be in total control over the room, the facts, and over Tyler. Listening was the key to his success, not just to what was said, but the how, the nuances and what was not said. The Boss took a moment to assess Tyler. Background he had, what he wanted was to gather a feel for the person. He could see he was insecure, scared, uncertain of himself and, most importantly, wanting to please.

The Boss, who had not introduced himself, spoke, "You know who I am?" His voice was strong and direct.

Tyler nodded. "You're the Boss."

The man laughed. "Yah, I suppose so." He never gave Tyler his name. "I've heard a lot about you Tyler. So, you want to become a member of the Hells Angels. Why?"

Tyler's throat was dry. He swallowed. "It's my chance out of Blue River. My chance to have a life, have some respect. The Hells Angels are the best."

The Boss, who had not taken his eyes off Tyler, nodded and said the following in a slow, forceful cadence, "We are the best. And I am looking for the best. Tyler, I need to see inside of you, your secrets. I cannot afford to have people I cannot trust. Trust is everything and you need to be completely truthful with me. Are you ready to tell me the truth about yourself?"

Tyler said, "I am, I will."

"Okay. I understand you have a brother, who is riding with the Rebels. That right?"

"Yes, sir."

"What's his name?"

"Alex.

"Older, younger?"

"Two years older."

"How do you get along with him?"

"Okay, I guess. We don't see much of each other. He stays out of my way and I stay out of his."

"You don't sound close."

"No, not close."

"Why not?"

"I don't know. He was always better at everything than me. We'd fight and I'd always lose."

"He's two years older than you, older and stronger." The Boss knew he had struck a chord talking about the brother. "You know that if our discussions with the Rebels don't pan out, we might have a turf war with them. Means you having to fight your brother."

"No love lost, I'd fight him."

"Kill him?"

Tyler replied with no hesitation, "If need be, yah."

"Why aren't you a Rebel?"

"To be honest, I don't think my brother wants me to become one. I did some odd jobs for the Rebels, that was it."

"Odd jobs, like what?"

"Oh, a few drops, few pick-ups. Nothing serious."

The Boss got up. "Want a soft drink? I'm going to have one."

"A coke would be great."

The Boss went to the minibar and took out two cokes, opened them and handed one to Tyler. "Rocky says you learn fast and follow orders. You're a big guy, can you handle yourself?"

"Yah, I've had a few fights. Won most. I don't go out looking for a fight, but I'll stand up for myself."

"Where do you work now?"

"Gas station in Blue River."

"What do you do there?"

"Man the pumps, change oil, fix tires that type of thing."

"How long you been there?"

"Started this past June."

"What did you do before that?"

"Odd jobs, unemployed."

"You good with cars, I hear you have quite the pickup?"

"Yah, I like to tinker." Tyler was getting more comfortable. He enjoyed hearing the praise.

"You do drugs?"

"Just pot, nothing else."

"Live at home?"

"Yes, with my dad. Mom left. My sister and her kids are with us."

"Get along with your father?"

"Not really. I'm looking to get out and I think he'd be happy to see me leave."

The Boss leaned a little forward. "Tyler we have lots of connections. We've already done a lot of looking into you. We got people in the right places, with real power. Now, I've been told the police have talked to you about the death of an uncle of yours."

Tyler gulped, "Yah, my Uncle Bill died in May."

"You close to him?"

"Him, no. Only saw him two or three times in my whole life."

"I don't like surprises. If the cops are on to you about something. I need to know. Can't help you unless I know the truth. You know Rocky, he was facing a serious rap. It disappeared. Now I'm going to ask you again, and I want the truth, were you involved in any way with your uncle dying?"

Tyler, his mind swirling, knew this was it. "Yah, I was there."

"What do you mean, you were there?"

"I was with the guy who killed my uncle. But I never knew he was going to kill the old man."

"Alright, alright, let's take this a step at a time. For me to help I need details. The truth." The Boss took a moment. He had to be careful. Detail makes the case. "Start from the beginning. Who was this guy?"

"He was a big guy in the Rebels. His name was Nevada. That's all I was told."

"Christ, you weren't straight with me." The Boss, his voice rising in feigned indignation. "You told me earlier you only did a few drops and pick-ups for the Rebels. Now you're telling me you were involved in a killing. You're not being straight with me."

"I am, I am. The killing was found to be an accident so I figured it wasn't important."

"Yah, well the cops are asking questions, aren't they?" The Boss cooled down. "Let's start again. This Nevada. Describe him to me."

"Solid, heavy set. Wore good clothes. Short brush cut. Probably in his thirties."

"Who called you from the Rebels?"

"I don't know. The person just called and asked whether I wanted to earn 500 bucks. At the time, I had no job, sure. Person then said to meet a guy driving a black Impala at the abandoned gas station on the highway just south of town at 7:30 pm. The person also said I was to bring my fishing stuff, which I thought a little strange. But what do I know?"

"When did you get this call?"

"That morning, late, around noon."

"Nothing else? That was it?"

"That was it. I figured $500, easy money. I did what I was told. I drove to the gas station lot early and waited. A black Impala came and parked back of the station. This guy, Nevada, got out. Introduced himself. He told me, we'd wait until about 8:00 pm, be getting darker by then."

"Tell me what exactly did he say to you."

"Let's see. Introduced himself. Asked me if I knew where my Uncle Bill lived. I did. Told me he had to have a little talk with him. Did say it might get rough. Asked me if I knew my uncle. I told him no, hardly saw the old coot. We waited. He asked me whether this was bingo night. That I knew, my grandmother always goes to bingo on Tuesday night. Asked me the time it started and ended. I told him 7:00 to 9:00 pm. I often drove grandma there and picked her up. He seemed satisfied with that."

"Whoa, let's slow down. The Rebels ask you, a non-member, to get involved. Why not your brother?"

"I wondered about that too. Then I found out Alex was supposed to be involved, but he took a bender evidently at the Rebel club house outside of Rostern and couldn't go. Nevada was really pissed. Said he needed it done; had to be the Tuesday. They called me. Alex told me all this when we were working on our story for the cops."

"What did you think he was going to do to your uncle?"

"Didn't figure he'd kill him. Rough him up a little. I knew my grandfather and dad were working on something with the Rebels and they wanted some land Uncle Bill owned and wouldn't sell. So, I figured he was going to be threatened a bit."

"Were your father and grandfather involved in this?'

"No idea. Though they were both pretty happy when they found out Uncle Bill was dead."

"Your uncle would recognize you?"

"I wasn't too worried about that; the guy's old, off his rocker a bit. Nobody would believe him. Just in case I wore a baseball cap and sunglasses."

"Alright, what happens next?"

"Nevada told me to drive my truck. Just before 8:00 we drove to the vacant lot north of Uncle Bill's place. We got out. I noticed the guy wore leather gloves. We walked through the bush to uncle's place. He was out, walking up the path from the lake, when he saw us. Told us to get off his property. Get off. Yelling at us, the old coot. Nevada just kept walking towards him and I followed. We didn't say anything. Then Uncle Bill went to a woodshed and grabbed an axe handle. He swung it at Nevada, who grabbed the head of the handle and ripped it out of his hands. Then as cool as can be he flipped it so he could grip the handle and swung it two-handed hitting Uncle Bill on the side of his head. The old guy fell right down. I was shocked. Nevada bent down felt for a pulse. I guess there wasn't any and motioned for me to grab his arms. I did. We carried him down the path towards the river. We stopped at the shoreline and checked. Nobody was around. We carried him to the dock and Nevada told me to throw him head first into a couple sawmill logs that were in the water. And I did. Uncle Bill slid off the logs, head down in the water. Dead. We left. I cleaned up a few of the leaves where he had fallen. We walked to my truck and I drove him back to where the Impala was parked."

"Okay, so let me see if I have this straight. Your uncle is facing Nevada, who swings the axe handle and hits your uncle on which side of his head. The right side or left side?"

Tyler took a moment to visualize, "He was hit on the right side."

"About the axe handle; Nevada never had that with him?"

"No, Uncle Bill got it from the woodshed."

"What did Nevada do with the axe handle?"

"Ah, I remember he looked at it. Gave it a wipe with his glove and put it back in the woodshed."

"What was going through your mind?"

"I was surprised. Didn't expect he'd kill the old coot. But what was done was done."

"You are now back at the abandoned gas station, does Nevada say anything to you there?"

"Yah, I now know why I was told to bring my fishing gear. He told me to head to the family cabin at Dore Lake, fish and stay low. Not to return to town until next evening. Told me, gives me an alibi and that's what I told the police. Me and Alex were at the cabin fishing. Worked."

"Alex was going to back you up?"

"Evidently that is what he was told to say. He was right out of it."

"Nevada say anything else to you?"

"Yah, if I told anyone I was a dead man. I knew that anyway."

"When were you paid the $500?"

"Right there, he gave me five $100 bills."

"What did you do with the $500?"

"Bought new tires and rims for my pickup."

"How'd you feel about him killing your uncle?"

"Didn't really care. I mean he was an old man and kinda asked for it."

The Boss leaned back in his chair, more relaxed. "Well, that was a pretty clean hit. Made it look like an accident."

"Yah, right. Pretty cool. That Nevada knew what he was doing."

The Boss was about ready to end the interview. "No other secrets?"

"None," said Tyler.

"Look you stay here for a few minutes, I've got to go and talk to a few people. Understand?" The Boss left and went to the adjoining room. Rocky, Colin, Rolston, Feeney, and Sergeant Frost of the Major Crimes Unit, were all there, along with two or three other officers. Tyler's confession was in the can. Audio and video were clear.

Rocky sadly said, "I was hoping the kid was innocent."

The Boss nodded. "Looks like he's in for accessory after the fact to murder, minimum, and manslaughter. I doubt we can get him for murder."

Sergeant Frost asked, "Tyler is a little fish. He'll be the key to getting Nevada. Do we have enough to convict Nevada of first-degree murder, a contract hit?"

The Boss replied, "You do if Tyler testifies. Might have to make a deal with the kid."

Rolston spoke up, "Sergeant is right, Tyler is a little fish. Nevada is a bigger fish, but I think we might be able to get him to turn on Laxon and others. Worth a try. Nevada's smart and I don't think he wants to spend the rest of his days behind bars."

"True." The Sergeant took command. "Constable, anything else we need from Tyler?"

Feeney answered, "His statement fits with the physical evidence: the murder weapon was the axe handle, it was found in the woodshed, Mr. Jones was struck on the right side of the head and the blow to the front of the head is consistent with being thrown into the logs."

The Sergeant asked, looking around the room, "Anything else?" Silence, and shaking of heads, no. "Good work all. Constable Feeney, this is your case, take a couple officers and arrest Tyler for the murder of William Jones. Take him to the station and we'll do a formal interview there. We can hold him 24 hours. I want this airtight. I don't want him changing his story. I want him to repeat his confession and have him do a re-enactment. Airtight."

The Sergeant turned to Corporal Rolston. "Gerry, I'll leave Nevada's arrest to your gang unit. Wait until we get the formal statement from Tyler. I'll let you know. Probably won't be until tonight. Put a surveillance team on Nevada so we know where he's at."

Rolston replied, "It will be our pleasure."

CHAPTER 42

Sunday, September 10

The RCMP surveillance team was in place watching Nevada's modest bungalow on the East Flat in Prince Albert. Rolston was of the view Nevada should be arrested now, not wait, but he was outranked and it wasn't his call. As far as Rolston was concerned Nevada was like a dangerous animal, better in a cage then out.

Sunday turned out to be a cool and blustery day threatening rain, a harbinger of fall days to come. Nevada was pleased. No one would want to be at Fishing Lake on a day such as this. He spent the day watching football waiting for the time to move into action.

The RCMP officers were bored. Nothing happening. That all changed at approximately 5:30 pm, when Nevada left his house on foot. The officers thought it was for an afternoon stroll. However, Nevada wasn't out for a stroll. He walked a block and a half to an auto repair shop, which was closed, there he got into a non-descript late model grey Chevrolet Nova parked on the lot and drove off. The RCMP were on his tail from a discreet distance. Rolston told the officers to follow, but not to intercept; authorization was still pending.

Rolston was suspicious. Why not drive your own car? Nevada was up to something.

Nevada left the city heading east on highway 2. He was in no hurry; it was a leisurely Sunday drive. He turned on to Fishing Lake Road and backed into the entrance to the abandoned homestead. The trailing officers continued on down the highway, without a glance towards Nevada; they knew better. The highway descended into a low-lying swale. The driver immediately braked hard, made a quick U-turn and parked behind a windbreak. One officer got out and hiding in the low shrubs focused his binoculars on Nevada, who was approximately 250 yards away. The second officer stayed in the car keeping radio contact; he radioed in for instructions.

When Rolston received their call, he was certain Nevada was up to no good. But what? Rolston responded, "Keep the Fishing Lake Road under surveillance but do not intercept. I repeat do not intercept. Report on any other people and vehicles taking the road."

Nevada parked the Nova and tried his CB, "Calling Goose Dog, calling Goose Dog – this is Vegas. Over."

Over slight static Nevada heard, "Goose Dog here; receiving you loud and clear."

"Goose Dog, all clear. Over."

"All clear."

The evening was turning prematurely dark because of the low-lying heavy cloud cover. A slight drizzle had stopped. Nevada smiled, everything was going to plan. All he had to do was wait the arrival of his invited guests. He smugly sat back in his seat and lit a cigarette.

Josef and Rebecca, were in a lazy relaxed mood and stayed at home. Sunday was a day to watch football or read a good book. They looked forward to the surprise party for the Morrisons. They dressed for the evening, casual upscale. As per instructions, no card, no gift. It was a little after 6:30 pm, time to go.

Rolston was uneasy. Nevada was simply parked and hadn't moved for over 15 minutes. The surveillance team reported nothing. Rolston radioed the officers, "I'm leaving and will be there in about twenty minutes. Continue to stand by."

Shortly before 7:00 pm Josef saw the sign for Fishing Lake Park, slowed the Parklane, signalled and turned on to the Fishing Lake Road. Nevada made the call, "Goose Dog, Goose Dog. Watch for deer. I repeat watch for deer."

"Roger, Vegas."

Derek shot the truck into gear, cranked up the volume of a cassette he had in the deck, Alice Cooper's 'Schools out for Summer' blared. Derek was stoked; he was ready to do this. He put the truck in gear and pounded the steering wheel to the beat of the music. The cab of the truck was an explosion of noise, as if the noise would drown out what he was about to do. The truck growled its way up the hill.

Rolston was five minutes away. The surveillance team called in, "A green Mercury turned on to the Fish Lake Road." Rolston froze. He remembered Manne drove a green Parklane. He reacted, "Intercept. Intercept Nevada now. Intercept."

The surveillance officers sprang into action. The officer, observing from the windbreak ran back to the cruiser. Once in, the driver activated the siren and lights and burst on to highway 2.

Josef wasn't in any hurry; they were a little early. The Parklane coasted along at 50 miles an hour.

Nevada saw the lights, heard the siren. He called into the CB, "Goose Dog, Goose Dog. Abort. Abort. Cops. Cops." The cruiser descended on him. The surveillance officers got out, guns levelled at the car and driver. Nevada put his hands up. He wasn't worried; he had just stopped to have a smoke.

"School's out for summer; school's out forever; school's been blown to pieces…" Alice Cooper sang. Derek shouted and pounded. There was no hope for him to hear Nevada's CB call. The truck neared the crest of the hill. He was pushing 60 mph. The truck rumbled, the engine revved, the transmission whined. Derek saw the glare of the approaching car lights. When he reached the crest, the oncoming car was fully in view, 500 yards away closing fast. Derek focused on those lights: 400 yards, 300 yards, 200 yards, 100 yards. Then Derek saw in the distance the flashing lights of the RCMP police cruiser. 50 yards. Derek was confused. Police lights. He veered towards the car, Alice Cooper sang, "And we got no principles; and we got no innocence." At the last moment, Derek turned the truck back to his side of the road and the gravel truck whisked by the Parklane.

Josef had seen the truck coming at him. He steered to the shoulder, not wanting to over react, and two of the right wheels caught the soft gravel. The car teetered on the edge between road and ditch. The truck pulled back and shaved by. Josef brought the car back to the road and came to a stop. His hands gripped the steering wheel, refusing to let go; involuntary sweat wet his brow and back. In the rear-view mirror, he watched the truck disappear. He also saw the police lights in the distance. Rebecca was as shaken, taking deep breaths, not saying a word.

She broke the silence. "What just happened?"

Josef replied, "I don't know, but I'm getting a funny feeling. Where are the other guests? We've seen no other cars and there are police back at the intersection."

Rebecca turned and looked back. "Do we turn around or do we go on to the lodge?"

"Let's continue on to the lodge," said Josef and Rebecca nodded her agreement.

Josef drove cautiously on down the hill to the parking lot. There were no cars. The lodge was dark. All was quiet. Josef slowly drove through the parking lot and turned to drive back. A police car arrived and blocked the exit. One of the officers got out, and came to Josef's driver side door. It was Rolston. "Are you okay?"

"Yes, we're fine."

"Thank God. Tell me, what the hell are you doing here?"

"It's a long story Corporal, but I have the distinct feeling we were set up. A gravel truck almost ran us off the road."

"We stopped the truck and are talking to the driver. Follow me back to the intersection."

Josef followed the cruiser back to the intersection. The gravel truck was parked on the side of the road. The driver was seated on the ground next to it. Nevada was in cuffs standing by a cruiser. For Josef and Rebecca, all fell into place.

Rolston spoke to one of the officers and came up to Josef and Rebecca. "Truck driver says he got spooked by a deer."

"There was no deer," replied Josef. "What's he doing out here this time of night on a Sunday anyway?"

"Says he was checking the parking lot to see if needed some gravel."

"And Nevada, what the hell was he doing out here? It's no coincidence," said Josef.

"Says he was out for a Sunday drive and stopped for a smoke. Look, I'm not buying it either. But tell me why you're out here."

Josef filled him in on the supposed phone call from William Morrison.

Rebecca glared at Nevada, calmly standing by the cruiser, he looked at her with a slight smirk on his face. Wrong thing to do. She strode up to him and without saying a word belted him with a solid right-hand punch to the chin and a well-placed hard kick to the crotch. Nevada fell to the ground, squirming, trying to get up and at the same time twisting in obvious pain. None of the surrounding officers were in a real hurry to come to his aid. Josef pulled Rebecca back.

Rolston stifled a smile, but had to act with authority. "Miss, that's enough or I'll have to arrest you too."

Rebecca turned to Rolston eyes blazing. "That bastard just tried to kill us."

Rolston nodded. "We'll get to the bottom of that. I'm sure the truck driver has more to tell us. Especially since Nevada's going away for a long time; we've just arrested him for the murder of Bill Jones."

Josef, holding Rebecca in a tight grip, broke into a big grin. "You got him."

Rolston answered, "Yes we got him."